A Sensitive Person

JÁCHYM TOPOL

A Sensitive Person

A NOVEL

Translated from the Czech by Alex Zucker

A MARGELLOS
WORLD REPUBLIC OF LETTERS BOOK

Yale UNIVERSITY PRESS | NEW HAVEN & LONDON

The Margellos World Republic of Letters is dedicated to making literary works from around the globe available in English through translation. It brings to the English-speaking world the work of leading poets, novelists, essayists, philosophers, and playwrights from Europe, Latin America, Africa, Asia, and the Middle East to stimulate international discourse and creative exchange.

Yale University Press books may be purchased in quantity for educational, business, or promotional use. For information, please email sales.press@yale.edu (U.S. office) or sales@yaleup .co.uk (U.K. office).

Set in Source Serif Pro type by Motto Publishing Services.
Printed in the United States of America.

Library of Congress Control Number: 2022934810
ISBN 978-0-300-24722-0 (paperback : alk. paper)

A catalogue record for this book is available from the British Library.

This paper meets the requirements of ANSI/NISO Z39.48-1992 (Permanence of Paper).

10 9 8 7 6 5 4 3 2 1

Contents

Translator's Introduction

In 2017, the Czech Ministry of Culture awarded Jáchym Topol the state's highest literary honor, for *A Sensitive Person* and for his body of work to date. As literary historian Ivo Říha noted on the occasion, "Language and style—these are what make Jáchym Topol an author recognizable to even a casual reader after just one paragraph."[1]

Language and style, as it happens, are also the primary tools of the literary translator, so one of my aims in this introduction is to highlight the hallmarks of Topol's language and style—what it is that makes Topol's prose Topolesque—and how I treated them in my translation of this novel. However, context is of course important too, and in this particular novel I felt it to be especially critical, so before delving into the elements of the text itself, there are a few facts I'd like to share about Topol's life and career to give readers of *A Sensitive Person* the same basic knowledge about the author and his background that most Czechs bring to the book.

Jáchym Topol's father, Josef Topol, was a famous poet and playwright, as well as a translator of Shakespeare and Chekhov, and his maternal grandfather, Karel Schulz, was a novelist, critic, and poet. Jáchym himself is one of those Czech novelists who cut their authorial teeth writing poetry rather than prose. As a twentysomething living under communism during the 1980s, he published several collections of free verse in samizdat (from the Russian самиздат, "self-published," meaning written, reproduced, and circulated outside of the state-owned and state-controlled publishing industry in order to avoid censorship), as well as composing lyrics for his brother Filip's underground rock band Psí vojáci (Dog Soldiers). After the fall of the Berlin Wall and the so-called Velvet Revolution in 1989, Topol wrote one final collection of poetry before making the leap to prose. Yet he has always been more than "just" a writer.

In the Communist era, Topol was also an organizer and activist, engaging both politically (mainly with the "monarchist-anarchist" initiative České děti, i.e., Czech Children, or Children of Bohemia) and literarily (mainly as a cofounder of the samizdat cultural journal *Revolver Revue*). More than once he was arrested and interrogated for these activities, which were illegal under the Soviet-sponsored regime of the Czechoslovak Socialist Republic. In the post-Communist era, Topol worked first as a reporter for the investigative weekly *Respekt* (where he was one of the few journalists in the country to cover racist attacks on Roma and Vietnamese), then as a cultural critic at the daily *Lidové noviny*, before joining the Václav Havel Library in Prague as its program director in 2011. In the 1990s, Topol and the other editors of *Revolver Revue*, drawing on their experience with Czech samizdat in the '80s, raised money for and assisted students from Vietnam living in Prague to organize, publish, and distribute samizdat literature in Vietnamese, as well as to translate and publish their own work in Czech. Today, at the Havel Library, in alignment with its mission (devoted to "people, events and phenomena related to the legacy of Václav Havel"), Topol organizes readings and other events featuring authors and artists who are politically engaged, Czech and non-Czech alike.

The influence of Topol's early days as a poet are evident in his prose. An urgent propulsiveness, the vivid depiction of oppressive atmospheres interspersed with candescent moments of intense poetic imagery, and a broad spectrum of themes (primary among them being the struggle of individuals both with the cruelty of the world and with their own demons), typically related with sarcastic detachment—these are central attributes of Topol's poetics, and they are on full display in *A Sensitive Person*.[2]

Apart from the rhythm of his language itself, the main device Topol uses to drive his prose forward is ellipses rather than periods or other more definitive connective punctuation. Topol's debut novel, *Sestra*

(Torst, 1994; published in my translation as *City Sister Silver* by Catbird Press in 2000), was relentless in its deployment of ellipses, a technique Topol adopted from French author Louis-Ferdinand Céline. Here is a passage from chapter 4 of *A Sensitive Person*, describing the scene at Budapest Keleti, the main train station in the Hungarian capital:

Then they pass through a door and find themselves in the sleeping area. People with backpacks sit on the floor, indifferent to the announcements, as passengers hurry past . . . They killed us, raped us, a guy hunched over his laptop types, pecking out the letters . . . Chased us, murdered us . . . They lie on inflatable mattresses, camping mats, surrounded by the hustle and bustle of the train station . . . We begged, we wept . . . the mountains couldn't hide us, the people wouldn't hide us . . . we fled to the sea, we are alive . . . the guy types out, deafened by the raspy soundtrack of departures and arrivals . . . And though the road leads nowhere, at least we are here on this earth.

Topol uses ellipses here like a movie camera lens: Zoom in: ". . . They killed us, raped us, a guy hunched over his laptop types, pecking out the letters . . . Chased us, murdered us." Zoom out: ". . . They lie on inflatable mattresses, camping mats, surrounded by the hustle and bustle of the train station." Zoom in: ". . . We begged, we wept"—et cetera.

In the final chapter Topol employs ellipses extensively, steering readers' eyes (and ears) from one character to another, again zooming in and out on the action, as well as in and out of characters' heads:

The exhilarated Solder is still expecting to find a band of kindred spirits waiting for them on the lawn . . . maybe Black Lukáš could even bless the tank, he thinks, grinning to himself for what may be the hundredth time now in the course of this sensational ride.

He gives the young Tater Tot a merry slap on the back . . . yes, they came prepared to salute the guests with live fire and get the funeral party underway.

Neither Solder nor Tater Tot realize, however, that the lady cop with the bandaged head is blocking the tank's path . . . Napalm blinks in bewilderment, this lady cop is saluting them . . . And what's that she's shouting? Welcome, comrades! Then she hurls her cap in the air and yells, Hurrah! . . . She thinks we're Russkies, the dirty rat, flashes through Napalm's mind as the officer opens her mouth . . . She recognizes the long-haired, bearded old geezer bowing to them from the turret, tattoos running up and down his neck and cheeks, fishbone in his hair . . . and he's a repeat offender! Dropping behind the police car, the officer levels her gun.

Turning now to the second key characteristic of Topol's style—interrupting bleak or oppressive scenes with radiant, poetic imagery—here is an example from chapter 6:

Conflagrations blaze on the plateau. The borders flicker with dying flames. There are multitudes of them, dozens, perhaps hundreds of fires. In clumps and individually, the distant ones like match heads, the nearer ones like torches kindled upon the dusty, withered earth. It is a scene reminiscent of the night sky fading to dawn, spilled out over the furrowed earth by a tug on the universe, or perhaps some divine whim of God.

In general, throughout the novel, Topol waxes poetic on the beauty of the natural world at quiet moments in between human acts of cruelty and violence, moments such as this one:

The man in the slicker patters along at a brisk pace. Papa clomps along elephant-style. As the humans squish across the vivifying floor, a vibration of the subtlest frequencies seeps up toward them out of the algae, visible only under a microscope, multiplying in numbers quantifiable only by astronomy. Myriads of tiny shells move in copulatory bliss amid the tracks left behind in the soddening moss. Intoxicated springtails and whole armies of stone flies, bacchanalian revelers of the aquatic realm, frolic in the splashings. Creatures that live hours, days, only to serve as sanctuaries for larvae, planktonic organisms, and enormous water bugs, mandibled warriors, water-striding boyars of the insect kingdom.

The juxtaposition of beauty and brutality may be seen as a tactic calculated to produce an effect, though I am inclined to see it more as an expression of Topol's feelings toward the world, and his perspective on it, suggesting a wonderment and fascination at times bordering on religiosity. Whether or not God exists is a question voiced by characters in all of Topol's works, more often than not strongly tinged with the hope that the answer is yes. Unavoidably, it was a subject that came up repeatedly in interviews with him about this novel in particular. And if Topol himself shies away from identifying unambiguously as Catholic, Czech critics have documented Catholic symbolism throughout his work.[3]

In addition to the elements of Topol's writing style that I cite from his website above, one more feature is absolutely integral: his rich use of colloquial (*obecná*) and spoken (*hovorová*) Czech, as opposed to the standard written (*spisovná*) register. The 2013 volume *Otevřený rány. Vybrané studie o díle Jáchyma Topola* (Open wounds: Selected studies on the work of Jáchym Topol), assembled and edited by Ivo Říha and issued by Topol's publisher Torst, contains an essay by linguist Petr Mareš on the use of written and colloquial Czech in Topol's work. Although the portion of Mareš's analysis devoted to Topol predates the publication of this novel, Mareš's observations hold true for all of Topol's prose, and certainly apply in the case of *A Sensitive Person*. For our purposes, the most pertinent observation Mareš makes regards the text's "heavily nonstandard [*nespisovné*] coloration" produced by "the high frequency of these occurrences [of colloquial usage], as well as the fact that they constantly draw attention to themselves when being read due to their graphic 'anomalousness.'" Mareš points out that Topol still maintains a differentiation in "the language of the narrator and the language of the characters," with the usage of colloquial Czech confined predominantly, though not entirely, to the characters. "However," he adds, "more essential is the fact that nonstandard and standard means of expression constantly alternate throughout the entire text, with the alternation almost never being predictable. The text steers away from regularity and clear motivation, instead uplifting dynamic and spontaneous creation as its main quality."

The phenomenon Mareš notes here figures prominently in *Citlivý člověk*, and it's one of the most challenging aspects of Topol's prose style for an English-language translator to render. In the space of a single monologue, the register of a character's speech may shift from colloquial to more colloquial as their emotion grows in intensity. Here, for example, is the character named Lomoz talking about the women he has known over the years at the brothel where most of the action takes place in the latter part of the book:

> Well, I won't live long enough to see the next crop of girls, I can tell you that. I knew their moms and aunts, before they got hitched or drank themselves to death, or both. Some of em're okay and have kids with their husbands or what have you.

Then, one page later, in the same conversation, Lomoz shares about his time in Pitești Prison—an actual former penal institution in Romania, notorious for the atrocities committed against people incarcerated there in the years 1949–51, under the guise of "reeducation" as part of a depraved experiment by the Communist regime.[4]

> Yeah. Two years I worked there, and not one person stuck it out. Poor souls took me for an actual devil. It wasn't just professors and brainiacs in there. There was also folks from villages, some of em pretty religious a course. It was them called me that. The devil. Pitești devil, they called me in that Romanian lingo a theirs.

In the Czech, there is a slight but discernible difference in register between these two extracts, which I represent in English by abbreviating the preposition "of" as "a" in the second instance. These types of subtle variations occur throughout the novel, particularly in the characters' direct speech, so I was careful to translate this variability, rather than enforcing a consistency that isn't there in the Czech.

The struggle of people to endure in harsh circumstances even as they wrestle with their internal demons, an enduring theme of Topol's writing as noted above, is front and center here, mainly in the attempts of the older characters (Lomoz, old man Bašta, Mr. Hrozen, Růženka) to come to terms with aging and death. It's also noteworthy that although the theme of individual struggle with life and death has been central in Topol's work from the beginning, it is particularly salient in this novel, owing to the fact that his entire immediate family—younger brother, father, and mother—passed away in the space of just three years while he was writing this book. As the author himself revealed in an October 2015 interview: "I've covered dozens of kilometers walking the hall-ways of hospitals over the past few months. Either I was going to see my dad or I was taking in my mom, and in between I was running out for shoots on a documentary about my brother. [. . .] His death unfor-tunately was long, hard, and painful. It's the same thing now with my dad."[5] This isn't just a matter of the author's own personal experience, however. The fear of dying a long, slow death, attached to a machine ("hookin folks up to revivers and prolongers even when they got a death notice stickin out their ass," as old man Bašta puts it), is a pertinent is-sue for Czechs in light of the steady decline in the quality and accessi-bility of care for the aging and dying, along with that of the health care system as a whole, in the Czech Republic over the past thirty years.

Indeed, Topol's fictional worlds always map onto present political and social realities—even insofar as the events that characters in his novels witness, undergo, or relate. As I learned in the course of my re-search for *City Sister Silver*, nearly all of the worst things that happen in his fiction are based on real life. Just as the fears of death expressed by characters in *A Sensitive Person* spring from what Topol saw his loved ones endure, the nurse from Rumburk, the "Angel of death" Lomoz mentions in chapter 13, who killed elderly patients by injecting them with potassium, is an actual woman who in 2014 was charged with the murder of six patients by giving them an overdose of potassium at a hospital in the north Bohemian town of Rumburk (she was eventually found innocent).[6] Similarly, a page or so earlier, in the same chapter, Monča shares the contents of a tabloid newspaper article about a plane crash in Ukraine ("Or was it Russia?" she says uncertainly within sec-onds of having read the piece, cloudiness on facts being a common trait of many Topol characters across his oeuvre—and of course we also see here the sarcastic detachment noted above):

Hey, you guys, look at these photos! It's awful! Bodies fallen from the sky, impaled on telegraph poles. Scattered across the field. And get a load of this girl. Will you look at her?

Who's that bimbo? the old man asks.

Some pro-Russian separatist. Dolled up in makeup she got off the bodies.

This incident too actually took place: a Malaysia Airlines flight crashed over eastern Ukraine on July 17, 2014 (a Dutch-led investigation concluded it was likely shot down by pro-Russian rebels who controlled the region of Donetsk), and as widely reported in tabloid papers internationally, a Ukrainian woman who described herself as a pro-Russian "separatist" posted pictures on Instagram of herself wearing makeup that she bragged had been looted from debris of the downed flight.[7]

Likewise, even events appearing only in the background are drawn from real life: the floods, wreaking havoc on the Czech Republic, and indeed all of central Europe, with increasing frequency as a result of climate change and referred to here in multiple chapters; the "tainted booze" that Scales the fisherman warns Papa about in chapter 19 ("Booze these days is garbage, people die from the stuff. It'll blind you on the spot."), which in 2012 led Czech authorities to ban all sales of liquor containing more than 20 percent alcohol after at least twenty people died and dozens more were poisoned from drinking bootleg vodka and rum.[8]

Although there are many more examples of the characteristic mixing of fact and fiction Topol deploys in *A Sensitive Person*, the last I will offer here, because of its ongoing importance to society and politics in not only the Czech Republic and the former East bloc but all of Europe and beyond is the way immigration, immigrants, and anti-immigrant sentiment surface repeatedly in this novel. During the period when Topol was writing *Citlivý člověk*, racist and xenophobic violence flared in the Czech Republic and throughout Europe, in reaction to what is now commonly referred to as the 2015 European migrant crisis. Consistent with his work as a journalist in the early post-Communist years, Topol has never shied away from depicting the darker sides of Czech society. The racism and xenophobia that abound in *A Sensitive Person* have appeared in his writing since his earliest prose, although they stand out most in *City Sister Silver*, which he wrote against the backdrop of the 1990s Yugoslav wars. One of that novel's central themes is tribalism as human nature and the violence it produces. Among the many variations on that theme, *City Sister Silver* contains an entire chapter devoted to the Holocaust, as well as scenes with skinhead attacks on Laotians (a fictionalized recasting of the sizable Vietnamese population in Prague) and recurring invocations of the genocides of Native Americans in the United States.

It is in keeping with this "warts and all" approach, then, that we see several characters in *A Sensitive Person* using racial slurs to refer to Black immigrants. Other characters use pejorative terms for Muslims. One character rants about organizing a militia to gun immigrants down, "Soon as they get off the boat." Another uses a slur for Chinese people as outsiders with sinister designs on the local economy. Nor is xenophobia directed solely along racial lines. Czechs throughout the novel refer to Russians in disparaging terms, in part as foreigners making investments that Czechs see as a threat and in part as former occupiers of Czechoslovakia, while Ivan, Papa's Russian brother, denounces Ukrainians using an insulting and derogatory term. And at the opening of the novel, Papa and Soňa, with their two sons, are driven out of campsites in England and Spain by xenophobic stone-throwing local militias. In short, no one comes out looking good.

As Topol stated in an interview when he was still writing the book, "I've detested politics for as long as I've been able to think, but I've got a feeling it might be a generational thing. The way I'm made, the way I grew up, I can't leave it out, even if I hate it. I remember envying these Dutch authors talking about writing novels set in the countryside about love and hate. If I write a novel set in the Czech countryside, there's going to be Nazis in it, or Communists, or nowadays Putin supporters."[9]

While Topol remains committed to portraying Czech society realistically, and without sanitizing people's shortcomings or opinions, at the same time he does attempt to lighten the heaviness by playing out his disturbing scenes amid a plot that is decidedly grotesque. For as harsh a portrait as Topol paints, when it comes to individuals at least he remains hopeful, even romantically so. For him, as I hinted at above, this is largely a matter of faith.

In a radio interview after *Citlivý člověk* was published, Topol said he believed there was an internal logic to the novel, as well as "an internal straining toward God," but the only way for him to write about the subjects that matter to him most is to embed them in the grotesque and the burlesque of everyday human life: "It's a very Czech thing: we don't like to use big words, we're afraid to talk about God and love . . . We act like we're tough, we make fun of everything. But I think if it wasn't for that, we wouldn't be able to take another step."[10] And so, amid the irony, the sarcasm, and the violence, Topol creates a curious landscape in which love crops up, surprising the reader in the bleakest of circumstances. The invitation is open to step into the narrative, following the colorful, true-to-life cast as they walk their crooked paths toward meaning and hope.

NOTES

1. "Jáchym Topol získal za román Citlivý člověk a za dosavadní tvorbu Státní cenu za literaturu," Aktuálně.cz, October 22, 2017, https://magazin.aktualne.cz/kultura /jachym-topol-ziskal-za-roman-citlivy-clovek-statni-cenu-za-l/r~5b22ac4eb75a11 e79090002590604f2e/.

2. See the author's website: https://jachymtopol.cz/desivy-sprezeni/.

3. For example, Klára Kudlová, a literary historian in the Catholic Theological Faculty at Charles University, observes that the Madonna is a recurrent figure in Topol's oeuvre, even going so far as to claim, "The various Madonnas—the Polish Madonna of Częstochowa [City Sister Silver], the War Madonna in fictionalised modern-day Russia [A Sensitive Person], and finally the Czech Madonna of Poříčí [again A Sensitive Person]—create a Christian counterworld in Topol's novels, and signalize the persistent role and presence of spirituality in the region [of Central Europe]." Klára Kudlová, "On Fields of Bones, Headsmen and Madonnas: The Symbols and Figures of Central Europe in the Past 25 Years of Jáchym Topol's Writing," Porównania 2 (27), 2020, 247–63, https://doi.org/10.14746/por.2020.2.13.

4. See the Piteşti Prison Memorial website at https://pitestiprison.org/ and "Piteşti Prison," Wikipedia, https://en.wikipedia.org/wiki/Pite%C8%99ti_Prison.

5. Jan H. Vitvar, "Starnoucí bílý samec," Respekt, October 11, 2015, https://www .respekt.cz/tydenik/2015/42/jachym-topol-starnouci-bily-samec.

6. See Ian Willoughby, "Nurse Charged with Murder of Several Patients at Small-Town Hospital," Radio Prague International, November 27, 2014, https://english .radio.cz/nurse-charged-murder-several-patients-small-town-hospital-8276606, and Simona Holecová, "Novináři jí říkali sestra Smrt, vypadalo to jednoznačně. Nebylo," Neovlivní.cz, July 26, 2016, https://neovlivni.cz/novinari-ji-rikali-sestra-smrt -vypadalo-to-jednoznacne-nebylo/.

7. "Malaysia Airlines Flight 17," Wikipedia, https://en.wikipedia.org/wiki/Malaysia _Airlines_Flight_17, and Rich Shapiro and Deborah Hastings, "Ukraine Woman Posts Selfies with Mascara 'Looted' from Malaysia Airlines Crash," New York Daily News, July 25, 2014, https://www.nydailynews.com/news/world/ukrainian-woman-re portedly-posts-mascara-looted-malaysia-airlines-crash-article-1.1880205.

8. Jason Hovet and Jana Mlcochova, "UPDATE 2-Czechs Ban Spirits Sales after Bootleg Booze Kills 19," Reuters, September 14, 2012, https://www.reuters.com /article/czech-alcohol/update-2-czechs-ban-spirits-sales-after-bootleg-booze-kills-19 -idUKL5E8KEKLR20120914; "Czechs Ban Spirits after Bootleg Alcohol Poisoning,"

BBC News, September 15, 2012, https://www.bbc.com/news/world-europe-19608461; and Dinah Spritzer and Dan Bilefsky, "Czechs See Peril in a Bootleg Bottle," *New York Times*, September 17, 2012, https://www.nytimes.com/2012/09/18/world/europe/czechs-ban-hard-liquor-sales-after-methanol-poisonings.html.

9. Jonáš Zbořil, "Topol nemůže být bez politiky, Šindelka zkoumá internet. V čem se liší dvě literární generace?" Radio Wave, April 24, 2015, https://wave.rozhlas.cz/topol-nemuze-byt-bez-politiky-sindelka-zkouma-internet-v-cem-se-lisi-dve-5215020.

10. Jonáš Zbořil, "Jáchym Topol: Česká cesta je sebeironie. V Citlivém člověku ale řeším i Boha," Radio Wave, May 4, 2017, https://wave.rozhlas.cz/jachym-topol-ceska-cesta-je-sebeironie-v-citlivem-cloveku-ale-resim-i-boha-5965676.

A Sensitive Person

1

BRISTOL GLOBE. WHY HE ADDRESSES BOTH. NIGHT
FLIGHT. SOŇA IN THE MORNING. THE NOTEBOOK.
THE TATTOOED BOY. CAMP ON FIRE. PISS OFF!
ELEANOR AND HER BOYS. AND ONWARD.

How the hell am I sposta concentrate here?!

Papa squats behind the wheel of their nomadmobile, bottle in reach, notebook open on his knees, scribbling away.

Almost finished writin a chapter last night, but what with all the commotion, I only got down an outline! And here Bristol always used to be so nice! *Treasure Island*, boys! Ever hear of cabin boy Jimmy Hawkins? He addresses both his boys, because, as he puts it, he wants to get them talking. The one in baby rompers as well as the one that's grown.

You know what's interesting, though? he says, turning to Soňa, who's heating a spoon over one of the flames on the portable stove. On the other, she gives an occasional stir to the little nipper's porridge.

Now I identify more with Long John Silver!

That just comes with middle age, says Soňa. She continues her morning ritual, rolling up the sleeve on her flamboyantly colored mandala shirt.

Papa's tattered notebook, covered with coffee and wine stains, goes sailing over the still-sleeping little boy and lands amid the piles of junk.

He stretches out his legs and settles his head back against the headrest, taking in the other nomads stationed around them. On his body, a grimy T-shirt and shorts; in his eyes, a relentless shine of curiosity. On the histrion's head, a crocheted hippie hat, his ginger hair, with tufts of gray, sticking out from underneath.

His gaze lands on the gated entrance to the campsite, a minute replica of the Globe Theatre, covered with light bulbs that flare to life only at night to form the numeral 400, a rather comical portrait of the playwright himself, and the legend HIS WORDS: WISDOM, FREEDOM, AND BEAUTY!

Due to the nighttime arrivals, there is an unusual amount of activity swirling around the site of the traditional festival, this year dedicated to the life and work of William Shakespeare. It was here, years ago, that Papa and Soňa marked the anniversary of the Czech Republic's accession to the Community with an ingenious performance, dancing their way to a splendid three hundred and thirteen pounds. Now, however, everything is different.

Papa stares, gapes, deliberates. Sniffs the wind, taking his bearings by the movements of his beak. There was a time when he considered having his nose lined with a thin coating of precious metal. But he wasn't *that* successful.

An urgently summoned team of immigration officials are stationed at the entrance gate, their desks, computers, and forms stacked with donuts, plates of pastries, cups of java.

The grounds were empty yesterday. Now, though, the site is strewn with people arranged in groups. Rows of sleepers on mats, women in long frocks with babies, little clusters here and there sitting and gesticulating. Old women with plastic containers plod to the water hookup, while adolescents hanging around in tattered T-shirts and jeans survey the women as if they were overseeing their work.

Police cars sit on the edges of the crowd, whose largely black garb gives them the appearance of a solid mass. Most of the nighttime arrivals stumbled in and bedded down right on the spot, assaulted by waves of uneasiness and fear throughout the night.

Man, do I love Bristol! Though we never did get a peek at the port. Maybe we can get down there today, what do you think? Papa hollers at the boy as he shuffles off to fill their containers.

The line for the hydrants extends past the gate. Could be the hose burst, or maybe someone damaged one of the water sources. Moving single file, the dark, veiled women inch forward, tramping through the mud with their barrels and bags of refillable bottles. Water squishes up around the boy's tennis shoes.

Hey you . . . The boy raises his head. A smiling young woman with a mane of blonde hair cascading over her shoulders hands him a chocolate-frosted donut out the window of the illuminated Globe replica.

He stretches up on his tiptoes, feels the jelly drip down his fingers, but just then somebody slugs him in the shoulder. Two dark, gangly boys. The taller one, with sleepy eyelids, grabs the donut and scarfs it down.

He, I . . . The young lady leans out and hands over the whole box of treats, the sun beating down on their multicolored icing.

A scuffle breaks out, sending the boy scurrying away. Suddenly he's lost in a sea of pants and T-shirts and blow-dealing elbows, reeling like a puppy tossed by its heartless master into the midst of a Doberman fight.

Peering through the advancing line of skirts, women's flats, sneakers, and sandals, the boy catches a glimpse of the overturned canisters and edges toward the women, who dodge him with furious screams, like he was a stinging insect. To his amazement, he discovers he's holding a box against his belly with the donuts squished into the corners: he won.

The boy holds the spoils close, now suddenly amid the sleepy crowd. Someone, still half buried in their sleeping bag, takes a swing at him, he jumps out of the way.

And finds himself staring straight into the face of a naked boy. Roughly the same age and height as him. His hard little face not only grubby but also thoroughly black. His cheeks, arms, and thighs are tattooed, strewn with inflamed needle pricks. The crowd streams past, giving them a long look. It's a long way to the fortress on wheels, where his parents are. He hands the boy the box. Turns around and picks up one of the plastic containers, claws the other one from underneath somebody's feet, waits his turn in line, then sticks the hose in them and fills them to the brim. The way he's always done.

The evening performance in Bristol is canceled under the clause covering unexpected events, catastrophes, and natural disasters (plus sixty-two pounds for Papa and Soňa).

Well, we wanted to blow this rainsville and head south anyway!

They fall in with the caravan of other cars and spend the day traveling on to a new campsite.

After the trip, Soňa and the boys are exhausted, so they get ready for bed right away. They don't even bother with setting up a tent, instead just cuddling up in the back of the camper.

Soňa cradles the little nipper in her arms, whispering in his ear. As the boy falls asleep, he catches a glimpse of his papa in the front seat, scratching away in his notebook with his chin thrust forward.

That night, someone sets the pikeys' camp on fire. The assailants hurl a Molotov cocktail into a tent, while another group ignites the wooden watchman's hut. As the caravan crews dash about, trying to extinguish the flames, the occupants of the camp rapidly pack their things. Papa urges the family to stay calm.

They intentionally threw it in a tent where nobody was. They know what they're doin, they're not tryin to hurt anyone.

They sure do want us outta here though!

Can you blame em?

All right, let's move it, we're goin too! says Soňa with her one seeing eye still glued shut and in an alarming state of disarray.

Papa objects that he really wants to finish writing his chapter. But maybe instead I should turn it into a play, he mutters. Just then some pebbles fly into the windshield. Cast from a distance, they land without force, drumming like raindrops.

Goddammitall! Papa shouts, flinging his notebook into the back, where it lands on a heap of other unfinished work.

LEAVE MEANS LEAVE! POLISH VERMIN!

A group of angry women and a few scowling older men hold up a homemade banner bearing those words, as well as a few others.

At the head of the procession, pouring out of the street toward the devastated campsite, swarms a pack of boys.

Leading the way is a severe-looking man, dressed in black, with a megaphone at his mouth. He chants the slogan at the top of his lungs from under a pencil-thin mustache, waving a black umbrella to conduct the passion-swollen chorus behind him.

They look like they just walked out of a Beatles video, don't they? Papa says to Soňa.

A toddler nails one of their fenders with a piece of brick. The others howl with pleasure.

Eleanor Rigby, that's it!

Another lad wings a brick at the caravan, but it falls short.

We're not Polish vermin, we're *Czech* vermin! Papa yells out the window. We fought for you! Battle of Britain! Ever hear of that, lady? he screams at a woman in the fast-approaching swarm.

You were definitely born by then, you old cow!

Take it easy!

You heifer!

He starts the engine. Soňa takes the boy's hand. With her other she points to a street of postcard-perfect redbrick homes jammed with local inhabitants heading in their direction. Men and boys in T-shirts and jeans stomp across the trampled lawns, baseball bats in hand.

The fastest of the bunch, an elegant-looking fellow with colorfully tattooed arms, in a T-shirt with stripes slicing the suspenders holding up his shorts, spits on the hood and proceeds to step around to the vehicle's rear.

I think we better go, says Papa. And they go.

2

TRAVELERS—NO HOLIDAYS! EXASPERATED
OFFICER. MEMORY OF SLOVAKIA, MEMORY OF
LOVE. ABOUT THE LEG. ABOUT ADDICTION.
ON THE BRIDGE. UNDER THE BRIDGE:
A SYMPHONY OF THE UNIVERSE.

Leaving England, they zip down through France, a day here, a day there, a little dégustation in the South. Papa's got his sights set on the calendar of events.

But on reaching the old campgrounds in Spain, they find the hookups all torn out or filled in with concrete, signs substituting vehemence for grammar, like TRAVELERS, LEAVE! WE HAVE NO HOLIDAYS! and calls for them to bugger off, spraypainted on the boulders and concrete walls around the designated sites.

In the hamlet of Peñascos, a traditional hippie meeting place, a citizens' militia stands at the alert, equipped with a water cannon and a banner reading NO! THANK YOU, ADIOS!, while just down the road from the old Travelers' site outside Toledo is a huge refugee camp, spilling into the city, where there are increasing numbers of demonstrations and clashes with the police, so the KOBKA festival, in honor of Edgar Allan Poe, is called off (minus three hundred forty-seven euros for both of them), and it's the same story in the market town of San Guzmán, where there's no interest in performances that summer (minus two hundred fifty euros for her, minus three hundred fifty euros for him, minus fifteen euros for the boys, who would've shined as Pucks, especially with the little guy suspended above the stage from a rope). And on it goes.

They cross back into France, where at a campground in one of many darkening twilights they are surprised by a wall of caravans and silent mustachioed men, mostly garbed in prehistoric nylon suits, some with red sashes stretched across their paunches. The women—squalling moppets clinging to their colorful flowing skirts, hair, arms, and fists covered in silver jewels and other trinkets—are not exactly what you would call quiet.

Hey, they pinched our spot, Papa splutters amid the general ruckus and screeching.

But before they can confront the usurpers, they are stopped by gendarmes with machine guns over their shoulders.

Papa takes the bottle he was just about to swig from and deftly tucks it under his legs.

A tall, somber-faced man in an officer's cap steps up to the window.

We should turn around and beat it. Fast.

No way! The boys're tired! Tell that bull we've been pitchin our tent here for a thousand years, for God's sake.

But clearly the gendarme doesn't like his tone.

He steps around the hood, his fierce gaze piercing Papa's pupils, which are roiling with a passion of equal ferocity.

He says that according to new regulations, the camp's only for French citizens. You gotta show your carte du nomade.

Mon capitaine, you must be shittin me, man! Papa yawps. What card? Do we look like gypsies? Mon colonel, noo nuh sum pa lay ciganes, we are Czechs! Noo sum bohèmes de la Bohême!

He says the best pension for foreigners is Au Trois Couilles de l'Empereur Napoléon Bonaparte, three kilometers from here.

And who's gonna pay for it, sonuvabitch! That Funès is out of his mind! Tell him that!

No!

Show him the children! Boys, slide over!

The cop takes a look at the desperately smiling Soňa and the terrified boy, pulls his gun from his holster, and presses it to Papa's throat.

Papa just stares straight ahead, feverishly licking the drops of sweat beading on his upper lip.

The officer's voice is soft and insistent.

He says he's very tired. He says this convoy from Romania is the fourth one already today. He says he hates Hitler, but he feels the need to remind you. He says we have no business being here. He also says you shouldn't make fun of him.

Fine, fine, grumbles Papa. Exkoozay mwa, muhsyuh, pardon mwa, he rasps now to the cop's back as he turns the van around. He says nothing even as they careen back down the shabby road in a cloud of dust, and he says nothing even as they hit asphalt again, passing a few familiar landmarks—it's not their first time through this dry and dusty landscape—and in the distance now he sees the bend of a river, there used to be a couple spots around here in the old days, some campgrounds where they stayed before they had the boys, and then with them too, that's right! The two of them know the area well, it's etched into their memories—and the boys? well, now it'll be stuck in their minds too.

You sure you don't want a sip? This stuff is precious, amontillado, seriously!

Don't drink and drive, are you crazy? says Soňa. She snatches the bottle out of his hand and glug glug glug.

Couple swigs of amontillado, nothin better for buildin bravado!

You can say that again, Soňa replies, tipping the bottle down from her lips. Her face, alarmingly rumpled, begins to take on a calmer appearance, a state of bliss spreading through her capillaries. She adjusts the bandage on her leg, pulls it tighter.

Frogs got all serious, don't you think?

Ever since Bataclan.

Batawhat?

Don't tell me you didn't see it, it's all over the news. Oh, never mind . . .

What kina clan?

As she finishes explaining, he rummages around a box on the floor, searches through all his pockets, and finally pulls out two pink rectangles of hard shiny paper, waving them in Soňa's face.

You see! We should've gone! I won these tickets from a friend of mine. He was practically bawlin, his favorite group was playin there, but a bet's a bet, what can you do?

Huh?

I was gonna invite you there for our anniversary, but I totally forgot! How many dead were there? Guess we got lucky, huh?

So you forgot our anniversary! Typical!

I'm sorry!

Mm-hmm!

I think I already asked, but where'd you learn all those languages anyway?

I just did.

I envy you. All we learned was Russian.

We won't be needin that.

You've got a Russian name, though. Doesn't that seem weird to you?

It's from my dad.

You're always dad this, dad that. What about your mom, though?

Soňa makes a sweeping gesture into the distance.

My name's hebish.

That's not how you say it.

Say what?

Biblical's better. Just say biblical.

Well, all right then! Hey, look . . .

They're coming up on the bridge now, its giant frame arching over the valley, the bridge they know from below. The two of them give each other a look, a dewy-eyed look from deep down inside, so deep that for a second of eternity you become that other person, though what's running through their minds right now is how they met. Back then in Slovakia.

He saw the girl again first thing in the morning. She stepped through the curtain of similarity enveloping the other participants of the theater festival and sat down beside him. He clapped his notebook shut, put away his pen, and stared.

Slim and gorgeous, colorful braids, her bosom practically sang.

To what do I owe this honor?

They were on fire. So they kissed. Meanwhile, a gentle breeze rolled down from the mountains enfolding the concrete and grassy surfaces of the Pohoda festival site, caressing and soothing their burning hearts.

You're such a man!

The early-morning guests seated around the table behind them burst into laughter, the one with the bone in his nose actually moaned, and another, a metrosexual covered in comics from head to toe, just hee-hawed and threw back his whole Mirinda in one gulp.

She smiled. A moment from the previous night stood out in her mind, when the stalwart conqueror, drained at last, came to rest in her tenderness-swollen palm, resting there like a satisfied, chubby little baby.

You really are an old fucker! You know, people say the generations are growin farther apart, but I like your generation.

Really? So what does your dad do?

We're from Benešov.

That performance of yours? Wow! You were the best!

So where'd you learn to act?

Art therapy—I was in treatment, he said, revealing the truth.

Yeah, you're really yourself up there. I also like that you're not tattooed.

I considered it, but I've got too much respect for prisoners.

He didn't elaborate. Among other things, on the landscapes of men in blue jumpsuits where sacks of acetone rustled and pederasts smacked their lips; the world behind bars, where the darkness of the soul is dense. Why scare the young lady away?

What?

They don't have that instinct for self-preservation.

I see. So where're you goin from here?

I don't exactly know yet.

I like that too.

Rumbling and jolting, Papa and Soňa vault out of their ardent recollection across the yellow-outlined speedbumps and onto the lengthy bridge. A structure seemingly spat out by a civilization from outer space! A steel edifice dozens of meters above the river! Arched vaults, filigree nuts and bolts, stones painstakingly carved to fit together precisely. Utter rapture.

Here under this very bridge, probably, who knows, she had given birth, about nine months after they met, give or take a week. Who could count all the individual moments in the rolling river of love and harmony that had surged from them in the beginning?

Beyond the parched landscape, the sea lies sparkling in the distance; beneath them, a French river, again soaking up the reflections of their souls, pulling them toward the bottom, down among the rocks, into the churning sludge.

She turns her attention away from the road, casts a glance at his jutting nose indicating the way. Peeks at the boys in back, the sleeping little nipper sweetly displaying his cute little face, the other one gazing pensively out the window. And she feels so sad! And so marvelous!

Hey! Maybe the present moment really is all there is!

You promised you'd stop.

There's no heaven and hell, ever, anywhere, I swear.

And she launches right back into it.

Life is beautiful! Sad and beautiful! That's the only thing I know!

You don't care about me, fine, but for God's sake, think of the kids!

The present is all that exists, for real! I just realized it now!

Look, this is our last performance, then we go home, and unless you stop, I'm droppin you off at the clinic first thing. How's your leg? You said it had been hurting.

It's swollen!

What from?

I donno. Life.

Needles're dangerous, you know.

It is swollen a little, that's true.

Look, in any case it's best to be ailing in your mother tongue. We'll find you some fancy private clinic and your daddy can spring for it. What do you say?

Like hell. What about the boys?

What about them? I'll take care of them.

Swear on the Mother of God.

Fine!

No, swear it, for real!

They come rumbling off the bridge, since he should have touched the brakes before going over the yellow but didn't, and go barreling down the asphalt road, past the bushes leaning out from the concrete-reinforced banks.

Hey, buckle up, all right? Where's your seat belt? If the cops pull us over, we got nothin to pay the fine with.

But then they decide to look back.

They were wandering lost in the dark. They could have sworn they knew the way to the nearest clinic, so they could go straight to the delivery room and get there in time, but things went awry.

He peered out the windows, trying to see the signs through the cords of rain, while she moaned, holding her hands atop her swollen belly. They must have missed the turnoff. All he could see was a red glow shining under the bridge.

He stopped and got out of the car. He would go and ask directions. With great effort, she wriggled out and tried to come along. He chased her back to the car, but she insisted . They probably both needed relief from that cramped space full of groans and cries. She was desperate for air. And besides, they had run out of gas.

He held her as they stumbled through the mud beneath the bridge's arch. The road was high overhead. Right away they came across a heap of paper boxes. She flopped down, unable to go on. At least she had cardboard under her back.

She stretched out and spread her legs, attempting to pull up her skirt. As he tore the rags from her trembling hips, her milk-filled breasts shook in time with her breathing. Rolling up his sweatshirt, he stuck it underneath her head, and good thing too.

The back of her skull slammed furiously into the pillow as she writhed in pain, her truly animal-like screams reflecting off the metal arch.

He tried not to blind her with the light from his headlamp. Besides, he didn't even want to see the look on her face as foam formed at the corners of her mouth. She continued to shriek in pain, her stomach bulging monstrously.

Papa kneeled at Soňa's feet, aiming the cone of light at the expanding opening between her bloodied legs, where a tiny little head had appeared. He waited, prepared to grasp hold of the infant. The head emerged. Then popped gently out. As if someone had pressed down firmly on Soňa's belly and squeezed out the contents. The newborn slipped out, softly plopping into his hands. He felt more than saw the umbilical cord. Using his finger, he untangled it from the coil of blood and mucus and sliced through it with his jackknife. He gaped in awe at the blood-covered child. It's a boy, he realized. He cleared the slime from its mouth using his little finger. Tried to wipe the little eyes, tiny as grains of lentil, and the child weakly mewled. Then burst into tears.

Probably that explains why he didn't hear the footsteps. Or the voices. It wasn't raining that hard anymore, but the little boy's cries drowned out the sound.

They came from somewhere on the other side, down below the bridge.

Soňa lay on the boxes, legs bent at the knee. Though no longer at the peak of her pain, her face was still contorted in spasms.

They came walking up and surrounded them. Black men in jeans, windbreakers. One young man held up a lighter, another had a flashlight, pointing it at the little nipper in Papa's hands.

In a gesture of defenselessness and amazement, with an almost apologetic grin, he raised the child to show the newcomers. Blinking in the light. His baby son fit in the palm of his hand, whimpering and howling. In the other hand he held the jackknife.

An old man with knots of gray hair falling in his face ran the cone of light over the newborn's crippled, bloody body. The young men bunched together, one of them gave a hearty laugh. Others began to straggle in from the darkness deep beneath the bridge, soles clicking over the rocks. A hint of rain reached them on the wind as they crooned and nattered. Of course to the newly turned father, kneeling with his small son against his body, every sound was an expression of nature, all the universe was singing its symphony, rejoicing to the heavens and conveying its support.

But these were men. So he stood up, and noticing the open knife in his hand, blood-covered and wet with slime and goo from the umbilical cord, he turned it on the new arrivals.

Sa va? inquired the shaggy-haired old man.

Sa va byen!

Shok vray um port uh kuto, said the old-timer, taking the knife from his hand.

Soňa was surrounded by women. And squeezed in behind them, a whole flock of girls. The womenfolk gathered around her, laying sweaters beneath her head, caressing and kneading her aching body. They had water with them. A few commands and the younger ones padded off into the darkness under the bridge.

Papa moved toward her. Clasping the tiny little boy gently in both palms. Soňa peered at the company gathered around through half-shut eyes. Then her face convulsed in a spasm. And then another.

The screaming started up again, and her belly began to swell like a sack. She jerked and thrashed, screaming and spreading her legs. The gaggle of twittering female assistants reached out to soothe her, holding her hands, wiping her forehead.

Papa hadn't thought he was capable of movement, but a power greater than his drove him toward her, toward the cluster. Through the women's arms and elbows he saw Soňa's thighs opening wide. Then a new tiny little head pushed its way out of her body, another child coming into the world.

They had helped them. They helped them out enormously. Back in their campsite they had water, hot water, as much as was needed. Their own besmudged little children were happy to do without a bath. And someone even got through to the clinic on the phone.

They sent Soňa on her way with a full baby bottle, clothes, wads of exotic cotton, a lemon, and all kinds of tiny sweet fruits the parents had never laid eyes on before. And in one final friendly gesture, the old-timer thrust the jackknife into Papa's hand. Rinsed and cleaned. Yep, it had turned out well.

This time they cross the bridge without incident, leaving it far behind in the distance of the parched landscape.

Hey, by the way, did you say ailing? Soňa says, picking up the conversation where they left off. Her voice is a raspy shriek, likely foretelling further unpleasantness.

That's like from World War II, no one says that anymore! she declares, patting down her jacket, digging through her skirt pockets for her drug paraphernalia.

Upon which Papa informs her that her current belief that her stoned consciousness is more expansive, more entertaining, and more expressive of the human condition than the consciousness of someone who is not ingesting toxins is not objective, but just part of her addiction.

There you go with the fatherly talk! Shit, I might as well be home!

But you're gettin older too, don't forget. Your eyes are like slits in the morning. You party constantly, not to mention you're gainin weight.

The fuck're you talkin about? My leg hurts is all!

Look, don't think you're immune. Nobody is. Like it or not!

Stop psychin me out!

And you constantly complain, have you noticed? That's also new.

This time, for a change, she pulls out a silver tube, which he snatches out of her hand and flings into the back of the car.

She belts him one. Though by now, of course, he is skilled at dodging her blows. He has also grown accustomed to her strident tone, whereas a normal human being would be numbstruck by the grinding buzz saw of her indignation. He just closes his inner ears. Papa yanks the wheel, steering them out of the way of the wildly gesticulating oncoming drivers, their appearances merging into a tangled mass that vanishes into oblivion, as she leans into the back, hugs the boy, and presses her head to the sweaty little notch at his throat.

3

CHARLEVILLE, LES POÈTES MAUDITS.
SECURING PROVISIONS. PREPARING THE
PERFORMANCE. BRIELLE AND ONWARD.
TO MUNICH. ZOSHCHENKO'S END.
TO THE LAND OF CHILL.

You know what Charles Baudelaire wrote? That the Belgians were cud-chewers who couldn't digest a thing, Papa says, smiling out the window at the organizers in rain ponchos directing them to the parking lot at the local house of culture.

Also, when he was in Belgium he lost the urge to smoke, but he couldn't help himself, so it was extremely unpleasant, Papa explains to the family on their trip to the bordertown supermarket.

Keep him distracted, Papa says, tipping his shoulder toward the guy creeping along the aisle behind the family, not letting them out of his sight.

Soňa, little one in her arms with the bigger boy in tow, collapses into the store detective's arms, and as she blurts out the international expression: water! shedding an actor's tears from her eye, Papa zips past the registers. A few moments later, around the corner from the supermarket, the family divvies up the fine Swiss chocolates and gourmet sausages, along with some minibottles of vitamin solution Papa managed to squeeze into the paper sacks that officially housed only a few croissants, which he of course paid for, plenty. And as the fab little bottles of Jim Beam and Jack Daniel's spill out of his pantlegs, and he tries to explain to the boys that those are just for him, Soňa is having none of it.

I'm amazed they don't have scanners at the registers like at the airports. Oh well. They'll get em eventually, but for now at least we're good.

Where are we anyway? Soña inquires, dark as a Moor herself as she wipes the boy's chocolate-smeared face with a spit-soaked handkerchief, clutching a pack of diapers under each arm.

Charleville, says Papa. A couple boxes of sardines come loose, dropping out of his sleeves. I throw a pair of undies over the cameras, he explains. Learned that back in commie days. I had a buddy who'd walk into a Tuzex in Poland or Hungary wearing a pair of shorts and walk out again in three pairs of jeans. We'd sell em around the corner and party for a week. Ah, youth!

What time do we perform today?

Yep, then in New York I had a friend that had these custom pockets sewed into his coat, and he'd go out and shoplift books, or sometimes even steaks. This one time he put a steak that he'd nabbed out of a freezer in the same pocket as this expensive picture book, talk about a stupid move, and this girl I lived with got all huffy whenever I'd cook up one of his steaks, like, "Stolen goods? I'm not eating that." It was just plain theft as far as she was concerned.

Girl?

One of those ones I knew back in the day, before you came into the world.

Mm-hmmm.

Oh, come on now, they were just mattresses that I practiced on until I met you. So you'd be satisfied! Anyway, the only thing I ever stole was some food, just a little, I was broke. Gavros was my hero. That scene where he steals the swan to feed his two lost little brothers, that is seared into my brain. We should do it someday! But of course your generation doesn't read Victor Hugo. Oh well. Can't say that I blame you.

You're mixin it all up.

That's true, but it is all mixed up.

Plus you already told me all that before!

Sorry!

Let's talk about somethin else.

What for?

During their siesta in the car, Papa proposes to Soña that as long as they're in the birthplace of the master Baudelaire, they should act out an excerpt from "A Carcass." She can play the starring role, and the boys can circle around her, playing the flies, while he recites the lines, but in a way that offers hope. She interrupts him to point out that Charleville is the birthplace of another poet legend as well.

Right, he went out with Baudelaire, didn't he? They were queer as all get-out! I donno if I could pull that off.

No, that was that other poet that went out with the guy from here, says Soňa, eyes glued to her phone.

Whatever, either way they were all accursed.

Fine, if you say so!

I can't remember everything, can I? Papa grumbles. Plus you know we weren't allowed to go to school! Not everyone's born velvet! All those privileges. Freedom! Yeah, I mean you! You're what they call a child of the Velvet Revolution.

Do you even have a high school diploma?

You bet, and a nice one too. Got it right here in my suitcase somewhere. Heh-heh-heh!

Though they did nail me in fourth grade. I ever tell you that?

Who "they"?

The ess-tee-bee, secret police! That's how it was in those days . . .

Don't bother. I know the stories from my dad.

Oh yeah?

Only he was on the other side.

Yeah, well, after that, in the nuthouse, that's where I found myself, art therapy. There was this nurse there, actually more than one. They brought me books, banned ones too. They enjoyed hearing me recite. There was a doctor too. Psychologist, actually. She was always on my side.

Uh-huh, the usual story.

Basically, she ended up as my slave. All of us nutjobs had to go on walks. Calisthenics, ping-pong, that sorta crap. She exempted me from all that. We spent the whole time in her office. She was great!

So actually it was a good thing.

The main thing was, I didn't want to go in the army. Who knew where the Russkies would send you? Afghanistan, Poland . . .

So you got out of it . . .

Yeah, I can tell you now, you're an adult. But supposedly I was the only one she ever had an orgasm with, so she didn't want to discharge me. Things got a bit tricky after that.

You poor thing!

Yeah, talk about a wild ride, but there's always someone you find who can help. That's the art of war.

Oh, spare me, what war? Nowadays? My dad . . . hey, these Pampers're amazing. I guess they gave em to me cause they thought I was a refugee.

Are you kidding? What do you mean, refugee? They give those out to all the women here. It's a rich country.

You think?

Sure.

Papa crawls into the space behind the sleeping bags and crates and heaps of paperbacks and boxes of Chinese soup and the stove and everything else they have back there, opens a notebook, and starts scrawling away.

This here set of wheels has got some serious miles on her, says Papa, patting the dashboard as they zoom down the highway through gale-force winds that batter and churn the windmill blades, spoiling the views over the swampy flatland . . . I probably already told you how I scrounged up the cash for it. Soon as the Czechs joined NATO and the EU, I took my poems out on the road. They invited me all over the place. When I was in jail under the Bolshies, locked up for my resistance poetry—man, that was the tour to end all tours! Yeah, that's not gonna happen again!

You've told me that story a thousand times. How the Westerners ate it up . . .

They were curious about us backwoods clods from Eastern Europe. That was still under Havel.

Right, but things're different now, huh?

Hm.

We've got problems now, huh?

Well, the scene is different today, for sure. Spontaneous poetry and Beatnik stuff, that's all gone. Fuckin committees all over the place. A million emails for every stupid little thing! And, as long as I'm bein bitter, the ethnic card doesn't exactly play to our strong suit either.

Oh, come off it. We've both noticed nobody ever invites us back anywhere.

True!

We're gettin tired, if you ask me.

Y'know, it's one thing puttin together a poetry evening and somethin else comin up with a play for a family. So it kina makes sense. Plus I had different needs back then. What're you gonna do?

Oh, cut the crap. They took us a lot when I had a belly, and how many times did they do it to take pity on the kids? I really don't think it has all that much to do with your genius.

Hey, look where we are! Check it out! Remember?

They zip past the highway signs for Bruges and Damme. And there's no use his inviting her to look when her eye has just landed on their little son's halberd.

It was like this.

He was rolling around in the back of the van fishing for ideas, but it didn't click until she googled where they were, that is, where the festival was taking place. In the south of Holland, Brielle, the festival of the Geuzen rebels . . .

Well, shit, then it's simple, he informed her and the boys. Damme is where Till Eulenspiegel died. In elementary school we learned that was the Dutch people's liberation struggle against the usurpers as part of the effort to install communism. I read it as a little boy in the children's hospital psych ward. The Geuzen? We got our show in the bag!

Soňa, high as a kite on whatever drugs she was doing that day, circled the stage in a hooded cape with cutout holes that Papa made from a sack of fertilizer he found lying out behind the local supermarket, which perfectly evoked the Inquisition. She played the role of the tyrant, the Duke of Alba, reaching out her claws toward the boys, who played the rebellious Geuzen.

The big boy banged a drum, weapon at the ready, with the little nipper suspended over the stage in a traditional clog-shaped cradle, representing the future of the Netherlands, while Papa with a loaf of cheese tucked under his peasant's frock, borrowed from the prop man, played the mighty Thyl Ulenspiegel. And as he bellowed out the Geuzens' battle song—

Tear out the Duke of Alba's intestines
whip him in the face with them!
the boy chopped away at Soňa till she began to totter and collapsed onto
his halberd, and apart from poking out her eye, she also nicely bruised
her ribs while she was rolling around on the floor howling in pain.

So now instead they just bypass it and cruise on through Germany,
weaving and dodging their way around the former wintering spots,
since the local officials have the boys in their sights, and moreover one
friendly squat, which in past years they had used to take a break and
supplement the boy's more than spotty school attendance with home
schooling, has burned clear down; another has been converted into
a youth hostel for young millionaires; a kulturhaus where Papa once
had friends from the days after the fall of the curtain is now a residence for writers fleeing Egypt, Algeria, Turkey, Syria . . . In other spots
where art-loving Eastern Europeans once flocked they find new asyl-
hauses for people in genuine distress; and in place of a small alternative farm they used to frequent is a brand spanking-new feminist zone:
NO MAN—NO PIG PLACE. Soňa is thrilled when she first sees it, but then
changes her mind. In another picturesque little town, they stumble
into the midst of a rowdy demonstration, with naturally no idea what
the residents are marching for, but when a couple of locals decide to
flip their vehicle, children or no, Papa shifts into reverse and the family
keeps on trucking. Everywhere they go, the squares and plazas where
people of similar appearance once strolled, trying to make up their
minds where to go and who with, are now lined with ranks of impover-
ished refugees, guarded by smiling police and soldiers, two meters tall,
blond and blue-eyed, slim, muscular, and armed to the teeth, dispensing goodwill at full blast.

Sometimes Soňa can't resist, veiling herself like it was just another
acting exercise, and as long as the other ladies don't hound her out of
line she comes back to the car each time lugging packages of groceries
and hygiene supplies, plus a cleaning agent or two, which she doesn't
know how to use anyway.

They don't really hit bottom till Munich.

The commissioner of the venerable Freies Theater festival insists that
they first undergo an interview and auditions, only after which he will

decide whether and in which category of the festival—now of course being held to mark the four hundredth anniversary of William Shakespeare—to include them, which is crucial, since that means money.

The commissioner has a metal cashbox open on the table before him, glowing with banknotes in every color of the EU. He's a good-looking fellow, too. The way the shine of his teeth accords with the sparkle of his obviously tailored-to-fit leather shoes makes the rumpled acting duo just a wee bit nervous. An artistic ringlet hangs down across the man's forehead, and when he speaks of literature, the commissioner's eyes glaze over with a sheen of dreamy awe. His gaze is flat, roving, perhaps even Hölderlinesque, as Papa excitedly whispers to Soňa.

The wide-open window of the ground-floor office affords a view of the other acting troupes in various stages of rehearsing or loafing about. A Tatar group called Crimea Sunrise is busy limbering up. Georgians from the company Papa's Sharp Sabre are practicing tricks with their various sharp objects. The mood is cheerful and lively as the smiling Afghans in their turbans and brightly colored robes shyly trickle into the courtyard along with a few Chechens from the line of refugees winding across the square. To the delight and curiosity of the international small fry, a group of authentic Ukrainian folk musicians are scraping the verdigris off their trumpets. But there are beads of sweat standing out on Papa's brow.

What does he mean we were supposed to mail in our application a year in advance? I've played here so many damn times I can't even count!

Well, that's what he says!

Hell! Used to be enough just to show up on time! They were glad to have us! They all know who I am!

You mean back in the days when Havel was president, right?

Well, there didn't used to so many troupes, I guess, Papa says, cooling down.

He also wants you to explain why Forefather Czech is in *The Winter's Tale*.

Well, when Antigonus lands on the Bohemian coast, the cabin boy cries: Beware! There lurk creatures of prey in this land! And Forefather Czech appears!

He doesn't seem convinced.

Well, it's very alternative. But seeing as we're Czechs, and this is the only Shakespeare piece about the Czech lands, it should be acceptable. It's our right!

He says it doesn't seem that way to him.

And you're sure you translated correctly?

Of course!

Look, tell him . . .

Forget it! We're just embarrassing ourselves. Let's go, c'mon.

Just then, a fearful voice echoes through the kulturhaus. The entire ground floor shakes with screams, including the room where they stand before the commissioner. He too gets nervous, nods to them, they rush out the door.

The spectacle that greets them upon entering the next room makes Soňa put her hand over the big boy's eyes.

The world-famous and renowned Shakespeare actor, the Russian genius Zoshchenko, known for his performances as Macbeth, Caliban, and Henry IV, reclines on a bed in a pool of blood. A dagger protrudes from his chest, its richly crafted hilt still quivering. The commissioner screams and fishes his phone from his pocket. As the whole courtyard rushes toward the open window, the frightened shouts show no signs of letting up.

They don't want us! Maybe the bossman here reads, says Soňa sarcastically as they stride across the oil-stained surface of the parking lot. And maybe he knows a smelly ham when he sees one!

He just isn't the type to appreciate a postmodern, alternative, multicultural approach!

That's old hat now!

Mainly it's bullshit. That was wild with Zoshchenko, though, right? You think the fest'll be canceled?

All you think about is yourself. Poor Vitaly Semyonovich, maybe he's got a family. Who do you think did it?

Hard to say. Besides, you never know with Russians! Maybe he got sad, maybe he was down in the dumps and just . . . I really liked him too.

You don't have to take the piss out of everything. Sometimes I'm not in the mood! What're we gonna do now? We're flush outta cash, Jesus and Mary!

Don't take the Lord's name in vain. And to no purpose. Maybe there'll be a miracle.

Now you're fundamentally pissing me off! You're a gasbag and an ego-tripper and a manipulator!

Now, now . . .

And an alcoholic and a clown and a nutjob!

I get sad too sometimes, you know.

Jesus and Mary, when you told me I was the best back then at the Pohoda fest in Trenčín! That was beautiful. And to think I believed you!

But it was true!

Waaaah, ach ich!

Y'know, Soňa, I always pictured our son as the cabin boy in *The Winter's Tale* shouting that line about Bohemia!

What?

Beware! There lurk beasts of prey in this land!

Jesus and Mary! Our son? Shout?

Well, speak, anyway. Maybe he'd like that!

If only! Soňa bursts into tears and kneels down and hugs the boy, sobbing into his neck.

Listen, Soňa, those poor refugees from bombed-out homes, families shattered, some of em with torture scars, those poor souls have no idea what's in store . . . we're doin pretty good!

Oh fuck off!

What do you say we go to Budapest and then on to Slovakia?

Huh?

By the time we get to Slovakia, we're practically home. Just a hop, skip, and a jump from there to Sázava. I told you how my dad and brother started those famous motorcycle races there.

You told me a thousand times how poor you were as a little boy.

My brother and me used to fight in the barn. He's a good bit older than I am. The barn was where him and my dad kept the bikes.

So he must be an old geezer by now! Those races're practically stone age!

As it happens, the motocross in Poříčí nad Sázavou's really something! To this day, I kid you not!

I'm sure.

Plus I'd like to show the boys!

Seriously?

You get in first . . . here, I'll hold the door. Hey, boys, come on, what's the fuss, up you go, settle in! We're goin to Slovakia. Home, here we come!

Home, huh? The only one here from Czechoslovakia's you, you old coot, Soňa says, now in the front seat.

That's right, and I'll never stop bein sorry that we split with the Slovaks. I'll be Czechoslovak till the day I die, even if my kids're just Czechs. Like you. What's it like bein just Czech? Don't you feel a little deprived?

Why should I?

Emotionally I still see Czechoslovakia as my homeland, says Papa, slamming his fist on the dashboard, spitting out the window, and honking the horn.

How come?

It's what I'm used to.

Basically, though, same difference, far as I'm concerned.

You're right.

Ach ich!

Please, come on, don't cry. You'll frighten the boys. Now, now. No need for tears.

But it helps.

All right then, it's all right.

I'm not even allowed to cry anymore.

It's fine.

Cords of rain beat against the windows. A little stream right by the rest area is taking a pounding, foaming up, bounding along the concrete gutter. The drain ripples with the incoming water.

The still-drowsy Soňa nudges Papa's tousled head.

So're we goin?

She gapes in disbelief at the wads of bills—not only blue and pink, but green, yellow, and purple too—shuffling through his hands. Her gaze slides down to the floor. The cashbox.

We're fucked. You're insane.

Not to worry. No one'll be any the worse! I guarantee you they're insured. They got the whole thing covered, relax! They know what they're doin.

They're gonna lock you up!

Are you kiddin? They'll just write it off.

You think?

You saw what it looked like back there. Nothing but suffering masses. No way will they investigate!

He rolls down the window and flings the empty cashbox into the drainage ditch. Now he's got a road map over the tattered notebooks on his lap.

We gotta go through Hungary. We can perform there. I know it there.

Yeah?

Yeah, sure. The Hungarians're great, totally chill.

You think?

You'll see!

4

MOMENTS IN SPA CULTURE. COMMISSIONER HOT
ON THE TRAIL. WHERE TO HIDE THE FUNDS.
KELETI PU. IVAN AND VASKA. DRAMA AT THE
POOL. SWIMMERS' TRAGEDY. WHO'S PLAYING
OTHELLO? WHERE'D IGGY FLY OUT OF?

THE ETERNAL YOUTH OF WORDS—OUR WORLD—SHAKESPEARE 400—
BUDAPEST! reads the poster outside the festival office that Papa just exited, smiling.

We go on right after *Othello*, he announces to the family, nose immersed in the program. A breeze from the river flowing around Margaret Island ruffles the pages in his hands.

Check it out, my buddies and I slept all over this place, says Papa. He points to the bushes around them. But we're about to find ourselves the finest accommodations of our life. We can take showers till the cows come home, and wait'll you see the food. Hungarian cooking's amazing!

Soňa smiles too, nodding along as Papa describes the pleasure and comfort awaiting them in the famed mud and thermal baths they're walking past right now at the heart of the Budapest island.

Their noses pick up the damp, not unpleasant odor of salty mud, and through gaps in the fence they can see bathers lolling about in the water. There are also people sitting reading half-submerged, and chess players buoyed up by the one-of-a-kind Hungarian water, urinating around themselves as they weigh their next move.

In a space over by the artificial waves, a small party coated in mud is slapping more mud on themselves. Then a battle ensues as they bombard each other with pungent cakes of mud. The boy's head is in a whirl from all the whooping and exultation, and he can feel a film of salty sweat all over his skin. A short way off, he spies changing cabins, kiosks selling all sorts of treats, and a greensward covered with people sunning themselves and just generally lazing about.

Oooh, Soňa smiles broadly, now we can really relax. Have a swim. And then home we go! You're finally gonna get to see your native soil, boys!

That's right, Papa chimes in, and we'll get us some proper clothes, too! I mean, look at us!

Yeah, yeah, says Soňa.

We'll buy tons of presents, Papa goes on, and throw out all the junk we've been luggin around with us, you'll see! We're gonna get rid of everything, down to the last camping mat!

All right!

Just do today's performance and fwoop . . .

That's right!

And once we get home we can start our own theater! Easy!

Now hold on . . .

I mean, after we've had a chance to relax—that's understood.

What about the boys?

They gotta go to school, I know! We'll be able to afford the best doctors now, the best care, all of it! Don't you worry!

Yes, yes, Soňa nods, her gaze suddenly absent, askew . . . Feeling a prick in her swollen leg, she drags the boy by the hand over to the nearest kiosk, yanking his shoulder as she stumbles.

By the way, it's really fascinating what they're doing with *Othello* here.

Soňa orders a glass of wine. They serve it chilled.

Having him played by a gorilla! It seems somehow more daring, having a white girl strangled by an animal. Why don't we all sit down, huh? It's really pretty hot. Hey, boys, cola, juice? Order both if you want! Hey, look, everyone, we're here!

And so they are. Right by the parking lot, so they can keep an eye on the car. They sit down on a bench, have a few drinks, eat a few hot dogs, melegszendvicses, roasted corn on the cob . . . they stuff themselves with treats, this time all purchased by Papa . . . whatever anyone wants, he jumps right up to the kiosk to get it. They dispose of their wrappers and leftovers in a stone trash can when they're finished.

Now that we're loaded, we're going to be orderly and economical! Papa exults.

You know with that ape . . . maybe there aren't as many animal rights advocates in Hungary as other places, Soňa says.

Well, maybe it's a tamed animal, from the zoo. Or the circus.

Could be. Gorillas are intelligent!

Boys, listen to your mama! Gorillas are almost as intelligent as humans. They might even be smarter! Why shouldn't they be able to act in plays? Your mama's right.

Told you, says Soňa, hand roaming through her skirt pockets.

Hey, boys, want a magazine? In our day all we had was that Pioneer crap. You've got it good! What'll it be, Martians or Indians?

Don't be stupid, they're all in Hungarian, it's just a waste of money . . .

They've still got the same pictures. Listen, boys, tell you what. I'll buy you both. Then you can trade. You're brothers, remember, so no fighting.

Jeezhush and Mary! Soňa shrieks. As she brings the tube of pills to her mouth, it knocks against a tooth so hard it throws off a spark.

Then they both see him.

The commissioner. The fellow from Munich.

In the same suit, as if he had marched right out of the office, hot on their trail. And he's standing at their camper. He leans toward the window, gazes inside. Drums his fingers on the hood, pursing his lips, perhaps whistling. Rises up on the toes of his polished shoes to peek through the windows. In his hand he's got a phone.

The whole family follows Papa, racing around to the back of the kiosk to hide. They take cover behind the trash can made of stone.

Soňa squats down, leans her back against the plank wall, little one in her arms. The bigger boy leans against her, peering out from behind the garbage can.

Soňa?

Mm.

If your arms start hurting, hand him to me!

Everything hurts right now.

Look, we'll wait awhile. If he takes off, no big deal!

We gotta get outta here now! Screw the camper, it's old anyway. I just feel bad about the phones. I wanted to call my dad!

Soňa, but . . .

We can get a hotel, right? We've got IDs, no big deal.

Soňa, I'm not sure how to . . .

You've got the cash on you, right?

I hid it in that old edition of *Moby Dick*. That dog-eared Penguin edition. Somebody might take those shiny paperbacks, but the Melville's all beat up. I've also got *Prestuplenie i nakazanie*, but that's in Russian, no one'd take that!

So you don't have the cash?

I just took enough for food. And we spent it.

No, don't tell me.

I also tucked some away in that Thrift Books edition of *Quixote*. No one would dream of looking in there.

They stumble across Margaret Bridge, trudging headfirst into the wind howling over the Danube. For one brief moment, it crosses Soňa's mind to pull the boys to her side and jump, skirt billowing . . . but that probably crosses everyone's mind walkin across the river like this, she thinks to herself.

It's straight to the train station for us! Keleti! We can take a breather there! Wash up! I can't even tell you how many times we slept there back in the day, no sweat—though I did get locked up one time . . . Papa shouts into the wind as it hurls wrappers and grit at them over the bridge's railing, which means they must be nearing the station, and that's a good thing, because Soňa's swollen leg is really slowing them down.

I'm amazed they let you in the country!

But don't worry. That was under socialism. It won't be in their database now.

Pushing their way through the crowd of people in the concourse, they sneak past the police station, pass a booth of humanitarian workers, trudge by a many-headed serpent forming a twisting line with clumps of five, ten people, children in their arms.

Then they pass through a door and find themselves in the sleeping area. People with backpacks sit on the floor, indifferent to the announcements, as passengers hurry past . . . They killed us, raped us, a guy hunched over his laptop types, pecking out the letters . . . Chased us, murdered us . . . They lie on inflatable mattresses, camping mats, surrounded by the hustle and bustle of the train station . . . We begged, we wept . . . the mountains couldn't hide us, the people wouldn't hide us . . . we fled to the sea, we are alive . . . the guy types out, deafened by the raspy soundtrack of departures and arrivals . . . And though the road leads nowhere, at least we are here on this earth.

Oweeeee, wails Soňa, as a newly arrived emir, in a flowing robe with a bundle of green fuzz under his arm, steps on her foot . . . The cries and shouts of the crowd fill the hall right up to the ceiling, like boiling water threatening to slosh out of a glass.

See, I told you we could spend the night here! At least we already ate! Idiot!

Vendors push past them with carts of sandwiches, newspapers, travelers dragging suitcases on squeaky wheels. Off in the corner, the boy spots a lone figure towering over the crowd . . . a roving, restless shine in his eyes, yes, the boy has a feeling the tall old-timer is . . . looking around for them. Now he's waving to them! The boy tugs at his mama's skirt. Grabs his papa by the hand.

I'm glad to see you so interested, boy. Yes, take it all in. Take a good look! Who knows when we'll be back again.

Back from prison, hisses Soňa.

The old-timer peels himself out of the corner and sways through the crowd of refugees, yep, shuffling slow and easy over the turbans and fezzes and caps, heading straight for them.

You dumbass, you ruined it! And the little one shit his pants . . .

As Soňa swears and fumes, the foul-smelling little nipper still pressed to her breasts, she drags her boy away by the hand, yanking so hard tears well in his eyes. She practically dislocates his arm, she's gotten so worked up.

Just then, somebody runs over Soňa's sore foot again with a cart full of pickled tomatoes and peppers and disappears into the clangorous throng rolling past like a whirl of shadows.

OwwwIwantouttaheeeere . . .

Soňa, let him go! Here, lean against this pillar! Son, you don't have to . . . Using his sleeve, Papa wipes away the tears suddenly spraying everywhere—down the boy's chin, around his nose, down his cheeks.

Look at you crying, and you're a big boy. You don't see your little brother crying like that.

No, but he . . . Soňa chimes in from the squat she's dropped into.

There, there. Take an example from your little brother!

But he never cries. Haven't you noticed?

All kids cry. You cried too. So did I.

But he doesn't cry, ever.

That's good, it means he's strong. A strong individual, I've been tellin you.

I think he doesn't know how.

That's a good thing, isn't it?

Actually, it's bad. Really bad.

Oh, please, it's always something with you!

They stare daggers at each other, the whispers of the refugees circling around them, the voices from the loudspeakers announcing station stops and delays, the sounds of children crying, screaming, coming from the endless line . . . So deeply absorbed are Papa and Soňa in their showdown that it takes them a moment to realize . . .

Please, just stop arguing!

. . . the words are in Czech. The two of them glance down at their boy's tear-soaked face, Soňa with a stunned smile, Papa gaping open-mouthed . . . believing the voice to have come from him, but their still-silent son is suddenly standing, along with them, in the path of a mighty shadow.

My dear friends, the big man says. He speaks in a bass voice, just as you would expect, but in a tone so smooth it's almost greasy, and velvety soft. With rusty-gray hair and a big, jutting nose, the burly man stands before them in a shiny blue tracksuit with yellow stripes running down the side.

The boy stares, realizing that the man looks just like his papa.

In his hand, Papa's double clutches a festival program turned to the page where there's a tiny little picture of their camper van and the whole happy family posing beside it. They're all done up in their costumes and makeup, but you can tell it's them. Then, filling a whole page, is a huge portrait of the genius Zoshchenko.

I come to welcome great artist Vitaly Semyonich Zoshchenko. And here you! I looking for you. The burly man taps his finger on their photo. You know who am I? he asks Papa, his gaze boring into him.

Papa's chin drops under the intensity of the stare. Then his eyes bulge and his face twists with the shock of recognition.

The man grins back at him.

I long time from motherland gone. In native speech I have gaps. I plan visit spas in your country! I am missing you!

He's a head taller than Papa. Stronger. Older. Brown spots on the backs of his hands. And the shoulders of the youthful, still-brawny old-timer? Like a rock.

Zoshchenko will no be coming, fascists killed, he says. But you here! Now you know who am I? I am Ivan, your born braht.

The boy stares at his nose. Then zooms in on his papa. Same cheeks. Big lips. Now Soňa sees the likeness too.

The man lays a hand on Papa's shoulder.

Moy mily braht!

B-r-o-t-h-e-r! stammers Papa.

They hug. The devils know whose bones crack louder.

This is my wife Soňa! And these're my boys! Twins!

I know, I know, the burly man says, nodding his head. Why you have come to vokzal? You are no performing? You are leaving?

Yep!

And where to? And to do what? Shit! You said we were gonna swim in the baths! Relax, enjoy ourselves! We're a grimy mess . . . Soňa sputters.

Which way you are going?

No way, Soňa says.

You will come with me!

Where to? says Papa.

Soňa bangs the back of her skull against the column, then goes rigid. Maybe she overdid it . . . She fixes an eye on a point in the glass dome overhead.

I Ivan, the man says, bending down to the boy. How they call you?

The car is driven by a smallish fidgety bald-headed guy. He's wearing a blue tracksuit too, though his is without stripes. He runs his beady eyes up and down, giving them the once-over. Satisfied, he smiles. They bundle themselves into the vehicle quite comfortably, and it's just a short way to the bridge.

This Vaska, Ivan says, gesturing to the driver, who steps on the gas with an Adidas-clad foot. You speak to him Czech. He is from Prague district Smíchov, they call him Tyran.

They hurry to the parking lot, then push their way through the formally dressed crowd straggling out of the afternoon performance in the festival tent, clogging up the entrance to the baths.

Othello's over. We should've been goin onstage now, Papa growls.

But we're not! Soňa adds grumpily, sending Papa chasing ahead after Vaska and the strapping man in the tracksuit. Soňa, along with the boy and the little one in her arms, limps along behind.

And they've turned up just in time. Just in time for the family to have to duck behind the kiosk again. They observe the tow truck. Cops in jumpsuits emblazoned with the word RENDŐRSÉG burble into their cell phone–walkie-talkies. Their antagonist from Munich, stretched on tiptoe, studies the heap of paperbacks in the back of their camper with a laser gaze, then watches with a smile as the towing service performs its work. He walks a few steps away, chatters something into his cell.

As their vehicle disappears for good, Soňa plops herself down on a bench. Papa wraps an arm around her sweaty shoulders as the little one claws his way to her breasts.

Then Papa gives Ivan the full account of their run-in with the commissioner.

Well then, Ivan declares. Vaska and I, we will give little think. No good for EU fascist to testify on you. You go swim!

What? Can we? Soňa exclaims.

I don't know about that, Papa mutters.

What do you mean you don't know? Soňa barks. We're goin! C'mon, boys, let's go for a dip! We need to get clean at least, right?

Ivan presses a bill into her hand. Go. Cleanse yourselves. Vaska will prepare fresh clothings.

The boy washes off the mud. Warms himself in the afternoon sun. The changing cabins are behind him, and somewhere over there on the grass are his mama and little brother. Sunning themselves along with the other naked people. A multitude of them, sprawled out on blankets for the afternoon siesta, the pulsing sound of Hungarybeat resonating from boomboxes. A small man pushes an ice cream cart across the lawn.

The sun-steeped water ripples in the bluish-bottomed swimming pool. Artificial waves lap against the boy's thighs at regular intervals, splashing on his boxers, just like at the sea. But he isn't clutching sand between his fingers, or shells, or pebbles. The pool bottom is wrinkled, bumpy, but the surface is firm underfoot.

Every time they've gone to swim in the sea, his papa has said the same thing:

Boys, you don't know how good you've got it! We lived behind Communist wires. We couldn't get anywhere near the sea . . .

The water here's not salty and smells to him of mud. He scrapes muck off his T-shirt and shorts, leaves them to dry on the wastebasket next to the pool.

He and his mama disguise themselves as mud people, giggling and carrying on. Everyone around them looks like savages, plastered in mud. He and his mama just copied them. And good thing they did.

Soňa started slapping mud all over her colored dreads the moment she spied the commissioner shuffling out of a cabin in a bright-colored two-piece suit. She grabbed the boy and they dropped to the blanket. The commissioner walked right past them. Didn't even turn his head. He slipped into the warm water and floated off into the host of bobbing heads and carefree bodies, buoyed up by the warm gush from the thermal springs.

Through half-closed eyes now, the boy spots Vaska Tyran hurrying after him. In a swimsuit; biceps, adorned with perhaps an excess of tattoos, flexing; bald pate shining. He hastens into the water after the commissioner, winks and gives the boy a toothy grin.

The emir, known to the other warriors of the Islamic State as Emir Yosuf, has come to the renowned baths straight from Keleti pu. The emissary of the divine state with the green rug under his arm didn't fare well with the young refugees at Keleti. One in a thousand is all it takes, though. As long as the giaours feed and care for them, a single walk through the half-naked whores in this city of depravity will surely make at least one of them into a man taking up the sword of God.

There is a moan from the dressing cabin next door. Emir Yosuf, prayer rug and God's instrument at the ready, places his eye to a knothole.

The moaning is coming from a petite blonde, in her mouth the swollen nipple of a brunette, whose fingers, yes, and palms are easing into the silky patch between the blonde girl's thighs. The emir moans too, beating his member, suddenly jutting eagerly from his green swim trunks, against the cabin wall . . . Then, steeling himself, he turns and walks out to the grassy bank . . . As he passes a group of women in their forties knocking around a beach ball, he turns his gaze not only on the she-devils' bare necks . . . Covering his lustful member with the rug, the emir then beholds a young man of stunning beauty, nakedness emphasized by his two-piece rainbow suit as he sinks into the waves up to the ringlet on his forehead . . . Horrified at his orgasm, the emir howls a howl not unlike the screech of the gates of paradise swinging shut . . . As he spreads out his green raft of salvation to pray for the giaours' death, the edges of his rug are overrun by a girl scout troop in minuscule swimsuits, led by a well-built blonde woman cheerfully singing commands . . . Deprived of prayer, Emir Yosuf unsheathes his holy instrument . . . The nearest whore, her immodestly colored, bizarrely tangled hair falling across her naked bosom, splashes about with a little devil in range of the prayer station. Uttering cries of Daesh! Allahu akbar! the emir leaps into the water, in one hand a knife, in the other an ax inscribed with the words of the prophet, swinging for the harvest . . . Then suddenly, a bald man, up until then peacefully floating on his back, rises up before the emir like an apparition, wielding a glittering knife, and moving at such speed that only an angel in flight could have detected the word DONBAS on the dagger, he slices the emir's throat, drags him under the surface, and, just to be sure, runs the blade through his heart.

The boy feels a chill on his back. Takes a few steps into the pool, so the water reaches his waist.

He hears the sound of a rasp over the pulse of the artificial waves. The chill that falls on his back, the shadow that swallows him up, he guesses to be from some giant-sized animal.

The boy looks up into a maw twisted in rage . . . No sooner does he inhale the stench wafting from its fangs than the gorilla's paws are around his neck, squeezing, choking . . . A claw scrapes down his thigh, tearing his boxers. The boy starts yanking out fur by the fistful, kicking his legs in the pool, howling amid the monster's whines as it shakes him like a leaf above the water's surface . . . Suddenly he hears the slap of sandals, the clump-clump of shoes dashing his way . . . You lowlife! The boy's papa clobbers the beast over the head with the stone wastebasket, jumps feet-first into the pool, picks the vessel up from the bottom, and bashes it over the animal's skull once again . . . He snatches up the boy, still coughing and swallowing water . . . and hurls him from the pool.

Curling up in the grass, the boy notices a squad of ants marching around the edges of the pool . . . and the last thing he perceives as he loses consciousness is a din of voices.

Papa continues stomping the corpse as it hangs limply suspended amid the bloody water. He tries again to hoist the container from the bottom. But at this point he's too drained. I've had enough, he mutters, rolling onto the ground next to the boy.

They bivouac on the grass right alongside the wire fence. The boy lies on a towel beneath his papa's sweatshirt. His mama, bent over him, gives off a clean aroma, humming a tune about the murmuring waves of the Sázava river . . . sun glinting on the ring in her lip as she holds his naked brother in her lap. The little guy's skin is covered with bites, old and fresh alike, all red. He waves his little arms around, big dong just hanging out. They can still feel the warmth of the sun.

The boy's head, shoulders, ache from being clamped. The pain is descending from its peak. From the water he can hear the shouts of the muddy nudists, giggling and squealing. Colorful balls fly through the air to the strains of bubbly pop.

Ivan and Papa sit on the grass, side by side.

Listen, brother, says Papa, teeth chattering. You know what happened? My son got attacked by a gorilla!

That one? Ivan points.

The cops have just appeared on the other side of the fence: Rendőrség in black jumpsuits, truncheons and handcuffs on their belts, bent over panting . . . They haul behind them the ice cream vendor's cart, propping up the enormous hairy body on top, its glassy eyes grazed by flies . . . pudgy flesh flies and midges dance over the bloody pulp of its muzzle, held together only by tattered strips of flesh.

Six cops push the cart with three pulling from in front . . . a cluster of people trail behind, children scamper about, the cops mop their sweaty brows . . . Somebody hides the corpse beneath a blanket and the womenfolk drag their tots away, covering the little rubberneckers' eyes . . . The nudists give up knocking their beach ball around and rush to the fence to stare.

Ivan and Papa lean in toward each other, both men in a squat, nearly touching foreheads.

Braht moy, here actors come after performance to bathe. This is why monkey came. It wanted to play. Misfortune happened!

Sonuvabitch! I kill anyone who fucks my son, you hear?

Clear! But here in EU animals have same rights as people. Remember! And you have killed monkey. You are in enormous mess! You must flee!

Hey, screw that. If somebody fucked my daughter, that'd be wrong too, right?

Braht, is pedophilia even crime in EU?

Now you're just pissin me off!

In Russia pedophilia is crime! This could not happen!

Hey, slow down, Soňa chimes in.

What?

It's not gonna be like you say! I mean, sure, he's got a few scratches on him. But what'd you actually see?

Sonuvabitch, that gorilla better not be infected!

Yeah, okay, but what about the car? We got a problem there too . . .

Othello, says Papa. Shit!

Braht, you must not take so hard . . .

Was that really an ape? Soňa chimes in again.

That's right! Papa says. What if it wasn't an ape? What if it was a man dressed as one? I didn't have time to get a good look! Maybe it'll be in the papers! Or on TV. I reckon they've got TVs in pubs here just like everywhere else. You know any Hungarian?

No.

Then we're fucked.

The wet but now clothed Vaska winds his way toward them through the clamoring nudists, track pants coquettishly rolled up over the tops of his shiny boots. He has a big box under his arm and a cluster of plastic bags, which he sets down in the grass. One of the bags is overflowing with Hungarian baby food and goodies.

Now you will change clothes, Ivan commands. Clean and new! What you say, missus?

Ooooh . . . Thank you!

Happy, Soňa? You have very pretty name!

Just then the buzz by the fence rises in volume again. This time it's a pair of white-garbed medics, trotting through the sunbathing vacationers and day-trippers to the water. More rubberneckers press up to the fence.

Here, Hungarian clothings . . . Ivan pulls T-shirts, boxers, tracksuits out of the plastic bags and, with a slight blush, lays a few little thingies down in front of Soňa.

But everyone, including Soňa, with her one bleary eye, is staring at the fence again.

The paramedics are coming back with a stretcher now. The boy again spots the commissioner's dreamy forehead, artistic lock of hair pasted in place with water now. He sees the arms strapped to the unbreathing body, the big toes pointing up in the air, the pale face covered with a sheet.

Munich fascist no will bother you now! Ivan says to the family with a smile. He gives a slap on the back to the grinning bald man, still lightly reeking of salty mud as the dampness evaporates from his clothes.

His Adidas now safely stashed away in a plastic bag, Vaska Tyran's feet sparkle in a pair of elegant boots.

And you will with me. My beloved family! Where else you would go?

You know, Ivan, says Soňa, deftly changing clothes beneath a towel, the way women have done for thousands of years. You've been really kind, but we're on our way home.

Papa stuffs himself into his new tracksuit. Shoves his and the boy's wet clothes into the trash with the beer cups, amid the swarming bugs.

Vaska Tyran hands Soňa the opened box, heaped with rompers, baby tees, baby caps, baby bottles, nothing but tender little brat things.

Ach, says Soňa, and lowers her head.

We will no have crying here, says Ivan. An oversized bottle of vodka appears magically in his hand.

The setting sun filters through the sheer liquid, glittering in the glass . . . and off roars the ambulance, those who gave their lives for art, though each in very different ways, resting on the floor, cheek to cheek . . . Only the emir's corpse floats in the mud as yet undiscovered.

There is nearly no one else left on the grassy plot with them now. As closing time approaches, a few visitors toss their towels into their bags, the janitors stab debris onto the ends of their trash pickers, no more sounds of whoops and splashing even from the wading pool.

We must drink to reunion!

If you insist, brother, Papa says, getting to his feet.

And you all will be with me. Like femily!

Soňa pulls the red track pants on over her aching leg, hissing a little, then tugs the Donald Duck tee on over the little one's head, and as he rolls around on her lap in his elegant new romper, Soňa zips the track-suit top up between her breasts.

Little taste for woman . . . Ivan hands her a thimble-size cup.

Are you kidding? Gimme that! Soňa says, snatching his full-size drink.

The boy stands up. The scrape on his thigh is bleeding. Vaska is at his side in a flash, rubbing the wound with a stinging wad of cotton soaked in vodka. The boy can tell from the way he presses a bandage to the scratch that it will stay there till it scabs. Papa hands the boy his out-fit. He slips into the new boxers, then wriggles into his track pants and wraps up the remainder of his achy, itching body.

Ivan, you're too kind, really. Thanks! So, where're we driving to? I mean, assuming we change our minds.

We no drive. We fly.

Where to?

Paradise!

Squeezing tightly into the car, they speed through Budapest and the flatlands beyond, driving into the twilight.

Vaska Tyran hands his papers to the guard at the gate, Ivan nods to the Rendőrség. Papa waves to them, but not until they've driven past.

There are only a few planes, buffeted by the winds off the puszta, which is pleasantly oxygenated by a tall stand of spruce trees enclosing the landing strip in a nearly magical ring.

They cram into the bowels of a small aircraft. Soňa buckles in the lit-tle one, now fast asleep, on the seat next to the boy, who has taken the spot by the window. She spreads out right behind them. Papa plops down onto the remaining seat, and Ivan folds himself in beside him. Vaska Tyran climbs into the pilot's cabin. Papa can't stop sniffing at his new tracksuit. He does rib Soňa a little over the color of her outfit.

You're on fire, baby!

Hm!

It hasn't escaped the boy's notice that his mama didn't throw out her old clothes. She bundles up her skirt and jacket behind her head. But then suddenly leaps up, snatching a barf bag . . . as, shaking and roaring, the airplane inches forward . . . The boy presses his nose to the glass.

Within an instant of takeoff, the vegetation below looks like a scale model.

If you see anything interesting, give a shout, Papa tells the boy, passing the bottle to Ivan.

The plane lurches a few times. Majorly.

From this tiny airport they have taken Imre Nagy, Ivan informs Papa.

Oh, really?

From here he has flown into enormous eternity! Ivan says through a spray of booze. The neck of the bottle is practically jammed down his throat.

What? Imgy . . . Who's that? Soňa chimes in from behind.

Imrigy . . . Nagyap . . . Ivan splutters.

Who? What?

He says Iggy Pop flew outta here! That time in Lisbon. We saw him, remember?

Oh, right, yeah, Soňa chirps. The Igster . . . she smiles a moment and shuts her eyes. Then lightly snores her way through the rest of the flight.

5

FATHER, GIVE ME MASK! THE AJVARS. VISION OF
A SPIRITUAL STATE. ON LITERATURE. SURPRISE
ATTACK. THE GREAT GÉRARD AND THE LITTLE
MONK. CELEBRATION OF NOVOROSSIYA—
UNSUCCESSFUL. A POLITICAL DISCUSSION.
TURNOFF TO SLOVAKIA. THE CITADEL.

I am glad to have younger braht, grins the old geezer, crushing Papa against the wall with his mighty frame, even with his athletic legs, covered in striped terrycloth, jutting into the aisle.

You have westernized, but only skin. We will peel! Maybe give younger braht thrashing.

Papa throws an elbow into Ivan's ribs. We always fought when we were little!

You always lost!

How many times did I sneak into the barn when you and Pop were gone and stare at that dirt bike track you built! Hey, Ivan, how come you still talk like a pig?

Ivan leans in, whispers something in Papa's ear, but as the little plane enters a powerful vortex, straightening out again with a roar, it's impossible to make out his words, so he makes a few faces, puts a finger to his lips . . . and taps his ears.

Oh, okay . . . well, I guess I can tell you now, lookin at yours and Pop's tire tracks all over the threshing floor, spare parts and rusty canisters lyin everywhere . . . I always used to wonder why you left me behind.

You were little and for nothing!

I see.

We were building practice arena in barn. There our father trained himself. For perfect ride of death!

I remember those bikes screamin all day long! And Ma screamin at you guys. And I remember toddlin in, lookin for you and Pop, and you

44

were nowhere in sight! The barn was empty. Do you have any idea how I felt?

Well, how many years you were in sixty-eight? Four? Fife? We followed Red Army to Russia.

Didn't you feel bad for Ma?

She was glad.

Yeah, well, I split soon after myself. Hung around the Sázava . . .

Homeless? Poor little boy!

Hey, I'm not complainin!

Big, tremendous moment to meet braht! Ivan declares, raising the bottle. He caresses his seatmate with his eyes.

Papa too fixes Ivan with his gaze.

And for an instant the two brothers seem to turn to stone. In a freezing-cold space, eternity gaping on all sides . . .

Listen, braht, rider of death, you know, in Russia it was rank! Ivan says, coming back to life.

Yeah? Really?

They loved Father there. Every soldat who sees him, turns his head and motorcycle vroom, vroom, and riding fast—will he fall? will he no?—every soldier whispers to himself, I wonder how would I do?

Hey, this place we're flying to, will . . . he be there too?

Will he be, will he no? Ivan says, throwing up his hands.

Goddammit, talk normal! Is our pop gonna be there?

Rider of death, this is our corrida!

Oh yeah?

Arena of death, sport of true men. Just man and machine! No entertainment for homosexuals and pedophiles like in West! And no animals suffer like silly Spaniards. In Russia the people love animals!

So he's alive?

Father? Not so easy to say.

What the hell does that mean?

Volodya himself wanted to see him. And Surgeon! Commander of Night Wolves combat units.

So the poor old guy cut himself up, did he?

Was big event at first celebration of Novorossiya! Father was turning eighty. And I say, Father, give me mask, I will ride instead you.

Oh yeah?

Well, rider of death has mask.

So what did he say?

To shut my mouth. He is man!

Hm.

What father we have, eh?

Mm . . .

And then he flew off track, ai-yi-yi!

Oh, really? How bout we have another drop, huh?

Ai-yi-yi! You know what it was? Assassination attempt! On Father!

Yeah, really? Get out!

Yeah! First celebration of Novorossiya and stands are roaring. Father rides and some nationalist Moslemin fanatic shoots him. Or it was Ukrainian fascist? We arrested them after and exterminated many!

I'm really sorry to hear that!

Pardon?

I'm sorry to hear that, you know, but . . .

What?

Ivan, look, I got by without you guys for years! Wait, no way did we finish that bottle already. You got any more?

Yeah.

I could do with another drop.

But your wife, braht, she is drinking, Ivan grumbles in Papa's ear.

Me and Soňa are goin home, and we're gonna get married, you hear? Papa gushes in a burst of vodka loquaciousness, rolling his head on the headrest and gawking into the darkness.

And forgive, braht moy, but your boys need home.

That's what I'm sayin!

Listen, braht, in our country, other side of Urals, we have special child camps, very good there, fresh air! Healthy upbringing. I will have your sons brought, they are also my blood.

Are you crazy?

All right, this side of Urals. As you like. And braht?

Hm?

Is many loose women!

What?

Ivan gets up, thrusting his mitts into the tiny storage compartments

. . . Papa steps into the aisle, examines the gently snoring Soňa, and, seeing her blink, flips her jacket sleeve over her eye. Another step and he's at his sons' seats, shaking the drying moptop on the boy staring out into the dark, listening to the metallic hum of the small craft in flight.

Hey, just came to say hi. I was worried how you were holdin up after that thing in the pool . . . Anyway, looks like you're fine, so that's great! I see you're interested in the sky . . . I myself didn't fly till I was a grown-up. Must be the former Soviet Union down there below. We weren't allowed to go there, cept on Pioneer trips, you would've hated that . . . How's your little brother? Snoozin? You're takin good care of him, all good!

Papa trails off into mumbling, struggles his way back up the aisle as the plane pitches and drops, and is just about ready to settle back into his seat again when he looks down and is paralyzed with shock.

There's a general sitting there. Chest covered with medals and ribbons, he doffs the flat cap from his head, freeing his touseled gingery locks, yep, it's the toothily grinning Ivan.

Sit!

Ivan plants a papakha on Papa's head, smears something under his nose, pastes something on, and voilà, he's got a mustache hanging off his nose . . . Ivan throws a heavy overcoat over his shoulders.

You Zoshchenko! On stage we will be in spotlights, we will welcome Ajvaristan into Novorossiya . . . We are going to celebration, yes? Second, grand celebration of Novorossiya expansion! And celebration of Shakespeare! In my country we love Shakespeare same as in West.

Oh, really?

Culture is common treasure of humanity, you do not think? All major world artists and actors are invited—you will stand in for Zoshchenko! Listen what you will say! And Ivan proceeds to read, eyes pinned to his laptop:

"So shaken as we are, so wan with care, Find we a time for frighted peace to pant . . . No more the thirsty entrance of this soil shall daub her lips with her own children's blood . . . No more shall trenching war channel her fields, Nor bruise her flowerets with tanks."

Good, no? Zoshchenko as Shakespeare's King Heinrich welcomes peace! You will be great! Ajvars understand squat.

Who? Avars?

Ajvars. And you great Slavonic braht. Zoshchenko everyone loves. The Tatars love Zoshchenko?

Ajvars! We are flying to Ajvaristan! This is tiny little corner of Ukraine, which has voluntarily attached to Novorossiya! This will be our celebration!

Hm! Since when do Cossacks perform Shakespeare? grumbles Papa, straightening his papakha and tugging at his mustache.

Learn it!

Excuse me, but I already know it, that's the first page of Henry IV . . . Papa grouses. He has put on the caped overcoat and, head settled comfortably against the headrest, is examining the enormous silver buttons.

Ivan's laptop purrs in his lap, the lowest-hanging medals on his chest clicking against the screen as he frowns gloomily, shaking his head and grumbling in discontent . . . Van Damme will no come to celebration! . . . Kharel Gott will no come either . . . or Drupi! . . . Mel Geebson also no! Braht, they have betrayed! And our father . . . he lays a hand on Papa's thigh and gives a gentle squeeze. Our father on motorcycle will no come! Ach.

Ivan stares glumly at the laptop screen a moment, but cheers back up after another swig and slugs Papa in the shoulder.

Braht moy, you want be minister of culture of Ajvaristan?

Huh?

Sure, minister lives nice! You have million-dollar bribe and eat salami every day.

You don't say . . .

We build spiritual state in Ajvaristan! It will be cultural oasis of Novorossiya! Except for miners, those bandits in Luganda and Donbabwe, ha-ha-ha! It will be plaything! Braht moy! You have in my country new home! I will be gubernator of Ajvaristan!

The general and future gubernator of Ajvaristan—a forgotten corner of Ukraine settled by the diminutive nation of Ajvars, who as far as Papa can gather were formerly steppe nomads—settles back in his seat, still studying the news on his flickering screen, though now with a bit of a smile.

Braht moy, when we will be there you can write! In Russian! You want? Russian literature is greatest! Even in West is recognized. Every-one knows!

Oh, baloney!

Pushkin!

So your greatest writer was a black man? Hey, go grab some refugees, I'm sure you'll find another poet!

You are disgust!

Taras Shevchenko? Now he was a poet. Born a slave and carried a knife in his boot. That's the way to write.

Braht. I love you even despite provocations. From artist allowed. You are forgiven.

Suddenly Ivan shoots up from his seat, banging his flat cap into the ceiling, and thunders in a voice so loud that he drowns out the roar of the plane.

Yes, we have lost greatest empire on earth without single shot! We have exchanged greatness for jeans and chewing gums! Slimy West has brought us to knees, because we no were strong! But Volodya Putin has this all changed! Yes, he has pointed way for us! It is religious and spir-itual war! And God is on our side! Eurasian giant has risen! Hurraaah!

Ivan hurls his cap the few centimeters to the ceiling, snatches it as it falls back down, jams it on his head, blinking, widens his eyes, taps his ear with his index finger again, says pssst . . . blinks frantically at Papa again . . . and shoves Papa against the seatback, crushing him with his weight. As the medals on Ivan's uniform dig through Papa's coat and tracksuit jacket into his chest, Ivan frantically whispers into his ear.

I could purchase you few commodities in lovely Sázava region! I love Josef Lada still! I want there to live. In Czech lands. I want to live. Braht, listen . . . I have money, seas of it!

And then suddenly, boom, boom, they're bumping along the landing strip, barreling at full speed, and it's almost a miracle one if not both of the siblings doesn't bite his tongue in two.

Soňa steps out of her seat and, shielding her head against the bumps, gropes her way back to her young sons and holds them close, wrap-ping them in her arms. The boy gapes out the window at an armored personnel carrier standing on the shabbily lighted strip under a pock-marked bent metal sign reading WELCOME IN AJVARIGOROD! Then, one after another, the faint lights go out . . . lightning flashes down through the darkness overhead, and thunder, distant but persistent, rolls toward them.

Outside they hear rumbling and thunderclaps accompanied by bright streaks of light across the sky. They fall and slip down the chute that pops out of the open door, Vaska catching Soňa with the little one in her arms, grinning at them from under his helmet; he's got on a uniform too . . . The boy slides down and gets tangled up in Papa's long coat. He recognizes him right away, even with the thick mustache . . . stares around at the big men in black uniforms, Kalashnikovs and long rifles strapped over their shoulders.

They follow Ivan up the metal stairs into the APC and squat down on a bench amid another group of heavily armed men. Looking out through the observation slit, the boy sees another round of lightning bolts ripping across the sky, missiles whistling past overhead. One buries itself on the very edge of the landing strip, exploding as they lurch into motion, the shards drumming against the shell of the APC.

Hold on to your hats, boys, Papa whoops. There's shootin goin on here! What've you gotten us into, Ivan?

This Ukrainian fascists firing Grad rockets! They no want Ajvaristan into Novorossiya! But here it will be like in Crimea, no worry, braht . . . The transporter jerks as it crunches over a barrier.

Hey, Soňa, what do you think? Were we better off at the baths? Papa shouts, but Soňa isn't listening. She's busy polishing off the vodka from the plane, in between gulps pointing at him and chortling with laughter.

Nice disguise! You should see yourself!

They barrel through the hangars, past a cluster of dark buildings, and into a series of twisting streets. Passing a small town square, they sink ever deeper into the narrow lanes of a quiet little town.

You really look awful. Like some seedy old Cossack!

What seedy! I'm acting!

Look, let's get rid of Ivan and Vaska, they're startin to get on my nerves, Soňa says. Vest over her red tracksuit top, she lays her head on the big boy's shoulder, holding the little nipper on her lap. The soldiers grin right in her face as the APC rounds a bend, tossing them out of their seats at her.

I'm tryin to tell you, I got us a gig! We're on our way to a celebration! We're gonna act! How bout them apples?

Oh, okay then, nothin new, just acting as usual, fine then, Soňa says, hissing through her teeth as they jerk back into motion.

Not exactly, my dear friends, Ivan says, smiling broadly. No! Now you act for your life!

The dark streets turn into a broad boulevard. No people, no lights in sight. As they drive along a wooden fence, the boy's eyes slide over a bedraggled cloth banner: SHAKESPEARE 400! VOTE PROSPERITY! Papa reads out the Cyrillic to his family. They drive past a bus station with shattered windows. In the dim beams of the APC's lights, the boy sees the filth swept by the wind from beneath their wheels; plastic bottles, layers of cigarette butts. As they pull onto the town square, the headlights sweeping across its expanse, it looks to him like the gathering place of giants.

An armed guard at a barricade of stacked tires flicks his light at them and they drive across the asphalt toward a huge illuminated stage, spotlights fixed on a sign that Papa translates out loud: SHAKESPEARE— UNITY OF CULTURE AND FREEDOM! AJVARISTAN—HOMELAND! WELCOME TO NOVOROSSIYA! The boy blinks, now able to see that the square is filled with people. Every now and then, the beam from one of the floodlights lands on the crowd and he can make out caps, fur hats, funny flattop hats on people's heads. He sees a wave ripple through the crowd.

They come to a stop at the stage. A coal-black luxury car sits beneath a tautly stretched canopy, headlights on. Soldiers bustle about. There is also a group of children. The boy is first to jump down from the armored vehicle's metal steps as its snout drives right up underneath the canopy.

They can hear the crowd distinctly now as the group of dark-skinned boys and girls emerge from under the canopy and walk out onstage, bearing artificial flowers. The sloppily tacked together bouquets look like brooms and carpet sweepers in the sloe-eyed children's hands. The girls in red skirts, the boys in shiny suits, arrange themselves into rows and circles like a band of imps in the palm of some gigantic being.

The boy hears a rustling, then the thunder of falling waters, which turns out to be applause from the crowd.

As the occupants of the APC come pouring out like the contents of a can, Vaska brings someone over from the car, leading them by the hand. A big blond man in a fancy suit, with a hard chin, a boxer's schnoz, dilated eyes. Soňa elbows Papa in the ribs, calling his attention to the new arrival. Next to the stiff-necked members of the military, the big guy looks like he's pitter-pattering off to a ball, and no wonder: there's a rope around his ankles. Not only that, but even with the helmeted Vaska keeping a firm grip on his hand, the fellow has a lasso slung around his neck. Holding the other end of the rope is a small young man clothed in a flowing habit. Yep, a little monk in a frock.

You know who that is . . . blathers Soňa, her lips almost eagerly parted as she points to the elegantly dressed movie star.

Ivan comes rushing up: Dorogy Gérard! he cries, and proceeds to kiss the rock of a man on either cheek.

Eh-hem, eh-hem, Papa says, sidling toward them, and as Soňa breathily enthuses into his ear, That's really Depardieu! he lifts his right hand and thrusts it at the man in ropes.

Sa va? Ji swee osee um duh tayahtrih, he says. The Frenchman, however, doesn't even blink, his gaze fixed somewhere on the black canvas overhead, or perhaps he is listening to the children now stomping and singing onstage.

Ivan shouts into Papa's ear, Only Gérard has no betrayed! Only world star who supports our Novorossiya! Besides you!

So then why is he tied up? Papa inquires.

For his safety we give him pills, Ivan says. Strong pills! All of a sudden Ivan turns, gets right up in Papa's face, and looks him in the eye. You want such pills?

No!

You are no traitor, braht, Ivan says through his teeth, then gives the actor a shove toward the stairs, prodding Vaska onward as he drags the divine servant of Thalia by the belt. Noticing the monk bow his head and lower his eyes, seemingly hesitant to move, Ivan steps up and slaps him in the face.

The next thing they know they're pushing onstage in one big knot, with the boy trailing behind. As they force their way through a row of little girls, the team of little boys stands in the spotlight at the edge of the stage, bowing to the darkened crowd, who clap and cheer them on.

As Ivan storms through the girls, they topple to either side like bowling pins. Papa in his papakha and long coat is just getting oriented when Vaska leans into him from behind, sending him flying up to the edge of the stage and into the cone of light with the boys.

Ivan hoists Papa's hand in the air and shouts into the mike in Russian: The Great Zoshchenko has come from the West! Somebody whistles, there is the sound of applause, and as sweat slides down Ivan's face, he grasps the lifeless hand of the Master from the country of the Gallic rooster and hoists it triumphantly in the air.

The great Depardieu, he cries, has come from Volodya Putin and Aleksandr Lukashenko! And he says, Da zdravstvuyet Ajvarskaya Novorossiya! Long live Ajvar Novorossiya!

The applause now drowns out the hostile cries, the whistling and roaring voices. Someone shouts for the cameras, Leave us, Russian VERMIN!, and something comes flying onstage. The girls in folk costume leap out of the way, and the next object smacks Ivan right in the forehead. The crowd's whistles and screams surge in waves as something goes whizzing past the boy's head and one of the young maids drops to the ground. Plastic bottles sail through the air, shoes, hats, papakhas, though none as large as Papa's . . . Vaska snatches up a little girl in braids and holds her in front of him at the edge of the stage as he aims his pistol over her shoulder into the darkness below, sparking a truly horrific uproar in response . . . Stairs or no, the little girls flee beneath the canopy, and when the first costumed boy leaps from the stage into the clamoring mass, there is the sound of applause again, even giggles, and the other boys go flocking to the edge of the stage. Some take a running leap into the melee, while those more cautious lower themselves down.

Just then the boy feels someone grab hold of him—the monk. Together they run for the canopy, with Papa hightailing it after them. He's thrown away his cap.

Vaska Tyran kneels at the microphones with his pistol. The soldiers in black line up behind him, taking aim. As the spotlight roams over faces, bodies, picking them out from the mass gathered beneath the stage, people run, fleeing the bullets, and the monk shoves the boy underneath the canopy.

Ivan, the Frenchman in tow, herds them into the back seat of the black automobile. The APC attempts to plug the hole in the barricade, but the crowd just pours right over it . . . The car goes blasting off, the beam of the spotlight, clearly now out of the light crew's control, frantically searching for it in the dark. They are on their way.

Ivan squats behind the wheel, Papa bent toward him, the boy snuggled up to his mama in back as she clutches his little brother, and thunk wham! a man lies unmoving at an overturned roadblock, while another lies broken-backed, flailing his arms and legs like a bug, trying unsuccessfully to pick himself up from the road.

Buildings, streets, go flashing past, then they barrel uphill through a series of sweeping hairpin turns, the darkness changing to a murky yellow light. The boy looks out and catches a glimpse of the crescent moon, the sharp outlines of cliffs.

As they keep heading upward, now more slowly, Papa turns to the back seat holding a little bottle he found in the overcoat. Eyes glittering above his long black mustache, he passes the bottle to Soňa, who affably tips it back and gulps.

Papa unscrews another little bottle with his teeth, takes a swig, hands it to Ivan, and the boy sees a trickle of tears sparkle under the wheelman's prodigious nose.

Geroy Vaska! Ivan says. Hero, like in Kiev. As Ivan lets go of the steering wheel to make the sign of the cross, Papa grabs onto the wheel with his left hand, with his right snatching the bottle out of Ivan's mouth.

Ai-yi! Ivan cries, beating the back of his head with the general's cap. Ai-yi-yi! he cries, and as the sounds of him swallowing his tears die away, they suddenly notice the sound of tapping and knocking coming from outside the car.

They drive up a long slope, and Ivan pulls to a stop right at the edge of a drop-off. He walks around to the back of the car, his ashen face clear to everyone in the light of the glittering stars, and opens the trunk. The monk sits bolt upright, and, tugging with all their might, together the two of them peel out the celebrated master. Given how contorted he is, it isn't easy. But they manage.

The boy and his mama, hastening to be of assistance, run their eyes over the cans and tubes of every sort, rolls of salami, boxes of juice, pâtés, vacuum-packed goose and turkey thighs, crates of wine . . . Before Ivan can click the trunk shut, Soňa scoops up a carton of Gauloises.

The quiet little monk, hair only slightly mussed, leads the actor by his rope to the edge of the drop-off, where—managing to stop before they tumble into the chasm—the two of them stand urinating. Just a few short steps from the vehicle.

Suddenly, out of the depths of the car, Soňa produces a baby seat.

She thrusts the little nipper, just opening his eyes, into his brother's arms. The boy keeps a tight grip on him, back pressed against the side of the car, chasm at their feet. The idea does cross his mind, but anyone in his place would get the same idea.

This car seat is totally cool! Soňa says, wind rippling through her colorful wisps of hair. I love French products! First-rate. Ivan and Vaska, though, I can't stand. By the way, have you noticed how nice the car smells?

The little monk leads the actor back to the car, and Papa and Ivan meanwhile hold a quick consultation.

I say we return and kill the saboteurs! Ivan fumes.

Where're we headed now?

The Citadel!

What for?

There my geroys! Ajvars, those whores, have betrayed us! Ivan raves, pounding his fist on the hood of the car. He explains that to get to the Citadel they have to pass through Ajvar villages, where the people know him well. And his uniform. The traitors keep watch even after dark. So Papa will do the driving. The boy will take the seat next to him, and Ivan will lie at their feet. And just for good measure, they toss a few blankets over him that they found in the back.

And they're on their way, breeze wafting in through the window, the shine of the moon, the light of the stars. The boy tugs at his track pants as the man at his feet rattles on, angrily muttering Slavic curses, Ajvars this, Ajvars that, going round and round . . .

Can't say I'm surprised they don't want you as chairman, Papa says, interrupting the stream of revilement pouring forth from the floor.

It is no people, is rats, Ajvars!

I mean, if they don't want you here . . .

Ukrainians, khokhol sons of bitch, they confuse Ajvars!

Right, right . . . !

Is treason! Is clear!

But listen, brother, the Ukies are out here like flies on shit, there's no way you can win, Papa injects quite sensibly, but then instantly falls silent, seeing the shine of reflectors from a fellow on a mule in the pass directly in front of them, dark-skinned, diminutive, the glowing dot of a papirossa in the corner of his mouth, and as Papa skillfully avoids the buckets strapped to the donkey's flanks, the Ajvar gives them a wave of his straw hat.

Ajvars too few, can no rule alone, grumbles Ivan, then squeals as Papa goes for the gas pedal but accidentally stomps on him instead.

That's just like you Russkies! Conquer, destroy, exterminate!

Shto zhe?

That's not how it's done anymore!

It is!

It doesn't work!

It does!

It's the twenty-first century!

Big deal!

Papa steps on the gas, zipping through a little village, just a few tiny shacks, not a soul in sight. Dogs bark, tugging at their ropes, but there is nobody here staring at them, nobody lingering in the dark.

At a crossing of roads, a long-distance coach comes motoring off the furrowed asphalt of a wooden bridge. More than one clearly packed bus is traveling through the moonbeam-diluted dark. Papa stops and waits for the panting machines to pass.

Tons of Ukies takin the coach to find jobs in Slovakia and Czechia, Papa notes.

Heh? Braht?

How far is it to Slovakia? Day? Day and a half?

A head without a general's cap, which must have fallen off somewhere, emerges between the boy's knees.

Maybe two?

Look! Ivan says, ashen-faced, eyes ablaze. He points upward, ignoring the buses vanishing over the bridge around the bend.

Above the little valley, in the light crowding through the clouds, a cross gleams atop a metal dome. The sheer walls of a fortress rise up before them.

There Citadel!

6

ARMED FORCES—WE ARE MANY! IN THE
MONASTERY CATACOMBS. GLOWING MACHINES.
DEAD VACATIONERS. ON MARRIAGE AND
CHILDREN. WHO'S ON THE OTHER SIDE OF THE
HATCH. WE'LL SEE! AND START PRAYIN . . .

Dawn is breaking.

They stop the car at the foot of the mighty, rugged, grapeshot-pitted walls. Even the monastery dome, towering above them, is cracked and riddled with bullet holes. The three-beam slanted cross leans askew toward the sky.

Ivan scrambles out of the vehicle, officer's cap on his head, and stands before the cathedral gates, surrounded by armed men, trying to explain something, raging and gesturing widely with his arms.

Wow, you'll never guess what that young guy is named, says Soňa, sticking her face into the front seat. Serafion, isn't that pretty? He's assigned to Gérard as his interpreter. But Gérard looks kina shaken, like he's in shock or somethin!

Conflagrations blaze on the plateau. The borders flicker with dying flames. There are multitudes of them, dozens, perhaps hundreds of fires. In clumps and individually, the distant ones like match heads, the nearer ones like torches kindled upon the dusty, withered earth. It is a scene reminiscent of the night sky fading to dawn, spilled out over the furrowed earth by a tug on the universe, or perhaps some divine whim of God.

The titushki linger around their vehicle. All done up in various bits of uniform, flamboyantly colored combat jackets, tracksuits. Rings, scapularies, crosses, chains around their necks. More than a few sport a chilling assortment of knives tucked into their belts, handcuffs, and various types of torture instruments. Guns and long rifles over their shoulders, Kalashnikovs. Heads shaved bald or in officers' caps, under sagging banners and monstrances, stripped of their orthodox Stalinist insignia in the course of rowdy punch-ups.

Little wonder the black sedan commands so much attention. However scratched and worn, it's still a proud and noble vehicle. Beyond compare with the banged-up, mud-spattered Toyotas puttering around them. The procession of men flowing down from the fires like a gray resounding river streams also around a few Gaziks, trying in vain to conceal their socialist origins with camouflage.

Papa, one arm over the boy's shoulders, the other twisting his mustache, puffs out his chest so the medals on his overcoat are clear for all to see . . . and they saunter over to Ivan. The men surrounding the general, eyes glinting with curiosity, willingly step aside.

Ivan gives Papa a hug.

Eto moy braht! From Czechia. Czechs, Slavic brothers and friends! Hurraaah, Ivan cries, flinging his cap in the air. The other men join in, and a few kisses and manly pecks alight on Papa's and the boy's cheeks.

Braht, look, brothers from Donbas, Russian Orthodox army, Ivan says with a sweep of his uniformed arm . . . Papa counts the tanks approaching over the plain, driving through and between the fires, and when he reaches the full number of fingers on both hands, Ivan draws his attention to the men in formation approaching at a steady trot. Next to them, the titushki look practically like farmworkers.

Is Phantom Brigade and Brigade of Death, our Chechen brothers, and Legion of Saint Stephen, Ivan says, pointing to a group of men in gray uniforms, the advance guard trotting past the half-crumbling walls . . . Is Essence of Time Battalion, true geroys! Dorogy braht, you know what you see?

Not bad, mutters Papa, kicking at a clump of gray dirt.

Is army of God. We are many!

Ivan takes an overcoat from one of the soldiers and slings it over the shoulders of the French actor, who totters along by the side of the monk Serafion as he leads the little family to the monastery entrance. He pushes open the cracked door decorated with carved saints in various stages of torture, and they find themselves in an enormous dimly lighted space.

Papa blinks. The boy shields his eyes with his palm, scout style. They stare into the feeble light, which falls onto the dusty stone floor through holes clearly punched in the walls by projectiles. Twisted shell casings lay about where they landed in the dust, fallen plaster, and piles of brick, along with shiny cartridges fired out of all the mess in response. Remnants of fires are visible on the cathedral floor, discarded cigarette butts, trash.

However, the holiness of the place is confirmed by a smoke-stained iconostasis depicting legions of saints, a flickering lamp behind a wooden enclosure, and more lamps hanging down from the ceiling on chains, thin and massive alike.

Braht moy. Ivan's iron arm coils around Papa's shoulders.

This special monastery. This monastery of War Madonna, mother of homeland.

Chill and unease descend through the openings in the perforated dome. There is just enough light to be able to make out the Savior in the frescoes. His feet rest on the bottom beam, prolonging the agony. Pictured around him, a throng of bulging-eyed rabble, eagerly lapping up every quiver of his body, every shed tear, as an absolutely extraordinary spectacle.

They stand in a cluster by the entrance. A pair of plank beds. A couple of fellows dozing in chairs, pried-open cans of tuna at their feet, leap up, a bayonet falls off a chair and rattles at Ivan's feet. Roused to action by Ivan's commands, the men can't keep their grinning mugs off Soňa. She repays them with a nervous smirk, dreads bouncing at the collar of her red track top, and settles in on a plank bed with the little one, stretching out her leg with a hiss. She fishes around in the pocket of her jacket, pulls out a tube. Serafion parks Gérard on the plank bed opposite. The boy strides off after Papa, who shoos him away with a wave of his hand. The guards here have a portable stove, the aroma of tea wafts from a glass pitcher into the surrounding damp. The boy returns to the warmth.

Ivan and Papa tramp along the smoke-stained walls, kicking the fires' remains from their path with their heavy steel-toe boots. Ivan stops in front of each of the doors in the iconostasis, bows, crosses himself, mumbling something, they move on. A metal circle stands out from the floor amid the fragments of shattered brick. Ivan seizes hold, yanks open the lid.

They climb down the stairs, a humming, churning sound rising from the catacombs.

I can hear the laundry humming in the basement, Papa jokes into the coat on Ivan's back, but mostly he's being careful not to trample on his own overcoat as it sweeps along the stairs. They step off the stairs into a sharp yellow light cast from bulbs housed in wire cages along the walls.

A clean-swept concrete floor. A row of lockers against the wall. Two huge, noisy machines. Mobile crematories, shuddering with the workings of their inner mechanisms. Their smooth surface is covered with scale lines and contacts, the black handgrips and lids of heat-resistant glass handily placed at eye level.

The machines, filled with glowing flesh spinning behind the glass, are anchored to the floor. Connected up to a generator. The orange tubing of ducts arches into the vault overhead.

Naked bodies recline on the ground. A young man, who Papa narrowly avoids stepping on, eyes open though unseeing, lies rigid, arms extended along his body, legs stiffly protruding. On his neck, an open wound. In it, bits of lint in a dusty, dried-up smear of blood.

Two tiny, dark-skinned men emerge out of nowhere and head toward them, dragging a trolley cart, its metal wheels scraping against the concrete. Ivan, speaking in an aggravated tone, says something to them about being in a rush. Hands garbed in pink rubber gloves, the two runts seize hold of the man with the broken neck, place him on the trolley, and raise the adjustable bed to the level of the oven door. A tap on the handle and the lid swings open. As heat breathes out of the open oval, Ivan and Papa back away one or two steps. The body slides into the furnace. And the two men bend down to collect another corpse.

Ivan grips Papa by the shoulder and forces him to his knees. By a redhead laid out on a camouflage tarp. A square-built man, formerly a rock, his stomach is now shrunken and collapsed, the lining of his belly split open down to his crotch.

Ivan points out the tattoos covering the man's chest.

That is sign of elite Russian airborne division, and this is name of geroy . . . Igor Lebed. You understand?

No. I mean yeah, says Papa, shaking his head.

To carve off is impossible. Is impossible to carve orthodox Russian hero. We must give him to fire. God permits! They are here only on holiday. But if Ukrainians or Americans find them, ai-yi-yi! What propaganda would that be!

Oh, right, yeah, yeah, Papa says, nodding frantically, and presses to his mouth a ragged handkerchief that he must have found in the pocket of his coat. The two of them are still kneeling on the concrete. No sooner have the Ajvars hurled the redheaded soldier into the oven and flung in the bloodied tarp than there is the sound of an explosion and the cellar vault shakes. Another mighty bang follows, and a piece of plaster peels off and drops from overhead.

Papa lies down, knees to his chin, presses his palms to his ears. Ivan bends over him, easily prying his cramped fingers away from the sides of his head.

Is Grády! Khokhols will come! Is clear! But we return and win back Ajvarogorod.

You think? squeaks Papa.

Celebration must be! We will be again onstage without Ajvars! You and I and Gérard and armiya! New celebration of Novorossiya! He is fine actor, Gérard Depardieu, what you think?

For sure!

You and I and Gérard will be on televisions of world! We bring culture and peace to Ajvars! EU will be happy! USA will be happy!

Well, I donno bout that . . .

Braht moy, we leave monastery. But first, here is one more person.

What? Who?

Our father.

Ivan gets to his feet and claps his hands to dismiss the two men with the trolley. At his command, they wheel it away and drift off to wherever they came from. Using the sole of his shoe, Ivan sweeps the fallen dust away from behind the humming machines. And marches across the room.

To a little hatch in the wall. It appears to be all metal, or at least metal-plated, Papa can't tell the difference, but there's a handle sticking out of it. Ivan must have had the rifle he now holds in his hands hidden behind one of the crematories.

There our father, Ivan says with a sigh. He points to the hatch.

No!

Yes! They have applauded him. And I was his mechanic. And I have guarded him, braht! In Moskva, Tbilisi, Sevastopol. In Riga they have applauded him. In Minsk, Grozny, in Ulan-Ude!

Seriously?

Everywhere they love our father, rider of death!

Hm. Pretty cool!

And I have guarded him with this weapon: Ivan taps the heavy rifle stock. I have guarded so no nationalist or Islamist can endanger!

Papa gets to his feet, and as he stretches out his hand, Ivan gives him the gun to hold, but only by the stock and he doesn't let go. The general's cap shades Ivan's eyes from the light bulbs a little, but not enough to hide the teardops sliding down his cheeks. He wipes his eyes with the sleeve of his general's coat.

First celebration of Novorossiya! In Donbas. I have already told you. Whole world was watching us! Even Volodya Putin!

Is that a fact?

But Father already was old! I have seen how he shakes when he climbs on motorbike. Old! Ivan hangs his head. He would not make ride!

Aha, Papa says.

He would fly from track, enormous disgrace it would be, and so I . . . Ivan's voice drops to a whisper.

Are you saying you . . .

I shoot him! You only know.

Oof, Papa groans.

So it was!

That's awful.

Ach, braht.

Awful!

Ach, you. Ty moy mily! Then we have arrested bunch of fanatics, Islamists and khokhols, nasty fascist nationalists. It was declared assassination attempt. Good name of Father preserved. Clever, no?

Listen, Ivan. Just lend me a car. It doesn't have to be Gérard's, I don't need anything fancy. Just loan me like five hundred euros, and me and my family'll skedaddle. Okay? How bout it?

Braht, good that you are here! Go to Father.

Ivan darts to the hatch, grabs hold of the handle, and ever so slightly cracks it open. Just a smidge.

Braht, impossible to take Father away! Out of question! And impossible to leave him alive. You open door and walk through gate.

Forget it!

Help Father!

Leave me alone, for fuck's sake, both of you! You're hallucinations.

This no hallucination! Careful!

Listen, Ivan. Just lend me two hundred euros. What harm'll it do you? A hundred! Please!

Braht! Be strong!

That is one thing I'm not doin! Out of the question!

Ivan springs to Papa's side and whispers in his ear: After, you will go home and purchase commodities along Sázava in our native land. I love Czech lands! There we will live together. And you will have new family! Czech lands is garden!

What're you talkin about? I already got a family! Papa springs away, wiping the spray of his brother's saliva off of his face.

Your wife is drunkard, shit on her. You will have new wife.

What?

You want Ukraine woman with big breasts and rosy cheeks? Two eyes? Not problem. You are of belief brunette is best? Okay! I respect you, braht.

Cut the crap!

New wives give new sons!

Papa manages to stay on his feet through the next few booms and bangs, but Ivan tears off his mustache, knocks him to the floor, and at the moment the ceiling trembles and another boom drowns out the thrum of the machines, Papa's older brother has hold of him by the neck, dirty fingers aimed at his eyes, pressing down so forcefully that the vanquished man ceases to struggle.

Like in barn, Ivan splutters. Remember? How we used to horse around?

Yeeeah.

You must help!

Nooo.

Before Ukrainians attack, before you hear hurrah, you will kiss our father with bullet.

The man underneath relaxes, stretching out his legs. He gives up.

Like a little dog under a big one. With the toe of his boot, he touches the rifle stock propped against the cracked-open door.

Ivan leaps up and marches toward the crematories. Papa, limply, fully defeated, picks himself up from the ground.

Your sons worth shit, Ivan says, fingers dancing over the controls. The circular lid opens. Papa can feel the blast of heat.

Your big one does not speak. He has fear in ass.

He's just shy, Papa mumbles.

Leave them. Forget them.

C'mon, I can't do that!

You must have thought before, if you are man.

Sure, I've thought about it lots of times, Papa says, backing toward the half-open door. Ivan bends over, gropes along the floor, snatches something up, head unguardedly at the height of Papa's knees. When Ivan straightens back up again, holding a sock in his hand, Papa's afraid he's blown his chance even as he feels around behind him for the rifle.

And your little one? Is retard! Ivan sighs. What to do with cripple?

He tosses the sock in the furnace. Watches as the lid closes again. When he turns around, he sees Papa holding the rifle and grins.

Good! You understand.

Ivan digs in his pocket and fishes out a shiny cartridge.

Take this. Go to Father. God wants!

We'll see about that!

Papa swings the rifle butt and bashes Ivan in the temple. As his general's cap goes flying, the second blow catches him in the chin, and Papa just keeps on hammering and pounding.

The next hellish bang that shakes the ceiling is now accompanied by lots of smaller ones. Papa tosses the rifle aside, rolls the big man over, tugs the coat off his body, throws off Zoshchenko's. Averting his gaze from the bloody head, Papa slips into the general's garb . . . and as he reaches for Ivan's flattened cap, he kicks the hatch, it latches shut, then he gathers up a gob of spit, as best he can, and spits on it.

He hesitates for a brief moment, weighing the heavy body on the floor with his eyes . . . but then he hears the sound of more explosions and something in the ceiling comes loose, creaking, falling . . . Papa tramps up the cellar stairs. One or two bulbs torn off the wall, along with the ceiling plaster, hang loose on the end of their wires . . . He throws a shoulder into the lid with all his strength, and just as he starts to get scared that the house of God has fallen down and he's buried inside . . . the door lifts pretty easily. No wonder. There are lots of hands circled around it, pulling on it from above.

The boy stares at his papa wide-eyed, then buries his face in the uniform. Grimy men in big papakhas, draped in tricolor flags, and men in uniform with them, stumble over the scattered brick toward the exit. Beams jut from the ceiling. Where there used to be a wall, now there is a clear view of the hillside opposite. Papa sees tanks, standing side by side, with blue-and-yellow masking.

Cap jammed low on his head, cloaked in the general's overcoat, Papa screams the one thing that springs to mind: Hurraaaaah . . . He grabs the boy by the hand and they dash across the beams and bricks toward the carved door, bounding across the toppled plank beds with a pack of soldiers at their heels, and as they come running out of the shrine, they make straight for the fancy black car, still sitting right where Papa parked it.

Apart from that, the scenery is unrecognizable. The troops they saw marching past earlier are either scattered across the plain, or taking cover behind the sanctuary bastions. The ones they ran out with hit the deck, taking shelter inside the uprooted monastery gates. As he fumbles for the car keys, paying no attention to the whiz and hum of artillery fire filling the air, he looks through the window and finds himself staring through a wisp of black smoke into the terrified face of Soňa. Collapsed beside her, cowering in his seat, is Gérard.

At last Papa and the boy throw themselves onto the seats, and Papa, enraged, lights into Serafion: What does he think he's doing, sitting there all huddled up behind the wheel? They need to make straight for the bridge, where the tanks can't get across. Just before he falls into unconsciousness, he bellows one last command at the monk:

And start prayin, man.

7

THE CARPATHIANS. SNINA PASS. WHAT SERAFION
HAS THAT PULSES AND BEATS. DIVINE DANCING.
LUCKY US! MASTER OF THE PASS. SOŇA . . .
ON THE D1.

The giant beeches that shield the hunting cabin on Mount Succor in Snina Pass, where Serafion drives them to safety, swim in the mist rising out of the valleys.

At every step, the burdock and wood ferns reach over the boy's head. He spots a strip of asphalt through the gloom of the dense woods, sharpens his focus; the mist breaks. Striding across the road is a deer, a hefty male, his antler velvet worn away from rubbing trees and locking horns with opponents. The hart stirs, disappears into the undergrowth.

The boy ambles over to the car. Stares through the glass at the dozing Serafion clutching an oval icon in his fist. Next to him, the coiled actor drools from his open mouth, covered up to his chin with the military cloak. The boy can hear his mama's shrieking voice from the upper floor of the cabin. Papa is up now too. So the boy goes to join them.

Soňa descends the exterior ladder, easing her sore foot down one rung at a time, holding down her skirt as she tips back a bottle of wine from their already considerably depleted supplies. Her dreads are bunched into a braid and beautified with glitter plucked from the surface of her jacket. Papa forgoes the ladder, jumping down and landing in the grass with a thud in front of a stake that juts up from the soil.

Soňa?

Hm?

It really terrifies lots of people that there's nothing beyond the borders of our consciousness.

Chickenshits!

Papa has his big brother's army pants tied around his waist with an electrical cable. Time to get busy with the ax. He splits the logs into sticks, which he and Soňa arrange into a neat stack.

But the thing is, for me, that huge field of nothingness actually gives me strength!

Oh yeah?

Yeah.

So how huge is it?

I donno, whatever.

I think you're onto somethin! Hey, this peppered camembert is really good, says Soňa, pulling a gooey package from the pocket of her jacket.

Yeah?

Does make you thirsty, though. Too bad we finished that turkey. We also polished off all those pâtés already. We were gonna leave you some, but we didn't.

I'll open the sardines instead.

They look good. There's bread around here somewhere. We've got knäckebrot too. And some canned stuff.

Brilliant!

Apart from that, we're almost out of goodies, Soňa reports. This is all we got. She raises a bottle of Pernod. It's actually makin me queasy, though.

I could do with a drop of Beaujolais myself.

Sorry, just ran out.

No biggie!

Wanna know what I'm really celebrating? Soňa says.

What's that?

That we gave those two jokers the slip. That creepy Vaska. The way he kept lookin at me. If he ever laid a hand on me, I would've screamed.

Well, that's not gonna happen now.

And that brother of yours. Sorry, but I don't ever want to see him again, for real!

Don't worry, you won't.

The cabin's lower floor is built of thick beams, with no windows. The upper-floor window is an embrasure and observation slit, for hunters to hide. Downstairs it's just benches; upstairs, there's a bed, a stove, sleeping bags, a stack of porn mags, empty bottles. The cabin door is metal, warped, scraped by the claws of the wounded bears that lash out at the hunter's nest every now and then. The ladder is reinforced with magdonite poles. Otherwise the hairy beasts would break it in two like a twig. The hunters tether calves and baby goats to the stake. Sometimes they cut them open. Predators are drawn as much by the anxious bleating as by the smell of fresh blood.

Wow, I tell you, that Gérard's some gentleman! We got stopped along the way, and they started right in yellin at us, but then they laid eyes on Gérard! He even autographed their guns. This country girl came walkin by, leadin a cow on a rope, and what does he do but get out of the car and kiss her on the hand. Can you believe it? Anyway, he signed an autograph for the chief, then took a picture with him, so they let us go.

Oh yeah?

Papa blows into the embers, kneeling on the ground, shielding the skimpy flame with his hand.

You slept through almost the whole trip. Day, night, you were out. This other time we got stopped by a band of Cossacks. But Serafion tamed them with his icon. He keeps it under that funny robe of his.

What're you talkin about?

Back at the Citadel, Serafion was a guardian of the War Madonna, mother of the homeland, as they call it. So when they gave him Gérard to guard, he took the Madonna with him. You think it's valuable?

How do you mean, tamed them?

Well, for some of em, just gettin their picture taken with him was enough, and the rest of em were impressed we were transporting a sacred icon.

All right, so where are we?

Blowing harder, Papa adds some twigs to the newly risen flames.

See, that's what you get for bein asleep! I was just givin the boys our last Hungarian supplements when all of a sudden we're surrounded. I'm tellin you, those Cossacks are armed to the teeth! So the monk opens up his frock and there's this glow comin off his body and it's, like, drumming, like that oval with the picture of the Mother of God is sending out waves. I mean, seriously, I wasn't even high, but there was this, like, light or glow, like, comin off that icon!

Yeah, that can happen . . .

I could actually hear the little heartbeats from the Madonna! So the bandits kneeled down and asked Serafion to bless their weapons! And he did it, though he was winkin at me the whole time. I don't think he took it seriously.

But, Soňa, where are we?

Snina Pass, she says, waving her arm in the general direction of the border, where the Carpathian massif rises up out of the mist from the Ukrainian plain. Gateway to Slovakia, you might say. Nice, right?

Very nice!

That's why Serafion brought the icon.

To take it to the monastery? Papa balls up the general's coat and adds it to the rising flames, medals included. As the fire heats up, he feeds the cap to it too.

He's got an older brother here that's gonna take care of him. And us too! Sposedly his brother's some big shot. He's the one guaranteeing us safe passage through the pass. Home!

Great!

Hey, so what were you and Ivan doin in that monastery for so long? Were you guys drinkin or what? You seriously have no brains! Tanks, battles, up on the hill, and you leave your wife and kids to go off with your brother and drink in some cellar.

Soňa, but . . .

I get that you guys hadn't seen each other in a long time. I do!

Oh, please.

I just thought you might act a tad responsibly, really!

Oh, c'mon now!

The little boy lies on the bed behind a wall of pillows embroidered with hunting scenes. He breathes gently in and out, peeking out of his unbuttoned, still mostly clean romper. Stretches his little hands and feet into the dancing light. Sunbeams frolic across the windowpane as featherlight wisps creep into the room from the misty formations assembled beneath the forest canopy.

The bigger boy covers his little brother with a shaggy blanket. And inhales the aroma from below. Shooting out of the smoke and crackling heat, the aroma of grilled meat.

That's a delicacy! What're you doin? That was our last one left!

I'm sorry, Soňa, I just really like grilling!

Hey, check it out: Gérard!

The little monk, cassock hitched up around his waist, barrels across the glade, tripping, stumbling, regaining speed again. The actor easily keeps his lead just ahead. He bounds naked through the tall grass, snorting like a bull on the loose, or perhaps a wild boar, driven mad by the scent of his own musk, reveling in the joy of movement.

Gérard breaks away . . . Here we are, over heeere! Soňa calls, waving a stick speared with flesh. Papa tosses a well-done piece to the boy, who has just jumped down from the ladder and picks the bread up from the grass.

And they eat. Greedily. And watch.

The little monk grasps at the actor, who slips free every time. Yes, Gérard Depardieu cavorts about the glade in a youthful and statuesque manner, resembling the fauns of myth. Leaping and gamboling through the tall grass, he suddenly stoops down and peers into the forest, one leg raised . . . then plucks a flower, again on the run. The little monk pants after him in vain. The actor easily avoids the monk's attempts to apprehend him, the sandy color of his hair blending pleasingly with the rays of the afternoon sun, which roll across the meadow like a giant ball of light. Gérard dances and dances in the shade of the forest titans . . .

Hey, nice ass! Like a toreador!

Any chance you've got the papers for the car on you?

They're in the car. Hey, look what I found in the glovebox. I took it out so it wouldn't get lost!

From the pocket of her skirt, Soňa produces two rolls of red-colored bills. Papa, seeing the three zeros, whistles long and low.

I'll give it back to Gérard later, yeah?

Of course!

As soon he gets dressed!

Sure!

But their conversation is interrupted . . . along with their admiration for the naked giant's dance creations . . . by a cavalcade of jeeps thundering up the road, then, with a roar of engines and squeal of tires, bursting into the clearing, a motorcycle with sidecar leading the way. They come to a halt in front of the cabin. Soldiers holding machine guns salute as they brake to a stop. A giant man, dressed all in black, hops off the motorbike, draped in guns, metal tools strapped to his belt, a helmet on his head.

I forgot to tell you that . . .

Papa barely takes a step and the barrel of a gun is pressed to his neck. He chucks the stick with the sharpened tip into the grass.

I was just going to explain to you that . . .

Everyone looks at Serafion. The soldiers approach him across the trampled grass . . . and it's as if the heart of the man himself were aglow, the regular pulse, the beating, causing the glade itself to resound, the forest titans themselves to vibrate.

The little monk stops short, smoothing the exposed shirt on his chest, looking as if he intends to run toward the assembled men . . . but he is so fatigued that he can barely walk. The only sound now is the rustle of his bare feet against the blades of grass. And Gérard is nowhere to be seen.

The little monk winds his way through the jeeps, and when at last, red-faced and out of breath, he stands before the warrior, he gets such a powerful slap in the face he topples over.

The hulking man seizes hold of him and lifts him in the air. Tears rolling down his cheeks, he plants a kiss on the little monk's lips, then covers his cheeks with ardent kisses. The tears flow onto Serafion, into the surrounding grass, and surely onto the little monk's sweat-soaked frock as well.

Serafion urgently points to the woods, chirps some words with lowered eyes. The officer shakes his head. Shoves the youth toward the motorbike.

The little monk wraps his arms around the driver's waist, the wheels dig into the dirt, and the roaring jeeps once again shadow the path of the lead rider, leaving nothing behind but the stink of their exhaust.

He could at least've waved goodbye!

No. Maybe not. Maybe his brother wouldn't have approved.

And what about us?

That's what I wanted to tell you. We cross the border at daybreak. The car's got Slovak plates on it now. Didn't you even notice?

No.

Well, it does.

Excellent!

Yeah, it's all been arranged. I told you his brother's a big wheel round here.

So I saw. But what about customs? Border patrol?

That was them! Soňa says, pointing to the disappearing cavalcade.

Aha!

It's gonna cost us two thousand euros.

Well, we're damn lucky then.

You can say that again.

Soňa hops aside, palm on her belly, doubles over, and spews a stream of vomit.

Soňa? Are you all right? I guess it wasn't cooked enough!

I just puke sometimes these days.

Really?

Yeah. It was cooked just right!

The darkness falls so suddenly, it's like the shadows leaped down from the branches. The vehicle is ready to go. They move all the blankets, sleeping bags, and comforters down from the upper floor to the fire. And wait for daybreak.

A wild mixture of squawks and howls resounds from the forest's depths, alternating with periods of total silence. Caravans of clouds pour across the moon, whose pale shine ripples through the darkened sky.

It just occurred to me, we should've stayed upstairs!

But how would you get up there with that leg?

You don't believe in bears?

Look, we're fine out here.

Or are you waiting for him to come back?

Gérard?

Yeah.

Serafion'll take care of him, you'll see. They'll have a search party comb the woods in the morning. Putin'd break their bones otherwise. Don't worry! His brother'll see to it. But we need to be gone by then. And since when've you been sick?

Well, I'm not really sick.

Then what are you?

C'mon, you know.

The boy tosses some twigs on the fire. Curls up with his parents squatting at the fire's edge. Waits for his little brother to fall asleep before lying down himself. The sleeping bag he pillaged from upstairs is big enough for two.

I threw up so much after those Cossacks, I thought it was from them. But it wasn't!

Oh no?

No. It's that.

Are you serious? That's amazing.

You don't seem too excited.

No, I'm happy! Look, don't worry, we'll get outta here. And tomorrow we'll zip through Slovakia, the dee-one's just a short ways away. We'll be home in a jiff. Aren't you excited?

You said I was gaining weight. Complaining and stuff. Well, now you know why! Truth is, I am kina beat. And these wrinkles're insane.

C'mon, not at all!

Listen, the main thing is for it to be healthy.

Oh, absolutely! Course it'll be.

I shouldn't drink. I'll just have a bit. To help me fall asleep.

Absolutely!

We'll be back home again soon. Then everything'll be fine, right?

Oh, absolutely!

8

ON THE D1. THE BRIDGE IN POŘÍČÍ. A MENTION
OF THE PAINTING OF THE VIRGIN. INSECTS AND
BROKEN GLASS. SPLENDID PLANS. SOŇA, IS THAT
YOU? IT'S TAKEN CARE OF. MALES. IN THE SHOWER
AND OUTSIDE THE SHOWER: MAMA.

Justshutthefuckupforaminute! Soňa screams in Papa's ear. He grips the
steering wheel, zipping along the D1, the highway that stretches east
from Prague, a tapeworm slipped from the city's bowels, carved into
the plain.

But I'm just sayin what I see, says Papa, having tumbled straight out
of the night into the driver's seat and launched into a nonstop commen-
tary on the world passing by outside the windows.

Glued to the D1, they go plunging into Praha-východ, the region east
of Prague. The boy, in the back seat, snuggled against his little brother,
takes in the factory buildings, the warehouses and assembly halls, multiplying like cells, one budding off from the other, the gas stations like
oases festooned with ads and garlands of flashing lights, even by day.

So what do you see?

That it's different here!

Home is elsewhere, that's for sure, Soňa says sensibly, flinging an
empty nip to the floor. One hand on her belly, the other one strokes
her swollen leg, where the whole way from the Carpathians a lump has
been alarmingly growing underneath the skin.

The boy surveys the landscape, the hot air slamming against him in
waves. The area east of Prague around the D1 is disarrayed by the hustle and bustle of construction, ads offering more products than anyone could count gushing from the planetary sewer of plenty, shopping
malls springing up alongside motels announcing themselves with plastic baskets full of condoms—love nests, as they say.

The little one, belted into the car seat, breathes with difficulty, whistling through his nose. The two brothers are connected to each other by a pool of sweat.

The bigger boy rolls down the window. As the fresh air dries their sweat, he stares out at the giant eagle of the Mattoni logo. Faces of politicians, their appeals. The car hurtles down a corridor lined with business slogans, the product of specialized brain trusts: CAIRO SAVINGS BANK: SAVE NOW, SPEND MORE LATER! Then a half-naked girl proclaiming that pussy isn't soap, or SOFTNESS, THY NAME IS WOMAN. And to round out the trio: JESUS = YOUR LORD.

Just keep that window open, AC's overworked as is! Papa whoops, tugging at his Hungarian T-shirt. He's traded his uniform pants for a pair of shorts he procured at a gas station along the way.

Oh boy, oh boy, Soňa sighs. Fishing a pill from a silver tube, she swallows, washes it down with a drink, deodorizes her sensitive leg with Rexona, young lady–style.

They go speeding through a rainbow, arching through the sky above the interchange like some huge gossamer valley. Asphalt roads ooze off the D1 here, shadowing what in days gone by were poachers' footpaths, dirt tracks, and cart ruts from village to village. The boy's attention is drawn by a billboard in the shape of a giant beer stein, depicting a black cat in a cap with a bag over its shoulder: VISIT THE U SEJKŮ PUB! He jumps in his seat as Papa offers greetings to the river with a long honk of the horn. The highway and the river here gleam side by side, backbone to backbone, as tenaciously as the highway sprays out asphalt roads, the river soaking up drainage, runnels, swampy meanders.

To get to Poříčí nad Sázavou, the village where Soňa was born, they head down a road that curves off the body of the D1 like a tentacle.

Every so often, one of the two in front taps on the window to signal their amazement at some familiar site . . . where there used to be nothing, the city had spat out whole zones of sheet-metal enclosures, warehouses stocked with lawnmowers, garden furniture, pyramids of sawdust briquettes, outdoor grills, statuettes and monuments with fragments of the baroque aesthetic, funereal creations seemingly made of sugar and whipped cream. They go zooming down blacktop roads between fields where the rags on the scarecrows flap in high winds, auguring heat waves or floods.

And then, speeding down a county road along the reinforced river-banks, they catch glimpses of the river through the stalks of corn, the treetops adorned with a layer of plastic bags and sticks deposited there by the floods, like ornaments woven into the hair of pagan chieftains.

And just after passing an inconspicuous cherry tree in whose branches they see a clot of mud baked by the sun like a patch of skin from the hide of a leviathan, they drive past the sign that says POŘÍČÍ straight onto the bridge with the marlstone saints.

Little do they know that they're following the long-ago path of the Order of Little Fools, who saw themselves as little bees sucking the wounds of Christ. Once upon a time, a flock of them strode barefoot across this bridge with penitential scourges, singing a song devoted to Mary, in rhythm to the lashing of their whips. Amid the rain of blood and tiny shreds of flesh, shot through with the perfume of the smoke of swinging censers, they carried the painting of the Virgin on the Mount into the sanctuary in Poříčí.

And just as back then, the vermilion-edged clouds tugged the dusk behind them, and with it the foreboding of a storm, as yet still coiled up in wait.

The family tarries only a moment among the saints and swarms of twirling dragonflies over the river, then enters the streets and lanes of the village, guided by details fished from Soňa's memory—here a mile-post, there the oddly still-flaking corner of the butcher's shop, the little church on the hill.

Hey look, Soňa says, poking her arm out the car window with a rattling of bracelets. They used to have Turkish honey!

A gloomy-looking pair of gents squat on the bench in front of the grocery store, sucking on bottles of beer. As the big black sedan cruises past, their eyes are glued to it. It's an event, a precious gem. A tall man in a ratty sports coat, shaved bald like a convict, even stands and waves.

Then they turn into streets lined with houses, cottages, and gardens, pass another church, some apartment blocks, including a few paneláks from the days of the comrades, and stop at one of them.

In front of a tall sheet-metal gate covered in curls of peeling paint.

So, here we go!

Soňa opens the door, pokes her head out, sun glancing off the ring in her lip, taps the swelling on her leg, thrusts her foot from the car.

So let's go!

Papa gets out, pushes against the gate, it swings open. Into a large, cool courtyard. So they climb back in and drive inside.

Soňa gets out, but trips over an abandoned clamp. Her bulbous leg slips out from underneath her and she leans against the hood for support, eyes wide as she takes in the scene.

A rusty chainlink fence. Of course back in the day it used to be slats. And there used to be squashes everywhere. In Soňa's memory they blaze in fiery colors, the freshly turned earth shooting energy up through their slender, fibrous roots. And a dazzling supply of tomatoes, yellow and red alike. Plantations of cabbage, patches of kohlrabi, obscene snarls of carrots.

Daddy! blurts Soňa, and takes a step, skirt brushing the stairs. We're here!

The curtains inside are drawn. He lies in the gloom, nestled in blue-striped comforters, blankets. They can sense his body, his truly colossal bulging belly, quite likely the source of all the stench. The parchmentlike skin of his face. And the hairs thrusting up from the gray patches of skin that cover his face like layers of bark. A sparse stand of hair, pasted into a clump with sweat, protruding almost comically from the surface of his veiny skull. His Pleistocene neck, with folds of yellowing skin spilling across the collar of his pajamas, hardened into a suit of armor with sweat, filth, and shit.

Soňa lifts her hands to her mouth, lets them drop, fingers groping in the pocket of her skirt.

We're heeere! Papa shouts from the hallway, stomping up the stairs and bursting into the room, little nipper in his car seat in hand.

Blob-strewn linoleum. Sideboard crammed with stuff overflowing into the room. Broken dishes veined with gray smears of hardened sauce. And, seemingly spilling over out of the wallpaper, stacks of newspapers and magazines, flyers and handbills grinning from within their yellowed pages, looking as if they've been whipped with a cane. Heaps of medications—tubes, tablets, pills—fallen out of the old man's bed in a jumble.

The sleepyhead stirs. Raises his wattled face, a patchwork of different faces joined together with wrinkles like the vestiges of a series of botched plastic surgeries.

Papa sets the car seat down on the lino, walks to the window, draws the curtains, and so sees the sudden rain.

It's fierce. Streaks of lightning across the sky. The storm wheezes like an animal. The sodden clouds gush and spit water down in strings, the drops hitting the window so hard it nearly rattles.

You wouldn't mind a little fresh air, would you, Mr. Hrozen? I brought the whole family for you!

Papa opens the window.

The old man's eyelids twitch, then crack open.

Soňa walks to the bed, skirt sweeping over the plates and trash on the floor.

Hi, Dad!

Soňa, is that you? says the old man in a voice unexpectedly loud.

Yeah!

And your grandkids're here too! says Papa, chiming in.

You should see yourself! You look a mess! And what the hell's that on your head?

Hey, Dad, we're gonna get settled in. Then I'll be back!

The boy lugs the car seat into the kitchen, next to the old man's bedroom, grease sticking to his soles. Soňa gets caught on something on the wall and trails a little behind.

In the corner of the kitchen is a shower cubicle covered with plastic. The stove right next to it, covered in junk. Broken glass and dead insects stuck all over the floor. Kitchen counter and cabinets dating back to ancient times. Couch. Stuffed deer head on the wall above. Table, clipped-on plastic tablecloth. Closet doors open, piles of clothes falling out.

Soňa pulls a broom out from behind the counter by memory. Slaps it around the floor, nudging the broken glass out of the way with her shoe. Takes out a blanket, spreads it on the ground. Peels the little one out of his rompers, lays him on his back. Dampens some napkins and wipes the boy's gently arched little forehead, little hands and miniature little nails, puckered little lips. Skin shivering lightly beneath the scratchy moisture, the little one gapes up at the colorful tufts of swaying hair, blinks, goggling his eyes like frogs, mice, little creatures do. Mama gives him a bottle, so he sucks.

Papa snoops around the cups in the sideboard, rummages through the kitchen cabinets, forks, knives, and spoons clinking, items in the interior banging, shifted to the wall with swift movements. Wrists relaxed, he combs over every inch, feeling his way with a gentle tap of the fingers.

The old man is starving to death and proud of it.

Long as death has settled in, who am I to chase her away? Hrozen had already made up his mind. They delivered him food, but he still had the strength left to shuffle to the front door, pick up the milk cans, as he called them, and flush them down the toilet. All of them that came to check up on him, that whole pesky web of helpers that sprang up with his sudden incapacitation, sensing the chance to get a lick of the honeypot, he just threw them down the stairs. He always had liked having his space. Not only that, but he'd stopped taking care of the building back when Soňa disappeared. It had never been easy living with him. In the end, he was left in the building alone.

It was sometime after that that he took to bed. Just lay around drinking, water.

I'm goin about it the smart way, while I can still control it, he thought, feeling pleased with himself.

And he dug in.

The panic, anxiety, fear come in waves. But Hrozen is dug in. And it gets easier every day.

He sleeps a lot. As much as he can.

Yeah, I'll do it myself, he thinks with satisfaction in his waking moments of clarity.

I'm a man, after all, he assures himself whenever he surfaces.

I'm the one who makes the decisions here.

And sometimes he even smirks to himself, shaking his head at his own cunning. He wants to nestle against the wall. But he can't even budge. The stiffness came only recently, as well as the gray membrane that the newcomers broke when they entered.

He feels some movement next to him and opens his eyes. It's Soňa, sitting beside him on the bed.

What's wrong, Dad? Anything hurt?

Ah, it'll be fine.

Does anyone come to see you?

Please, there's nothing I need.

I'm gonna rinse you off, okay?

That time in the yard. The little daughter peers at her father through the fence slats. Daddy, look, I know how to run, watch! she blurts. And runs a short way. Vanishes from sight for a moment. Then stops and peeks through the fence again.

An ordinary moment. One out of a thousand. But it felt like something happened. Something astonishing. The two of them, together in a rift in time, with ordinary, everyday life going on all around them. Everything going on revolving around them. Him standing there in coveralls, scratching his army crewcut. Nailed to the ground by the vision. And how did it all happen? And why? It was the most intense feeling he ever felt. Many years have passed since then. Now he has death in his innards.

Hey, Dad. I'm gonna rinse you off, okay?

Soňa, what happened to you? You only have one eye?

You need to wash.

You look a sight, girl!

Wait here, Dad. I'll be right back!

If you say so.

Check out this jacket! Badges and everything! Czechoslovak People's Army, oh shit!

Papa pulls the jacket out of the closet and and tries it on.

Medals, too! Son, remember the medals your uncle Ivan had? And look, a police badge. You could start a nice collection. I used to collect badges when I was a boy. Hey, these're some pretty nice suits. But hardcore stone age! Hardcore.

The little boy, now all cleaned up, lies on the kitchen couch, padded in pillows and a rolled-up blanket courtesy of his mama.

I didn't know he was that bad! I'll give him a wash in a bit.

Hey, Soňa? I feel bad bringin it up, obviously. But the building is gonna be yours.

I guess so, right?

So that means we can finally get married. What do you say?

That you're stupid. And pretty old, in case you didn't realize.

Sit down. Relax. I'll make us something to eat.

Seriously, I had no idea how bad off he was! Shit! How could I not've known?

I think he'll be better now. Just havin you around! And the boys can go to school here. Regularly.

And we can shower right now, Soňa says, pointing to the cubicle in the corner.

I really think we oughta take a look around the place!

Hey, give it a rest, would ja? I'm gonna peek in on my dad. Rinse him off a little.

I made some coffee. But uff, it's awful. Is that Czech coffee?

Don't look at me. I never drank coffee till I got outta here!

So how do you feel?

I could lie down right now, but that shower is callin my name!

You know what I was thinkin, Soňa? We could start a theater here! Soon as we get settled in. I can drop by my ma's place later. But we could really pump some blood into the culture here in Sázava. What do you say? And our theater café will have awesome coffee. Good strong espresso. You could be in charge of that, Papa nods to the boy. Like a part-time job, you know? After school.

Slow down!

Only part-time job I could get in soshie days was workin in the potato field! Or in the factory. You can definitely do better than that!

But we're flat broke. And I am plumb tuckered out.

Checkin out that doe, son, huh? That is really something! I never knew your dad was a hunter, Soňa.

First of all, he's still here, he still exists, got it? So don't talk about him like he was already dead.

Sorry. I think I'll make spaghetti. How's that sound?

You bet he was! There's a boar's head in the best room. He brought it home for me on my birthday one year. I open my eyes and whoa! There's this wild pig there beside me. Huge head, glass eyes bulging out at me, right. But he meant well by it! He was head of the Gamekeepers' Association.

He was head of everything, wasn't he?

Papa brings the spaghetti in from the car. The oil and salt shaker are on the shelf over the stove. The spaghetti is delicious—French, he points out. Before long, the water's heating in a pot atop the stove.

We can make it with sardines, I saw a can here in the cabinet! Apparently he liked fish. Did you and your dad used to go fishing?

Yeah. And don't talk about him in past tense. I'm asking you kindly. I'll go look in on him in a minute in case he wants to eat with us.

You said he had a field. And other stuff. Forgive me for bein practical. I'm just tryin to think of the family.

And which family would that be?

You said he had some land.

He does!

Papa dumps the spaghetti into the boiling water. Hey, you guys. We still have another bag of cheese. Parmesan, hooray! But this really is the last one.

Now the plates are on the table, a mound of spaghetti on each one. A dusting of cheese. The kitchen is filled with steam, rising up toward the beaded chandelier. Papa serves the salted and peppered sardines on a Victorious February plate from the Poříčí collective farm. The tiny bones jut up through a thick coating of oil. The family members take their seats.

You know what? We're not gonna be travelin that much anymore. That cheese is great, right? Lucky for us Gérard was such a gourmand.

Papa opens the bottle he found. The label shows a hunter holding a bottle with a label showing a hunter, etc.

You should probably abstain, though.

No biggie. I don't like the hard stuff anyway.

Still, we can have a toast. To makin it here in one piece!

I'll drink to that.

Hey, Soňa says, tapping the boy on the shoulder. Ready for sleep yet? Actually, know what? Go take a shower first.

Not bad, Papa says, swirling the glass of brown liquid.

I'm tired! I'll check in on him later. And I'm not goin anywhere else, in the apartment or the building. Not till tomorrow!

Mostly I just think it'll be easy here.

What?

Finding a quiet corner. To write in, y'know? I'd really like to get somethin done!

Hm. You've said that before.

Papa slips into the old man's room on tiptoe.

How are you, Mr. Hrozen? Feelin any better?

He snatches a moth out of the air, pitches it into the darkness, closes the window, the light from the kitchen bursting through the glass door onto his back. Treads carefully over the lumps and debris on the floor, lifting his knees like a stork. Peeks under clothing, lingers at the closets, the table in the corner. Probes and examines, inspecting everything. Kneels down by the bed, slides his fingers up the clammy sheet to the headboard, feels around behind there.

What the hell're you're doin? You skunk, says the old man.

I came to see how you are.

The fuck're you talkin about?

I came to help you, Mr. Hrozen.

Papa lifts the blanket, lowers it again, slides his hand under the pillow, all around the old man's head, twitching beneath the sticky hair.

And for fuck's sake, don't call me mister. Talk normal. There's nothin I need.

But you need help.

What do you want here, you punk?

I'm just lookin around.

I don't care. Call Soňa.

Lemme just fix this here. Make you more comfortable, kay?

Leave it, I said. It's fine as is.

The boy stands under the shower, the stream of water washing out the dirt from scabs, abrasions. The plastic floor around the drain turns black with dust, flecks of mud from the soles of his feet. Looking out through the frosted curtain into the room, he sees his mama slip from the couch onto the floor.

He wipes himself down with his palms, quickly shakes himself off, pulls on his track pants and a T-shirt.

She lies twisted in pain on her stomach, thick, oily blood flowing

out of her. She rolls over, pawing the floor with her hands, leaving behind burgundy specks. Her skirt is hitched up, exposing the opening
between her lightly golden-haired thighs. A bloody glob of fetal tissue
oozes out. His mama's pale face, as she rolls over toward him, looks
tiny in the light of the chandelier. The boy stands over his mama, frozen with fear, as she reaches up, feels for the handle. The door opens
so hard it rattles the glass.

Soňa!

They lift her up. With difficulty, her legs keep sliding out. But she
manages to stand up straight. Papa grabs a dishcloth off the stove and
starts to wipe her off, but the rag is instantly soaked. He throws it away,
grabs a blanket, wraps it around Soňa's shoulders, takes her in his arms.
He and the boy can hear her breathing as they tramp across the spattered linoleum. She holds on tight while they help her down the stairs,
until her palm slips off the back of the boy's hand and she grasps hold
of the railing.

Take care of your little brother, he hears his papa say. And don't you
go anywhere! Just wait right here for me.

9

LADY COP. CITIZENS' ASSEMBLY. RICHIE THE
SCOUT. BAŠTA, LORD OF THE JUNKYARD. A LITTLE
DIFFERENT KIND OF HOSPICE. HUN RAIDS. RIVER
CLEANSING. GETTING THROUGH TO THE HOSPITAL.
BIG BOYS DON'T CRY.

The boy opens his eyes to daylight splashing into the room. He lies on
the couch where he fell asleep curled up next to his little brother. Also
now blinking his eyes open. The kitchen door is open. Two men in gar-
dening overalls carry a large body on a stretcher out of the room next
door. And disappear around the bend in the hallway. He skims his gaze
over the bloody footprints on the kitchen floor.

I know my rights! Just try and kick us out! The kids haven't even had
breakfast! he hears his papa say. A lady cop steps into the kitchen.
Gapes open-mouthed at the spattered floor and the little nipper stren-
uously smiling up at her with his whole little face. She kneels down to
the couch, taps the boy on the shoulder with a gloved hand.

On your feet, sonny!

The officer has a round young face with a wart in the dimple of her
chin. A wooden baton hangs from her hips. Attached to her belt are
handcuffs and a gun.

You're gonna go to a boardinghouse, boy. They'll give you breakfast
there. Both you and your brother, of course, the lady cop says, word by
word, slowly and emphatically.

Do you understand me? Do you speak Czech?

He nods.

What's your name?

She draws herself up to her full height, uniform stretching tight across
her breasts.

Don't touch anything. This has to be photographed, alla this here. She wrinkles her nose at the bloodstained floor, exits the room, leaving the door open.

Things stand out in the light of day. The clock on the wall. The deer head. The peeling cabinets. The table with glasses and plates. All the dirty corners with dust balls.

What do you mean sick nurse? We're fine! the boy hears his papa again from the hallway.

He turns around and wriggles into his track pants.

And here comes Papa, carrying the baby seat. He snatches the little one up off the couch, into his arms.

C'mere!

Slips something into the boy's pants. An envelope.

Put it under the elastic. Move around, walk to the door.

The boy walks to the door and back, adjusts the envelope against his behind. The elastic holds.

Walk more nonchalantly. Take Mama to the hospital here. She needs to relax.

Papa seizes hold of the car seat with both hands and bounds down the stairs, the little nipper gripping his bottle between his fists.

Crossing the courtyard now, in the bright light of day, they see sparse yellow grass growing up through the weed patch of odds and ends, discarded metal and wooden scraps. Their car is parked on the road in front of the building.

Surrounded by lots of people. Including the short lady cop. And other officers. Neighbors in T-shirts and shorts, work coveralls. Whoever just popped out of their garden to see what was going on, now clustered shoulder to shoulder, studying the intriguing foreign automobile. The panelák windows are bedecked with faces, everything here is right close by, everyone is watching. Papa digs in his feet at the gate.

You can't run us out of my daddy's home, he cries.

He's got a child, somebody shouts. A little kid, for God's sake!

Morning, madam commander, says an old-timer with a rake over his shoulder. So is it true Hrozen's passed?

I was here when they carried him out! Eyes shut. I says to myself, he's probly not even alive, a neighbor testifies, cheeks flushed with excitement.

The police close the gate.

What'd they do?

How come there's no TV here? Somebody call the station, a guy in camouflage shorts demands.

Let the brothers go home! someone shrieks in a fake-squeaky voice.

I know that guy from somewhere, mutters somebody.

Here they are lockin up kids and citizens like it was Russia, somebody grouses.

Yeah, soon it'll be like Karlovy Vary. Russkies overran that place like roaches, mutters the guy in camo, tipping back a box of plonk. He hands it to the old-timer. The two of them burst out laughing at his joke as the short, busty lady cop shoves Papa toward the car.

Little Soňa was here. I saw her! But that guy's some actor. The whole thing's fishy.

They show up and next thing he's dead. If it were me, I'd investigate!

Please, not in front of the children.

Did you see what a mess those kids were?

Papa fishes the car keys out of his pocket, sets the baby seat with his son in it on the running board.

We're takin him in for questioning, ladies. Just calm down.

You calm down, you dirty rat.

What? What's that you said?

Sittin on her ears, the dirty rat, mutters the red-cheeked neighbor, and with the toe of her sneaker draws something indecipherable in the gravel.

Papa opens the door, pulls in the baby seat, buckles it securely in place, the boy climbs in the car.

The lady cop swings up on the running board, Papa lowers the window, the lady cop sticks in a gloved hand, grabs hold of the handle over the door.

I'll direct you!

Where to?

We're headin over to The Three Tykes boardinghouse, get you boys fed. The lady cop smiles. They got a social worker there, too.

What?

Nice car! shouts the lady cop, gripping the window with both hands.

Once we get the boys settled in, we'll pop on by the station and write up our protocol with you.

They pass the last paneláks, the grocery, take a turn after the church, the lady cop on the running board giving directions.

We'll question you, then off we go to technical inspection, says the lady cop. She rocks up on the running board, stuffing her breasts through the half-open window, stuck to the side like she's melted on.

As they weave their way through the last lanes of the village and emerge onto the blacktop winding toward the bridge, the mist and vapors drift toward them from the waters below, and, seeing a flash of the river's surface through the mist, Papa speeds up.

He suddenly cocks his fist and launches it out the window, catching the lady cop with an uppercut to the chin. Her cap sails off, hair flying around her head as she tumbles over the railing, landing hard on the slope, rolling down to the water, and hitting the surface with a splash.

They reach the statues on the other side of the bridge and Papa slams on the brakes.

Flatbed trucks drive onto the bridge toward them, emerging from a cornfield, the columns of light from their headlamps tearing through the mist, transporting timber, tree trunks with slashed, resinous bark. Another vehicle carries a load of young sows beneath its sleet- and mud-stained tarp. They hear the sounds of snorting and grunting as the ripe whiff of pig stings their nostrils. Another car hauls scrap metal— pipes, ovens, battered stoves, tossed higgledy-piggledy one atop the other. The vehicles pass with millimeters to spare.

We gonna sit here forever or what, grumbles Papa. Finally, the last vehicle drives past and the way is clear.

As they jolt over the speed bumps coming off the bridge, a scarecrow catapults out of the field, crashing into the side of the car. Just keep it straight! he yells as he crouches down on the running board.

They're the only ones on the road now, driving fast.

Hang a right!

Papa cuts the wheel and takes a sharp turn onto a dirt track. Tall stalks of corn flicker past, scalps fluttering in the breeze. He brings the car to a stop.

Startled you guys, huh? Sorry bout that . . .

What's goin on here?

The scarecrow steps down off the running board, opens the door, climbs in next to Papa. Long-limbed type, smile stretched wide across his thin, pale face, clean-shaved head. He spreads out on the front seat, baggy-kneed polyester pants, shabby sports coat.

Just keep on goin thataway, he says, waving up the track. And take it slow.

What is this?

Gave ya a start, huh? How bout you, young fella? He turns to the boy. Scare ya?

They jounce along the rain-carved rut. Then down a gravel path into the woods and across a creek. Foamy water spits against the windows like someone flinging sand, clumps of mud kick up from underneath their tires.

Then they head uphill, stiff white roots jutting across their path, tree branches whipping at the top and sides of the car. A glow rises from the clearings overgrown with lush green grass.

The fellow next to Papa starts to chuckle to himself.

That was some resolute action you pulled back there. On the bridge!

Where're we goin?

Not much place ya can go now, is there? Just keep drivin.

So where're we headed?

You'll see!

I haven't slept a wink, and the way she was bossin us around!

C'mon, you killed her, are you kiddin? Me and the boys were watchin from down under the bridge. You punched her and she got all cut up down there on the rocks. She's dead meat! Why'd ya do it?

I didn't mean to, really!

So I came chasin right up the hillside, look at me, clotburs all over, he says, tearing the thorny clumps off his jacket and flicking them out the window. Caught ya just in time!

We've got a heck of a trip behind us, I've hardly slept. She really put a scare into us, Papa says defensively.

Listen, that dyke's an asshole. There's somethin wrong with that woman, for real. So your patience snapped, that it?

Right, Papa nods.

She was takin ya down to the cop house, that it?

Yeah, Papa nods.

You're in a hell of a situation, I tell ya.

Jesus and Mary, I mean, you saw! Jumpin up on my window and screamin at me! Scarin my boy!

Pretty decent set of wheels, the fellow says, patting the dash. Hail from Slovakia, do ya? And where ya comin from?

So where're we goin now?

This guy I know, Járin, had a Slovak chick and ever since then he insists that Czech women're tired, more like boring, what do you think?

Seriously, I have no idea.

But not all of em, he says. Not all.

Hm!

So ya don't remember me, huh? A drink to reunions, whadda you say? The lanky man produces a bottle from his jacket pocket. Pulls out the cork with his teeth, takes a swig, hands the bottle to Papa. Papa accepts while keeping a close watch on the road.

I'm Richie! says the guy.

Look, I haven't been here in years.

You don't remember me cause I was young. Good bit younger than you, in fact.

They whip along through the woods, down a hard, well-traveled path.

Ya know, I remember little Soňa from the Hrozens back when she was just a bare-assed pixie splashin around the creek at our place.

Oh, really?

Musta been five or six, now whoa there, don't get angry, kay?

And they're there.

A bar across the forest road. On the other side, wrecks of cars, wedged into one another, tossed here off of dump trucks. Jagged bits and scraps bristle in the yellowed grass like traps. Sheet metal, rusty iron, crushed glass everywhere.

At the center of the junkyard is a trailer. Someone squats at a fire in front.

Richie leans out the window and waves. The keeper of the flame stands little by little, struggling up with the help of a crutch. A chain around his waist is holding up his track pants. The old geezer is all tightened up, and his chest is laced up too—aha, he's got on a corset. It's hot here in the junkyard quiet, sunlight bouncing off of all the metal and glass.

Richie lifts the bar.

They drive in.

Richie guides them, flattened cars towering over their heads. They veer off toward a low-slung metalworking shop. It reminds the boy of the highway, all the warehouses, garages, hangars.

As the car enters the shop, the boy's gaze lands on canisters scattered about, a heap of colorful work gloves, piles of bolts dark with oil, thick sheets of metal stacked in the corner, two or three automobiles in various states of disassembly.

Two young men stand in the sharp light, watching. Even with the fan blowing they have black knit caps on, probably so the seams of their skulls won't come unglued in the heat.

The name Miran, stitched in bright red thread, stands out on the chest of the guy who steps up to their car, swathed in orange bib overalls, hair in a clip. There are pictures, scrawls, and dots tattooed all over his naked arms and face.

Waving a pair of long pliers, with blue spaghetti tubing in place of grips, he points to a ramp along the wall. Papa inches the car up along the yellow lanes, following the arrows, until he hears a click and the wheels lock into place.

As the boy undoes the seatbelt on the car seat, sweat beading on his forehead, he sees the sparse patch of hair budding atop the little one's head is also matted with sweat. He blows on his brother's head in a vain attempt to cool it, but his breath is hot as well.

You know them? Richie waves to the workmen as they approach the car.

No.

Be surprised if ya did. Bašta's boys're even younger than me.

Oh yeah?

If you didn't know em before, you will now.

I can't wait.

Come on outside.

But that's my car.

Come on out.

Give me one good reason why.

They could just as soon take that thing apart right over your head!

One of the mechanics is already knocking on the car from underneath. It takes all the strength the boy has to lift his brother out of the seat. Not long ago, he still carried him like it was nothing.

That car of yours needs a goin-over, needs repairs. Let the boys take care of it.

No need, Papa says. We'll be leavin soon anyway.

Don't be silly!

So Papa wriggles out. Steps onto the ramp.

Should we take our stuff?

Just leave it all there!

Papa kicks a tire.

Come with me! We got lečo. Or soup maybe, not sure.

They follow Richie, single file, Papa carrying the car seat, down a narrow path between the piles of flattened wrecks, tramping through the heat-baked mud over thick clumps of yellow-bleached grass dusted with rust, oil puddles on every side.

Sit down, orders the gimp by the fire. Reigning from atop a wooden crate. A small heap of branches lies at his feet.

They take a seat, one by one, around the fire. The boy, shifting the envelope in his waistband, squats on a brick. Papa settles in on a stump. Puts the baby seat with the little one at his feet.

Richie heads off to the trailer, steps inside, claps the door shut behind him.

Hello, Mr. Bašta.

Fine pickle you're in, Tab, the old man replies after a moment's pause.

His drooping, toadlike eyes water. Chest imprisoned within a plastic corset, his stomach bulges out from his red track pants below. Bašta's face is swollen, sunburned. His arms are like logs stuffed into his track-suit top. Palms, a firm layer of solid flesh; callused, as they tend to be on people who use crutches. Snarls of knotted gray hair tumble down to his shoulders from beneath his knit cap.

You're damn lucky Richie saw that whole thing! Other boys also called right quick, let me know what was goin on on our bridge.

The old man pushes out his breath, wheezing and rasping from deep in his throat, the skin on his neck collapsed into a series of leathery gullies. His Adam's apple, small and hard, hops when he talks.

Could you loan me your cell?

Could.

Thanks!

But no signal here nohow.

Aha!

Boys hoisted her up from the bottom, leeches already on her. Big crack in her skull.

Oh boy!

Why'd you do it, Tabby?

Ah hell, oh boy.

Look, nobody round here liked her, the old man says. She shit in everyone's den. You and the kids can lie low here with us. You wouldn't last a minute out there on the road.

Thank you so much.

She shouldna tried to act the man, stupid cunt. Tell me, what man'd ride on the running board so everyone could see his ass. Man woulda set inside with you. And you'da gone where he wanted, right.

I feel bad about it, Papa says, blowing his nose.

Lemme explain to you how it is, says the old man, spitting into the fire. He glances briefly around the scrapyard's wooded surroundings, the tree tips gently quivering as they stab into the heatstroked sky.

She threatened you with her nightstick. Talked aggressive at you! Angry like, yeah? You were in shock after the death of your father-in-law.

Yep!

Protectin your kids, am I right?

Yeah, of course!

And you're a man, aren't cha? So you stick up for yourself, right? Only normal, right?

I was swattin a fly, she let go!

There, you see. Shit! Your boy here saw it too. What's your name, son? You dumb or what?

He's shy.

Thing is, why'd you run? From the scene of the crime? That's the question, see.

Aha!

You were in shock! In shock, get it?

My mother lives nearby. We're goin to her place.

I'm not sayin you're not fucked. You are. But there's things can be done.

I gotta leave the boys with my ma.

She where she always been?

Yep. Pyšely.

You got a real Pyšely horse face too, not in a bad way. Listen, I knew your mama, even before she hooked up with your daddy.

For a split second Bašta turns serious, raises his head.

We admired your pa. Heck of a motorcycle rider. How is he? Last time I saw your pa, he was on his bike, ridin off into the distance from the Poříčí bridge! He still alive?

I donno. Papa lowers his eyes to the fire.

I breathed a sigh of relief when he headed off to Russia. He wouldna had it easy here.

Hell, I didn't have it easy here either!

So that's why you went off into the world, son, is it? But you're back on your native shores now, that's nice.

Yeah. Please, I just need your people to stop workin on my car.

Those aren't my people, those're my boys.

I'd like em to stop.

Don't be stupid.

Plus I was thinkin I might sell you my car.

You already sold it, boy.

Huh? For how much?

You'll see.

Huh?

First things first, lad, let's have a drink. To old man Hrozen! We've known each other since we were kids, did you know that?

Bašta pulls a small bottle from the pocket of his track pants, unscrews the cap, takes a swig, wipes the bottle with his palm, hands it to Papa.

Papa tips the bottle to his lips and keeps it there.

Strong stuff, huh? This ain't that crap from the bottling plants, the old man says, slipping the booze back in his pants. He pokes the fire with a branch, raw and green. Sticks it into the coals. White steam rises up, till the fire burns it to dust.

Old Hrozen was hard. Like me. I don't give two shits anymore that he joined the Communists back in the day. He had it out with death like a man. Might not look it but I been thinkin about it myself these days.

We appreciate the hospitality, but we'd best be gettin along now. Sunshine's not good for junior here.

He's asleep!

Still!

The old man reaches into his pocket, takes out an enormous handkerchief, and hands it to Papa.

Make him some shade.

Papa gingerly takes the snotrag in two fingers, shakes it out, and tosses it over the little one's head.

He'll be fine like that, says the old man. Help with the flies too.

No doubt!

We got a district hospice in Čerčany, you know? The Good Shepherd it's called. But Hrozen said fuck that. I wouldn't wanna have to move when my time comes either. Long time I thought I'd have my own folks put me down. But you know that's no good.

Oh no?

I got an idea, though. I'm gonna convert our business here into a hospice, see? Decent chunk a land, right? Bašta surveys the field of cars through the rippling wave of heat.

Already got a name. The Good Bailiff. What do you think?

Pardon?

I figure it's good havin the hospice by the water, so clients can look out the windows, see the water flowin by, like the thoughts runnin through your head, and the worser off you get, the better death seems compared to life. And that's the moment, see?

Aha!

You gotta catch the moment! That's the thing, that's all it is.

Oh, I see . . .

Just gotta set it up so there aren't any shits and carcasses floatin under the windows. That'd be distasteful, right?

Sure would.

Yeah, that part's simple. Send a few guys with nets upstream and that takes care a that. I think we'll be such a success that folks'll line up just to get in the door. We'll suck up all the customers from the Good Shepherd, what do you think?

I don't entirely understand.

My boys don't get it either. Pokin around in machines is their thing. All this here used to be wilderness, and everyone and their uncle wanted a Western car. Now half a Prague's out here and every halfass cunt's got a set a wheels. We'll end makin more money off a my hospice than we do off a cars.

Really?

Yep. It won't be just your everyday kina hospice, if you know what I mean.

A-hah!

The old man slips his mitt off the crutch and rubs his fingers under the corset.

Sonuvabitch eczema.

Thank you, but we really have to go!

Listen, you know what pisses me off most about dyin?

No, what?

Resuscitation devices. In my hospice, there won't be any a those machines that breathe for you, shit for you, talk for you. No sir, I swear! The Good Bailiff'll be an express hospice.

A what?

Folks should be able to die fast as they want. Rotted throat? See ya later! None a those artificial throats, so you can keep coughin another year. Forget it. Is your liver shot? Get outta here! Brain fucked up? Lungs withered? So what? Your time has come. Look, when you're done, you're done, what's the big deal?

Guess so.

Hey, the relatives'll be happy! Way it is now, their loved one's on their mind all the time, takin up space in their head. They've already said their goodbyes ten times, then the doctor comes along and starts em up again. Filthy business, I'm tellin you.

Hm.

Folks're unconscious for weeks, years, but nobody gives a fuck. How do they feel? Who the hell knows? Then when they wake up, beggin with their eyes for it to end, too bad. Doctors gotta keep draggin it out. That's the law nowadays. Who wants that?

I donno!

The old man pulls a stick of kindling out of the heap, runs it under his corset, rubs awhile with verve. Then pulls the stick out, and a flattened ant along with it.

There he is, little shit. And flings the wood in the fire.

Czechs're still used to dyin in Hun raids. Not this drawn-out death stuff. Know what I mean?

Huh?

Here, get a load a this!

Bašta reaches up to his neck, feels around for a string, pulls it out from underneath his plastic shell. Something swings on the end. Some kind of sharp-pointed pendant.

Real bronze!

What is it? A knife?

Arrowhead. My boy Kája found it in the river. Avar relic. That means Huns.

A-hah!

See, the Huns come ridin in, cut the throats on half the village, shoot em down with arrows, while the other half hides in the woods. Then the Huns pull out, our folks come back. The women mostly sobbin and cryin, the men take up their arms. And then what? Then nothin, life goes on. That's what our folks're used to, shit. Not that resuscitation crap they're bringin in from the EU. You with me?

Oh, for sure!

So you sold us the car at a bargain price, thereby contributing to the new hospice. Through this charitable act you've now erased your ill-considered deeds. You're a good man, the old geezer says, slapping Papa on the back.

Listen, guys, it's great chattin with you, but I'd like to take a peek at my car now, if you don't mind? Papa says, getting to his feet. My boys're practically smoked sausages out here in the sun!

Sit down.

No.

I give the whistle, my boys'll be here in two shakes. What do you think?

Calm down.

Oh, I'm plenty calm, but the main difficulty is personnel, you know.

Czech lands for Czechs, no argument there, but Czechs've gotten spoiled, hookin folks up to revivers and prolongers even when they got a death notice stickin out their ass. But I found a solution.

Oh, really? What's that?

I got Richie and other guys out on the byways keepin their ear to the ground. See, I'm tryin to track down the type a folks that, like it or not, are already on friendly terms with death, the type that've drunk it in through their pores in whatever fucked-up regime they come from, then again in their death-defyin escapes to countries that'd rather beat their asses than give em asylum. They're the type a people that don't fuck around, and I got work for them.

Oh yeah?

And mind you, I couldn't care less if they're niggers! Now I'd like to invite you all for lunch. The whole family. How bout you, young man, where's your mama? Don't you talk?

I took Soňa to the hospital, Papa says from the stump. We had a bit of a mishap, he says, glancing at the boy. Women's stuff! And Mama had a nasty thing with her leg, too, isn't that right?

Oh, really? Is that so? Huh, so that's what happened, is it?

I want to call the hospital, but there's no signal here, says Papa.

I been callin there too! Won't tell me a thing since I'm not from the family! Why'm I callin? Well, on Sázavan they said some young lady at the hospital jumped out the window. Or maybe she fell? Somebody helped her?

What? I even told her goodbye. They said they were takin her straight into surgery.

And what if I told you Richie's sister is a cook in the Benešov hospital? She didn't have much of an innuendo what was goin on. But she saw the two a you. Standin by the window together!

We were sayin goodbye!

Place was full a patients. But Richie's sister said she recognized Soňa for sure. Saw her standin by an open window with a guy. Had to be you!

Guess so.

I always did have a soft spot for Soňa. Taught her how to shake nuts down from the tree when she was little. She used to graze our kid goats! I'd give little Soňa pears, always the best ones, big and sweet. If someone were to cause her harm, I donno what I'd do.

Just then, a voice calls out: Chow time!

Richie pokes his head out the trailer window.

Comin right up!

You'd never guess it, but our chef Richie here's a regular scholar.

Yeah?

He used to be somethin like a professor, but then he went haywire, y'know?

Yeah, that can happen.

But hey, he wasn't cut out for school! He's too much the flighty type. But there's still times when it'll come over him and he'll lecture the boys: You better listen, better study! Specially when work is busy, am I right?

Yeah, that makes sense, mutters Papa.

Richie slams open the trailer door with his forearm. Balances on the steps with a full tray of food.

People say all sorts a things about him, but it's just talk. Our Richie's a good guy.

Here it is, gents, munchies are served!

Richie is decked out in a grease-stained apron, his outstretched arms wielding a scratched plastic tray loaded with dishes. He flicks his tongue as he walks toward them over the puddles, avoiding the wires, all the junk.

Well so I says to him, Richie, come stay with us. I don't see or hear too good, you can be my eyes and ears. Though back then I could hear like a lynx still, lemme tell ya.

That was kind of you.

Spoons jingle in Richie's apron pocket as he skillfully carries the tray, not splashing a drop. The soup is grayish-colored, and piping hot.

We used to cook on the fire, now we use the microwave, the old man informs his visitors. He pulls his own personal soup spoon out of his track pants pocket.

Listen, Richie, so what did Dora say she saw again?

A man and a young woman by the window. Get a load a this swank apron I got from her—my sis is a cook, ya know. Assistant cook, actually, she's a bit on the slow side. Bon appétit, guys.

The boy takes a dish from the tray, and as Richie bends down to serve him, he pulls a soup spoon for the boy out of his apron.

The server hands the other dishes into the outstretched hands of the old geezer and Papa. Settles down on a free brick.

Anybody can tell it's you by your sniffer, Tabby, Richie says, balancing his soup on his lap. There was a whole mess of bandaged and other sick folks in the hallway, but only one young woman, actually a girl. Dreads and all, so it was obvious. And one-eyed to boot.

The detectives might be interested to know that Richie's sister saw you standin there by the open window, don't you think? Although, tell us, Richie, is Dora even sane? Would that hold up in a court a law?

That I don't know. Better blow on it, it's hot.

Tasty though, the old geezer says.

Right?

You don't like it? Bašta asks Papa.

Oh sure. I'm just a little out of it. I wish what happened hadn't.

Like everyone else, says Richie, smacking his lips.

I'd also like to say that reality takes on the qualities of a dream, the guest elaborates, soup spoon in hand.

Whatever, Richie says.

Certainly would be nice to be able to cancel time, mumbles Papa. If it didn't exist for me the way it doesn't exist for the Sioux. I'm not that advanced yet, though.

Grunts and cunts, odd ducks, shaggin's all they think about! the old geezer howls.

The boy plugged his ears while they were talking about the hospital. Now he holds the hot dish of soup on his lap. Scoops up a spoonful, shovels it into his mouth. Polishes off the bowl.

Stands up and in one step moves beyond the fire's heat. The wrecks around them shimmer in the hot morning air. He stretches up on tiptoe. Wants to walk it off, but the soup has him feeling plugged up.

Then something even worse happens than bursting into tears. He can't stop it, it just comes spewing out.

Yuck, we're eatin here! Your mama would slap you good, you pig, Richie yells.

What're you tellin him that for! the old geezer blurts. What's this crap about his mom! You're a heartless bastard, Richie, an animal, I tell ya!

The patriarch, groaning and sighing, straightens his spine, stretching his chest inside the plastic corset. He leans into the hot air, digs his palms into the crutches.

C'mon down to the water here, boy. Just a little bit of a ways.

The boy dawdles along behind the old geezer, through the blazing heat of the scrapyard. Laboring on his crutches, the old man walks straddle-legged, sweating profusely.

I'll think what I want about microwaves, boy, the old geezer mutters. Nothin you can do.

The crutches leave holes behind in the ground. Nearer the riverbank, the boy sees stabholes all over the place. They hobble down to the water. Thick, untrampled grass bristles among the trees. Water slaps against the stones.

I come down here to fish, son. Take off your clothes.

The boy strips off his track pants. Using the tips of his fingers, so as not to soil them. He glances back at the old geezer.

Everything.

He sheds his jacket. Takes off his boxers and T-shirt, slips off the riverbank with his little bundle of rags. It's shallow there, before he knows it he's amid the current. The water splashes in his face, all over his body. He rubs the fabric together, dunks his head underwater. That's the best part.

He climbs out to see the old man wiping the envelope on the grass. Weighs it in his hand, bends it in his fingers. Shoves it in his pocket.

Step up in the sun, boy, dry yourself off. I gotta make a call, okay?

He pulls a phone from his pocket, puts it to his ear.

Hello, hello, is this the hospital? He turns to face the boy. Shhh, quiet, I'm talkin to the doctors!

He screams into the phone so loud it drowns out the rush of the current.

Yeah, I heard some lady jumped out the window, yeah? She fell? It's all over the radio! A-hah! I understand. Mm-hm, okay. Mm-hm! Well, thank you very much for that information, doctor.

He sticks the phone back in his pocket, turns to face the petrified boy.

Well, boy, seems some lady really did fall out the window there, but it mighta been a cleanin lady, not your mom! So just calm down, all right?

He takes a step toward him, closer to the thundering water.

Get dressed.

Leans his forearms on the crutches.

The pay is lousy for those cleanin ladies there, and on top of it some of em drink, you know, so it isn't hard to wind up with an accident. Just let your clothes finish dryin on you. It'll be nice and cool, you'll see.

He whips the crutches forward, stabbing them into the soil as they climb the path through the trees.

Sheet metal gleams through the leaves. A branch nearly swipes the knit cap off the old geezer's head. He runs his fingers under the cap, clawing at his scalp.

A young man blasts a line of cars with water from a hose, while someone else works the hydraulic press, compacting wrecks. The sound of clanging metal rings through the forest, the blows of iron on iron. Rusty sheets of scrap hang from the jaws of a small crane. Boom and thump and bang! The bundle of sheets falls atop the pile with a furious groan. The crane operator leans out, the small man waves.

The old geezer leans against the boy's shoulder, crutch tucked under his arm, pushing off with the other. They reach another line of cars.

The odor of paint fills the air. The vehicles freshly repainted and squeaky clean. Passenger cars, vans, all they need now is to be put back in circulation. A territory of auto paint, linseed oil, gasoline, and motor oil. They accumulate used oil here by the barrelful. And in every direction, smashed windows, ripped-out gearshifts, loose bearings, heaps of greasy rags, rusty nuts, clamps, wires, odds and ends.

I think you should stay here, the old geezer says. Your daddy's a nutcase, they're gonna run him in sooner or later. And that brother a yours isn't worth the gas out my ass. Look, nowadays a baby's born big as a finger, and steada lettin it die, they stick it in an incubator. It's alive, but it's got no idea. It's a piece a shit, son. A piece a shit.

The boy stares down into the sun-baked mud, studying the round holes left behind by the crutches.

Any rate, that's some weird tracksuit you got. I'll get you a perfect set of overalls, a spread for your head, and my boys'll train you to be a mechanic.

The boy doesn't even know why, but all of a sudden his eyes are wet.

The old man raps his back with his knuckles, gives him a little swat.

You stop that! Stop that right now! Big boys don't cry.

Bašta fishes around in his track pants, fishes out another snotrag. The boy shakes his head, wipes his eyes with the back of his hand.

You're gonna have fun with my boys, you'll see! Some of em're mine and some of em I took onboard. What boy wouldn't like workin with cars, right? Meanwhile I got a great job for you till you get trained up. You can walk upstream with the dip net, scoopin out turds and carcasses. You can handle that, right? So we keep it clean under our windows.

The boy shakes his head again and studies the mud beneath his feet.

You wanna be with your own folks still? Fine by me! You change your mind, just ask for Bašta's boys. Everyone in the area knows us. How could they not?

The old man leans against the door of a small car, gently strokes the hood, gives a tire a kick. Sticks his mitt in the open window, feels around, and presses down.

The horn is an earsplitter, almost cuts the woods in two.

I can lend you the purple Fiat. Bet you'd like that, huh?

10

GATHERING OF THE CLAN. A LAUGH WITH
THE ENVELOPE. BREATHING UNDER A CLOTH,
GROWING, GETTING HEAVY. THE MAN WITH THE
PANS. INTO THE STORM. SOMETHING FROM THE
SKY. THE GREAT PYŠELY FAIR. BISON APPEARS.
AND THE GIRL.

As the branches smolder out, the others fully consumed by the fire, a smelly, red-hot heap spills across the firepit.

The caravan's open door knocks back and forth in the breeze that has finally kicked up.

Hey, folks, c'mon over! Richie waves from the cluster squatting around the fire.

The boy follows the old man, draped over his crutches. The tips scrape across the rocks, lift with a sucking sound from the mud. And there they are.

Richie kicks a figure lying twisted by the fire. Papa, face down on the ground. Attired in orange coveralls. His former clothing smolders in the ashes.

Case a Beaujolais in a Beemer, well shit, man, thanks . . . Richie gives the recumbent man a slap on the back, his other hand wielding a bottle with a French label on it. There are a few more being passed around the fire.

The boy notices bits of singed fabric floating above the ash heap, flames licking from beneath the broken crates. He recognizes their road maps, baked together by the heat, various other remains of his family's meager possessions. The junk from the door pockets and glove compartment, constantly rolling across the car floor, now glows red and disintegrates, disappearing before his eyes amid the stink of plastic bags.

And the boy searches. Eyes roving about in the sun's glow and the warmth from the bonfire of trash. Till at last he spots the little one.

In the car seat, in the shade of the caravan. A rag has been thrown over his head, a thin piece of cloth. In the place where the boy guesses his brother's tiny mouth to be, he detects a faint, delicate swelling. He walks over to the smaller boy, pulls the wet wipes, baby bottle, out from underneath him. He should take him out, wash him up. But next thing he knows, Richie is there on top of him.

Don't worry, young man! Your daddy gave your brother a pill and the little buster went out like a light. I put a curtain over him, see? Got his breathin holes right here and the skeeters and wasps can't get to him. Nice, right?

Amid the cluster gathered around the fire, the boy recognizes Miran from the hangar, tattoos squiggled across his thin, sharp face, shaggy ponytail hanging down between his shoulder blades. He squats on a brick alongside Kája, a somewhat younger hulk. The two of them chew in unison, coveralls unzipped, sleeves rolled up, lightning bolts and arrows tattooed across their chests and forearms. The pair next to them, in identical black caps, are twins. Solder is the little guy who waved at them from the crane. Then there are a few other boys and a young cub named Tater Tot, bottle opener at the ready. Whenever anyone gives a whistle, he scoots into the caravan to grab a beer from the fridge.

Everyone in the collective sits sociably snacking, tipping back Beaujolais in the dreamily shimmering air.

Till suddenly their attention is captured by a sound. Old man Bašta dodders his way to the fire, parks himself on a crate. The next thing they know, there's a sound of ripping paper and he's waving around a torn envelope. Then, reaching in his fat, crumb-coated fingers, to the onlookers' amazement he pulls out a thick wad of bills. Five-thousand-crown bills.

Holy Virgin! gasps Richie. One of the black-capped men's jaw drops.

The old man extends the hand with the riches over the fire, letting the heat lick at his fingers for a second, but all he drops into the flames is the envelope. It flares up and everyone practically bursts their sides laughing.

As Papa struggles to raise himself into a sitting position, the old man gives him a kick.

You sure've wandered a long way from your home in Pyšely, I'll tell you that, the old geezer says, shaking his head. On a slippery slope if ever I saw one. You should be ashamed. Robbin a dead man, shit. Where'd old Hrozen keep it?

Under the pillow.

Well, he never did have much brains. You're lucky he was dead when they took him away. I'd have to make you pay if you'd caused him any suffering.

He was dead. Everyone saw.

All right, Pyšely boy. At first me and the boys here figured we'd help you just outta brotherly love. Seein as that card-carryin dyke pissed us off. Way I see it, a woman like her's got no business bein in the police. You dealt with her like a man, Tab, and I appreciate that. But now I believe you've been sent down by heaven itself.

Papa straightens to a sitting position, brushing off the particles of ash stuck to his coveralls. The boy stares at the bruise underneath his father's eye. The imprint of somebody's fist on his jaw also suggests his costume change was accompanied by a tussle.

Tab, your contribution increases the chances that my project will succeed. Not only do I like you, but I'll give you a lift to Pyšely. Then you and your boys can go where you like. Sound good?

Coffeeeee is seeeerved! Richie shrieks, deftly balancing a tray full of plastic cups as he makes his way among the men.

Meanwhile Papa accepts the Beaujolais offered him by Miran, sucking eagerly and urgently from the bottle.

Where'd you find this? he asks the tattooed man.

Under the rags in back.

Damn, we didn't look there!

I gave your young son here a choice, the old geezer continues. Bein a sensible boy, he chose the Fiat. But now you listen. Nothin beats friends sittin around the fire after a good meal throwin back a cup a joe. And havin a chat. Would you agree?

Sure.

Papa settles in, fingers clenched around the bottle's neck, and also accepts a plastic pipe handed him by Richie.

So look, there was this man that used to sell pans. Which isn't the best business, but the man knew how to hustle, kept his wife and daughter fed. He sold pans in train stations, pubs, rang the bell at people's apartments. His pans were good and not expensive—there's a market for that stuff. Carried samples with him, a whole set. Always worked hard, lookin for new outlets. And then one day he came our way. And he ran into Richie here. Where? At our favorite spot, the Distillery, right here down by the river, under the ruins of Zlenice castle. To this day they still got a wooden bar there, painted by Máťa Píťa. Anyway, they got to talkin business, life and whatnot, right off the bat. Had a drink together, why not? Then Richie here, bein a bighearted guy, the type a guy who trusts people, brought the salesman back to our place. This was back in the day before all that nonsense with microwaves. And our pans were all tarnished and dingy. One word led to another, and we sent the man off to deliver some things to our friends in the villages, here along the river. He was a sociable type, could carry messages, noticed things, no big deal. Likable enough. Remember, guys?

Sure do, Pops! someone shouts.

Yeah, yeah, the pan man.

Another person nods.

So not only did we give refuge to this man selling pans, we even offered him a vehicle. Person like that and he's gotta go schleppin around on the train? But you wouldn't believe it, one night this man just ups and walks off through the woods. And goes and defames our livelihood at the nearest police station. I mean, can you believe it?

No.

Traitor couldn't even find this place again. Brought the cops with him. Yeah, that little bulldog bitch with the big tits was their leader. Some of the local officers were none too pleased about it. Trudgin through the swamps, all those prickly branches. Who'd wanna do that? They asked him the way so many times he got completely lost. Couldn't find a thing. But my boys found him all right. Then his wife and daughter wept. And wept and wept and wept. I felt sorry. Isn't that a sad story?

Yeah.

All right then, Bašta nods. We've eaten well, had a chat. You'd best be on your way. I know you and your boys are no prisses, but it's lookin like rain.

He pulls two, no, three thousand-crown bills from his bulging tracksuit pocket and hands them to Papa.

The little purple car is already nosing its way toward them. Compared to the wrecks in the background, it looks kind of cute. It comes to a stop a few steps away from the fire.

Papa, boy at his heels, strides over to the caravan, lifts up the car seat—carefully, so the curtain won't slip off of it.

Oof, he grunts. Seems your little bro's gained some weight, he says to the boy. Think he started growin? Now that he's finally back in his homeland, Czech country?

And Papa bursts out laughing. Puts the seat back on the ground and laughs so hard he starts to cough.

Hurry now, Tabby, the old man says, thwacking Papa on the back. We don't have any raincoats here. And we thank you kindly!

Now Bašta roars with laughter too. Bent over double, he laughs so hard it may be hazardous to his health.

Richie's choking too. Even the long-haired Miran flashes a toothy grin. Along with the smiling hulk, they stand up and march toward the little car. And the musclemen in black knit caps? The two of them are hammering their thighs.

All aboooard! Richie yells through his hands rolled into a cone.

Now everyone is laughing.

Kája takes the sleeping bags, sweaters, whatever comes to hand that didn't go up in flames, and arranges them over the boy and his little brother.

Get down on the floor, he tells Papa. Tosses a blanket over him.

And breathe through your nose, dude. Or better yet, don't breathe. Locals get their hands on you, it's not gonna be pretty.

The forest patriarch was right.

It's raining.

Hard.

Mounds of dark clouds dominate the sky. Water gushes down as they burst through a curtain of rain and lightning into the woods on the other side of the gate.

Miran drives like a madman, the merciless whimsy of nature detached from the instinct for self-preservation. As the car hurtles around the bends, Kája howls from the seat up front, muscular frame barely crammed into the Fiat, elbow to elbow with his brother, their tattoos linked in an ever-shifting labyrinth. Dirt clods flying, wheels spraying pebbles, they plunge headlong toward the drifts of light, goggling at the spectacle, unable to discern amid the celestial fusillade where the thunderbolts leave off and the twilight begins.

The boy presses up against the car window, fiery lightning balls whizzing low across the sky, hissing, glittering yellow and green at the edges as they punch through the mist and disappear into the woods.

Suddenly a shadow flits overhead as a solid body crushes the treetops, throwing a pall over the earth, which it splits open wide with a plume of yellow smoke, in the blink of an eye dissolved into mist, leaving behind a crater reeking of phosphorus.

Amid the cacophony of buckling clouds, the Fiat's surface shines like a suit of armor. The car and its overflowing crew go barreling down the road through the woods and emerge into the midst of cornfields, when a light flares out of the darkness ahead.

They come to a stop.

The boy raises his feet off the living mass beneath him.

The cannonade above and around them has fallen silent. Wind, buffeting the tassels of corn silk, whistles through the field, but the rain at least has let up.

Papa sighs, wriggling impatiently.

A wall of cornstalks rises up on either side.

Why aren't we moving? Kája asks.

There's something there—in the field, Miran says. See?

A light is bouncing up and down in and over the field ahead.

This is where that cop chick always used to lurk, man, that weasel dyke, Kája says. Doesn't want a guy to do her in the pussy. Gotta have a chick that takes it in the pussy, that way she'll listen to you, take care a you, Kája says. He blushes at his own guy talk, but no one can tell in the dark.

Shut up, mutters Miran.

The light in front of them splits into three smaller lights.

They're coming toward them.

Cops in black rain ponchos. Two shine their lights onto the hood and sides of the car, circling it. The third steps up to the driver's side. Knocks on the window.

Miran hands the officer his papers without being asked.

After all the crashing and thunder, the cop's voice sounds like a newly invented human tongue.

You aren't comin from a party, boys, now, are you? I don't have to give you a breath test, right?

We're on our way home from work.

Hm.

C'mon, Rudy, you know us, right?

I do.

Then you know we're always good.

You're good? Then I don't have to see this, do I?

He sticks his black-gloved hand in the window. Miran takes his papers back. The cop peers into the car. Looks straight at the boy.

That one a Bašta's boys I see?

Yup.

You folks been multiplyin.

Sure have! You know us!

I do.

So can we go now then?

Go on ahead.

Thanks a lot!

By the way, boys, did you all see that? Somethin went down over there, says the cop, waving his beam into the field.

Oh yeah? says Miran. We didn't see a thing.

Plane maybe? Glider?

Maybe a duster? guesses Kája.

We're goin to take a look, says the cop.

We didn't see a thing. But it probly went in the woods.

Don't come through here again. We're closin it off.

What for?

Move along.

In some spots the dirt track turns into a drainage ditch, with runoff from the woods flowing through, dragging gravel along with it. The car bumps and jerks, spraying water, till they land back firmly on asphalt again. Barreling down the road.

Too bad we got no tunes, says Kája, humming to himself, drumming his fingers on the dash.

The young boy blinks, having a hard time keeping his eyes open. A deep space opens beneath them as they rumble onto a bridge. He hears music, the whistle of fireworks overhead, their colorful, flickering light exposing statues on either side, in hoods and miters, bareheaded. The light of the fireworks skids over their stony hair and outstretched arms, shatters on the marlstone.

Miran slows the Fiat to a creep as they come off the bridge and find themselves in the midst of a noisy crowd.

The sound of laughter and conversation, the aroma of roasting meat, penetrate to the car's interior. A full range of hips, buttocks, bellies, and elbows is on display. Every few seconds somebody stops, bends over, and flashes a friendly grin, then raps the hood with their knuckles.

Passing down a wide street with fences on either side, they drive through an arch festooned with chains of artificial flowers. WELCOME TO THE PYŠELY FAIR! it declares, the exclamation point of light bulbs blinking on and off in the calming rhythm of breath.

They catch sight of the white tip of a maypole decorated with garlands. The sound of pop music fills the air, the clank of Chair-O-Planes ratcheting into motion, the shouting and uproar from the other attractions. Gondola cars decked out in colorful streamers sail through the air as the crowd of fairgoers thickens, though they more than willingly make room to let the Fiat through.

Men in shorts and T-shirts adorned in all manner of slogans and images brandish plastic cups of beer. There are also a few staid gentlemen in summer suits; they walk alone, most likely ruminating on their surroundings, while the other men walk side by side, hands frequently intertwined with women's. Tough-looking boys, glowing cigs between their lips, flock in circles around the girls, underage, thin as a whip and even more problematic.

Every few minutes the girls burst into cascades of ringing laughter, punctuated by a disparaging remark, while their aunts and mothers, trying to keep a handle on their already nearly plastered husbands and rampaging small fry, offer expressions of genuine disgust amid the glow of fireworks, with a rush of inner sadness welling up here and there.

The crowding is especially thick around the beer stands, with their grills of roasting klobásy and sizzling chunks of pork. But the liveliest stretch of all is along the caravans, the shooting galleries on wheels, with their spinning colored targets and the deafening pops, squeals, and laughter that accompany the efforts of lame shooters and brilliant marksmen alike.

Stop, Kája barks.

Someone has broken off from the crowd. A tiny but truly statuesque girl, bosom straining against her T-shirt, jumps in front of the car. Despite her somewhat protruding belly, what she resembles most is a doe, apart from the sloshed and cunning eyes. As she tosses her head, a wave of red obscures the already limited view of the men inside the car. She bends forward, pressing her breasts to the windshield.

Kája, heeeyyy!

Miran brakes to a complete stop. The wail that issues from the mouth of his massive brother is so feeble it's almost shocking.

Světla, outta the way, will ya, Miran says from the window.

In the blink of an eye, the girl is surrounded by burly men with earrings screwed into their beet-red farmers' ears, most of them in khaki tees and camouflage shorts, arduously stretched over their swollen muscles. The leader, gold chain encircling his bullish neck, wedges himself into the window face to face with Miran.

A rapid-fire battle of glances ensues.

The Fiat moves on and the burly man nonchalantly waves to his gang to indicate that the matter's been taken care of, but he only reverts to the mode of jolly king after planting a few humungous slaps across the redhead's face. In terms of impact symbolic, but to spectacular effect.

She squawks.

So loudly they can hear it in the Fiat. And again they stop the car.

Calm down, Miran tells his pale-faced brother, drooped down in the seat next to him like a speared puppet.

Světlana's got her week this week, you know that, Miran says, trying to soothe him.

I know.

She's just walkin around the fair with him!

Sure.

She's just messin around. Bison knows damn well he can't go grazin in that meadow, Miran says coolly, studying his brother's angry countenance. Which suddenly relaxes.

Sure.

113

So're we good?

We're good.

The curve that emerges between the young boy's knees is Papa's head.

Now go straight!

Get down.

I can't breathe anymore!

Get down.

Now go left!

They drive uphill through an alley of trees, past gardens and wooden sheds, cut off from all light and noise inside the tunnel.

Stop, says Papa. So they stop.

The Fiat's rear lights merge with the light from the little house. Low and stooped, a single window shining.

Papa climbs out first. The boy is right behind. He shakes with cold. It rains down on them as they stand on the grass. Papa tries to do a squat but falls down. Slams to the ground, face first in a puddle. So hard it makes a splash.

Richie tosses the sleeping bags and sweaters out of the car. Unfastening the little nipper from his car seat, he lays him on his back on top of the sleeping bags, still wrapped in the curtain.

The boy lifts the curtain. His little brother opens and closes his mouth, maybe trying to catch raindrops.

Papa talks into the puddle. But no one can understand. He sits up, wiping black trickles of mud from his face. Now his coveralls are spattered too. The rain is still spitting down.

Kája slams the trunk shut.

You guys take care, he hollers. And climbs in the car. They drive off.

11

REALLY, MA? MÁŤA. THE TANK. A RUSSIAN WHORE
SPUN FROM THE SAME YARN. TIRADE AGAINST
THE HEAD OF STATE. WHERE'S MONČA? CRAWLING
AND SUCKING. MISIMPRESSION AT THE DOOR.
SCARF WITH STRAWBERRIES, ETC.

They swiped our car seat, lousy bastards!

Papa settles back into the damp grass, takes the little boy in his arms. Notices the baby bottle lying on the ground and sticks it in his pocket.

Oh well, we'll make do. Listen up, boys! Lemme tell you a story people around here tell about my ma.

He struggles to his feet.

My ma had a cat. And that cat had kittens. Pretty similar looking, looked pretty alike. So people asked, Hey, lady, how're you gonna tell em apart? And she says, Well, shucks, this one I'll call Tabby and the other one I'll drown.

Ha-ha-ha, Papa guffaws. Then gives the boy a gentle slug in the shoulder. But you met Uncle Ivan, son. So she didn't actually drown him. She isn't that kina person, you'll see. You're gonna stay here with her awhile. It'll be better that way.

She sits on the couch in a nest of pillows facing the TV. Nodding her head, her slapdash gray bun shaking in time to her own vehement private soliloquy, driven by a pugnacious up-and-down of her chin. Garbed in a polka-dot apron tied over a tracksuit, she taps her slipper-clad feet against the linoleum floor. The stove glows with heat, and the pipe leading out of it into the wall above the coal scuttle is red-hot too.

Ma!

Sweet Virgin on the mount, you startled me! What're you doin here?

Brought my boys!

Papa snatches a handful of pillows off the edge of the couch, sets them down on the spattered linoleum, lays the little fellow into the nest he's created. As the curtain slides off his pudgy cheeks, the little nipper fixes his gaze on a point above their heads. Papa nudges the bigger boy toward the sofa.

These're your grandsons, Ma!

Well, now, that's nice. How long's it been since you were here? You know, they just brought me back from the hospital day before yesterday, I believe.

Really? Well, you're lookin good.

And you're lookin negro, boy. What's that mud all over your face? You helpin out with the floods? Hey, did you see that movie with Menšík? I adore that man. Got a touch of negro blood in him, did you know that? Not that I care.

Good for you.

What's that orange thing you got on? If that ain't a faggy color now, please.

This is what people are wearin these days, Ma.

Well, our Máťa Píťa was fond of orange, or more like bloodred, I suppose. My whole time in the hospital I was lookin at his pictures. After he got famous for paintin the walls at U Sejků, they wanted him everywhere.

Hey, Ma, I'd like to feed the boys first, do you mind?

Course not, I love kids. But I'm afraid I got nothin here for you.

I'll just take a look in the cupboard, okay?

You know, after Máťa Píťa painted the hospital, they wanted to hire him for that hospice in Čerčany too, but by then it was too late.

Really, Ma?

Back when he broke up with Růženka, that dipsomaniac slut, not that I got anything against her, I wish everyone the best, he went off and holed up in some cabin somewhere. And what do you think he did there? Well, he wasn't drinkin, says he was makin drawings, but then he decides he could use a drink after all, sit and chew the fat over a beer like normal people do. So he makes a trip to the pub in Pyšely, and he's barely finished his first one, lookin around to see who to talk to, and up on the TV they show some head cut off by some Arab in France. Boy, if you'd walked in there then with your face all smudged up, I don't know what would've become of you!

Hey, Ma, we're just gonna rinse off a bit and have somethin to eat, okay?

So then he heads down to Čtyřkoly, like he'll have one there, why not, and in Čtyřkoly they got a TV too and by then there's been two or three heads sawed off by those Moslem fellas. You think he got loaded there? Máťa Píťa? Not on your life. He cleared out down to the Distillery on the riverbank to have a drink in peace. Looks around to see which fellas there he might have a gab with, bout the floods and fish and who's got what kina tomatoes this year, only the old drunkards're all dead and the young ones just sit there and stare at the TV, portable they got there, smallest one on the river, and there's more noggins chopped off. So he swings down along Šmejkalka Creek, pops over the hill, and finds a chair in the pub at Senohraby station and orders himself a beer. But the place is dead quiet, they're all starin at the TV, and what's on? More Ayrab handiwork.

Hey, Ma, we're gonna take some lunchmeat. Pack's already open! Got any bread?

And Máťa Píťa Longleg's like, I don't need to look at that, so he figures he'll go have a gab at U Sejků over in Hrusice with the paintings of Mikeš the black tomcat with his hikin stick and boots. But now they've got a TV at U Sejků too, and what're they watchin? Same chopped-off heads as everybody else, followers of Mohammed wreakin terror left and right. So Uncle Píťa picks himself up and heads up over the hill, all the way to Ondřejov, and sticks his head in that bar there called Hell, but the TV's in charge there now too, everyone's just starin at it, and what're they showin but . . .

Ma, I know!

Papa takes half a loaf of bread in a plastic bag from the cupboard, slices it up with the first knife he finds, slaps a thick slab of lunchmeat on one slice for the boy and does the same for himself.

Well and then, if you can imagine, Máťa hoofed it all the way to Chlum, down under the ruins there, and fell in the creek and drowned, sad to say. If he hadn't drowned, I think he'd've stopped drinkin, just out of spite. Like me. I almost don't drink anymore.

The boy, glued to the sideboard, studies the black-and-white photographs of social events, gaudy dolls in embroidered skirts, old-time devotionals. A decorative spoon from the village fair with the face of the Poříčí Virgin Mary and a bowl bearing the legend JZD RUDÁ ZÁŘE PYŠELY—Pyšely Red Glow Collective Farm. Decorative plates sit piled in stacks, including one enormous one with the words GREETINGS FROM KONOPIŠTĚ! and a picture of a deer rearing up on its hind legs, its flank clearly wounded by buckshot.

You mind if I also make some tea for the boys?

No tea here. I wasn't expectin you!

Hey, Ma? Don't suppose you might have a swig for me?

I told you, I stopped drinkin alcohol. But if I do, I make sure not to overdo it.

Sounds reasonable, Papa grumbles. Pushing away the plates and mugs, he goes snooping through the dishes, digging all the way into the cobwebs in the back, where the yellowed paper is peeling off the cupboard wall.

He pulls out a bottle, the dark liquid glistening like amber, like a jewel, like a mystery. Uses his teeth to remove the cork. And empties half the bottle in three or four gulps. He leans against the cupboard, suddenly calm and above it all.

Well, if that don't beat all. You stole my bottle! You know, I don't even think you're mine. Well, who knows whose you are. Only thing your daddy's dick was good for was peein. But I needed a real man. Someone who was solid. A woman's got a right.

Oh, c'mon, Ma!

How many times, while you were out there futzin around the yard, good for absolutely nothin, did I wonder, where'd he get that from? The milkman with the wide jaw? That young buck from the woods that steals trucks, stinks like a truck, but gives the same dependable ride? Was it the postman that delivered him? Whose stinker is this?

C'mon, Ma, cut it out, at least in front of the kids!

Yep, you and that little brother of yours, Ivan, they should've choked that one with a pole, what a good-for-nothin he was. Just followed your daddy around all day, covered in grease and gasoline. Almost caught fire more times than I can count! Had to send em both out to the barn finally, let em sleep out there with those bikes of theirs.

Look, Ma, that was a long time ago.

Yeah, you've stirred up some memories, showin up here outta the blue. Boy was I glad they cleared out after that mess with the Russian tank. That dad of yours strutted up a storm on that motorcycle! Nobody round here hobnobbed with the Russkies, but the minute they gave him recognition for his bikemanship, he practically bent over backwards to help em. How was he gonna stay here after that? So he cleared out with the Russians and took your little brother with him. Thank God for that! I had enough on my plate just with you.

Ma, stop it.

Divers tried to fish out that tank. It ran off the bridge into the river. All they drug up was skeletons. There was five of them there in that tank, four men and a female. And what slut you think it was climbed in there with those Russkies, huh? You think some Pyšely girl? Bullshit, it was that Russian whore from Poříčí, from the Hrozen family. Wouldn't surprise me if the old Bolshie had sent her over himself. Anything's possible with them. More likely, though, she was boy crazy. And that little Soňa of yours is spun from the same yarn! Your choice, boy. But then don't be surprised that your kids're like this.

Wow, Ma, you haven't changed a bit!

And you didn't invite me to your wedding.

There was no wedding! Listen, Ma, has anyone been around askin for me?

No one, you thief. I still got one more bottle, though. Just seein you's makin me thirsty, you scoundrel.

So they didn't come lookin for me?

The old lady scrounges around in the pillows and comes out bottle in hand.

I thought you'd gone off somewhere chasin after your daddy and brother, and now you turn up here again! Where's Soňa?

The bigger boy pulls the curtain from his brother's face. The little one blinks in the light. Then, catching sight of the bits of fragrant lunchmeat, his whole body starts to twitch, thrashing back and forth. The boy sweeps some tiny crumbs of bread into the little one's mouth. Takes out the baby bottle, reaches toward the sink in the wall. Returns the bottle, full, to the tiny little fingers.

Listen, the way you busted in here, all covered in mud, I got scared we were bein invaded and you were one of them chocolate rapists. You know, I kina blame the president for hatin on refugees like he does. Personally, I could use two or three. And those folks sayin they should be gassed, well, I don't agree with that either. I'll tell any fool, straight to his face!

You've got guts, I'll give you that.

Me and Mama were standin right there on the roadside when our Jews went to the transport, and one of them was my good friend, Lojzík, we were real close. Mama said she wouldn't want any boy who wasn't spun from our yarn, but gas chambers, that was goin too far!

Hm!

Look, swear to God, I could do with two or three refugees. Have em dig out the cesspool, fix up the barn. Did you take a look back there yet?

No.

Fine with me if they're chocolates. Long as they got solid muscles.

How's Monča?

Well, if you can imagine, when Monča came back from traipsin around out in la-la land or wherever she went, she thought she was gonna have herself a little bundle of joy, and then zip. Her man walked out on her. And she'd already bought a carriage. So she put the carriage away in the barn and just stared out the window all day. Talk about a sad sight!

Where is Monča now?

She's workin at U Paručky down in Městečko, runnin the show. Moved there so she could be by her pops, blind old Lomoz. Guess she needed someone to take care of, seein as she lost the little one. Lemme tell you, I don't know what got into my head when I decided to shack up with him. And not just my head, ha-ha-ha!

Sure, Ma.

Old Lomoz sure did like my looks, though, back when he could see. Maybe you're his? Say, when were you born anyway? Somehow slipped my mind.

Papa tells her.

Really? Never thought I'd have a child that old.

And these're your grandsons right here, Ma.

Jesus and Mary, what's wrong with him?

The plump little nipper puffs himself up and struggles out of the pillow nest, rolling himself over the edge.

Isn't he the restless one! His rompers're filthy, look at all that mud. And his face is so old. What's wrong with him?

Ma, lend me your cell phone. I gotta call the hospital.

Not on your life, it'd cost me a fortune. Besides, I don't have one.

Papa slams the door so hard the windows rattle. Stomps out into the hallway. Then the boy hears the sound of another door banging shut.

He unzips his little brother's rompers. The stench of filth comes pouring out, clogging up his pores.

Little kids smell, that's a fact. But God knows I served my time. Three little rascals I had. No more for me, that's it. Here, wash him up. Grab the basin from under the couch.

The boy kneels down, reaches in between the tapping slippers, slides it out. It's full to the brim.

Toss that out. And don't spill on the linoleum.

He lifts the washbasin with both hands. Not a drop sloshes out. Using his elbow, he opens the handle on the glass-inlaid door. Opens the main door the same way. One step, two, he's in pitch-black darkness. The smell from the basin makes him want to vomit. He splashes it out into the dark. Shuts the door.

Goes to the sink, runs the water.

Now the little boy is lying at his feet. But closer to the stove. Did he crawl on his back? Can he crawl?

Put the basin on the stove. And don't scrape the enamel!

He sets the washbasin on a metal sheet atop the stove.

C'mere. Sit down with me. The old lady pats the couch next to her.

Come closer. They say huggin's good for old folks. But nobody wants to touch you anymore once you're old. We need hugs too, just like kids. But old folks're disgusting.

She pulls out a bag of candy. The wrappers inside rustle.

What's your name? If you tell, I'll give you a candy. You won't tell? You one of those outy-stick kids? Hey, keep your hands offa me! Don't you dare. Just stay right where you are, okay?

She sticks the cough drops somewhere underneath her.

That mother of yours, Soňa, she always was an awful one. Even as a little missy, all dolled up in makeup all the time like a gypsy girl. And how come she isn't here with you?

A giant moth, drunk on the humidity, staggers across the linoleum, drawn toward the stove. It disappears in a tiny fist.

So you came for summer vacation, huh? Well, you can't stay here with me. I don't have room, understand?

The boy kneels, tries to twist the moth out of his little brother's grip. Crushed but still alive, the slimy blob coated in wing powder disappears into the little one's mouth. He sucks, then swallows.

Someone raps on the glass at the door.

A woman in a scarf. Mama.

The boy seizes hold of the handle, opens, and stands glued to the spot. It's not who he thought it was.

The woman wears a flower-patterned scarf on her head, and the blouse over her large bosom is dotted with flowers too. A long skirt flows from her hips.

Startled you, huh?

Papa flipflops across the floor in sandals, then leaps in the air, skirt aflutter, landing by the couch.

Ha-ha, you didn't even recognize me!

He grabs his mother by the shoulders, tugging her from the couch. The old woman gives him a smack in the face, flailing at his throat, his face, wherever she can reach.

Holy Virgin Mary, such a fright! What nosy old lady's that, pokin around here, I said to myself. And here it was you in disguise? What're you tryin to do?

Look, Ma, if anyone asks, I wasn't here, okay?

They just reported somethin crashed into the woods in Poříčí out of the sky, you know? Some UFO or giant rock? Police got it all closed off. Whole area's crawlin with cops. Course Sázavan reports on Poříčí all the time. How they grow the biggest radishes, got the best soccer team, on and on. Yeah, those folks in Poříčí always know how to get their way.

She takes a belt, returns the bottle to its hiding place under the cushions. And wriggles down into the blankets and pillows.

Papa's holding a package. He thrusts it at the boy.

I brought you this from your aunt Monča's room! Change into these.

If some little green men came wormin out of that flying saucer, the eyeballs on those Poříčí folks would pop right outta their heads! But I don't wish any ill on em. Like I say, we all do what we can.

It's a girl's outfit. Scarf, skirt. Hoodie. The scarf is patterned with big strawberries, instead of flowers like Papa's. The sweatshirt is pink. Pair of sandals.

Papa bends down and ties the boy's scarf.

There!

Papa squirts soap into the basin of heated water and lathers up, rubbing suds on his cheeks.

Pull that skirt on, boy. Disguised we've got a better chance they'll let us into the women's ward to see your mother. If we need to. Get my drift?

The boy leaves his track pants on under the skirt. Pulls on the hoodie.

Just be glad you're little so you don't have to have breasts.

Papa pulls out a silver tube, slides a tablet into his palm, tosses it in his mouth. Squats down next to the smaller boy. Crushes another pill in his fingers. Clutches the little nipper's cheeks, pours the powder into his puckered mouth.

Bring water. He nods to the larger boy.

What's that you got there? What's that you're givin him?

Vitamins, Ma. To help him sleep.

I could use some of those myself. Well, thank God I've still got a little gulp left. But that's for the show. Show's comin on soon.

As Papa strides out, little one in his arms, he doesn't even notice his skirt sweep across the coal scuttle. The boy slips out behind him. Papa slams the door shut, rattling the glass.

12

WITH A CARRIAGE. YOU'LL BE FINE AT MONČA'S.
IF ANYONE, EVEN SOMEONE MALEVOLENT . . .
SHOOTING GALLERY PROMENADE. THE TERRIFYING
FLYING LOG. HELPING HANDS. THE REDHEAD
AGAIN. ESCAPE.

Their things lie on the grass where they tossed them. Sweaters, a T-shirt, somebody's sneaker, sleeping bags, a ragged toothbrush.

Wait here a sec!

The moonlight gives a nice view of everything. He tugs at the skirt with his fingers. Runs the scarf back and forth over his hair.

Papa comes bumping along with a blue baby carriage.

The boy peeks inside. His little brother, rompers unbuttoned, looks back at him.

Papa flings the sweaters, T-shirt, whatever else is left, into the net beneath the carriage.

Let's see! Good thing you got such a soft girlish face.

Papa tips the bottle back, finishes it off, and tosses it over his shoulder.

Bet you'll get whiskers growin in soon, though.

With one hand gripping the handle of the carriage, he looks the boy up and down in his scarf and skirt, pink hoodie draped casually over his shoulder.

At your age, I already had a beard. But that's okay!

And off they go.

Walking warms them up.

They flop along in their sandals, skirts aflutter, behind the baby carriage, striding down the street past yards, fences, sheds, windows aglow in people's homes, they tramp along the smooth asphalt down the gently sloping hill. All the trees around here are covered in protective mesh.

Then Papa comes to a stop. Fiddles with his artificial breasts for a moment. Smooths his skirt and flowered blouse.

Quiet here, huh? Finally we can talk. The two of you're gonna stay with your aunt Monča awhile. It'll be fine, you'll see. Ooh, look, isn't that gorgeous!

They tilt their heads to the spectacle in the heavens.

Rockets go sputtering across the Pyšely sky in geysers of sulfuric yellow and cobalt, lighting up the treetops, causing chains, door handles, any and all metal surfaces to scintillate, sweeping tufts of phosphorescent light along the gutters.

And as the fireworks die away, they can clearly hear the distant commotion of the fairground, the chirping and chatter of a distinctly human crowd.

Your aunt Monča lives in Městečko. You'll like it there. And know what? You've got your whole life ahead of you. You can travel the world, go to college. We never even dreamed of that.

Papa hitches up his skirt, holds it bunched around his waist. Next to a tree jutting out of the sidewalk.

We can pee here.

Urinating onto the trunk, they sprinkle the cobwebs quivering over the wrinkled bark in the milky light of the moon.

Papa keeps a tight grip on the carriage as they make their way down a sloping street toward the light and noise, the sound of disco intensifying with every step they take.

And assuming that anyone, perhaps peering out from his hiding place among the sheds, from behind one of the trees, perhaps even someone malevolent and bitter, were to catch sight of the woman with the carriage that bore within it the smooth-skinned treasure that was the peacefully breathing child, the woman striding along with her barely full-grown daughter, whose sandals slapped devotedly along in her mother's footsteps, heading in the direction of the fun and entertainment . . . perhaps even he, however frustrated, might conclude that all is right with the world, and quite possibly comprehend, if with a slight prickle of envy, that unremitting actual good and motherly love are commonplace things in the world.

And then they turn the corner and are in the thick of it.

Really, just a few steps in off the dark street and they melt into the crowd. Sucked in by the promenade of shooting galleries.

They stride, or rather are dragged, down the lane of shooting galleries, bang! and bang! the shots running together into salvos, pellets thwacking into multicolored wooden targets big as wheels on an automobile. And at every shooting gallery, dolls and balls on a stick, flying monkeys on rubber bands, party horns, gingerbread hearts, all there for the taking if you can shoot a bull's-eye. Clumsy giants and hard-eyed runts squint down the barrel, stock pressed firmly to their shoulder, as giggling young ladies cluster around, squeezing giant stuffed animals to their bosoms, balloons on thin strings straining to break free of their hands with every gust of wind. From time to time, a shriek rings out amid the crack of rifles, a colorful ball full of fairground gas lofting into the air.

The balloons fly over the stalls, drifting past the foliage, blending in with the higher darkness, the carnival barkers' cries fusing with the shouts and laughter.

The young boy swallows. His belly growls. A draft blows up his skirt, he furtively smooths it down against his thighs. Inhales the aromas. Licks his lips.

And suddenly they burst out of the lane of shooting galleries onto the town square, really a village green.

Towering up from the center of the swirling crowd is a monumental tree trunk stripped of bark, festooned with lanterns, light bulbs, and brightly colored paper chains.

This is where they have most of the stalls selling bric-a-brac, the grilled meat carts, the beer stands. And the fairground attractions, the Chair-O-Planes, the swing rides, the Ferris wheel's upper seats thrusting toward the gleam of the stars as the more courageous fairgoers surround a giant giraffe with gondolas hanging off its ears. The thrill seekers are sent soaring up with a metallic swoosh, then plunged shrieking back down to earth, stopped by a true miracle of technology exactly one meter above the ground.

Papa, aggressively protruding breasts facing the rear of the crowd, one hand white-knuckled on the baby carriage handle, with his other hand thrusts a thousand-crown note at a vendor and fumbles for the paper trays of bread and frankfurters. He waits for the dollop of mustard, then slides the food to the boy, who meanwhile stands breathing in the juices of the hot meat, the beery ozone, the heat of the grills . . . and as the boy takes hold of the tray, at the sound of a terrifying, ear-splitting creak, he raises his head and sees the maypole sway . . . hears the crowd cry out in pain, rage, and astonishment, like the outbreath of hell itself . . . sees the wobbling tip and after that the monumental, crushing trunk flying straight toward them.

Ahhhhh, screams the crowd, the baby carriage squeaking as it bangs against the wood of the stall. The tree trunk slams to the ground, bounces up, rolls in the air, buckles, and falls again.

It demolishes the beer kiosk, the lanterns bursting into flame. Somebody falls on top of the boy, then quick scrambles away. A flood of heat pours from the overturned grilling stall, whose wreckage protects the crouching boy from the people running back and forth, shrieking, from someone hobbling in tears, people toppling left and right.

The boy, squatting on his haunches, bites into the frankfurter. Fumbles around for more, lands on a coal from the shattered grill, slips his burned fingers in his mouth.

And the horrible tom-tom of the trunk thudding against the ground suddenly falls silent.

Screams, creaking, and the rhythmic groans of the rides separate out from the mixture of cries. And the machines, one after the other, fall silent. Even the shrill, ear-splitting music goes quiet.

The gondolas hang motionless from the giraffe's ears like earrings. The swings have come to a stop. The Chair-O-Plane has stopped spinning. Even the hardiest tots sag pale-cheeked in their chairs.

In the spot where the trunk crashed into the shooting gallery, a portly gypsy woman scrabbles through the splintered targets, felled dolls, scattered stuffed animals. She pulls an air rifle with a cracked stock from the wreckage with a wail.

Even the Ferris wheel has ground to a halt.

The groaning of battered adults, children's tears, swearing, pain, and bewilderment resound across the battlefield in a chorus of lament.

Get up, honey, for fuck's sake!

Heeelp!

Pepík! Jesus and Mary, where is he? Pepííík!

Somebody cut down the tree!

The boy wriggles out of the smashed stall. The canopy, greasy with a thousand grillings, caught fire at the first touch of one of the lanterns decorating the tree. Its burning edges flap in the wind.

The flattened carriage lies at his feet. Crushed by the maypole. Its sharp tip, adorned with a wreath, juts toward him.

But no blood beneath it, no tangled mass of flesh, nothing.

Aha.

The squirming little worm in rags is clutched in Papa's arms. Flowered scarf pushed up on his forehead, Papa squats down, like a Madonna of the ruins, cradling the little boy in his arms. Soot from the grills drifts through the air, whipped by the burning canopy.

The boy comes running over. Presses his palm to his little brother's tummy, lays his head on the skirt gathered around his father's knees.

The emergency floodlights switch on, illuminating the scene. The rhythmic, mechanical noise of the rides is replaced first by the generators' quiet hum, then the sound of approaching ambulances, fire engines. The screams of police sirens.

Fairgoers wander the sprawling grounds in a daze, regathering friends and families or not, struggling out of the shattered kiosks, climbing down from the silenced rides.

A handful of battered survivors stop at the sight of the Madonna with the scarf over her face. A few more step up from behind, many themselves newly freed from the rubble, surveying the devastation.

Did the tree land on you, ma'am?

The lady's been hit!

She's got a little kid!

Bison, the big man with the gold chain around his neck, marches up to the pietà and throws out his paws to the little boy cradled in Papa's arms, blurting some inebriated comment, while the red-haired lass hanging on his arm, who seems to be in total shock, sobs loudly.

The vendor from the frankfurter stand, flattened fire extinguisher under his arm, tries to assist Papa to his feet.

Just take it easy, ma'am, don't try to move on your own, he says, dispensing advice like an experienced Samaritan. Papa ducks away from him, and bats away the grasping hand of the chain-necked pest.

The carriage is smashed to smithereens!

Jesus on the cross, Virgin on the hill, it killed the baby!

Give the mom a drink, all right? Stop pushing, let them breathe, all right?

The tree was notched!

Those Poříčí bastards!

Peeeepíííček . . .

Papa slowly rises to his feet, little boy in his arms, and stealthily adjusts his breasts, ducking everyone, clumsily trying to worm his way out from all the pesky attention.

But the man with the redhead girl steps in front of him.

Somethin fishy's goin on here!

Papa shakes off Bison's hand, which is wandering over the shoulder of his flowered blouse, elbows the gaping hot dog vendor in the stomach, knees another onlooker out of the way, and goes bounding off, skirt aflutter . . . The young boy takes off after him as the crowd looks on in shock . . . Bison shoots out his claw and tears off Papa's breasts, the redhead shrieks and falls to the ground . . . Papa, protecting his full armload, holds his skirt rolled up around his waist as he hotfoots it past the fairground stalls, hurdling fallen beams, young son in tow . . . They go racing into the lights of an incoming fire engine, and for a few ear-splitting moments weave their way through a tangle of ambulances and police cars, all blaring their horns and sirens.

From the edge of the ruined fairgrounds they dash off among the buildings. Then settle down in a dark passageway.

Dammit all to hell, boy, we lost that thousand crowns. But thank heavens we're all right.

13

IN THE GARAGE. LOMOZ. MÁŤA'S TRAIN TRIP.
MONČA. KÁJA: PRAGUE-EAST AND D1. THE PLANE.
BEING A PIECE OF MEAT. POTASSIUM. ARRIVAL OF
THE WHORES.

The shock and horror at the felling of the maypole, symbol of a red-hot summer . . . the falling tree, the various injuries, the destruction of several fairground stalls . . . gives rise to alarming rumors throughout the region.

The turmoil partially dies down during the night as the revelry moves into Pyšely's pubs and taprooms, especially after the official finding that the numbers of wounded, bankrupted, and otherwise affected have been considerably exaggerated.

Firefighters, paramedics, continue to keep watch over the devastated fairground site, and, with one version that made its way into the national coverage alleging it may have been a terrorist attack, there are also security units milling around the attractions, militiamen swaggering about, and reporters descending from all sides to issue canards the locals pull straight out of their asses.

And meanwhile more and more people, curious to see for themselves, are drawn to the site of the desecrated fairground. Like everything else in the area, after all, it's just a ways down the road.

Miran is woken by the persistent sound of squeaky, jabbering voices.

Wrestling himself out of the blankets, he finds his way by memory to the garage door, throws open the metal sheet, and peers out. His shaggy hair, combined with the confusion in his eyes and the scary tattoo on his booze-reddened face, ignite a spark of merriment in the assembled flock of boys. Already feeling a bit tired of vacation, the little stinkers thrill at the sight of the raggedy bum blinking out at them.

The saboteurs who cut down the maypole, envious hicks from nearby, most likely Poříčí, might well be hiding out in this tin shed on the outskirts of Pyšely.

A fistful of small rocks bangs against the garage door. Half-naked, half-asleep, Miran staggers two or three steps toward the boys, who dash out of reach, jeering at him, then resume their attack from a safe distance, hurling their projectiles with rapid-fire skill.

Miran takes several painful hits and, stumbling back inside, slams the garage door shut.

It's dark, but he leaves the lights turned off. He wags his head, a bit shaken at the youths' insolence.

Their dads and older brothers would never have stood for this.

They knew him.

He stares at the mattresses, the heavily breathing sleepers, the concrete floor strewn with engine parts, tools. A bra hanging over a lamp atop a wooden crate. A plastic table and chairs, a gooey mixture of food on plastic plates, cigarette butts, empty beer bottles.

The cars sit along the opposite wall: their new, very advantageously purchased sports car, black and majestic, and a sorry junker slated for a new paint job and general makeover.

The breathtaking black BMW was a newcomer to their fleet. Solder, the clan's master technician, had taken charge of it the moment Miran and his brother drove Tab and his sons out of the scrapyard. Now, after a brief discussion with a certain greased-palm someone at the relevant authority, the car sported a shiny new license plate, as beautiful and Czech as anything else in the area. Miran strokes the car lovingly.

Meanwhile, Solder had driven the Fiat back to the scrapyard. The Great Pyšely Fair held no interest for him. He knew the workings of the rides there inside and out, had ever since he was little, and they didn't have the impressive innovations in robotics that you saw on the attractions at St. Matthew's Fair in Prague.

Monča is stretched out on Miran's side of the bed, her curls flowing across the pillow. Still snoozing away. Kája lies huddled in blankets in the corner, whistling through his nose. They'd had their hands full with him after picking up Monča by the maypole in her new dress, tight across her belly, all tarted up and raring to go.

So much so that Monča had left Macinka, Janinka, and the others to saunter around the fair on their own, blowing off all the fun and festivities to be a loyal friend and help Miran out with his younger brother.

Kája had spotted his sweetheart with Bison and flown into such a rage that Monča and Miran had to take him to the nearest tavern and talk him down. Miran stood him drinks while over and over again Monča explained the purpose of holy week, so popular with the local girls.

Dude, it's a sacred tradition, she said, reminding Kája as if he didn't know. The week before the wedding, the girl has one last fling, tells all her exes goodbye, and after that she'll be sweet as a lamb—it's tradition, you can't break it! Look—she held her fingers spread apart in front of Kája's face—that's how many days she has left! And she loves you so much, I give you my woman's word, don't be a fool . . . It took so many rounds to calm Kája down that both brothers were in a fog for the maypole's collapse and the madness that ensued.

Miran drops onto the mattress with his friends and slips back to sleep, relieved.

A few moments later, old man Lomoz opens the garage door again, sliding it into the steel fixtures, the undulating metal creaking and squealing.

The old man, blue and yellowy veins cording his forearms, cocks his head, sniffs the air with his beak, feels his way into the space with taps and blows of his weaponlike hands. In wire-patched coveralls and steel-toe work boots, he storms in, dressed for battle. Hard on his heels, the sun bursts in behind him like the exhalation of a fire-breathing giant.

Wrinkling his nose at the stenches issuing from the drowsing crew, tripping over boxes and tools, he curses the workplace chaos. He gropes his way to the cars, kicking away the odds and ends that block his path, taps around to check what's there. Paint cans, brushes, scrapers, sandpaper, all just where he left it.

Hey, Pops! Monča greets the early worker.

She stretches a moment or two, yawning amid the blankets. Then jumps up, barefoot and naked, belly proudly swollen, decorative trinkets—rings, studs, wedges—in her lips, cheeks, nipples, and the navel of her protruding belly, either gently dangling or firmly lodged in flesh.

She kneels down at the kettle, takes a sip, makes a face, sprays a geyser into the trash heap of remains. Then pours water into the kettle out of a plastic container. Plugs the appliance in, tugs on her panties, squats down on her haunches.

Coffee, anyone?

Everyone, somebody answers.

But mine without milk, no milk for me! Kája shouts.

Calm down.

It pisses me off how they always bring me milk in those little pitchers, even though I don't want any. Didn't used to have em, before.

Probly one of those new EU regulations, says Miran.

Fuck that shit, says Monča, getting all riled up. No business of mine is gonna have any little EU pitchers, I can tell you that!

What was it like with milk in the old days? Kája asks Lomoz.

I've never had coffee in a pub. And at other people's place, I just drink whatever they give me.

Oh, okay . . .

The old man opens some cans and jars, a bottle of thinner he plugs with a rag. Has it all spread out on newspapers. Kneels down alongside the machine, the broken-down junker: his job for today. Time to get down to business.

You can see the county road through the open garage door. In the distance beyond, a line of trees along the river. No agitation in sight.

The old man runs the sandpaper over the bumps, the spots where the vehicle's paint is peeling. Probes the edges with his nails. Certain spots he scrapes. It's mainly the scratches and dings he's after. He grabs the brush and has at it. The job is to paint the thing.

How does he know which color to use if he can't see? Kája asks.

There isn't much they can do with that junker the old man's working on. But Uncle Lomoz is buddies with their dad. So the job is important.

Lomoz smiles, turning his schnoz toward the sound of Kája's voice.

The eyelids sewn in place of his burned-out eyes are wrinkled and cracked, as if the artificial skin had aged along with him. Behind the leathery curtains, it's nothing but empty sockets. He used to have glass eyes. Back then, insurance paid, no big deal. He smashed them to dust—seriously, to dust. When? Where? He had no idea. He was a wreck in those days.

Monča taught him how to wash out the sockets with boric acid. When he got sloshed, which was never a one-day affair, the holes in his head would fill with all kinds of secretions. Insects would get stuck in there, crumbs.

Downright nasty! Monča would say.

She'd been looking after him quite a bit lately, in fact. So did the other girls. With a whoops and a giggle, finding one of his many pairs of sunglasses, which he constantly misplaced. He practically lived at U Paručky now. Downstairs, in the kitchen.

Who needs eyes anyway? Lomoz always was handy. Whenever anything at U Paručky needed fixing, tightening, smashing, or, say, repainting, he'd always sniff it out somehow. He did all that. Plus upkeep for all the other buildings in the area too. They liked talking with old man Lomoz, everyone. Guys looked up to him. Because of how he took out that tank, back in the day. People knew. But it was more than that. The way he told stories, sometimes folks would almost forget to breathe. He'd tell them things that made their jaw drop.

Lately, though, he kept dropping everything. Where before U Paručky sometimes even used him for security—big, threatening guy who commanded respect from the local hayseeds and out-of-towners alike—now he mostly just lolled around the kitchen like an old housecat. He liked it there. In fact he loved it, it was his water of life, what with the coming and going day and night and squabbling and girlish chatter, inhaling all those body sprays and perfumes of theirs through his mighty proboscis, savoring the authentic zest of female adolescence that permanently hung in the air.

In the days when he was still interested, many of the young women indulged him quite willingly. Perhaps out of comradely and collegial affection, they viewed him as a natural part of the male inventory.

And a few of the congenitally randy little minxes simply came to realize that, especially in boring moments such as autumn sleet storms, this Lomoz guy was one naturally talented fucker.

It was only now, as he made the inexorable transition from old age into the next phase, that the girls sat around with him chatting over coffee and cakes. That's how it is in the sweetest paradise, assuming there's any time left there.

How can I tell the colors apart, young buck? By their warmth! Like a shaman!

Kája's eyes go wide. Monča gives him a wink. As in, the old man's full of it. Miran asks if they caught them yet.

Caught who? Kája inquires.

Those lowlifes that attacked the fair.

Hogwash, the old man grunts. The maypole was just poorly secured!

It got cut down, Kája blurts. Everyone said.

No sir, Lomoz insists. It was poorly secured. I worked on it.

Ahh!

Listen, kid, that thing with the milk in the pitchers reminds me of my old pal Máťa Píťa. His thing was he couldn't stand the new-style trains!

Uncle Máťa, Miran shouts from bed. He used to carve those little boats for us out of bark! Kája, remember?

Mm.

Looking at the streak of paint trickle across the floor, Kája decides he won't be hiring the old man to do the floors in his new residence, whenever that happens. All due respect.

That's him. Well, Máťa Píťa lived out in a log cabin for years, but then one day he decided to get out and see some people again.

Lomoz laid his brush down on a can and straightened his back till it cracked.

Also had himself an urge to go look at some girls! He'd been all holed up and off the booze, but then he says to himself, What harm would one do? Boy, did he hit bottom hard.

What happened? Kája squawks.

Walks to Čerčany to catch the train, passes the pub there, the Vulture, where he spent years just one long blur. I'll try somewhere else, he says to himself. Feelin adventurous. Then it all began when he got on the train.

What, what? the young one nags.

I learned how to milk cows from Uncle Máťa. Criminy jickets, time flies, time flies, Monča sighs.

Well, he gets on the train and goes straight to the window to open it up, ridin in the fresh air's nice, but the windows on the new trains don't open! Plus he's used to askin where he is, get the conversation goin—folks just love to argue over that—but he can't!

No? yelps Kája.

No. On the new trains, they hammer the names of the stations into your head from the PA, plus they got those flashin signs, so everyone always knows where they are! He's also used to strikin up a conversation about what's new or old outside the windows, and he can't do that either, since somebody put up a wall between the tracks and the countryside.

A noise barrier, Kája exclaims. That wasn't there before?

Máťa just sits there starin at the wall, like he's ridin inside a cow pen, and next thing you know here's Čtyřkoly, no riverbank or river, and bang! Senohraby, bang! Mirošovice, and the wall's right there the whole time, and he'd like to talk about it, but he doesn't dare, what with everyone else on their phones or starin at little TVs on their laps.

Ha ha ha, laughs Miran.

And it's gettin to be night, so this bright light comes on inside the car and startles Máťa, since now, with the window locked, he can't even see out at the wall, all he can do is stare at his reflection in the glass. It's no wonder his spirits sink. And he doesn't know yet what's in store!

What's that? Miran says.

By the time they reach Strančice, he can't take it anymore. Gets off the train and heads straight to the pub. The waitresses there are topless. That's a new one on him. Walks in, a girl comes over, naked breasts right up front, smiles and hands him a beer. So he downs it, orders another, and another naked girl comes up and hands it to him. Then another beer. And another naked girl. And on it goes.

Yep, that's it!

People afterwards said he was almost out of his mind with joy.

He should've come to our place, Monča says. He would've been totally calm, no big deal.

Máťa's suckin down his beer, drinkin in the fabulous nudity with his blurry vision, and so he has one more, and on and on as usual, and the moment he slams his empty stein down on the table, another young lady's there with a full one, breasts swayin or pokin out nice and hard like a statue, and Máťa can't help but think that this is his reward for life and he's in paradise, this is the end, and sure as hell, he keels over and that's all she wrote.

With that, the old man kneels down to the car, picks up the brush, and gets back to work.

Must've been a Wednesday, muses Miran. Wednesdays are topless nights there.

How do you know? Monča asks.

The guys've been sayin, Kája says, backing up his brother. And how do you know what it looks like inside a train? he asks the old man.

Folks've been sayin.

C'mon, Monča, get dressed. We're headin out soon, right?

Monča pulls her bra off the lamp, turns around, cocks out her elbows, snap.

Turns back to them.

That Monča. Standing there with the light cascading over her. Nails, studs, rings, resplendent barbarian ornaments, all gleaming, sparkling. As she spins around while getting dressed, the men stop and gape, the only sound the creak of fans and the stirring of summer insects like the engine room of eternity.

Well, her complexion may be a bit ragged with pimples, and her schnoz may stick out a bit too much, she isn't twenty anymore, not by a long shot, but who would want a young thing when he could have a goddess?

Good thing she got dressed. The brothers are following her with their eyes like sunflowers follow the sun. She doesn't even notice. Hardly a surprise. She got her start behind a window in Amsterdam, where the girls go naked all day long.

Wow, that's great how it just snaps, Kája enthuses.

It's embarrassing for a guy to struggle with a bra, he muses to himself. You buy your girl a bra and you can't even open or close it. But sure, some other guy can. It sucks. Maybe it's like a test. Like a contest for who can be the biggest dork when it comes to bras. Probly the winner'd be some salesman from Tesco. From the ladies' department. In other words, probly a fag. Serves the girls right.

Kája still can't stop thinking about Světlana.

Every day and every hour of the day.

He frowns, remembering how he saw her at the fair.

They've known each other since they were little, but they didn't really pay much attention to each other until Světlana was at Monča's.

Once they started paying each other a lot of attention, she stopped working at the brothel, it was only natural.

For now, though, she can get up to whatever she wants. It's her holy week. Seven days when a girl can run wild.

Kája's looking forward to the end of the week.

Then will be the wedding.

And the hulking man sinks into reverie.

Because in spite of his immaturity, and his natural instinct for violence, so readily salable, Kája has a very strong urge for tenderness.

For breakfast they have tea, coffee, slices of bread with something or other. Monča, now clothed, serves them on a plastic tray brushed clean of the remainders from the previous night's meal.

Afterward, she and Miran lie back down again. Have a smoke, shoot the shit. Wrestle over a copy of a tabloid newspaper lying around the garage. Monča wins. Miran grumbles. But Monča's the kind of person who takes her reading seriously.

Kája gets tired of staring at her. Grabs a crate and moves it over by the blind old man. Squats down and studies him from up close, making no attempt to hide it. Old people are still like another species for him.

Old Lomoz has dried up with age, Kája notes. But he's still a big man. Hasn't shrunk like others around. His skin, a map of heat waves, cold snaps, windstorms. Wrinkles so wide you can fit a finger in them, trenches like lashmarks. Grips the paintbrush sideways in his strong, crooked fingers.

His hands are like elongated tree roots, with nails like pliers, Kája reflects. The kind you only see on old folks in the country. Yeah, I'd rather see em dried up. Better mummies than tubs a lard. How many times you see old folks all potbellied and bloated like pigs. This one'll still have some muscle on him when we put him in the ground. That's how I'd like to be. When I get old.

Kája tries to be helpful. Slides the can over, wipes the brush on the newspaper.

Hand me a rag! Open the thinner!

Say, Pops, how old are you anyway?

You're still fifteen, aren't cha? Still a puddinhead.

Not me. I'm about to get married.

I know. I'm just fuckin with you.

That's why I went in with Miran. I need the money, right. The wedding, my dad's birthday present, and after that you won't be seein me around here anymore. I promise.

Old man sweatin you, huh?

Got that right.

Kája lays his head on the hood, coming to rest, mulling things over.

In his mind, Prague-East, where he and Miran operate, is a gigantic territory, constantly buzzing with the stream of traffic along the D1, crossing hills and valleys, the zoom of cars in places merging with the river's burble.

Prague-East, a motley district, here clotted with log cabins, there built up with opulent villas from a planet in another time when the parcels around Sázava, just a short way from the capital, catered to the luxury tastes of the cosmopolitan well-to-do. They remain here fence to fence with workers' apartments from Communist days, while a bit farther on, dilapidated farmsteads teeming with gypsy children loom up from the nettles, their walls chipped and cracked like the skin of an iguana.

Moments from Kája's debt-collecting trips circle around his mind. The hungover-tear-drenched hundred crowns pulled from a rubber boot after a gentle educational slap and a string of curses in the forest alehouse Stick Up the Butt. Or the wads of five-thousand-crown notes from the affluent debtor in Senohraby, whose refusal to comply had so rattled the two brothers that he puked all over the greenhouse from the ramparts of an overblown villa with sugary-pink brickwork.

Everyone had to pay back their debts, that was nonnegotiable. Any lenience would have destroyed the Bašta clan's good name as surely as machine-gun fire.

The occasional pinch of violence was needed, but Bašta never had more than two or three guns within his bailiwick, which came his way as collateral or as part of repayment on one of his long-term loans. They hadn't yet given any thought to modernizing their arsenal, as Miran and Kája tended to solve disputes in rather medieval fashion. Guns fell under Solder's jurisdiction. As master technician, he kept any prospective firepower in working order. They had only needed to use it in a few instances so far, to eliminate some exceptionally bad motherfuckers.

Where and when would they go? Who would they hit up? Whatever their dad tasked them with, Miran kept the details filed away in his head.

But either way, Kája wants to make a break. No more trips. He wants out of the junkyard. And he wants Světlana with him. The big day is drawing near when they'll give their dad his birthday gift and he and his girl will get married. That's Kája's plan: Live with his wife. Have children. Be together with her. So what? What's wrong with that? That's how everyone used to live, he shouts in his mind, as if arguing with a big, noisy crowd.

So how much money you need? Lomoz asks.

Well, enough for my wife to have a house with lots of furniture, a garden with flowers, a washing machine, dishwasher too, all the modern stuff. Car of her own, that goes without sayin.

Damn, you really do love her. What's she up to now?

Oh, you know. Holy week. Then we got the wedding!

Just as long as nobody goes and gets her in a family way, Lomoz says, reciting his standard line.

That's already taken care of, Kája boasts.

I always did nudge her in your direction. Spoke very highly of you!

Really?

Look here, girl, I says. Don't hump your way through your beautiful years. Marry the fool while he's still dumb enough to want you.

Aw, Pops!

Just fuckin around, don't worry. You two'll be fine, you'll see.

You think?

I know!

They dip their brushes in sync. Kája's amazed how well the old man handles things. How can he tell where to paint and where not to?

Whole thing needs paintin, the blind man replies. So it's not like it depends on any particular little piece. Don't overthink it. Just get in there and get er done.

Pops?

Mm-hm.

I still don't understand how you do it all. I mean, everything. If I went blind, I think I'd kill myself on the spot.

Go on, it's not as bad as all that.

Oh no?

You think it's easier to kill yourself than not to see?

I donno!

Well, I'll kill myself when I get old, the blind man says.

But you are old!

Not yet. Long as you got strength to kill yourself, you're still all right. And that's the problem. Fuck that up and you're nothin but a piece a meat.

How's that?

Man, don't even consider it. You're gonna have a baby.

How do you mean, piece a meat?

Just that you're useless, like you shit yourself and you don't even realize.

But what's it matter to you then, right?

True, the blind man says.

So what's the big deal?

I'm weighin my options to keep it from gettin that far.

Oh, shush now, Dad, Monča says. How bout some more coffee?

Monča keeps twisting around all funny, Kája notices. She's got her belly propped up with a pillow, her reading matter too, but every few minutes she keeps making this funny hissing noise. Spluttering. Miran must be tickling her or something.

Hey, says Kája, how bout I put on some music, huh? How bout some tunes, guys, what do you say?

Try the news, the old man says. Sázavan was sayin somethin crashed out there in a field. By Poříčí. Field's surrounded, cops got barricades up. No clue whose field. And part of the woods is closed off to traffic. Could a plane've crashed there?

There's a few of those shutdowns around, says Kája. Cops come trottin in, take over a spot. And nobody's allowed in. What's up with that?

Probably a property seizure, says Miran. Either that or a highway bypass.

Get this, Monča chimes in. I'm readin about it in the paper right now. But the plane crashed in Ukraine. Or was it Russia? Shot down, she says, waving the newspaper to dissipate the paint and paint thinner fumes.

Hey, you guys, look at these photos! It's awful! Bodies fallen from the sky, impaled on telegraph poles. Scattered across the field. And get a load of this girl. Will you look at her?

Who's that bimbo? the old man asks.

Some pro-Russian separatist. Dolled up in makeup she got off the bodies.

Let's see. Nice, Miran reports back to the painters. Kája, check her out!

But Kája's connecting the wires on the car radio, pounding the battery. It won't play. What do you expect from a wreck, oh well.

Jesus, how sad is that. The Russians shot down the plane, then zip, went right in and robbed the bodies. And their girlfriends nabbed the dead girls' makeup. Pretty nasty, if you ask me.

People there are poor, says Miran. It's not that simple! You can get makeup whenever you want. But what about a poor Russian girl? Think about it for a sec!

You feel more sorry for Russian girls than those people that got shot down? That's just like you! You think that separatist is hot? Why don't you just go to Russia!

It may seem wrong to you, the old man joins in. But for them it's normal. They take it as spoils. You shoot it down it's yours, period. Is makeup all they took?

I can't read this anymore, says Monča. Makes me wanna puke.

Russians're white, same as we are. Plus they're Slavs too. They're like us, only different, the old man tries to explain.

Hey, Miran, get up and get dressed, would you? I'll save you the picture, all right? Monča says.

You all are too young to remember sixty-eight. They came stormin in here on tanks, burst into the rectory, somebody flushed, and soon as they heard the splashing, they shot the toilet to pieces. That's Russians for you. Ask your dad.

Ukies are cool, though, Kája says. I worked with a crew of Ukies. Got along with all of em. They're almost like us.

They were both Soviets! barks the old man.

Sorry, I didn't know, Kája says.

As of today, there won't be any Russian girls at my place, Monča says. Imagine if I had to check their makeup.

The old man chucks his brush onto a heap of newspapers and folds his arms, those age-old logs, across his chest.

I could do with a sip of that coffee now. Shame the radio doesn't work. On Sázavan last time they were talkin about that nurse from Rumburk. Angel of death, they call her. She was killin old folks, shootin em up with potassium. I was wonderin what potassium was, though. Radio didn't say.

I don't know either, says Kája.

So potassium, huh! You think that comes in pills? I wonder if the pharmacy sells it.

Oh, shush now, Dad, Monča says, slamming down the newspaper.

How bout a piece of potassium under the Christmas tree for me, Moni, huh? Does it only come in injections? Or do they sell it as a drip? I could use some potassium on hand. It's summer now. But winter's comin, fall. Then those thoughts start right back up.

Oh, shush now, Dad!

Heey there, everyone! You all up yet? Janinka calls out. Coming in out of a brief shower, braids damp and clinging to her glowing face, she gushes greetings and questions, filling up the garage. Macinka echoes her. The girls aren't alone, having left a pair of young men waiting for them outside.

Hey there, girls! Miran warbles.

Monča's girls. Firm asses squeezed into tight jeans, nylon shells unzipped down to their overflowing breasts, the kept young women sport tiny, colorful rucksacks on their backs, with cute little travel bags in their hands.

Kája, ciao! exclaims Janinka. What's Světla up to?

Kája, turning beet red behind the hood of the car, droops his head, the crestfallen control center of all that mighty musculature.

I was gonna ask you, he mutters.

In that case, never mind, says Macinka. The two young prostitutes giggle, exuding good cheer and carefree spirits from every pore.

Kája rises from his squat, his whole body and facial muscles tightening into a mass of knots. Hands on hips, he advances, leans against the garage door, cooler in the rain now than the rest of the hangar, and grunts at the boys.

What're you starin at?

Take it easy, sounds the reply, now from a safer distance. The pair unglue themselves from the gate and slowly walk away, maintaining their dignity.

The girls burst out laughing again.

Světlana sends her *best* greetings!

She's having the *best* time!

They laugh and laugh. And their laughter, their gaiety, embraces everyone.

14

A COUPLE SLAPS IN THE DARK. WHICH WAY TO
MĚSTEČKO? IT'S NOT SO MUCH THE FUCKING.
BUT? HOWDY, BROŇA! BRONĚK'S ELDER.
WHAT KINA JAIL YOU THINK I'D GET? CHLUM.

The boy wipes his singed fingers, smeared with grease and soot, on
the front of his pink hoodie. Papa, in a headscarf that hides his long
hooked nose, cradles the little nipper in his arms.

They tread across some desolate garden, furrowing the soil. Their
sandals slap almost in unison. But they're taking a slightly labyrinthine
route out of Pyšely. As they circle the paths tramped by locals to the
edges of the fields, the trails keep leading them back to the village, between the fences.

Every now and then, a streetlamp cuts across their path and they plod
through the fuzzy yellow of its light.

Papa grumbles at every step, constantly stopping to take a rest, the
little boy clinging to his chest like a monkey.

Suddenly they hear voices. Papa freezes midstep, his boy right behind. The last homes in the village stand to either side.

And at long last, here's the road, a broken white line tracing its hump,
hurtling into the unknown. A ditch full of rusty cans, jars. Rippling nettles, prickles moist with rain.

The car's lights are turned on, moths flutter in its beams. A tall, spindly man sways on his feet, a girl, short but solidly built, skipping and
prancing around him. The only music is the slap of their soles and the
riverine stream of anger and bitterness coursing from their mouths.
Papa chuckles. He straightens up, tugs down his scarf, adjusts his one
remaining breast with an economical shrug.

It's her again, he whispers to the boy.

And so it is. The girl from the fair hops around her partner, landing a slap or two here and there, the smack of her blows a refrain to her litany of curses.

The man or boy staggers. Reaches out his arms to the girl. But all it gets him is another whap.

I always have had a weakness for redheads, Papa says.

Now they're right up close.

Good evening, says Papa.

Nothing. The guy staggers. The girl hops.

Evenin! shouts Papa. Would you mind givin us a lift?

Heh? says the guy.

I have my kids with me, Papa says by way of explanation. He holds up the little one, so the headlight beams illuminate the quiet creature in his arms.

Piss off, the girl wheezes, stepping away from her reeling partner. The long-limbed man squints, totters. Is he crocked?

Please, miss, Papa says, flashing a grin.

And with a leap over the ditch, skirt aflutter, the girl is bye-bye, pushing her way through the bushes, a bobbing spot in the darkness.

The rangy fellow sits down on the road, leaning his back against the car. Collared shirt, jeans—young guy, a passerby would say. But once they get up close, they can see his face is grizzled, with sunken cheeks and wrinkled skin lined with ruptured veins. To their surprise, they're staring into the vulturelike face of an elderly man.

Can I help you? says Papa.

Yeah.

Will you give us a lift?

We can give it a try.

We'd like to go to Městečko, though, Papa specifies.

First just help me get in, says the owner of the burning eyes, their glitter flickering within his aging skull.

The boy has a sharp sense of how and why everything happens, and how the universe within a universe turns along with them. The clinging feeling of unreality is intensified by the faint light of the distant lamps. By the crescent moon, sprung from the canopy of clouds above the distant slopes. The strangled barking of a dog. The friction of his skirt against the twigs in the forest. Everything happens bit by bit, in a subdued way, in the honeycombs of the coming night. With a creaking so barely perceptible that only a truly sensitive, or hypersensitive, person would notice.

The man sinks down on the front seat. Papa gets behind the wheel. But, he protests, he is all drunk out, so to speak. At which their rescuer pulls out a bottle and Papa enters upon his task with vigor.

Soon, however, their rolling voyage is cut short by a roadblock. The yellow barriers of a traffic closure.

Not even waiting for instructions from the black-jacketed officer with a flashlight, they turn around and make their way to the forest road, following the instructions scraped from the head of the beanpole in the front seat.

Every now and then a branch swipes across the car roof, rattling the foliage, or glances off a window, supple and petite.

So what're they keepin watch for? Papa says, attempting to strike up a conversation.

They say somethin landed in the forest.

The Tungus meteorite?

Ha-ha, wouldn't know.

A Russian Tungus observation balloon?

More likely.

And how bout you? Bit of a spat with the young lady there?

Fallen branches crack beneath the wheels as they drive. Every so often, they run over a rock or bounce over a tree trunk stuck in the mud of the road.

Well, I choose to depart this world by my own hand, as they say, and she doesn't wanna accept that, the man says. But I'm killing myself. And that's final.

I beg your pardon, says Papa, clearly taken aback.

She wants to get married. One a the local boys. It's utter nonsense. She's crazy. Fucking's all she cares about.

You're kidding!

Well, for her, it isn't the fucking so much as the hugs, the sharing, the reciprocity, all that stuff, y'know? She says she was neglected as a child, so she lacked the basic security of parental affection. I think they found her somewhere.

Oh, gimme a break, that's just an excuse.

Yeah, well, so now she wanders lost, seeking that intimacy through sex. Without it she feels incomplete.

Please, there's lots of folks like that!

Not like her. She's a genuine succubus. But I hear there's another one like her in Lensedly.

Really?

Yeah, for them, everything else is a living hell, apart from that sublime moment of orgasm when they merge with the universe. All the rest is gray.

Oh yeah?

It's practically a religion for her.

I see!

I proposed to her that we go out together, in a blaze of love. And you'll pardon all this in front a the kids, I hope?

Which way we headed? Papa asks. We need to get to Městečko.

These your children? Nice-lookin.

All right if I take another swig? So I can see where I'm goin?

And can you?

Like a lynx.

That's excellent then.

Excuse me for putting this so bluntly, sir, but I'm sure she'd just sleep with somebody else. Then you'd have peace and quiet, and as long as you love each other, things'd be hunky-dory, right? I mean, there's more lasting values when it comes to human relations than just, you know, sex, right?

Oh, baloney!

I guess you're right.

Listen, it's a pleasure to talk to you, really. It's unusual to come across an intelligent person here at night. It's just, pardon me, but I'm a little put off by the fact that you're wearin women's clothes.

We're on our way home from the fair, you see. We were part of an allegorical float.

Oh, well, that explains it! You wouldn't be an actor, would you? Do I know you from TV?

I do act from time to time.

Are you in any series?

Everything's a series.

But it's not. Because it ends. In death. And darkness. Sorry, but I'm convinced.

Well, I have noticed you tend to see things a bit on the dark side, Papa says. There're other opinions on death, though.

So do you believe? Is there such a thing?

Um, Papa said.

I mean, you don't look the hallelujah type. And you aren't about to claim after we round this next bend that you've seen Christ, are you? Cause I sure haven't.

Wow, look how dark it got! Are you sure this is the way to Městečko?

I haven't been lookin outside.

Oh no?

I just keep lookin inside my head.

Oh yeah?

And honestly, I can't wait.

But, sir, Papa says, trying to soothe the vulture man, what good does it do to worry about the girl? She'll have kids, right, eventually, and settle down, sure! She'll get fat, go to church, tend to the garden or what have you. It might be pretty nice!

It won't.

Or maybe she'll go to the city, work at some company in a nice jacket and modern skirt, right, maybe do yoga, and her husband'll be a good man, and well behaved, and if she goes and gets out of control, as you say, then so what, for God's sake! And havin kids, well, that's a sheer delight, lemme tell you! It'll be a good life.

It won't.

Oh, please.

In the end, everyone's broken, they die alone and in sickness. Nothing lasts—friendship, love, it all fades away, and in the end there's nothin left but dying and pain. And when you're in pain, you don't even remember the good times, as they say. And if you do? Then all the worse for you. There's no point in goin through it all again. You know that yourself.

You just had an argument is all, Papa says.

And if she does have kids, she'll just piss em all off and there'll be that many more unhappy creatures wandering the earth. And then they'll go and produce even more shattered unfortunates, so they got somethin to live for, right? I wanted to help her break the chain once and for all, this twisted cycle of passing on the cellular torch. The vanity and futility.

They hurtle through a clearing with stumps of trees bowed like living creatures, and Papa comes to a stop at another roadblock.

Amid the screech of the machine and the clatter of suddenly shifting objects, the man's head rams into the headrest, causing a slight cracking sound.

Two cops, dressed all in black, stand at the barricade, which is propped on a tree trunk lying across the road. Knocked down and split lengthwise, probably by lightning. The moon decisively dominates the forest scene as one of the lawmen pokes his head in the car window.

Howdy, Broňa! he sings. Fraid you'll have to turn yourselves around an go back.

All right, wheezes the man.

Look at you, bein driven by a lady! Middle of the night like this, ha-ha! Evenin, ma'am.

Papa squeaks out some reply.

On maneuvers are you, Rudolf? the man inquires.

Official secret, grins the cop, leaning against the yellow barricade.

Or did the Russkies invade again?

Hah hah hah!

So they turn and go back. Papa wipes the sweat from his brow with the scarf. The man named Broněk hands him a bottle as they drive back down the forest road, dark, muddy, and full of potholes, then leaves it clinking down below, probably against the man's ankle, it sounds like stone striking stone.

I showed him, huh? I'm not afraid to make a joke. But I'll tell you one thing, sir. Straight up.

What's that?

You've got some verve in you. You help me and I'll help you.

Jesus and Mary, when're we gonna be in Městečko?

You're takin the Lord's name in vain. And to no purpose.

Hm!

I had a good childhood, unlike her. I had a pop and a mom.

That's how it oughta be!

When she died, me and my pop fought over the urn. It ended up at his place, along with everything else, and one day he says to me, Y'know, I never had as much sex in my life as I have since your mother passed away.

Ouch, that smarts!

But then he started to croak himself. Only it dragged on. He spent the last bit in a special place for old folks in Benešov, and guess how much that cost? Nine hundred a day. Just for the room! And when he told me that about my mom, I got to wonderin what he was thinkin about when the two of them were, y'know, when they made me, if you know what I mean. So I asked him, you bet I did.

And what did he say?

No idea, I was plastered.

Hah hah hah!

You sure do have a cheery disposition, got some life in you. Take a left, we're headed down to the river.

We should've been in Městečko by now! says Papa. The kids're tired, he practically screamed.

We were all children once.

True enough.

Y'know, my pop's been on his way out a good ten years now, and he wants me to kill him. Stab away, he says. Be a man! And I'm so messed in the head, so mesmerized by it all, that when I pull the knife that he keeps in his slipper out from under the bed and ask where I'm sposta stab him, he just gets all pissed off and hollers, Between the eyes, you good-for-nothin, what kina question is that, how stupid can you be!

Don't let him make a slave of you!

I just can't help myself.

Tell him to go to hell.

I've done that already ten times.

Everything has its limits, right?

Not this.

With a knife, huh? That's brutal.

I said to him, Pop, you know they'll lock me up for this, right? And what kina jail are they gonna put me in? Patricide, are you kiddin? But he doesn't think about that. He grew up on all that wartime atrocity stuff, so to him it's nothin. Old people nowadays: Hitler in their child-hood, Stalin in their teens. They'd barely bounced back from socialism and got their feet wet in freedom when bam, the crisis hit. Refugees by the millions and a new Russian war to boot. The whole technological revolution's over their heads as well. Tell me how're we sposta get to Europe with old people like that?

It isn't gonna be easy! Papa shouts.

How bout your father?

Nothin much.

You see, and you're a dad yourself. That's nice. Hey, look up ahead, there's a tear in the dark. Or is that mist over the water?

Can't tell!

Anyway, now his childhood's all comin back to him, how he and his friends used to throw grenades into cellars. Hell, they didn't care who was down there, Krauts, Russkies, Ukrainians—meaning the Vlasovites, of course.

Oh yeah?

Yeah, there was always some army or other comin through, so the boys knew the soldiers'd go hide down in the cellars and lie in wait for the next ones, and my pop and his friends snuck up on them and chucked grenades in there!

Really?

They'd come crawlin out with their guts hangin out, and the commanding officer would come and tell the boys, Bravo! or Molodtsy!, depending which side he was on. And whenever some new soldiers attacked, they'd go hide down in the cellars and the boys'd sneak up on em and boom!

That was a hundred years ago!

Actually just seventy. And our Benešov was practically a model SS town, and . . .

Papa stepped on the brakes, bringing the car to a squealing halt.

Boys, let's go. Thanks a lot, Mr. Broněk, but we can walk the rest of the way.

Look, I still got some Fernet left here. I got practically a bar on wheels, more than I can drink, even.

The way you're goin on, it hurts my head, I swear.

You're not gonna walk all that way in the dark? With the kids. Be reasonable!

What flavor Fernet? Citrus or lime?

Both.

They drive on. Both putting so much effort into their silence you can practically hear it. The car jounces over the potholes. A milky mist creeps toward them, diluting the darkness. As the bushes drift past on either side, there are moments the boy feels like the car is afloat in a sea of white.

So you think there's any such thing? asks the man.

Any such thing as what?

God, of course. And don't start in on me with that there must be somethin jazz. Some universal intelligence or some such crap. It's all the same thing.

Yeah, sure I do.

You believe, or you know for a fact?

Same difference.

Don't try to weasel out of it!

Well, the devil exists, for damn sure.

That's not enough for me.

Oh no?

But we'll find out in the end, won't we? We'll all find out, huh.

I guess.

Ah well. She helped me so much, too. That love a mine really helped me. You saw how strong she was!

Well, there's more than one flower under the sun . . .

She's so beautiful, you can lay her on a wound and her supple young body just sucks it out, every bit a that pain. But she wants something in return.

What?

Everything.

Uh-huh.

Hey, look at that, we're here.

Where?

Chlum!

15

BLACK LUKÁŠ. LEAK-FREE MORGUE. HIGH UP AMID
THE SHREDS OF PLASTER . . . A WARRIOR'S DEATH.
I WANT YOU TO EXIST.

They zoom through the mist billowing up from the river to a broken-down little church atop a knoll. The ruin has been here for as long as anyone can remember, surrounded by graves with crosses, some knocked over and overgrown with ivy, thistles, all sorts of herbaceous plants.

The hazy twilight, bearing the hesitant promise of dawn, is torn open by the almost erotic squeal of a bat, plunging headfirst through the structure's broken roof, like a twisted rat comet in flight.

A tower, rather a turret, juts skyward from the hunched little church. Mortar between the stones eroded, weedy grass coiling through the cracks and crevices, mosses dripping.

Papa pulls the car to a stop a few steps from the graveyard wall, by a low-standing little house.

I got a friend fixin up the place here, Broněk informs him with a grin probably elicited by the pain in his crooked limbs. He opens the car door and slides out on his bony butt, hanging from the frame.

We'll find somethin inside. You can't go trampin around like a woman! Somethin instead a that skirt for the boy. Way he looks, it's a disgrace.

Papa snoops around the house, peeking in a mortar-splattered window fouled with cobwebs.

He's been workin on it big-time. Black Lukáš, they call him. Hermit, says the fellow, unentwining himself from the car like a spider. Got the house all fixed up now. Used to be a morgue. Dry, though. Nice place, least it doesn't leak.

That's crucial!

He swore he'd restore the place. Puttin all he has into it. He was in the can, of course.

I see!

Awful long time, all the worst prisons, Minkovice, Valdice, alla them. Whoa!

Awful lotta years. This Black Lukáš did awful things, supposedly.

So he was locked up under the Bolshies, or after?

Both. He didn't qualify for any a the amnesties.

Oh-oh-oh.

When they let him out, he just walked and walked. Till his feet brought him here. Covered a good chunk a ground. Could never come to rest, as they say, till he ended up here. Dropped from exhaustion and slept. And when he woke up, he started right in gettin the place whipped into shape.

So why do they call him Black?

Nobody knows. They're all afraid to ask. It was just him here, but folks spotted him right away. What's he doin here, jailbird like that. Maybe plannin to rob some gardens? So the local fellas staked the place out to get a look and saw him draggin boards in here, cartin bricks over there. Greetin all the grannies that bring flowers to lay on the graves. Even brought em a watering can. And this Lukáš fella was always polite. Had a real nice way of talkin to folks. He was so chatty, they started comin just to see him. And you could tell he was the handy type, had a green thumb when it came to repairs, and folks appreciate that.

So where is he now?

He's got tons a helpers now. Invites everyone he meets to come out. Right now he's out there leadin around a procession, collectin funds for repairs. I won't be around to see it, though. When they make the place sparkle, as they say.

Creak and slam!

Papa turns the door handle and slips inside.

The boy kneels down to his little brother. Wrinkles his nose. The rompers and everything have dried. Waves his hand over his little brother's eyes, watches the eyelids flutter. And the little boy opens his eyes. Spreads his cute little mouth open wide. Plump as a hippo.

He snatches up his little brother, carries him into the house. Either the little guy's gotten bigger and heavier or he's gotten weak. His legs are shaking.

Plank-board, dusty floor. The imprint of a cross high up amid the shreds of plaster; amid the flyspecks, the cobwebs, the outlines of a body, like something from Pompeii. Sacks along the wall. Sand. Coarse particles of lime, whipped up by the open door, cling to the skin. The suicide elbows his way in behind them, folds himself onto a chair. Bony legs in baggy pants, arms hanging spindly from his sleeves like spider legs.

Clotheslines crisscross the space, fastened to the walls with hooks. Clothespins hold bags of paper and cloth, sacks stuffed full of grass, plants. It smells, it reeks, intruding on the nostrils acridly. Tall rubber boots, trowels, a saw on the floor. Papa trips over bricks, screws, discarded clamps. Rummages through every corner, digs through shredded old newspapers.

Scuse me, sir, but could you fetch the wheelbarrow, please? It must be out back somewhere. I got my spot all picked out.

Papa lifting lids, poking around in cans and jars, opens and closes a desk drawer, sniffs the contents of a pot. Actually a pan. A huge pan, handle wrapped in spaghetti insulation. There's something in the pan that looks like meat but isn't.

Best to ask.

Burdock burgers, a hermit specialty! Go fetch that wheelbarrow and bring it here, all right? After that we'll take a look around for some outfits for you and the boy, all right?

Don't suppose there might be any pasta here at least?

I donno bout that. Best take another swig. My buddy Blackie's not the pub-goin type. Signed all my worldly alcohol over to the Lord, he says. He knows what to do with it.

Nice trick!

He just trusted in faith, what can you say? Not me. No matter how I try.

I know, right?

Listen, you help me out, I'll give you the car. You can sell it. You'll find a way. But if you don't mind, I'd just as soon we leave the notary out of it.

Hm.

I noticed you weren't eager to get too close to the cops.

You got that right.

Look, take my wallet too. Not bad, eh? I won't be needin it anymore.

Wow!

You take me down to the river in that wheelbarrow and I'll leave you the car, the cash, everything. We toss the wallet in the car, you take me down to my spot, and I'll give you the keys, deal?

Gee, I donno.

I'll never make it on my own. I'm tinglin all over my body. Look, I can't even open my throat hardly anymore, see? This hand here doesn't listen to me, and forget about the other one.

You're serious, huh?

You saw my bar on wheels. I don't want another drop! I'm done drinkin as of today.

Hm.

A heap of rags by the wall. A wooden tub full of pears. The boy lays his brother down on top of the soft heap. Peels a gob of roasted burdock from the pan, sticks a pinch in his mouth. The smells from the bags and sacks blend with the aroma from the mixture in the containers. He scrapes another lump from the pan, breaks off a few bits and feeds them to his brother. They slurp, they chew. The boy eyes the pears in the tub. They look soft and sweet. He stuffs a few under his sweatshirt and tucks it into his skirt.

Papa carries a chair outside for the spider man. They hobble over to the car. The man puts his wallet in the glove box so Papa can see, and snaps it shut. Papa sits him down on the chair, walks around the back of the house, and a moment later comes trudging back pushing a squeaky wheelbarrow. It's loaded up with stones, plus a few enormous roulders, with a big solid cow chain gleaming in their midst.

I loaded that on there back when I still had some strength!

Uh-huh.

Let's wait a little longer, though. There's somethin else I want to tell you.

Go right ahead!

So you know what happened next with my pop? I got the idea that I'd smother him with a pillow.

Seriously?

Well, what I noticed is, if you say the sickest thing on your mind, that makes it real in a way it isn't when it's just a tangled mess rollin around inside your skull.

I get it!

Why would I wanna drag somethin like that with me into the magnificent void, right?

All right, so tell me.

Doin it with a pillow, though, isn't too manly, right. Pushin that soft, squishy thing down on his soft old mouth, it's disgusting, right. Even if his body is thrashin around with the strength of a bull. But what's the use. Anyway, I'll tell you one thing. Long as you don't ease up, in the end you can smother anyone.

Scuse me, but you're crying, Papa says, mortified.

And he's right. The man's eyes well with tears, the whole fine mess running down his jutting chin, dripping through the stubble onto his Adam's apple as it slides up and down.

He's tossin his head side to side, the man says, whimperin, cause how could I humiliate my pop like that! He had to be disappointed—about the pillow, y'know? It's only natural. Knife to the heart, bullet to the skull, that he would've liked. Or at least a leap into the abyss. A warrior's death. They all threw themselves from the battlements, right? The ancient Greeks, the Incas, the Hebrews, Masada, right?

And don't forget Hrabal!

Right, of course! My pop had a balcony in that ritzy place where he was. But he couldn't get out there on his own. And I couldn't drag him. Just don't have the muscles. So in the end I grabbed the pillow. Maybe it was a low blow on my part. But that's the way it was.

The man blows his nose and wipes the tears from his cheeks with his fleshless, nearly see-through palms.

Now hold on a second! Sir! What about Richard III? The Lionheart? Do you mean to tell me he wasn't a man? Don't you dare. And he killed two boys with a cushion, right?

Oh yeah, I forgot. You're an actor. Was it that Richard, though?

Who cares, they were all knights. And they did it just like you. With a pillow!

Bless your soul . . . y'know, you're right!

And what about that Indian bruiser, Chief Bromden? He flew over the cuckoo's nest, in that Forman movie! Papa says, now practically screaming.

Man, you are on fire!

There's plenty more examples where those came from! Papa cries.

You are a truly excellent person, sir. I feel very relieved. Listen, I'm through drinkin as of today, but how bout you and me have a shot, what do you say?

Sure thing, Papa says. I grabbed the citrus from the car! He pulls a bottle from out of his grimy, tattered skirt.

Well, isn't that a coincidence, I took the other kind, says the spider man, clutching a bottle in his claws. I don't suppose Black Lukáš'd be too pleased. He's a bit opposed to booze. Well, but then again, it's true, he knows lotsa things. Including probly the most important thing of all.

That's exactly what I was wonderin, says Papa.

If he exists or doesn't.

Who?

You know. Him!

There you go with that again . . .

Well, you know, now that I got that, ahem, trip ahead of me.

Oh, c'mon! You can still change your mind. Look how beautiful it is outside!

I don't give a shit.

C'mon. Papa seizes the man by the shoulders and gives him a gentle shake. Come on!

So, do you want God to exist? the hermit asked me one day when I was mullin it over. Don't think, just gimme an answer, Black Lukáš said.

And?

Yeah, God, I want you to exist! I blurted. Just like that, automatically. Aha!

Then that's enough, Black Lukáš said.

I want you to exist.

Yep. Exactly.

That's enough?

Yep.

I never knew, says Papa.

Well, there you have it. Can I pour some in your cup here? A splash a lime, yeah? Or know what? Let's just have it straight from the source, who cares, right?

Listen, Papa says in a low voice, gripping the man's shoulder again.

Yes? What can I do for you?

So but seriously, you're sure there's somethin more than just this wild world of ours? This grind here we call life?

Yeah.

Definitely?

Yeah.

That's good, says Papa.

Excellent choice, that citrus, the man says. Keeps you warm. Mornings it gets pretty cold out here. Wouldn't you say?

That's cause we're on the knoll. Mists gather up here, Papa says.

But eventually the breeze'll blow it away, I think.

So, to your health!

And to yours!

16

TO MĚSTEČKO. PIOUS FLOCK. ABOUT LUKÁŠ.
A MENTION OF PROKOP. THE DEVIL'S FURROW.
THE MYSTERY OF THE OLD LOG CABINS. IN THE
BENDS . . . THE MILL, NEW SNACK BAR.

Miran steers the fully occupied black Beemer through the rain toward Městečko, the woods outside the windows rippling like splashes of water. And crack, a bolt of lightning slashes down through the wet sky, flickers across the travelers' retinas, disappears.

The two young lasses want to sit next to Kája and whisper in his ear! Wedding, ha! So they can torment him, teasing and cuddling him like a bunny rabbit.

Monča makes them get in the back, on either side of the old man. He runs his paint-crusted hands over their breasts, multiplying the squealing and explosions of laughter, patting them to make sure which is which, then plunges into silence.

They drive on, the sky opening up above the field and meadows, spitting water down on and into the heat-cracked earth, feeding the river's flow, and it's more than the dry ground can contain, the muddy current rising, flooding into the ditches.

As the muck from the deluge spills into the roadway, carrying reed grit, detritus, the surging river leaves behind a trail of mud, a plastic teddy bear floating next to a cat's carcass, the planks of a toolshed smashed to bits against the rocks, sawed logs swept from unknown banks, somebody's pink bathtub.

Here's a truck with a crew of local residents in waders and rubber boots, instead of the usual platoon of Ukie day laborers. They're building a flood wall, sandbags sailing out of the bed of the truck as they race against the overflow.

Miran honks, slowing as he approaches the roadblock, while Kája hollers greetings and jibes at his buddies on the crew, but suddenly Miran frantically brakes, the girls shrieking in terror, even Monča screams as the vehicle, swerving toward the shoulder, nearly strikes the head of the pious flock.

As the Christ-bearers jump out of the way, someone lets go of the poles and the medallions hanging off of them sway wildly, the clusters of wax candles jiggling as the wooden platform to which the Savior is tethered juts over the water, threatening to tumble into the river's murky depths . . . but in the blink of an eye the strapping man at the head of the throng leaps in, a red-eyed albino, bare skull towering over the crowd in the rain, stretching out his arms to grasp the teetering figure. He holds tight until the startled litter-bearers regain their grip on the poles. Then strides off again, the others following behind. As they pass the vehicle's hushed occupants, the truck wheels are nearly touching the stream.

What's goin on? asks Lomoz, lifting his nose as if to sniff the action outside.

Men and women march shoulder to shoulder in raincoats and dark-colored jackets, some still clutching doused candles, a close-packed dark group, caps, hoods on their heads, fresh blushed cheeks of young lasses side by side with faces like withered potatoes. The pilgrims pass the stranded car and disappear around the bend.

A procession, Pops!

Miran starts the car back up.

With Blackie leadin the way, Kája says.

Miran nods.

Black Lukáš, eh? says Lomoz, coming to life. So that was him, was it? Back again, is he?

We've seen him around, Miran reports. His mind churns with the rumors he's heard about this guy. They'd locked him up for dirty deeds eons ago, back when Miran was just a boy, locked him up tight. Now he'd reappeared as a righteous man, and with followers. I'll ask my dad what the story is, Miran thinks, returning his focus to the road.

And good thing too. The famous tree towering by the side of the road for nearly three hundred years had been struck by lightning amid the sudden storm and split in two. Now the mighty giant was strewn across the road, and Miran had to wend his way through the bits and pieces.

So, Pops, Kája inquires. You know Black Lukáš?

You bet I do, son.

So what'd he do?

Awful nasty things, boy, awful!

And how long've you known him?

Since I could still see!

Phew, whistles Kája.

Yep, says the old man in the back seat, puffing out his chest. Back when he was still just a little shit, heh-heh-heh!

So why do they call him Black? I mean, the guy's like an angora.

You don't wanna know, son. Better if you don't!

They head downhill, back toward the river, whose sloping wooded banks, laced with meanders, serve as home to the Old Log Cabins.

Hey, Pops? says the inquisitive young man, refusing to give it a rest. Just tell me at least, did he kill someone?

If only that, boy. If only!

But you killed someone, and I know it, whispers Kája, sorely misjudging the blind man's hearing.

I hear you gibberin up there, says Lomoz, jaw jutting pugnaciously.

The girls listen in, hanging on every word, when all of a sudden everyone gasps as the car crunches over a huge branch, flung onto the road by decree of the lightning.

So tell us then, Pops, says the red-faced Kája, turning to face the back seat.

If I killed someone? Nobody's ever pissed me off enough! thunders the old man, having nearly bitten through his tongue. But you'll be the first if you don't stop joltin us around like that!

The girls burst into giggles, Macinka giving the old man a flirtatious poke in the ribs. So, did you kill somebody or not?

Little girl, I'm of an age where in my day it wasn't that big a deal.

Cabiiins! exclaims Janinka, nose pressed to the glass.

It's only a few, though. One set back just off the road, the others still oozing resin in a deep ravine, hidden in the trees.

That the ravine has been called the Devil's Furrow since time out of mind is a fact the vehicle's occupants have known from the cradle. But what few of them realize is that the black wood structures here once stood in the wild, in spots known only to poachers and a rare few hermits, men of solitude and prayer, living off the air and the occasional minor trespass.

And that a certain one of them named Prokop—perhaps because of his uncompromising stance on the question of sin and his vehemence in combating it, later known as "the dreaded abbot"—hitched the troublemaking devil to a plow and forced him to plow a trench, a deep ravine tailor-made for hideaways, shacks, and log cabins, in short, the illicit dens that later sprang up along it, well suited for runaway slaves and heathens, the latter of which were fleeing the flaming borderlands, wooden granddads in their arms. The ravine went on to hide all sorts of fugitives from civilization, on the run from its executioners and tax collectors, then from billboardists, belligerent left-wing feminist activists arisen from the psychomuck of riverine deposits, Zemanite homunculi sprung from the mire of condom-choked quaking bogs and tampon-clogged toilets, and so on and so forth.

As far back as ancient times, the apostates constructed interlinked systems of well-ventilated caves, inhabited sometimes by robbers and murderers, at others by humble followers of Christ and other fugitives.

And being within spiritual reach of the monastery named after the river, which the illustrious Prokop erected not far from the Furrow, the inhabitants of the forest hideout generally did quite well.

Hard to say whether it was the mystical appeal of the place, the legends of the indomitable local population, or sheer coincidence, but long before the birth of Miran or anybody else in the car, the first bands of tramps had washed up here in the Devil's Furrow and the environs of the capital along with the spiritual seekers just as the smog industry was in bud and the first trams were beginning to run.

These protohippies and paleopunks, with their camping pots and hatchets, and often home-forged guns, founded utopian communes along the riverside. Women and men, boys and girls, luxuriated in nature, and in one another, washing away in the swamps and silver-foamed streams what they scornfully referred to as the skin of civilization, including the most revolutionary views on politics and gender. Devotees of the romantic cult of cooling morning dew, fiery evening skies, and personal armament, they didn't read the newspapers or bother to vote. Persecuted at first by gendarmes and later by commie secret police, hidden in the deep forests around the river, professing the all-embracing love of the creators for the created and vice versa, they were great admirers of the noble savages of the Pacific Coast and cavorted around rough-hewn totem poles carved with demon faces, wolf fangs, and bird beaks, based on the archetypes of the brutal, plundering, slave-taking Kwakiutl and Bella Coola tribes.

In the bends of the Sázava, sliced into the regularly inundated woodland shores, the dreamy tramps built their preapocalyptic communities by the light of nothing but campfires and the heavens and, apart from raucous potlatches held to the accompaniment of their own barbaric music, in deep sylvan silence, ruffled only occasionally by the smack of a beaver's tail or the squeak of a female muskrat being covered by a male.

Miran and his companions, however, know nothing at all of this past.

Their friends live in the Old Log Cabins where they are soon due to arrive, and more than that.

He and the rest of the vehicle's occupants intend to say hello to old man Lojda and their other besties, cousins, and in-laws—who can even remember them all.

It's not as if they have a choice.

Which is why Miran is shocked at the devastated cabin they're passing now. The others in the car are also stunned into silence.

The cabin yawns open, front door ripped off, windows hanging from the hinges. Where usually the yards and gardens stir with little children while the grown-ups lounge around in hammocks and folding chairs, there is no one.

The building even shows signs of fire.

The brothers exchange a quick glance, Miran nods, and Kája slips out of the car, disappearing into the woods.

One of the girls in back asks Miran whether anyone from the cabins happened to call recently?

No.

Miran snatches up his phone. After a moment of tense hesitation, he lays it down again.

What's goin on? Lomoz inquires.

They tell him what they see.

Macinka and Janinka wonder if maybe they should go take a look at the cabin. See how Kája's doing and help him check it out.

Nobody answers them, so they don't budge.

It's takin him long enough, Janinka says crankily.

Monča tells Miran to honk the horn.

Just then, Kája emerges from the forest. They can read the bleakness and ruin on his face as he reaches the car.

Same everywhere? somebody asks.

Yeah, says Kája, describing the fate of the other homes he's seen.

Anybody there? Janinka asks.

No.

So where did all the people go? Macinka wonders.

Must've gone somewhere, Kája shrugs.

Richie'll know where they are, Miran concludes.

Sure, we'll have Richie look into it, Monča nods. Now let's go ask at the mill!

So Miran throws the car into gear and they're off.

And we can grab a hot dog at the gazebo, Janinka says eagerly.

And soda pop and peanuts, Macinka adds with delight.

Head back, mouth open, Lomoz snores away, giant-sized arms folded across his chest, so the two girls pass the rest of the trip in whispers.

Y'know, Black Lukáš and those people of his're comin over too. They're invited to the wedding.

Wait, so why do they call him Black again? Was he locked up for real?

That's the funny thing about it. They locked him up and left him to rot, and he came out a changed man. Not only that, but now he's albino.

What? I thought his name was Lukáš?

It is.

You just said his name was Al Bino!

That's not his name, it just means his hair and skin are white.

Oh, all right. That's almost like my tomcat's name.

What do you call him?

Baltie.

Aww, that's cute.

By now they're coming up on the mill. Everything here is all in one place. They pass under a bridge rising high above the river, reminiscent of the Roman aqueducts guarded by legions and towering over forests full of trees marked for extinction but not yet laid low. The burble of water through the aqueducts sounded like a death knell to the barbarians of the time. In the same way the sound of cars whizzing along the D1 today forecasts the pending retirement of the last tall trees standing, antlers still scratching the sky, on either side of the river, not to mention the wolf pack inhabiting the plentiful gorges and gullies in the vicinity of the Furrow. And here they are at the old-time water mill on the broken-down weir.

Miran slows. He always relishes the sight of the colossus. Though it sends chills down his neck. The mill, which blocks the view of the water, seems indestructible, despite being constantly destroyed by humans and nature in unison.

At one point, the wrong make of turbines was delivered, or they weren't delivered at all. The drainage gullies and channels were clogged by the floods, and the runaway water damaged the iron fencing erected to protect the nonexistent pumps. It bristles up from the cracked walls at varying degrees of uprooting.

The colossus of the mill, pocked with holes and mangled by vegetation, looms over the Sázava. Birches sprout from the roof, the uninhabited rooms covered with old footprints and scraps, their walls puckered with mold. The mill was probably planned and built as the first developers arrived in the wake of the starry-eyed tramps and men of means began erecting villas along the river.

In the time of the comrades, though, many of the luxury villas' inhabitants were flushed into work camps or hounded out of the country, and athletic fields and swimming pools were symbolically transformed into junk depots and potato warehouses. Completion of the mill has constantly been foiled by either war or revolution, so it has never been anything but a shock to the eye, in a state of natural dilapidation calling to mind one of Gaudí's celebrated creations.

Now the mill is surrounded by socialist workers' plasterboard apartments like parasitic fungi on a fallen oak. And up to his waist in the overgrown prickly bushes nearby stands a Red Army soldier, machine gun in hand. Frayed by high winds, battered over the decades by stone throwers bored and hateful alike, the dishonored soldier keeps a vigilant watch, the eastern empire's forward patrol in the Bohemian forest. Perhaps waiting for his still-distant company, already hard on the march. Someone has slapped a pair of sun-bleached blue-and-yellow-striped boxers on his head. His weapon remains steadily aimed into the bushes.

The former workers' apartment blocks have long since been abandoned, windows shattered, doors and window frames pried off, wood consumed by the occasional visitors' fires.

The vehicle's occupants just stare in silence.

A temporary nesting site has sprung up near the apartment blocks along the riverbank, an improvised camp, a little town of tents and shacks, each year washed away by floods or beaten down by autumn.

And the welcoming gazebo, operated by longtime residents at a safe distance from the occasionally falling masonry, is gone.

All that remains are the imprints of wooden boards in the grass.

In its place stands a new, at first glance fairly shady-looking snack shack, kiosk, tap, or bar, wedged directly into the ruins of the mill.

17

The boy bends down to the heap of rags where his little brother lolls on
his back. Gropes around to see if he can find a T-shirt. Anything, rather
than wear a skirt. Even wrap a towel around himself. But all there are
is rags.

He bites into a pear. Sweet juice drips down his chin, blazing a sticky
trail through the coating of soot and dust, little bits of plaster.

He sees his papa out the window.

Veins standing out on his temples, nose sticking out, skirt rolled up,
pushing a wheelbarrow through the wet grass with the spider man inside. The man's arms encircle the stones he holds in his lap. Sharpened
cramp irons jut from the rocks, the cow chain trailing through them
and wrapped around his waist.

The boy takes a big bite of the pear and holds it out to his brother,
who seizes the fruit in his gummy little fingers, bites in, chomps and
slurps.

The ruin is behind them now as they slope down toward the river,
Papa holding tight to the wheelbarrow's grooved handles. Pushing it,
crushing fallen twigs, through the puddles, through the thickets.

The man raises his scrawny arms, flashing through the mist like flying snakes, shielding his eyes from the slashing twigs.

The wheelbarrow carves a furrow in the layers of decomposed duckweed. Water floods into the groove, a grass snake slithers through the
wet. Even the frogs, respectful of the thunderous funeral cavalcade,

rise off their bellies and emerge from the grass in long hops, ruffling the dew-drenched stalks.

Collapsed and shaken by the ride, yet filled with an inner longing for change, the man looks back and sees the shadow of a tall and mighty being upon the water's surface, someone in a flowing cape, horns jutting from his head.

Sonuvabitch, he shrieks softly. Looks at Papa, sees him bent toward the ground cowering, eyes wide.

The apparition vanishes in the wisps of mist.

So you saw it too, says the man warily.

I sure did, mutters Papa, clearly shaken.

Thought it was the devil in my head, come to welcome me, says the man, but looks like it's not that simple.

Some younker on his way to a jamboree, some costume party or what have you, Papa says.

Know what? Keep goin.

Papa nods and they start back up.

Soon, soon, soon we'll will be there, soon, soon, soon, any minute, is the mantra the man whispers as he jolts toward change in the rickety wheelbarrow, full of a joy that inspires him with hope.

The boy watches his papa's flowered blouse and flappy skirt until they vanish into the grass on the downward side of the slope. He stares off into the haze. Glimpses a light, a fiery spot blazing through the mist. Rises up on his toes. Sees the flaming stick the man clutches in his hand as he runs, hears a scream, then the shouting of many throats. The boy cowers at the sound of the roar, which sends a shudder through everything around him.

He runs to the other window. Stares out at the ruin with the tower rising high, at the suddenly crowded graves. They came from the fair, he realizes.

The invaders leap to the ground from the crumbled cemetery wall. Others, having kicked in the flimsy wooden gate, rampage through the graves on their machines, while still others, amid a raucous medley of honking horns, hammer the wall with pickaxes and metal rods, the light from their torches like giant burning match heads.

Garbed in leather jumpsuits, faces covered with animal masks, they leap about among and on the graves, digging away at the hard soil with rods and shovels. A handful of burning torches land on the small church roof.

Someone with a cape fluttering on his back leaps through the fiery mist onto the wall, horned helmet on his head, screeching as he flings to the roof one burning stick after another.

It suddenly hits the boy where he's seen the hulk before: the rock from the fair. And gripping his little brother to his chest as tightly as he can, he stumbles out the door and makes his way over the gravel on his knees. Stained girl's sweatshirt bulging with pears—the skirt pockets don't fit a thing—he crawls along the sharp groove carved in the mud by the wheelbarrow.

Behind him, two louts are smashing the car hood and windows, while someone in a spine-bedecked helmet breaks down the door of the welcoming morgue.

The leather-reinforced men pound away at the car, enthusiasm undampened by the spray of broken glass into their faces and beards, in fact celebrating their wounds, offering up their bloodied faces almost like a sacrifice.

The boy draws himself to his feet. The church tower is behind them now; he can hear the din of destruction. He drags his little brother along through the damp grass, supporting the back of his head with his palm—there are stones in the grass, sticks.

Then he sees his papa.

Papa hurries up the slope. Drops flat when he reaches the top, taking in the scene at the church. Picks himself up, runs, crouching, through the grass to them. Despite his shakes, a wave of warmth washes over the boy. He sits next to his little brother, waiting.

They torched our car, the fucks.

Papa squats. Blouse in tatters. Hair poking out from under his scarf.

If you hadn't seen em, I'd say I was hallucinating. But you did.

The boy nods.

He can feel his papa's palm, stroking his cheek.

Good thing you got outta there. You're a pretty smart kid. For real.

The boy, blushing, doesn't raise his face, leaves his eyes closed. Papa gives him a slap on the back, a love tap to the chest. The pears that had been bulging out of the pink sweatshirt are gone, irretrievably, except for one. Must've rolled out along the way.

Maybe the hicks're on their way to a costume party, son, what do you think?

Papa, pear in hand, takes a bite, talking through the sweet crush of fruit.

No, not them. Fuckin hayseeds.

They trudge along the hillside, step by step. Papa, little nipper in his arms, stops every minute or two. The little one drowses. He reeks to high heaven.

Then they drag themselves back uphill, skirts ripping on the thistles. Papa tears off his lower layer. They sit down, try to rip it up into diapers. But the fabric tears along the threads, it's in shreds before they know it.

A low fence of rusty barbwire extends in front of them. They step over it, entering a gardeners' colony.

They wade through the pliant soil of flower beds and vegetable patches. The boy gets tangled up in a prickly gooseberry bush. Papa joins in as he stuffs berries in his mouth by the fistful, and they stand there, stuffing their faces. Cucumber patch. Papa pulls out one after the other, but they're bitter. He tosses several out before he lands on one he can share with the boy. They walk on, knocking over a ladder holding up an apple tree branch. Trample a few apples bending over to pick it up. Papa swears, kicks in anger, gets tangled in a rosebush. Soil sticks to the soles of their shoes. Papa boots a watering can off into the bushes, knocks over a little fence standing in their way.

Shovels, rakes, spades amid the dim light of the wooden sheds. Stacks of garden lounge chairs like wrinkled, layered tortoise shells.

A branch sweeps the girl's scarf from his head, his skirt chafes against the shrubs. They hop over a thing or two, then crawl under the wire again, looking out for stones, potholes, the boy up to his waist in grass.

They descend along a drop to where the mist seems to gush from the grass. Can't even see their fingertips when they reach out their arms. In the distance they hear a roar. They walk toward the swelling sound until Papa staggers and falls to his knees, keeping a firm hold on the little one, who never so much as bumps the ground.

I hear a river, Papa says.

And lays the child in the grass. Takes out a tube, knocks out a tablet. Breaks it in halves, puts one in his mouth, the other in his son's. Holds the child's mouth shut until his saliva dissolves the pill. Then stretches out on his back. Instantly begins to snore. Softly, eyes closed.

The boy squats down. Squeezes as close to his father and brother as he can.

And stares, eyes bulging wide.

Someone is hastening through the grass straight toward them. Hood on his head. Something glitters in his hand. Striding noiselessly amid the roar of the water, bending the tall grass underneath his feet.

18

THE WATER GOBLIN GANG. CROSSBOW THREAT.
LITTLE CALF. NEWSCAST. WHERE'S LOJDA?
FLUSHED AND SMILING . . .

THE WATER GOBLIN, announces the poster, rendered maybe in lipstick on a strip of gauze or bandage, apparently from the flood aid supplies. It's nailed to a stick that serves as a gate to the new establishment. The place looks truly bleak compared to the gazebo operated by the Old Log Cabineers, but the house is packed. Wired-in radio provides the entertainment, and as the newscast winds down on Sázavan, a dance tune intermingles with the voices of the high-spirited guests.

The early drinkers sit gathered around a keg of beer, ensconced in plastic chairs or just squatting on their haunches. A big man in coveralls and running shoes leans against the keg, old man Bajer, as he's familiarly known to the lushes, a leather waiter's wallet draped around his neck. A blubber-faced patron dumps in a fistful of change while blowing into a harmonica, accentuating the newscast with variations on the theme from *Once Upon a Time in the West*. It's hard to count how many bums there are, since even when they're kneeling down, watching the pan on the propane burner, they're in constant motion. The raggediest of them all, resembling a giant frog, pokes the chunks of meat with a fork torn from a tree.

Beyond the guests, a counter protrudes from a dark rift amid the brickwork. Stacks of Tatranka and Fidorka chocolate-coated wafers, bags of chips and pretzel sticks, candies in bright-colored wrappers, by the bag and individually, Russian-style. Colorful bottles of liquor, bottles and cans of beer, and other riches of the earth. The smell of plenty wafts from the concession window, burnt fat. And perhaps even a tang of blood hangs in the air.

Another resident shouts out a request for surplus change, examining the sores on his calf as he sits on the wooden steps hammered together from logs.

You can have a soda at home, Monča says like some school bus attendant.

Clearly the mill has been abandoned by the amiable Old Log Cabineers. Monča regards the ragtag strangers with disgust.

But Janinka and Macinka have already leaped from the car, dashing up the steps with the voraciousness of baby goats, while the beggar, taking the rush of thighs, knees, buttocks whooshing past his nose for a mirage, goes back to minding his business, attending to the shooting pains in his leg.

The girls crowd into the window, totally blocking it. Waving his fork, the man guarding the pan extends a few predictably lascivious offers their way, rasping in a high, thin voice. The fat man with the harmonica turns out to be a real nuisance, burying his instrument in his pocket to give Janinka a slap on her black denim–clad ass.

She wheels on him with a few clear gestures.

The drifters' laughter is almost jubilant.

I just want a soda, the girl tells the clown, sticking her head back in the gap. The musicman is still all over her. Meanwhile, some overtattooed suitor grabs Macinka and tries to sit her down on his lap. She resists so successfully, she knocks him over and the chair along with him.

Oh boy, says Kája, opening the car door.

Janinka's screams freeze him dead in his tracks. It's like somebody in the concession window has her head clamped in a vise, braids and all. Her whole body thrashes and jerks, but her head remains trapped. The screaming stops. For an instant. Then, for a few cruel, eardrum-slicing picoseconds, it intensifies again almost to the level of a circular saw.

The lecherous harmonica player is long retreated at this point. But there's something in that window.

Kája drags Janinka away from the opening, and a man they haven't seen till now suddenly appears. Aiming a crossbow at Kája, he extends the loaded weapon through the aperture.

No one's giggling now. Even the frogman at the pan stops croaking. The only sound is the announcer of world news rattling on from the radio, choking on the importance of his message.

Kája pushes Janinka behind him, facing down the crossbow with his chest. Stares a second or two at the double-edged arrowhead. The margins have been filed down to ensure that they penetrate as deeply as possible.

We're leavin now, Kája announces to the window.

Avoiding the mendicant, still asking alms, they walk down the steps, climb in the car, and drive off without delay.

What were you screamin about back there, girl? The news get you that upset? Lomoz asks.

They killed a calf, Janinka blurts. They shot a little calf with an arrow back there in that nasty hole in the wall. The butcher had a headlamp on, so I could see it perfectly, the whole execution.

That's no execution, the old man grumbles. That's illegal slaughter. Execution's somethin else, silly.

What kina animals are these guys? Where's Uncle Lojda? Who're these people he let come crawlin in here? the driver rages, practically gnashing his teeth.

They were just sayin on Sázavan how the workers from Ukraine here don't wanna stay. Were you tryin to change some Ukie's mind, zat what you were screamin about? the old man inquires.

I wasn't listenin, Kája admits. So where'd they go? he asks politely, peeking over at Miran.

Sittin on your ears, I guess, the old man says with a touch of brusqueness. They were just sayin how the Ukies back home are buildin a wall two thousand kilometers long.

What for? asks Kája.

Keep out the Russians, someone explains.

Will that help? Kája wonders.

No, somebody else opines.

I can picture it now, the old man says. The men buildin a wall, standin watch with guns. The women cookin borscht, pelmeni, whatever they got over there, sittin around the kettles at night. Keepin warm, eatin, waitin. Will the enemy tanks come, or not? Just like the old days! What I'd like to know is whether they already got any concentration camps.

I read in the paper they were swappin prisoners!

That means there aren't that many of em. Don't worry, we'll see concentration camps yet. But don't get mad at me, folks. I seriously don't care anymore.

The old man falls silent.

Hey, girls, I got some sodas here, Monča interrupts. Who wants a Mirinda?

Bro, Kája says, nudging Miran in the ribs. Old man Bajer was there. I'll go back and deal with his boys later. I was just itchin to smash the place up, he whispers into the driver's ear, but I booked cause of the girls.

Any Fanta? asks one of the girls.

Fanta too! says Monča.

You handled yourself excellently, bro, says Miran.

I'll take a Fanta then. Or Mirinda, whatever, says Kája. And, slightly flushed and smiling, he gazes out the window.

19

REUNION WITH SCALES THE FISHERMAN. HER
FADING FACE. AT HOME WITH SCALES. WASHED-UP
STUFF. LOVE IN THE SHACK. THE COLONISTS'
REVENGE. INTO THE BOAT. AND IN THE FLOW.

And that someone bending the grass is hastening toward them.

The boy tugs on Papa's leg.

Hey there, ladies!

From up close he's more stocky, a square-built man, smelling of aqueous ozone laced with the scent of rot. Black hair curls from under the hood of his rain slicker. He clutches his fishing rod like a gleaming sword.

But suddenly he wavers. Takes a closer look at them, bursts out laughing.

Papa rubs his eyes.

Stares a brief moment.

Hello, Slavoj, he says.

Tab. Well fuckin A, Tabby! What're you doin here?

What about you?

Look, get yourselves together, we're gettin outta here, the fisherman orders them, still grinning as he scours them with his eyes. I'm talkin *now*, yeah?

So they stand, Papa scooping up the younger boy, sleepy little head bobbing on his father's shoulder. Birds chirp nervously as they make their way down the slope. A blanket of mosquitoes descends out of nowhere, clogging their pores. They can't even close their eyes without wiping away a bloody shred.

The fisherman leads the way. Papa stumbles along right behind, and trudging in the rear is the boy, water clasping his ankles with every touch of his foot to the ground. As he scrambles to keep up with the men, the young puck's tears, both caked-on and presently gushing, combine with the grease from the grill shack on his face to form a much-needed antimosquito mask.

He wants to call her forth within himself and bring her to life. Her face. He could scrawl her name in the mud with his finger. He remembers his mother's scent. Then forgets it so quickly he's almost amazed. He is absorbed in everything going on. Looking out for sharp branches. For stones beneath the soggy moss. Her image within him dims with every step, with every nearly obscene slurp as his sandals sink into the footprints of the men ahead of him.

The man in the slicker patters along at a brisk pace. Papa clomps along elephant-style. As the humans squish across the vivifying floor, a vibration of the subtlest frequencies seeps up toward them out of the algae, visible only under a microscope, multiplying in numbers quantifiable only by astronomy. Myriads of tiny shells move in copulatory bliss amid the tracks left behind in the soddening moss. Intoxicated springtails and whole armies of stone flies, bacchanalian revelers of the aquatic realm, frolic in the splashings. Creatures that live hours, days, only to serve as sanctuaries for larvae, planktonic organisms, and enormous water bugs, mandibled warriors, water-striding boyars of the insect kingdom. The humans make their way through this kingdom with great self-assurance. Yet it seems the orator in Papa has perished entirely under the onslaught of all the stinging and sucking and biting.

Now, nothing but sonuvabitch, piece of shit, and cunt spews from his mouth as he strains to exhale the insect bodies crushed in his teeth.

Every few moments he stops to readjust his son on his chest, scratching his belly, yowling, slapping at his behind, and the air rings with the sound of the fisherman's hearty laughter.

Exasperated, Papa yanks off the flowery blouse, tears off his remaining breast and flings it into a puddle. Then peels off his thorn-tattered skirt, dotted with knots of clotbur stuck to it like adhesive tape.

Exposed to the bugs in nothing but briefs and a T-shirt of indefinite color, he trudges after the fisherman, little son in his arms.

The fisherman plants his rod in the muck and opens up his slicker. Unwinds a laundry line he has wrapped around his hips and fastens the child to his chest with the help of sailor's hitches, as he makes sure to emphasize.

The stench and heat pouring off the snoozing little boy don't seem to bother the man. The child's head bulges roundly from his chest.

Someone stumbling across them, with no insight into the situation, might even marvel. Perhaps they would take the fisherman for a freak of nature, a polycephalic creature, hidden from human view in the swamps.

The boy watches his little brother breathing noiselessly through parted lips. Notices, too, the mosquito bites on his tiny little cheeks.

But what can he do? Nothing.

He uses the break to liquidate the colony of mosquitoes on his own face.

The fisherman reaches into his pocket, takes out a tin box, removes a rolled cigarette, lights it with a match, and exhales the smoke right into the boy's face.

He lights one up for Papa too, hands it over the boy's shoulder.

Thank God, sings Papa. He comes to life, sucking in hit after hit, exhaling, blowing smoke all over his body.

The two men stand side by side, puffing away, bending and twisting and slapping each other on the back, issuing smoke to the four winds and every other which way.

I got loads a these, says the fisherman, patting the pocket where he sank the box.

We could do with some threads.

Got those too.

They puff away, intently.

And here I thought you was some stray whores, says the fisherman. You know there's whores out here stealin babies.

Seriously?

Yep. Fuck round the clock, but that still ain't enough for em. They want a kid. Only natural, they bein women. Some of em's so worn out, though, they'd rather just steal it.

Papa sucks the last of the butt through his fingers. He hisses in pain, then stabs it into the moss. The fisherman hands him another.

I ain't talkin prostitutes from some bar, though. I just mean regular women.

Seriously?

But these ones here ain't no garden colony women, uh-uh, I says to myself. Is it gypsies, come to ransack? And turns out it's Tabby! Ha-ha! Dressed like a broad! Tab and his boys! I recognized you right away. And you recognized me too. That's great.

Yep. So how you been?

What're you all decked out like that for? Look at you! Ha-ha-ha!

The fisherman laughs so hard he chokes. Takes a few steps back and sizes Papa up. Slides his gaze to the boy. And guffaws. The whole time puffing away, his free hand relentlessly batting smoke into the face of the attacking hordes.

First off I says to myself, this short one's got her hair cut like a boy. Aha, she must have lice. Imagine someone in our class at school havin lice back in the day! I mean, gypsies, sure, but otherwise? Lice under socialism? Talk about a hoo-ha! Now the kids today got em all over again.

Oh, really?

Oh yeah, nature's healin itself. Beavers comin back, we got muskrats, eels. Man, herons got nests where there used to be nothin.

Muskrats? I heard it was wild nutrias!

We got both. Only difference is nutrias have yellow snouts. What're you doin here, Tabby?

Me and the boys stopped by to see Ma.

Okay! You know what? Come on back to my shack, long as we're here.

Have you got something to eat?

Sure do!

Is it far?

Nope!

So what're you doin here, Slavoj?

I don't get up to the colony much. Only for a spell, when none of em's around. Steal me a turnip now and then, some carrots or squash here and there. Mornins only. These weekend gardeners, they're so stupid they can't even tell.

Ha!

You ain't gonna give me away, are you?

Of course not!

C'mon then. We'll get eaten alive out here.

And the fisherman bundles down the hillside.

He waits on them once they reach the spot where the steep slope changes to soggy riverbank. They tramp on across the wobbly marsh.

The hollows of their footprints fill with greenish water. They pick their way across slippery boards, dotted with leeches. Epidemic-inducing mosquitoes and buffalo gnats rise from all sides, sating themselves into a state of vegetative bliss on the hairless carcass of a dog. Hopping from one fascine to the next, the fisherman and his weary followers make their way to the river.

Water dashes against the rocks along the riverbank, and standing amid the fast-moving current is a shack on stilts. Black; through the nettles and hogweed, the thickets and scrub, imperceptible.

The fisherman gropes in the nettles, leaning into the undergrowth. Pulls out a lengthy ladder-ramp hammered together with rusty nails.

He sinks one end into the slippery mud of the bank and lets go. The other end, weighted with slant-nailed blocks of wood, bangs into the planks of the rugged walkway that runs around the shack.

The fisher slowly steps onto the first rung, ostentatiously demonstrating the gangplank's stability. Then, using his fishing pole for balance, he sprints across, the small boy safely attached to his belly, and leaps straight through the door in the blackened wall of the shack. Papa follows right behind. Undies hoisted, T-shirt flapping, grasping the sky with outstretched arms, he teeters precariously on one of the rungs before finally making the leap and vanishing from sight. The boy shoots across, practically with his eyes closed, sailing in behind them.

Into the darkness and stink of fish and musty rags.

As he slips on the threshold, he suddenly realizes that the damp, slimy alabaster is actually fish scales. Sucked into the dark of the shack, he bumps into a pail full of water, spraying some of it across the floor, so decides he'd better stay put.

He hears a rustle of paper. The fisherman lights a ball of crumpled newspapers under the brushwood in the stove. After that, the square-shouldered goblin, casting a feeble shadow, lights a candle, revealing the dwelling's cozy interior.

A table and chairs hammered together from warped tree roots. Stumps hatchet-sculpted into chieftain's thrones, with burly armrests of planed branches recalling antlers. An evident relict of tramp culture, the pride of Sázava DIYers, a ritual site unquestionably created with people in mind.

Indeed, any visitor younger than the boy might well have taken their host for a water sprite, a creature, despite his foul-smelling earthiness, created out of mist, marsh gas, algae, fins, crayfish shells.

The brownish dry rot relentlessly growing through the dwelling's walls, foaming with a pinkish mold around the edges, may also have contributed to the effect.

Peering into the corners of the room, the visitors see charred mugs and cups, canisters, stacks of bulging plastic bags, mounds of rags, plates, a heap of unmatched utensils.

Behind the snooze pit of mattresses, clearly damp and sticky, their host keeps a smallish, homemade workbench with a vise and clamp, a rusty engine for something or other lying underneath.

The boy peeks into the pail he nearly kicked over. Little fins slosh inside, jaws flash. Dare he stick his finger in? Something crawls along the bottom.

The fisherman unlatches the hook and opens the window. Light bursts into the room. The murmur of the current beneath and around them intensifies. The boy steps up on his tiptoes. In the distance he sees the treetops on the riverbank opposite.

And there's something else in here.

As the sunshine fills the room with light, they suddenly see the shack's rear wall.

And the face of the Virgin appears. Warped with moisture, collapsing inward on itself, making her ardent features seem somehow coarser and wilder. Yet in spite of the turbid water's roar, the gloom descending from every corner, and the processes of decay all around, she still retains a trace of girlish comeliness. Her noble figure garbed in typical desert attire. Her simple sandals. The knoll. The knoll where the Virgin stands awaiting the Holy Spirit.

In fact the onlookers need not be either chin-stroking biblicists or ruminating polymaths, or even venerable, high-frequency meditating art historians, for it to be obvious that this is the painting.

The Holy Madonna of Poříčí. The Expectant Virgin, aka the Virgin on the Mount.

Either that or a reproduction, familiar to them from countless publications, textbooks, postcards, tourist trinkets, and buttons, not to mention the blurry caricatures and smudged obscene cartoons spewed from rotary presses over the course of numerous anti-Church campaigns by feeble-minded Communists and pathetic Zemanites.

The lustrous gold picture frame alone, studded with apples, lambs, angels, figs, and other similar flourishes, feels like an embarrassment of riches amid the crudeness of the shack.

As father and son study the picture, the fisherman tidies up around the room. Feeds the stove with brush and wood chips, runs a broom over the tree-root table. Only then does he finally shed his slicker. Kicks it into the corner and unfastens the child.

Gently, using both hands, he lays him on the table. First spreading out a tablecloth or whatever it is. He agilely and quickly undresses the child. Wipes him clean with a newspaper scrap. Rinses him off with water, which he scoops from a pot on the stove.

You fellas're pigs! Why, this boy's in shit to his ears. And fuller a pee than a pisspot. Christ, look at the bambam on him! He's all covered in hair! How old'd you say he is, Tabby?

Mmmm, says Papa, still absorbed in the picture.

Boy, the fisher says, tossing his head. Hand me a rag.

The boy pulls a T-shirt from the heap in the corner, takes a sniff. It's huge, so he tears it in two. His mama would have done the same, she wouldn't have asked anyone.

Jeepers, we aren't a wee little babykins anymore. No more cuppy-cake, are we? Jeepers, look at us, isn't that right? Isn't that right?

Papa settles into a tree-root chair and, making himself at home, carelessly reaches under the table, pulls out a two-liter plastic bottle, opens it, tilts it to his mouth, and drinks.

As the little boy stares up at him, tiny mouth spread wide in a smile, and gently fidgets under his paws, the fisherman wraps him in the diapers torn by his big brother. He rolls the newspaper and rags that he used to clean the child with into a smelly ball, flings it out the window into the watery abyss running beneath and around them.

Kneels down to the pail of creepy crawlies and washes off his mitts. From under the table between Papa's knees he fishes out a big wicker bag. Tosses out what's inside, kicks it to the wall, lays a few rags on the bottom after holding them up to the light. Lays the child in the bag. Fits him like a cradle. The fisherman puts him under the table.

No yellin or cryin? None at all? Now that's what I call a big little kid. What's with him anyway?

Never mind, Papa says with a wave of the hand. Just let him get some rest.

The fisher turns to the boy.

Now don't look!

From a sack on the floor he produces one, two turtles, and one after the other slices off their heads. Tosses them, eyes rolled back, into the corner.

He opens the stove door and lays the shells, limbs dangling out, onto the glowing coals inside. Leaves the door open a crack.

He takes a little fish from the pail, chops off the head, scrapes off the scales with a knife, collects them together with his foot, digs out the innards, sweeps them up with the scales, kicks them into the corner along with the bladders and heads.

He prepares four fish in this way.

Placing a good-sized gleaming skillet on top of the stove, he melts a lump of butter spooned out of a mug. Lays the fish in the pan. Salts and seasons them with a variety of spices stored in plastic containers decorated to look like Snow White and the dwarfs.

How'd you come by that? Papa inquires, nodding toward the picture.

Didn't walk outta church with it, did I? Got it outta the water.

Shit, that looks like the Poříčí Madonna. The Virgin on the Mount. Is it?

That's her.

Hm, says Papa.

So tell me, what were you wearin those women's clothes for? Wouldn't happen to have any bread, would you, boys? Used to have potatoes, but I forgot and they went rotten. All I got now's some old bread. I can throw it in the pan, though, soften it up. Put it in with the fish, soak up the juice. I got cucumbers too. Tomatoes. I could maybe chop some up for salad, yeah?

Mmmm.

Don't drink that whole thing!

Shit, that'd kill me. Božkov rum, am I right? What're you doin keepin it in a beer bottle, man. Hm, I could do with a beer, come to think of it.

I'm not much of a drinker myself, tipplin was more Dora's thing.

Booze these days is garbage, people die from the stuff. It'll blind you on the spot.

Maybe before, when people were distillin it themselves.

The hell're you talkin about? There's five thousand people gone blind in this country, and some're even more fucked than that, some're even dead. Saw it on the TV, down at the Vulture, that pub at the station in Čerčany. Good klobásy there. Don't have a telly myself.

Tainted booze?

TV's always goin on about thefts at the bottling plants. Tabloids too. It's everywhere. How many people gone blind, outta their minds. You think maybe the Islamists poisoned our booze? That'd be just like em. I don't have a telly myself, like I said.

Hm.

I got condensed milk, though. Dora used to put it in her coffee.

The fisherman punches open a can. Hands the boy a lump of hard bread.

Make a pacifier.

The boy tears a morsel of bread off the lump, drips milk on it. Takes a lick. And pops it in his mouth. But there's still plenty left, so he crawls under the table, thrusts a sopping morsel into his little brother's mouth. The little nipper practically inhales it.

So he gives him another. And another. The little mouth just laps it up.

The fisherman turns to Papa. So it's true what people said, that you were outta the country and don't know the news. We got a booze epidemic here. Thank God I don't drink too much, just tie one on every once in a while.

That's true, Slavoj, I was gone.

Folks said they saw you on television. Said you were in Italy and all over the damn place. Me I don't go nowhere, I just stay put. Doesn't bother me none.

She really just floated in on the water then, yeah?

So you were all decked out like that for a play?

We were down at the fair.

Oh, okay! Little stinker eats that pacifier up, don't he?

The fisherman takes a piece of fish in a spoon. Brings it to the mouth of the little nipper, resting peacefully at the bottom of the bag. He sucks it in and swallows.

Give him a drink from that watering can. And come eat, before it gets cold!

Between the three of them, they devour every last bite.

What do they call you, young one? Kids call me Uncle Scales, go figure. What's your name? Don't you talk? Hey, Tab, don't your boy talk?

Not yet.

Oh well, kids're like that sometimes.

Scales, ha-ha, Papa chuckled. Is that what they call you now, Slavoj?

Yeah, well, I sell folks fish here and there. By the grocery, down the pub, wherever people's at. Glad you remember my name! Famous actor, seen the world, and still hasn't forgot his old buddy.

Oh, gimme a break!

The fisherman takes out tobacco, papers, rolls a smoke. Hands the first one to Papa.

You got that right, Papa says. No pussy, no tobacco, ain't no fun in this house, Jacko. Know who wrote that? Hrabal.

Yeah, well, Dora used to be the one did the sweepin up. Now it's up to me, yup.

Hey, you know this shack of yours'd make a great place to write. I could write a chunk, take a walk along the riverbank, write another chunk.

Of what?

Or I could write, go for a boat ride, and then come back and write! Writing needs a healthy rhythm, know what I mean? That's the main thing. Anyway, who's Dora?

Dora, you know, the fisherman says, reaching for the broom in the corner. He sweeps the fish, turtles, and remnants of God knows what other lives into a heap by the threshold.

Pick somethin out, he tells Papa, gesturing at the heap of clothes. You too! It's horrible, you runnin around in a little girl's skirt! Dora washed all that, it's from the water, good as new. Whenever a flood sweeps away the fences and clotheslines, there's clothes every time, always.

The boy digs around for a tracksuit and he'd like to get hold of a sweater too, but his papa's rummaging through the heap, trying on shorts and suspenders.

Blue as the ocean, Papa delights, pulling a striped T-shirt from the bottom and slipping it on. Have you got another slicker?

Sorry, Tab. I spend all my time down here by the water, y'know. No cell phone, no TV, none a that. What do I need a fridge for? Nobody comes lookin for me. But down there by the Vietnamese grocery, the fellas sometimes meet up out on the playin field, and we talk. One of em works in the forest, nother one up and down the river. There's a campground manager comes sometimes, few other boys. Great bunch we got, I tell you.

Oh yeah?

I mean, I don't drink, but I'll have a few beers. The Vietnamese stays open all the time, so we shoot the shit.

Yeah?

I heard old Hrozen passed away. So congratulations, old buddy. I mean condolorosa. Shit, I mean condolences, is what I'm tryin to say.

Thanks, Slav. You know, we all gotta go someday. Don't suppose you might have a wee bit of sugar to go in that rum? Not used to it like I used to be.

Well, you're not obliged, y'know? Nobody's forcin you, Tabby! My boy lost his taste for Czech rum, runnin around out there in the world?

Not entirely, Papa grins, refilling his glass.

Nothin wrong with Soňa, I always did like her. Great gal, no doubt. But old Hrozen, well, can't blame you for that fallin-out.

The boy is still poking around the clothes heap. Coveralls, too big. Rags and patches of cloth, an old tarp, string shoes, a brassiere. A green bathrobe, large. He gets tangled up in an old net, crashes to the floor. So after that he just sits.

Hrozen was an animal when it came to young folks, you know that. Any vagabonds came passin through, he just kicked em out. But if they were from around here, boy, he gave em the business. Anybody had long hair, police'd cut it off and kick their ass, sonsabitches. You wanna disgrace my district, you cocksucker? he'd say. And then it was off to the races! Slapped me across the ears, piece a shit cop. How was I sposta climb up on scaffolding and roofs with my head ringin after that, huh? I wanted to be a roofer. It's his fault I'm rottin here! But whatever, I'm all right. Down here by the water where the air's healthy and all.

You got it set up nice here. No phone, though, huh?

What for?

Well, so what's up with that picture anyway, Slavoj? It's weird you havin it out here in your hut, you gotta admit!

Like I told you, I found it washed up. Caught in the branches. A ball of lightning hit the church in Poříčí twice. Everything in it washed away, even the pews, must be from that. Me and Dora heard it on the radio.

You got a radio?

Yeah. No batteries, though.

Hm.

Vietnamese fella's got batteries cheap, but he don't take fish. Got this rice he makes and fries up with frozen fish in there. Said he doesn't like the taste a things from the river. What're you gonna do?

Uh-huh.

The fisherman finishes sweeping up. Sits down at the table, hangs his head, broom in his fist.

You think that picture was stolen? he says after a moment or two. Like some church thiefs took it out on the river, lightning sank em, and it floated away? Man, if I had to go and report everything that washed up here, I think I'd shit my pants. And besides, nobody gives a shit about me either. And so what? It's not a bad thing. Doghouse washes up, pile a clothes still on the line, armchair from time to time, you'd be amazed. That all can be bartered, understand. You know how much soup costs at the Vietnamese? Six crowns, for cryin out loud! Four crowns! You wouldn't believe the stuff that washes up here.

But is that the real picture, though?

It's her all right! Man, I spent years standin under that painting as an altar boy. Scored me some points with old Hrozen and the other commies later on. And she floated right up here to me, there you go.

Yeah, but shit, I mean that thing's worth millions. You're rich! Smuggle it into Germany, you could get millions! We just have to find a collector. I'm tellin you, all hell would break loose.

What Germany? I ain't budgin. It's stayin right here, just like it is. For prayin to, why not? Only place I ever go is Čerčany for some gizzards or maybe a run down to the grocery and back. I don't go to Benešov no more. Who wants to put up with that, ridin the bus back and forth like an idiot. Not to mention how much it costs.

So does anyone know you have it here?

189

Nah. Folks couldn't give two hoots what the river brings my way.

That's true, says Papa, and pours himself another drink.

Listen! Those were the days! I used to ride all up and down this river, all over the place, fishin, and when I came home, Dora was here. That was the nicest part.

What do you mean ride? You floated! On a river you float!

She's a strange one, I guess you'd say. No beauty, but a good woman, believe me, boys! We'd buy chicken gizzards, liverwurst. She used to come to the gardens with me. We never took anything cept a melon, couple tomatoes, stuff for soup. Those dummies don't even notice. And when I was out on the water, she would wait for me. Anyway, where would she go? Only then that fella showed up.

What fella?

He shows up all beat up and spit out, and how'd he even find out about my shack is what I wanna know. Did he know the place from before? Some little boys tell him where I live? And right off the bat he's all, "Buy a pan, shiny, brand new, like the dogs just licked it clean." Had all sorts. Luggin em round in a pack on his back. From little guys for eggs to this big fella here—the fisherman taps the pan on the table with his broom. And he's like, "Could you let me rest up here a few days, you think? I can pay! And take any pan of your choice." So he stayed holed up here a couple days and I went out like normal. Didn't suspect a thing, just took him for one a those rich fresh-air hounds from Prague. Guy's nuts, I says to myself. Wants a taste a nature—wake up early, shit in the water, that sorta thing. Experience somethin new. Course I didn't realize he was scared, that they was lookin for him!

Who?

The boys, that's who. Local boys.

What for?

Well, he pulled a fast one.

Okay.

So I come home and Dora's nowhere to be found. And neither is he. Dora coulda gone out if she'd wanted. Whole time she was here. She coulda got outta the shack on her own. I mean, it's not like the door is sturdy. I did used to lock her in, it's true, but it's not my fault she didn't have the brains to open it herself. Kick down the door, though? She wouldn't a dared do that.

You had her trained.

We loved each other! Whenever I came floatin up, I'd touch my chest and feel that cord with the key. And I'd say to myself, Now I'll open the door and get to see Dora.

So you did lock her in then?

Yeah. And maybe he felt like somehow he was settin her free. But what did he want her for? So he could bang her off in the bushes! Sorry to be so down to earth, boys, but that's a load a crap. They coulda been shaggin here easy, I wouldn't a known shit. And like I said, she was no beauty. Maybe he took her to carry around that backpack a his. Ordered her to come with him, so she went. It was awful. I come home and she's not here.

Leaning on the broom, the fisherman breaks at the waist, crushes his fists into his eyes, stays like that awhile. Shudders. Gives out a series of whimpering groans. He is truly sobbing.

Papa descends from his tree-root throne.

There, there, he says, patting the fisherman on the shoulder. It'll be all right!

Grabs a bottle, pours till the liquor splashes over the sides of the glass, slides the shot in front of the teary-eyed man.

The fisherman straightens. Reaches out, snatches up Papa's glass, and drains it. Only then does he notice the glass that Papa poured for him, and he downs that as well.

For Chrissakes, folks! he says, smacking himself in the forehead. I forgot all about the cucumbers! We got radishes, tomatoes. I'll make us up a salad!

And the fisherman starts right in, chopping and slicing away on the workbench, at his feet a plastic bag that looks to be overflowing with dirt—soil, sand, it fairly flies as he pulls the vegetables from it.

Slavoj, buddy!

Heh?

Look what I got for you.

Papa lays down a thousand-crown bill, then another, slapping them against the tabletop. Then slides them under a heavy ashtray overflowing with butts.

This is yours!

What?

You're talkin goose gizzards, liverwurst, buses to Benešov or whatever armpit. Batteries—I don't know what all. Look, I can take care of it. Two thousand Czech crowns. Cash on the barrel!

Look, I donno. The fisherman is rinsing off the sliced vegetables in a little plastic bucket.

I promise you I'll get the most amazing copy made. You'll still have the picture hangin here. What do you care as long as it looks the same, right?

I donno, I donno.

Slavoj, I'm tellin you, use your head!

You said yourself it was worth more than that.

But I don't have more.

A-hah!

So how about it? Who else'll make you an offer like that?

I donno. It washed up here, now it's here. I can tell you the rest a what happened with that fella, though.

Slavoj, buddy. One more thing. The way you take to my little boy, it got me thinkin. You and Dora had a little one here, didn't you?

A little one in a shack like this? Sick all the time? He's better off in the hospital. And that's where I ran into him again.

Who?

That fella with the pans! Stumbled on him by mistake. I was lookin for the floor with the newborns. I had dropped the little one off at the reception so they could take care a him, but how was I sposta know where they put him? So I'm wanderin around the place, and suddenly I'm in the men's ward. And there he is, in a wheelchair. By the coffee machine. Is that really him? I says to myself. It is! And he's totally beat down, can't even walk. Well, shit! Did I wanna kill the guy? You bet, for causin me that disaster. But I took it back right there on the spot. Revenge belongs to God, they say, and boy, did he get it bad. Who did it? Hell if I know! Hey, help yourselves, dig in! Your tastebuds're in for a treat, you'll see.

Another pan lands on the table. Piled high with finely chopped tomatoes and cucumbers and radishes. And something gluey besides, little lumps. Some fish thing or other.

The boy plants himself on the armrest of the tree throne, swinging his feet, his dirty-nailed mitts eagerly snatching up the fruits of the earth.

They chew, smacking their lips. Every minute or two they spit out a grain of sand, a little piece of twig.

The fisherman slides Snow White to them, filled to the rim with salt. Pours them each a brimming glass of water out of the watering can.

So I ran into him again, there at the hospital in Benešov. And I see his wife just got there, beautiful lady, nicely dressed, little daughter with her. They're sittin with him, sad as can be, strokin him and cryin. And their daddy don't even notice em. Doesn't even talk. Poor guy. Lovin family like that and he just ignores em, carryin on. So he got his punishment. But why should they be punished too? Just the way it goes. Well, but like I said, I ain't goin there no more.

Not even to see the little one?

Far as they're concerned, I ain't his father. What do you want here this time, says this one nurse, fuckin cunt. Get outta here! says this stuck-up cow. What're you raisin your voice at me for, shit. Can you believe it? Like I was trackin dirt in or somethin! They're just nasty there, no joke. I brought a plastic bag a fish, brought em some kohlrabi couple a times, always checked in like you're supposed to, but I couldn't get through!

So they tossed you out every time . . . no pasarán?

But anyways, I said to myself, he'll be better off there! He'd catch an infection here! Boy had hives from everything, scabies. Little nipper woulda coughed himself to death. And Dora, well . . . she didn't understand. But I knew it was better to put him there than keep him here to die.

I'm amazed they even let you stay here.

I wish you'd a been here to tell Dora that. All those checkups from the office, personnel and all that stuff, I don't even know . . . she didn't have a clue.

Shit, Slavoj, Papa says, choking. Are you sayin she had the kid here?

That's right. And I took him away while she was asleep. She looked all over for him. I'm tellin you, it was sad!

So you didn't tell her?

Tell her, not tell her . . . you think she'd a understood? When she went off with that Prague fella, I said to myself, Uh-huh, she's still tryin to find him. And I kept on goin to the hospital, thinkin I'd run into her there. Thinkin Dora might hunt him down by intuition, or somethin, bein a female. But she ain't that smart.

Bam! Something hits the wall of the shack from outside. Then again. What's that? wonders Papa. Hail?

Boom! So loud the fisherman jumps in the air. Then again, a solid shot to the roof.

The fisherman flies out the door, Papa's boy at his heels. Their adversaries are standing on the riverbank.

Come on out! cries one of them, apparently weak of sight. The boy and the fisherman are standing on the plank walkway in plain view.

The stones fly. And not just little ones anymore. The attackers have wrenched some hefty rocks out of the muddy bank, and two or three have already banged into the roof.

Hey, Scalester, what's that you got in your hand? Who's that for? hoots a gangly fellow in a straw hat, stepping out onto the first rung of the catwalk.

How many of them are there, hopping around on the riverbank over there? Seven, nine, maybe as many as twelve locals . . . plus someone on the slope . . . another creeping through the reeds . . . a woman in men's boxer shorts and a lilac bra, shaking her fist at them from across the water.

I was choppin vegetables, shouts the fisherman, slipping the knife behind his back.

Exactly, snorts the woman. Our vegetables!

There are also a few children there, sliding down the slope, giggling, making funny faces, hiding behind the grown-ups. But one young lad comes running up, stops on the bank, drops his track pants, and flashes his bare behind at the fisherman and the boy. The lilac woman tags him so hard he staggers.

Listen, neighbor, this has gone far enough! a somber-faced fellow with whiskers declares above the hubbub in a mighty bass. He pokes at the ramp with a tennis-shoed foot. Just first put down the knife, please, if you don't mind? Then c'mere so we can talk man to man. Or do we have to come get you? The spokesman raises his hands, signaling to the others with the rocks and stones to stop.

One tumbles into the water right in front of him, dousing the sturdy man with a geyser of dirty water.

The fisherman dashes into the shack, then reemerges, now wielding a broom instead of a knife. He bends down to the catwalk and, with a few sharp blows of the broom, knocks it into the rush of swirling water below. It circles in the current, stirring the foam and duckweed along the bank, and poof, disappears into the passing flow.

The bearded man, hands cupped at his mouth so his voice can be heard above the waters, declares, word by word, as if attempting to cast a spell: This . . . isn't . . . about . . . some . . . onions . . . man . . . but . . . what . . . about . . . our . . . fences? You trampled our plots like a herd of pigs! You're through here, Scales! he says, now shrieking in rage.

You crushed it all, you bastard, someone chimes in.

My roses, wails somebody else.

And where's my watering can? the lanky man in the straw hat demands. That was my favorite!

Greedy thief, screams the hussy in boxers, arm comically cocked, ladylike, at the elbow. She flings a stone, which barely reaches the middle of the stream.

At which the garden colony youngsters, all boys, start hurling rocks again, with fiendish accuracy. This is no longer just a warning shot or two. The fisher takes one or two hits right away, and the shots rain down around the boy while he cowers under cover of the partway open door.

Two or three men from the wrathful flock return to fishing serious roulders out of the mud, casting them at the roof with gales of laughter, causing the hut to shake with cracks, bangs, thunderous blows.

A couple of younger fellows come racing back down the slope bearing ladders, planks, and so forth, aids to enable them to conquer the water castle. They have oodles of tools like that at the garden colony.

Make a torch, Járin, the hussy urges the bearded man. Wedging a heavy stick between his knees, he wraps it in rags and ties the rags on with wire, giving the stick a puffy head. The woman pours something over it. The stick bursts into flame. The man with the beard steps up, shoe tips poking over the riverbank's edge, brandishing the torch. Still, he hesitates.

That stinky shack of yours has got to go. You've gone too far, Scalester. Sorry, pal!

The shouting dies down, stones and pebbles remaining in fists.

The fisherman edges along the walkway toward the water and calls across the gap: Járin, don't be stupid, that fire stuff is no joke!

You've been warned, Scales. Surrender now, or I'll throw it, for real!

Come on, Járin. Can't you see the little kid? the fisherman pleads.

There's no kid! He's got a whore in there! the woman barks.

As long as you all come across the water here to us, you'll be fine, says Járin, waving the torch around. You stole together, now you're gonna get wet together too. But the shack's gotta go.

The fisherman just grins.

You'll never throw it this far! You don't have the strength.

Oh no? Járin rears back, waving his arm.

No! You're too old! You won't make it.

Catapulting into the air, the flaming stick lands at the fisherman's feet, and he sends it into the depths with a kick.

Again the stones come raining down from the little guys on all sides, thunk, thunk—and boink, the boy takes a painful blow to the thigh, then another to the shoulder.

They burst into the shack, blinking to adjust to the gloom. Papa, wrestling with the picture, pulls it down from the wall, only to have it fall on top of him, mashing him against the table.

The fisherman shoves him aside, pushes away the table, bends down, seizes hold of a trapdoor in the floor, lifts it. Into the boat! he commands.

Rocks and stones continue to pound the walls and roof, a distraction until the members of the punitive expedition bring in the ladders . . .

Papa unwinds himself from underneath the painting, hands the fisherman the bag with the little nipper. The child dangles above the water for an instant before the fisherman grabs hold of him and deposits him on the floor of the boat.

He slides the oars into the pins. No mean feat with the skiff, tied under the shack, spinning in the current. The boy tumbles in headfirst, grabs for his little brother.

Papa just lies there groaning, having banged his head on the gunnel. The fisherman yanks the rope out of the hook, and they lurch into the flow.

As they shoot out from under the shack, the boy glimpses a blurred tangle of T-shirts, shorts, summer garments, hears cries of laughter and shouting . . . and then they drift with the current, under cover of alders, bushes, thickets, domes of hogweed, all the wild riverside vegetation, the fisherman steering the way.

He digs in with both oars as the current helps them along. Puts his back into it, working hard. A few powerful strokes in the turbulent yellow water and they've crossed the narrow throat of the Sázava. The fisherman drops the oars and reaches for the punting pole.

A few furious stabs of the pole and they're gliding through the muck along the riverbank, amid alders and young willows whose peeling bark hangs loose in strips.

The bow rubs against the sand, chatters over stones. And at last they come to a rest. The fisherman tosses the pole to his feet, gently rocking the boat.

And they stare. The boy in a squat, not letting his hands off the wicker bag; Papa bleary-eyed, mid-drink; even the fisherman, back in his slicker—all gape at the opposite bank.

Thick black smoke climbs up over the treetops, a glint of flames visible through the archway of leaves.

Smells like tires burnin, damn, stinks all the way from here, Papa rasps.

Cradling his bruised elbow, he spits into the water, rubs his battered head. Fresh scratches on his nose blend in with the marks left from the fair.

Jesus and Mary, he howls. What about the picture? That thing survived the Thirty Years' War! Scales! Why didn't you tell em what you had in there? They never would've torched it! This is insane! Fuckin hicks! he bellows his lament into the waters.

The fisherman turns to Papa.

So we're hicks, are we? How come you didn't say nothin? You're the one that's an actor all over the west and God knows where else! They'd a listened to you! You coulda protected the Virgin! I got scores to settle with them, but what about you, huh? How come you didn't show your face, Tab? Fishy, if you ask me!

Jesus and Mary, I left that two thou in the shack, says Papa, rubbing his forehead.

I didn't think they'd go through with it, but they actually torched it, the fisherman says. Hey, look what I found for you, he tells the boy, thrusting the heap of fabric into his hands.

Slavoj?

Mm?

How far is it to Městečko?

Not too far. Dependin.

And which direction?

Just follow the river. You know what the worst part is, though, Tab?

No, what?

If Dora were to come back, not that she will, she'll never find me now.

She still might. You never know!

Jesus and Mary! For God's sake!

What is it? Papa says.

I forgot the turtles. Christ on crutches, I could just! Talk about a delicacy, turtle meat in the shell . . . specially cold, you wouldn't believe it.

Dropping his head almost down to his knees, the fisherman clenches his fists.

A few of em in that sack were still alive.

He sits down on the edge of the boat and drops his feet into the stream.

Get a gander, boys.

Above the trees now, instead of black smoke, a whitish column curls upward, placidly blending in with the lowest-hanging clouds.

The fisherman pulls off his slicker, tosses it on the bench, sidesteps out of the boat. He shuffles across the shallows a bit, slips and falls, it looks like, growls under the water. A moment later his head and broad shoulders emerge. He doesn't turn to face them. Disappears again. Did he hit his head? They spot him a ways downstream. He floats along with the current, goes under again.

Scales! Quit screwin around!

Ashen-faced, Papa steps into the water. Scuttles back and forth through the shallows, sploshing about.

Scales, come back!

Up ahead is a pool, the current. Papa walks back to the boat, suspenders dragging his soaked trousers behind him. Climbs in. Sits down.

Son, it would seem our friend has sunk into despondency. But you won't solve any problems that way, remember now!

The boy squats on the seat, the bag containing his brother between his feet. He unpacks the gifted heap. Track pants and a T-shirt, both washed too many times. But both look good. And they'll fit him just right.

20

BRIDAL SALON. THE GIRLS, THE OPERATION.
MONČA'S TRICKS. MONČA'S A GOOD ONE.
THE CESSPIT. RIDERS OF RIGHTEOUSNESS.
A DISPUTATION ON PROGRESS. TRANSFORMED
RIVERBANKS.

The sodas are all drunk up. What with the heat rising from the sun-baked asphalt, they really hit the spot.

And as Miran steers the Beemer past a brand-new, high-end, glass-walled showroom offering Bushman outdoor supplies, he honks the horn out of sheer exuberance, and Macinka and Janinka give a whoop of salutation from their newly refreshed throats. They're almost home.

And indeed, they are zipping through Městečko, as is plain from the road sign, bearing the village's coat of arms. The village was built by the ancestors of the vehicle's occupants, among others, sometime in the twelfth century, and its coat of arms features a horse-drawn hearse, which the local residents prefer to pass off as a postal carriage.

The brothel U Paručky, aka Wiggie's, hidden in a cluster of trees on a side road stashed in the bushes, is a two-story cuboid block, originally colored gray, then spray-painted over in the expectable pink. The land and the building fell into the Baštas' lap as the result of somebody's unpaid debts. Monča began operating a disorderly house on the premises after going out into the world to gain some experience. And after the Baštas shook hands on it with Miran.

A roadside advertisement with a purple heart reading HOUR OF LOVE aims to pique passing drivers' interest in intercourse, with the price of a room, truly modest, scrawled in chalk.

Sales, or perhaps better put, bodily rentals, are conducted on the second floor, where the girls and visitors take turns, for the most part—aside from the occasional peccadillo and faux pas brought about by a guest's drunkenness or insolvency—in a companiable and generally good-humored rotation.

If there's one thing Monča doesn't like, it's gloominess.

Her command post is downstairs. A plain little den she shares with Miran whenever he's back from his business trips. The lower floor is also home to a pub, aka a taproom, aka a bar, featuring darts, a classic selection of booze, and assorted other frills. Adorning the walls are a few life rings, a gift from some pleasure-boat owners. They lend a certain distinctiveness to the atmosphere, along with the odor of river water.

Miran, threading the car up the bushy trail from the county road, passes the small homes at the end of the village, taking great care to steer clear of Monča's rose bushes, and pulls to a stop in front of the bordello, where they are met with an eruption of whooping and excited chatter. Zděnka and Vendulka are out on the lawn in the flood of sunshine, hanging out a rainbow-colored assortment of laundry to dry. A basket of similarly rainbow-colored clothespins sits on the large stone step at the entrance.

Apparently, the girls are too busy to mind the smell wafting up from the ground beneath the building. They've gotten used to it. The ones getting out of the car, on the other hand, as they weave through the laundry, wrinkle their noses. It's the broken cesspit.

The bras and skirts and panties fluttering on the clotheslines all around the gazebo are Monča's idea. They flap in the wind, come-ons, turn-ons, spottable from the road through the shrubbery. Subliminally they instill a message to passersby about the excellent hygiene practiced here.

It's also Monča's opinion that the fluttering laundry, drying and ripening in the sun and fresh air, gives a bit of a homey impression.

She's got all sorts of tricks up her sleeve for creating a pleasure paradise. The girls love their stud-and-earring-bedecked worldly-wise boss. They chalk it up to her tummy that she tends to be tired and snippy these days. And that's so cute!

Yes, the boss's protruding belly is a landmark.

It's all about the bundle of joy in the end, after all.

For now they were still enjoying themselves. "Now" being very impermanent.

Going to work for Monča at U Paručky was more like going to work at a club than it was drudgery.

They liked the money they made off their animality. It was easy to blow it on booze, clothes, squander it all away, of course, but they managed to save some too. That way, once the impermanent time of the brothel was ruptured, they wouldn't be walking into a serious relationship bare-assed broke.

Monča was happy to let them stay overnight in case of emergency. They didn't even have to work. There was always a bed here for the regular girls. Shower stall and all. Plus Monča and her buddies had enough of a reputation that it frightened off the worst of the dickheads, numbskulls, and rapists. That made life much easier. The hookers welcomed her views on life. Whenever anyone needed, she was there to give advice, even just standing there in the doorway, or to wipe the tears off that pretty face.

After all, fucking for cash, and doing it all day long, with a different person every time, wasn't exactly normal.

So there was suffering, albeit concealed and infrequent, involved in attaining peace of mind. If there was a flame of an impassioned "no" flickering within the whores, it typically sprang from the bowels of their psyche in a state of inebriation.

That was when the fleeing into the night, the sobbing in bushes, would happen, followed by a return, pale-faced, shaking, and covered in vomit, then by comforting and calm. Then again, other times, glasses flew, chairs toppled, and the guys were outright bewildered.

But here in the family bar and bordello U Paručky, troubles can always be touched up somehow. If there's one thing Monča has time-tested it's this: goodness is the way to go.

Then the days and nights follow one after the other as naturally as the road running by outside the windows.

So how does it happen? How is it that they become whores? Probably no special reason. Some people are just born that way. Plus it gets to be a habit.

Take for instance the lazy, good-natured Vendulína, the one with the braids. She arrived like a lamb, skittish and fresh-faced. At this point, she just takes it for granted that there are times when she turns into a whore from hell. Lets the guys fuck her brains out, comes or doesn't, no big deal, but the main thing is, when she falls asleep she no longer dreams about burning it all down, but instead whether a canary might pretty up the bordello, or how nice it would be to put new curtains up in her room.

Janinka caught on to the language right away, too. I like sucking, I like fucking, she says, trying to energize one ragged wreck as his head slumps to his chest. Stretch me with your giant prick, she whispers to the stunned milksop. He nearly faints, then returns to his male self.

Please, just do me now, she says, rubbing up against a husbandman who just came to get a peek. You're such a stud! she says, stroking her breasts, twisting her nipples.

She figures it out quick. What brings the cash. She knows how to give a guy the most important thing of all: self-confidence. Once she's mastered pussy talk, it fits her like a glove.

And the main thing is, it's temporary. Janinka: Selling yourself when you're single, that's no biggie, who cares? But selling yourself when you're in a relationship with someone you love? That I don't get!

The truth of the matter is, this is a business that tends to draw the more adventurous types.

You know, sitting around all gussied up and perfumed behind the cash register in a smalltown Billa may look great, it's clean and friendly, it isn't toiling in a field or the woods, but it isn't for everyone. Not to mention the other jobs out there. How would you like to work in a factory, on the shop floor, on an assembly line? Shit, you've got to be kidding . . .

For some of the girls, Monča's little roadside whorehouse is a downright oasis amid the turmoil of the world.

They come and go, but they find the current lineup particularly agreeable.

Yeah, they're happy here, especially the ones that have done a few stints in the so-called sex industry before. The stories they tell about the appalling and unnatural acts to which they have been witness at times border on the very edge of inhumanity.

It's livable here, from their point of view. Janinka, Macinka, Zděnka, Vendulka—alias Amanda, Xenka, Lou, and Sandra. They would say the same to anyone who asks.

*　　*　　*

Today they welcomed back the boss and the crew, especially Kája, with particularly great joy.

Their everyday routine of lazy, sleepy-eyed late mornings is extra-exceptionally livened up.

The night before, they were closed. And the bordello had limited hours the days before that, too. They all worked their tails off cleaning, and especially decorating, the bridal salon. Closed off to whorehouse visitors, the chamber was modeled on the "best room" in a country home, which only Sunday guests are permitted to enter, or the parish priest himself, should he grace the house with a visit, and where typically, enthroned on the piled-high bed, beneath a picture of Jesus Christ or the Virgin on the Mount, there was some kind of brightly colored doll, in the modern era more likely a charming stuffed animal. The wall was covered with a cabinet displaying an assortment of postcards, decorative mugs and coasters, figurines, and other knickknacks. The girls brought in all kinds of armchairs and comfortable seats, set up a series of large and small tables in a line, and covered them with a white tablecloth. They even decorated the chandelier with wedding ribbons, the freshly washed curtains gently billowing.

When the time comes, a sparkling bouquet of flowers will appear and the compound table will sag under the weight of food and drink. And of course the entire house has received a thorough cleaning. The apartment on the lower floor, jokingly called the guardhouse, which Monča and Miran occupy, will be readied in time for the wedding night. Once the festivities were over, where else was the young couple supposed to go, right?

The mood is spoiled a bit, though, by the smell wafting out of the cesspit. Lomoz comes rattling in with his tools. But doesn't make it past the kitchen. He squats down in his usual spot and just stays put. Doesn't want anything, not coffee, not water, not even a tipple. He just squats. It sometimes comes over him lately: fatigue. And this time it's major.

And Kája? The future married man? Janinka and Macinka goad and needle him, tugging him out of the car to look at the preparations, but he doesn't budge. Peers out at the cluster of girls. Yapping away about

Světlana, obviously, what else. Teasing him, the groom. Flitting around the car window, puckering their lips at him, pressing their palms to the glass. But the big day is still to come. The day of Světlana's arrival.

So they hit the road. Kája sucking a Fanta. Miran gripping the wheel. The old man and the women settled in at home. Off they zoom in search of prey, in search of cash, determined, fierce, merciless. In Kája's boyish imagination, they are like military drones over the desert, pursuing a sheikh who, in keeping with the commandments of his god, the infinite, the merciful, is at this very moment using a corner of his burnoose to polish a medal he received for running over some babies with a truck, slitting a pilot's throat, or something like that.

Yes, the brothers Bašta, motorized emissaries of the time-honored Sázava clan, barrel through the Ladaesque countryside like riders of justice, first to collect a sum owed by Hrom, owner of the camp, and then they'll catch up with a certain Koryčan in Mirošovice, a man defiant beyond comprehension.

These tasks were rather negligible, and predictable. What they had foremost in mind was a meeting with their other brothers. Over at Napalm's place. Regarding a truly important matter: a gift for their dad. A gift for which they had worked their fingers to the bone.

And passing again the stately glass-walled premises of the Bushman company, which occupied fields where before there had been nothing, Kája reveals to his brother that he once paid a visit to Járin—who, dressed as an alligator hunter, tries to entice the locals into buying broad-brimmed UFO hats and special bushwear, shirts and pants manufactured from top-secret outer-space materials, two-meter-long digital machetes, anti-shark harpoons, mega-splitters and super-mowers ... while for their part the locals, quite content in tracksuits and coveralls, with their ham-fisted hands and broken nails, if not from opening bottles of beer then from their use of such ancient and primitive tools as the ax and hammer, harbor a strong suspicion that the goods are intended for some other race of people, namely the ones who will come after them and take their place.

Kája bursts out laughing and glances over at Miran, taking in his shaggy hair, the intimately familiar sunken tough-guy cheeks, and he can't help but cackle, imagining his bro dressed in alligator hunter getup . . . or, for that matter, in a uniform from Mickey D's, which they're also building here, in a spot where there used to be nothing, or in one of those stark white outfits, punching the clock at the Mars bar factory, in that spot down by the river where there also used to be nothing at all. In uniform. Groveling, greeting, thanking. Day in, day out. And what for. For a couple of coins . . . like those pathetic losers who, stifled by their wives and kids, keep their drinking in check and take up employment with the companies expanding along the Sázava's bush-congested shores.

The brothers wrinkle their noses, squirming as they drive along the quickly developing riverside. The sight of the Old Log Cabins, burned down and abandoned, flashes through Kája's mind, and again he hears Macinka saying, Where did all the people go?

He doesn't know.

Entering Poříčí, on the left-hand side before they come to the bridge with the saints, Kája glimpses two or three gypsy dwellings amid the willows and reeds. They've always been there. But otherwise, the fields around have all been built up. Where once drainage ditches used to flow, the crossroads gleamed with battered wayside crosses, and run-down bolshie cowsheds rusted, sprouting heaps of manure, today there are assembly plants and warehouses.

Almost everywhere within view, foundations are being dug, corrugated fences are going up. There are helmeted men at work, in orange, yellow, or rainbow coveralls, even in the riverbed thickets, on the islets mid-river. In the summertime they swarm even in the spots where the brothers are accustomed to keeping an eye on the more or less unpredictable local population, the nomads who hold their summer gatherings in the surrounding woods, quarries, caves, and hastily made dugouts.

Kája stares out the window and is astonished by a sudden feeling of sadness, as if something had come undone.

He stares again at his brother, grinning and muttering behind the wheel. Miran is still here, just like their dad and Uncle Lomoz and Uncle Lojda and old Napalm and the others . . . The young man's gaze carves into the river again and he feels the power and strength of all those buddies and pals like a web, like intertwining roots, the thin but solid bonds between the people he grew up with, playing hide-and-seek and soccer, trading and dealing, eating like pigs and drinking like fish, living life, the face-smashings and peacemakings. Only something is different now . . . the stories his uncles tell, especially of course the one about the tank they knocked off the Poříčí bridge . . . all their sawed-off shotguns and forest hideouts, and above all, how to outslick everyone, always and no matter what, and cash in on everything, and never fall on your back and wiggle your legs like a bug, and don't beg, and if you do, only for appearances' sake . . . what to make of it.

Look at that shit, he says to his brother, waving his mitt at the fast-growing development on either bank. I'd like to smash it all to hell!

Dude, that's progress. That's civilization.

For real?

It's totally okay, says the older brother.

For real?

I mean, what else do you want?

Dude, but the whole thing's kina like weird, isn't it? Kina like nasty.

Otherwise we'd be runnin around bashin each other upside the head with rocks, know what I'm sayin?

I guess you're right.

So is that what you want?

I donno. But if that's what's comin, I'm ready.

And Kája falls asleep, abandoning his philosophizing, his mind now undividedly on Světlana, so much so that he can feel her—her weight, mouth, breasts, hair—as he whistles through his nose in his sleep, and the whole thing is so beautiful it can't even be described.

21

LONG SLOPE. OLD HROM, YOUNG HROM.
THE ARRIVAL OF THE CARDINAL. VENDULKA.
TIED UP. A CONTRACT. HOW HAPPINESS IS MADE.
NEW CZECHS. A FATEFUL TOAST.

The lower cottages of Long Slope camp, which Miran and Kája are now speeding toward, were almost all carried away by the floods, but young Hrom never got around to making repairs.

After returning from his military mission, he occupied the most spacious tent, known as the scout's tent because of its wooden frame. Hobbling from the riverbank to the woods and back again, he would settle in on his black crate and, joining in the circle of circulating bottles, talk about his plans to restore the decaying camp.

Long Slope, the patch of land that Hrom's camp occupied, looked like a page out of a glossy brochure.

A rolling hillside stretching from the woods down to the river. The forest provided the campers with cool shade, with the slope's lower edge made up of cozy sandy beaches licked by the Sázava. Young Hrom inherited the camp from his father, but, given that most of his customers were of the same disposition as him, he had never bothered to work at it all that hard. He was actually quite explosive by nature, and agonized over it. He didn't let anyone boss him around, that much was for sure.

Young Hrom's childhood, relatively undisturbed by school attendance, was spent as a cabin boy, cook, lumberjack, and camp worker—in short, as a slave to his old man.

Then one day, after the gyppos turned up, he rebelled and joined the army. Shortly after that, his mother, Líza, drifted away and old Hrom took to drinking. A lot. Little Vendulka Hromová bounced around the area, moving from aunt to aunt. When young Hrom came home from the military, decorated in tattoos and with multiple amputations, word was he'd had a nasty time of it, fighting in the Balkans, among other places. The moment he returned, though, he picked up his old man from the alcoholic treatment center in Benešov, where old Hrom had landed on a drinking spree straight from the slammer, and tended to him in one of the huts at the camp. And, just like his old man, he began to borrow money from the Baštas. Apparently he forgot he had a little sister nearby.

He remembered very well, though, when the gypsies came to Long Slope camp. He had been cleaning the kitchen in his mother Líza's forest snack bar when suddenly a cluster of them appeared among the trees. Dressed in tattered jeans, T-shirts, and tracksuits, dejected and cold, they crowded together in front of him.

Sir, would you mind if we picked strawberries in your forest?

They aren't growin yet, you twit, he enlightened the lankiest one, rocking side to side wrapped in a blanket. Raw-boned, skin nearly black, features sharp as an Arapaho, the leader of the pack, nicknamed the Cardinal.

Well then, sir, could we pick blueberries in your forest?

Them either, dude.

Well then, sir, could we gather mushrooms in your forest?

We already ate em all.

Well then, sir, then could we . . .

Pick whatever shit you want, it's all yours, the young Hrom said with a loud laugh.

That's very kind of you, sir, said the Cardinal, lowering his gaze. He got on best on his own. The rest of his kin loitered around the camp awhile, then disappeared. But Líza Hromová soon got used to the Cardinal gathering bundles of kindling for her and readily helping out with sweeping, cleaning the kitchen—in short, practically everything, apparently in an effort to refute the fallacies about the incompetence of his race.

The Cardinal sold Tatranka wafers to stray crews of Boy Scouts, pulled beer and soda from the tap, always gave correct change. Eventually, the Hroms considered him trustworthy enough that, while they and their visitors were asleep, they let him pick over the goods left behind by the lushes in the cabins. But as summer got under way, things went awry.

This was shortly after young Hrom made his escape and commenced his army career. The camp was still full, old Hrom was brimming with vitality, the huts, cottages, and tents were occupied, the grill spots and the soccer ground were full, nudists blanketed the riverbank, beach balls floated through the air. To this day the black campfire stains in the grass and the mounds of broken glass and rusty cans serve as testament to the wild nights of merrymaking.

In the corner of the woods where Líza's snack bar was, the trees were strewn with hammocks of relaxing campers, enveloped in the country music that blared from the radio, while as many as a hundred little rascals sunned and splashed with their families, and everyone in the camp was more or less happy.

LOW-COST HOLIDAYS ALONG THE SÁZAVA! announced a banner strung over the water, riddled with BB gun fire and singed around the edges from water enthusiasts setting it on fire just for kicks.

The floods came as per tradition, and the tiny snack bar was perpetually crowded. The Cardinal and Líza were busy as bees, and often it would happen that even after the last guests had called it quits, the Cardinal would serenade her on guitar until the early morning hours. They would be awakened by the faint voices of children and a gentle knock-knock from the other side of the locked door. Vendulka Hromová, sometimes with a pack of ankle biters, would knock and whine for as long as it took for the Cardinal, busy in the kitchen again, prepping for the morning rush, to open up and give the little girl Tatranky while her mother was still sleeping off her liquid breakfast.

And on one such hazy morning, as the sun edged its way up over the thundering river like the damp, bleary eye of a dog peeling open, then broke through the mist and burst into flames in all its age-old glory, no one gingerly knocked; instead, old Hrom kicked down the door. It's hard to say if he had simply overlooked the affection up to that point, but now he seized the Cardinal by the throat, slammed his head against the snack bar door, and dragged him through the still-smoldering coals of the campfire. Old Hrom carried the man, howling in pain, down to the river, and tossed him in the bottom of a boat, threw the very drunk

Líza in after him, then grabbed a pole and shoved them as hard as he could out into the dirty, murky current. They somehow made it over the first weir, but the churning waters smashed the boat to pieces on the rocks. This proved fatal to the lovers.

Old Hrom was fortunate. No one took it as murder, and his reputation preceded him wherever he went, so he had it good in prison. After serving out a basically symbolic sentence for what the judge deemed to be a crime of passion, and after young Hrom brought him back to Long Slope from the rehab in Benešov, old Hrom doggedly threw himself into work.

He didn't let it bother him that someone had set fire to the camp's wooden toilets and the handful of changing rooms in the time while he was away. He fixed up what cottages were left. Scrubbed, painted, took to the woods with a brushcutter. And eventually Vendulka came back around as well. She was quickly maturing into an intoxicatingly beautiful teenage girl, and would trudge around the woods after her dad with a cant hook or rake, deftly gathering the branches into a pile whenever he decided to clear a patch of snags. She would patiently tidy up the broken glass and general mess whenever old Hrom had a fit of nostalgia, raging through the night with a bottle of hooch. Trudge along the shore after him with a bucket full of nails, screws, and bolts while he mended the rowboats, the dock, and the diving boards the summerers had set up by the water. Et cetera. But old Hrom didn't say a word for the most part, or even look her way. Every time he caught sight of her budding beauty, he saw Líza.

So one day Vendulka hurled the bucket of screws into the water, packed up, and left. No one was surprised. The folks from the Old Log Cabins, who had resumed booze deliveries to camp before the season began, said the one old Hrom was really waiting for was his son.

He had obtained some funds to restore the camp from old man Bašta, and he soon went back for more. In fact, his growing debt had been the reason for Miran's initial visits to the camp. And after young Hrom came on board, they steadily continued.

Old Hrom even used to show off the postcards from his son to Bašta and his boys. Ancient stone bridges in valleys, picturesque towns with red-tile-roofed homes and slender white minarets rising up into cloudless blue skies, but also motorcades with bazookas and armored vehicles. Foreign stamps and postmarks that old Hrom and his friends struggled to decipher, bearing the unintelligible and, to them, funny-sounding names of towns and cities being torn apart by genocidal wars. Every time he stuck a postcard back in the pocket of his snot-stained coveralls, he would say, "That boy of mine might be comin home any day now!" Or, "Damn, I wonder where is that young fella?"

However, the state in which the young Hrom—amputated below the knee, missing several fingers, and with a jaw-dropping scar running across his belly—found his father upon his return made any deeper relationship seem rather unlikely.

Once the son had resettled his father, out of his institutional cage and into the fancy cottage, some of the old man's buddies began to trickle in. They brought him all the drink he wanted, it was like paradise for him. If only he'd kept it under control. But fat chance of that.

When it came time, young Hrom had old Hrom declared missing and laid him to rest himself. He buried him in the best spot, a shady corner of camp where the hammocks used to hang, near the ruins of the old snack bar. He totally disregarded the old man's considerable debt, and ended up even more in hock to the Baštas than before.

Young Hrom's first and in fact only change to the camp itself was to hang a new banner over the river. RIVER OUTDÓR CENTRAL, the new ad declared, and in smaller type, TENT 50, CAR 100.

I want the place to be international! Foreigners welcome, see? he stressed when Miran came by to talk to him about his debt.

Mm-hm, Miran nodded.

We're buddies, right, Miran?

Sure thing, pal.

So gimme a little longer. Camp'll get back on its feet.

No can do, pal.

You want this? asked Hrom, holding up a postcard with some young women and little donkeys burdened with packs. When Miran shook his head, he dropped it in the fire.

This one here's good, check it out. A bunch of guys, draped in knives and firearms, grinning out of a jeep wrapped in camouflage netting. And that's no postcard, that's a photo!

Nice, said Miran.

My squad! Five minutes later they hit a mine and got blown to shit. Every fuckin one.

You took that?

Yeah. Know what my dad said? He said as long as the mail was workin, it couldn't be that bad.

Oh yeah?

Yeah, then they sent me someplace where the mail didn't work.

Where was that? Africa?

Close! And one other place.

Sell us the camp, Hrom.

I'm surprised Vendulka hasn't stopped by. One day this whole place'll be hers, said Hrom, gesturing with one arm. My sis is quite a bit younger than me. And I got my wounds, Miran, don't forget.

Vendulka's got her hands full. Popular gal. But she says hello.

My dad wrote me once: "Come home, son!" And a couple sentences, good stuff.

Really?

When I flew back home and went to pick him up, I said, "Dad, do you want me here?" "I wanted you till you were born," he says back. Man was a joker, right up to the end.

Right!

He was a sorry sight, there in that cage.

Right.

It's good when a guy's got buddies, Miran.

I agree.

Lemme show you somethin.

Young Hrom dipped the two fingers remaining on his left hand into a cloth pouch and pulled out two thin, dark gnarled crescents.

Those're Taliban ears.

For real?

Take a sniff. They still stink.

How is that even possible?

Beats me. I'll show the boys when you bring em around. But no way am I lettin you dig up my dad. And even if I did, this ground here's sacred now because of him bein in it. You get my drift, Miran?

I get your drift, Hrom.

Would you sell the land your dad was buried in?

No, said Miran.

You see? You convinced me.

Over time, Hrom's merciless conduct, combined with the lax hygienic norms and torrential downpours, drove away even the most hardened guests. Even the Old Log Cabineers began to steer clear of the insolvent Hrom. The only visitors were the occasional woodland misfits, for whom the decrepit cottages were still a luxury. The amount of booze they and Hrom consumed was such that the once-famous Long Slope came to be known as Camp Hallucination. Due to the owner's difficult nature, eventually even the vagrants disappeared, leaving Hrom to limp through the ruins alone. Rummaging through the war souvenirs in his black crate, feeling around for his trophy grenades with trembling fingers, sweaty with pre-d.t.'s, he pictured the barrage of flames he would unleash, badass that he was, once the right moment came.

The tent site and parking lot yawned with emptiness. Torn Kofola parasols lay piled in a heap along with tablecloths and mats, courtesy of Staropramen, smelling of must. One morning, Hrom mistook the ice cream freezer box for a jukebox and kicked it, trying to make it sing.

Just then, two men in wetsuits came striding up from the river, and one of them said: We'd like to pitch a tent here.

First let me break your faces.

And so forth and so on. Until finally, at the forceful urging of their father, the two Bašta brothers set out to see Hrom. They had no doubt that in the end he would consent to sell the land. But they weren't excited to make the trip. They liked Hrom.

They emerge from the woods at the top of Long Slope like ghosts, an effect heightened by the mist, clinging to the brothers like a thick shag of cotton candy. But as they stride downhill, toward the river and the scout's tent, through the wreckage of huts, all that remains of their misty cloak is a few playful wisps, fluttering between their legs until the breeze wafting up from the river breaks and scatters them.

They see the first pit. A funnel in the soil, dirt and rocks, cut roots around the edge. The explosion must have been pretty recent. They pass several more. And, looking down through the mist to the river, they spy a white vessel with a red cross on its side.

Anchor dropped.

An ambulance boat.

There's a roar from the scout's tent. A bull's bellow that dwindles to a whimpering falsetto.

The brothers slide each other a glance.

And move fast.

They breeze through the peeled-back corners of canvas into the scout's tent. And stop dead in their tracks.

A bald man sits on a field cot. Chest wrapped in filthy bandages, he grins, observing them through narrowed eyes. Squatting behind him, in the shadows, someone truly large. In a wheelchair. IV drips snake around the mysterious creature hulking menacingly in the gloom. Flanking the man on the cot, two figures, standing silent and rigid. A fellow in a business suit with an attaché case, whom Miran recognizes as a well-known real estate agent, specializing in riverside property. And a woman in a medical gown.

And Hrom.

Lying on the sun-bleached, trampled grass in nothing but a pair of dirty boxers. Wound in rope, noose around his neck, hands bound. By his head, an overturned bowl of water, another one full of black globs.

I was here just the other day, Miran says distinctly.

Kája kneels down to the bound man. Hrom grunts, dark bubbles frothing at his lips. Fresh welts on his hands, chest, and abdomen merge in some spots with the old scars, making them look like whip marks. His face is disfigured with yellow bruises, and all over he's covered in shiny sweat, more like a layer of mica than a bodily secretion.

I was here and Hrom was fine. What happened? asks Miran.

Kája urgently gets to work loosening the knots.

We have arrived yesterday, says the bandaged man. He thrusts out his hand with a click, exposing the blade of a hefty jackknife with engraved lettering, and before anyone can say a word, he slices the noose from around Hrom's neck, saws, cuts, and the ropes fall away from his reclining body.

And your friend in bad shape. He drunk out total. Raving. Very bad shape, very degenerately he drinks, says the man, kicking at a heap of plastic bottles on the ground. For the most part, dark one-and-a-half-liter beers. And of course a mound of Božkov spirits.

Slurpin booze like a baby from its mama's breast, grins the suit, giving them a merry wink.

The two brothers can't help a twinkle of merriment coming to their eyes as well. But it fades as the woman shuffles out of the darkness, wielding a syringe. She bends down and jabs the needle into Hrom's arm.

Mr. Hrom will be taking the boat to the hospital with us, she says. Along with the gentlemen here. Mr. Hrom should be grateful to them. For what is more valuable than life? Nothing! That's how we in the medical profession see it. Still, we can't be sure whether delirium will occur.

This is nurse from Benešov hospital, the smiling bald man tells the brothers. We have enlisted her. There she has treated us. We ourselves are needing care, especially my friend, he says, pointing to the big man slumped in shadow, drips curling around him. And out of the half-light steps the well-known real estate agent. He hands Miran a business card.

I only have one, the man says with an apologetic shrug. Hopefully that'll do for the two of you gentlemen.

Miran hands the man the card back.

Thank you, it'll come in handy. You know, every day I go out with a whole stack of business cards, and next thing I know, poof, they're gone! Real estate in our region is moving fast these days, as it should be. But I'm of no use here anymore. The sale is complete. We've got the contract signed by Mr. Hrom and our witness here, the medical worker. All the essentials are taken care of. Wish it went this smoothly everywhere!

It will soon, says the man on the bed, nodding his head as he gets to his feet. Even with the brownish bandages encircling his chest, you can see how strong he is. His firm bottom is encased in khaki shorts. He stands tight as a clenched fist.

My name is Vaska. I know who you are. You two brothers! We will turn your fucky-fuck house into paradise.

Kája laughs so hard he brays.

The nurse bends down to the faintly gurgling Hrom and mops his face with a bandage.

Should I wait another minute? the real estate man asks.

No need, says Miran.

Getting the nod from Vaska too, he steps over Hrom and exits the tent with a clear look of relief.

So Hrom sold it to you, did he? says Miran.

We know you have just claims. Here is what Hrom owes you many times over. Vaska pulls several thick wads of bills from the pocket of his khaki shorts and lays them on top of Hrom's crate. The brothers stare at the heap of grenades on the floor, mixed in with the bottles. Hrom's large black handgun rests on the crate lid.

This camp is sold to me, Vaska says with a wide grin.

Who do you work for? Where're you guys from? Miran asks.

Are you guys Russkies? says Kája.

You two brothers, what good fortune you have come! We are wanting to speak with you. I have worked in brothels before. It is gold rush. Everywhere will be necessary accommodations for many people, for tourists we need brothels. It is gold. At your scrapyard will be brothels too! We will make agreement. Vaska offers the brothers a golden-haired mitt to shake.

The rattling at their feet quiets to regular breathing.

He's no longer vomiting, says the nurse.

Ayiiii, screeches Vaska. He slips free of Kája's grip only once Kája allows it.

The fuck're you talkin about? says Kája.

Vaska takes a seat on the bed, massages his hand a moment or two with a slightly theatrical hiss, then says: Nurse now will serve glasses for us three. We make pact and drink like brothers. I buy your brothel.

What did you do to Hrom? Kája says. To get him to sign like that.

Vaska plays with Hrom's pistol. Walking his fingers over the barrel to the grip and back again.

We have done nothing to Mr. Hrom! We have helped him.

As a matter of fact, Mr. Vaska was the one who secured these grenades, says the nurse. Mr. Hrom was trying to blow up our boat!

He missed! Miran exclaims.

We will be happy to make a sworn deposition with our attorney, says the nurse. More than happy, I assure you.

I'll ask again, says Miran. What did you do to Hrom?

Heh-heh, nichevo, sneers the big man.

Cut it with the Russian shit. Talk normal, you cunt.

My, my, so sad this is, the big man says, wagging his round, hairless skull. I was born in Czech family. Near Chernobil. I am eco-refugee! Czech!

Vaska fixes his eyes, blanketed with darkness, perhaps with a grief rising up from within, directly on Kája, who towers over him, clenching his fists.

We from Chernobil are pure Czechs. But here, at home? Vaska shakes his head again, focusing now on his dirty thumbs. For you in this country I am Russkie. Here I am no man, no Czech. For me, shovel, pick, shovel, pick, shovel, pick . . . Holding his head in his hands, it looks he may be about to sob.

Guess you shoulda done better in school!

I am standing on corner in Prague, Andyel metro, Smíchov, I see man beating girl! She is crying. So I fuck him up, she is my girlfriend, we love, but she works in brothel. Brothel's name is Tyran. Humiliation, no problem! This is brothel slogan. You know how it works? Humiliate, humiliate, humilate, then one day you no humiliate, and that is happiness! This is how they are training girls there. It works like charm.

He kicks at Hrom. You ask him! I no sign, I no sign, I no sign, and then: okay, I sign! When he says, I almost startle.

Pervert! Humiliation, no problem, huh?

Ever read Dostoyevsky? a powerful voice emerges from the lump that has remained silent up until now.

Nurse! Four glasses, shouts Vaska, springing up from his seat. Leaving the gun where it is. His bald head only comes as high as Kája's shoulder, but his build is so stocky that even with all the bandages and gauze, he doesn't look all that much smaller.

I am no Rusák, I Czech. And my commander Ivan also!

What?

We are New Czechs.

Eat shit.

And you will be New Czechs too.

Piss off.

I know from Hrom plan of your father. Hospice. Is bullshit. We will make here huge forest tourist brothel paradise. Gold mine! We buy your lands. Right now. You will tell your father, you will convince him.

We'll never sell, Kája declares. Not as long as my dad is alive.

Miran steps on his foot. And crushes down so viciously, tears spring to Kája's eyes.

Vaska just smiles. And nods.

I understand!

He turns around and takes the tray of glasses from the nurse, serves the figure in the wheelchair, and comes back out of the dark to the brothers.

Now we toast to health of your dad!

22

SHAKESPEARE AGAIN. ON LIFE WITHOUT HEAT.
REPEAT ENCOUNTER. SHOT THROUGH A BAG.
BISON'S SQUAD. PETTING AND A MOMENT OF
BLISS. YOU CAN TELL ME.

Papa and the boy drag the skiff up on the bank. Toss in the oars. Papa
puts a slicker on over his sailor's T-shirt, stuffs the plastic bottle in his
pocket. Peels back a few of the bushes. They cover up the boat, camou-
flaging it nicely. Squat down amid the grasses on the sloping riverbank.

The boy leans over his sleeping younger brother, shoos away the flies
over his little mouth. Is there something lying there in the grass? He
wrinkles his nose. Smells the stench and wet. The cloudy waters churn
at their feet. Mud bubbles swell from the shallows. The sun flares
through a haze of insects risen from the grass. Slap and smack, the boy
fidgets.

You're going to make a mess of yourself.

Papa takes a swig.

The boy whacks a serious blowfly with turquoise armor. Wipes the
flattened carcass on the grass.

As flies to wanton boys are we to the gods, they kill us for their sport.
Shakespeare wrote that, the swan of Avon. Now I can be Sázava's swan.
Just have to spread my wings . . . find a quiet place and write. And I will,
I promise you that. Shakespeare's boring nowadays. Yep, our tour's over
now. You'll have a great time with Aunt Monča, you'll see! And from
there it's just a hop, skip, and a jump to the hospital! First we have to
get there, though.

The tattered skirt dangles around the boy's thighs. The dark, sticky
bodies of flattened mosquitoes and flies dot the fabric.

Leave the clothes from Scales in the boat. It's easier hitchhiking with
a little girl.

Papa strides down the bank. Fishes around in the river, pulls out a large scarred rock, carved by eons of time and water.

In the folds and cracks, grubs writhe.

Papa lifts the heavy stone.

See that, boy?

The larvae quiver in the sun's rays, tiny members of the aqueous realm playing hide-and-seek in the stone's clammy rust.

Life without heat is possible!

The sound of rushing water is pierced by the roar of an engine.

They waste no time clawing their way up the bank, Papa lugging the bag with the little one as the boy holds on from behind. Clutching at tufts of grass, roots poking from the soil. They reach the top nearly out of breath.

A sandbank comes into view on the other side. Above it, the curled ribbon of a road.

A motorcycle approaches at fiendish speed. Drives into the sand, engine rumbling like a storm.

Papa drops to the ground. The boy, too, lies down amid the bug-infested grass. The bag with the young one cradled inside bulges up between them like a hump of earth.

A girl, behind her a man in a helmet. Her red hair flaps loose like a banner of war. Breasts pressed to the handlebars, she shrieks, sun flashing in her mouth like split lightning. The man, bull horns jutting from his helmet, has his arms wrapped around her, clutching the handlebars, possessively clinging to her back.

They bump along, jolting up and down, gravel spraying from beneath the wheels, until the bike falls on its side, burying itself in the sand.

As the man picks himself up from the ground, the girl dashes into the river. She disappears, reemerging a few strokes downstream. The horned man struggles through the shallows after her, submerged up to his waist. Papa slides down the turf into the sand. The boy follows after, dragging the bag behind him, carefully, so it doesn't bump.

Papa lifts the machine. The bike slips, crushing his foot. There is a sound of metal scraping on metal intermingled with Papa's howl of pain.

The horn-headed lug meanwhile drags the girl out of the current by her hair. Choking and spluttering, she barely gets to her feet on the rocks of the shallows before he chases her out of the water.

Stop! Police! Papa cries, hopping lamely around the machine. A pistol pops out of the belt bag attached to the handlebars at his feet, landing in the sand with a thump. He quickly snatches up the gun, fires off a deafening shot.

A black entry hole appears in the bag the boy grips in his hand. He opens the bag. His little brother blinks eagerly up at him, wrinkling his nose.

I'm confiscating the bike! We're the police, stop! Papa yells into the face of the man charging toward him.

They thrash about in the sand awhile. Tumbling in a ball. Then the man gets to his feet, swearing a blue streak. Rubbing the spot where Papa bit him. He gives Papa a kick in the head. Snatches up the gun from the sand, puts it in his pocket. Returns to Papa, kicks him again. Lifts the machine by the handlebars, wheels it onto the packed sand of the trail. Fires up the bike, at first teetering along zigzag. Then, finding his balance, he barrels off in a sandy whirl, vanishing onto the road.

The girl kicks at the ground with an unshod heel, sprinkling Papa's face with sand. He looks up, fixing her with a squint, and his whole rumpled face lights up.

Get up!

She stands there, barefoot, skirt drooping from her waist. Drops of water spattered across the downy skin of her arms and thighs.

Papa studies her cautiously, from below.

Perhaps nature itself, incarnated in the waterlogged woman, miraculously causes the twitch in his testicles to pass through his pummeled body and stomped head, spreading his lips in a lustful smile and wreaking havoc deep down in his itsy-bitsy brain cells, where the little pixies control his motor function. He attempts to get to his feet.

The girl is smiling. As if, fresh off a motorcycle crash and a beating, she hadn't just nearly drowned. Her ginger hair flows down around her shoulders. Her rounded breasts, large in proportion to her rather petite frame, darken the horizon from Papa's vantage point. Along with her protruding belly. Her nipples jiggle ever so slightly as she walks, moving targets for the seated man's attentive eyes. Sun at her back, the redhead is enveloped in a veil of spicy female musk. She must have been sweating in the water.

I lost a tooth, says Papa, picking a tooth out of the sand. And I think I've got a broken leg.

You got some pep in you. Almost took down Bison. Not bad!

Bison?

You shouldn't a shot at him, though. He's a cop.

You think he'll come back?

For sure, nods the girl.

Ah, fuck.

But maybe the other guys didn't hear? He'll come back with them, is my guess.

Well, that's just great then.

Know what? It's good you shot that gun! He doesn't want those guys to be worried he shot himself. That's why he went back.

I was tryin to save you, girl.

He thinks I can't get outta here myself. But he's a fool. I will.

He sure is, Papa agrees.

He coulda taken you out easy. But he didn't want to kill you.

What the hell're you talkin about?

He can kill whoever he wants. Self-defense.

Oh, right.

He's head of the militia.

Looks more like a metalhead.

He's got his crew, they keep order.

What the hell're you talkin about?

You know, they go where they want, do what they want.

Is that that shithead that was with you at the fair?

Hey, Pops, you got a car?

No, no car.

Guess I'm gonna float then, says the girl. I donno what you're gonna do. But I wouldn't wait here for them.

You were the one slappin that guy around! On the road.

So what's Broňa up to?

Don't even ask.

You can't walk along the bank here, though, Pops. There's houses, fences. I'm gonna float.

Are you pregnant?

Yep. I'm gettin married!

You don't say!

But first I gotta get to the wedding.

What would you say if I told you we had a boat?

The boy follows the girl and his father down the slope, pulling the little one in the bag like a sled. It isn't too hard in the sand.

The girl, hearing him pant as he trudges along behind them, turns and splutters in astonishment.

She sees a little girl, a girl pale as a ghost, hair cut short, in a tattered skirt and mud-spattered pink hoodie. And that bag.

She says nothing, but bends down and opens the bag.

Jesus and Mary, you've got a kid in there!

Yep, Papa says. He lowers himself to a kneel, then gradually straightens back up with a hiss.

I mean, that's an actual child.

Take her to the boat, Papa directs the boy. I'll repack the squirt. Make him comfortable!

The little one rears his head from the bag. Waggles his hands, lips pursed, eyes twinkling. But the smell, the stench oozing out of the bag is truly prodigious. It easily overpowers the mud.

Sweet Virgin Mary, what're you doin draggin that kid around in a bag? What kina freaks are you?

Hurry, before that stud of yours gets back! The skiff's over there, says Papa, pointing to the grassy ridge they just climbed over top of.

Go back up there and show her the boat!

The red-haired lass flashes a glance at the boy, whose face has suddenly turned bright red, and marches off, practically dragging him up the hill. Which, really, she is, since the boy's eyes are glued to her. He walks in her footsteps as sand flies from her heels, watching the subtle but fierce undulation of her behind. Treading in the shallow imprints of her bare feet, over the depressions left by her toes. The girl's inner glow burns off the drops from the skirt pasted to her body.

The wind rushes in with a sudden whoosh as they clamber up through the grass.

Hey, where's your mom anyway? Don't tell me it's just you and your dad!

When they reach the top, the girl comes to a stop, panting.

She can't catch her breath.

Gimme a thump on the back!

He winds up and slugs her.

Ow!

Being already midswing, he slugs her one more time.

Enough! Where's the boat?

He points down to the water. The girl grabs him by the skirt, pulls him toward her. Seizes his chin in her warm palm. Stares into his eyes. He feels himself turning redder.

Head over heels'll be best, I think.

She squats down and off she goes, tumbling through the grass.

A few somersaults later, he's lying next to her. She rolls over, sits astride him, he feels the weight of her swollen belly. The girl hisses in his ear, runs her hand under his skirt. Caresses it, fondles it, grips it in her fist.

The moment you whacked me, I knew. Girls don't hit like that. Only boys. You got some pep in you too. Just like your dad, huh?

She keeps stroking, squeezing.

You tried to trick me, now get ready to be tortured!

Catapulted with pleasure into the unknown, the boy almost loses consciousness. As he claws his way back from the abyss, the crickets' whir is unbelievably acute, the flies' buzzing like the hum of a power plant. Even the slightest sonic hints of frolicking insects unknown to him come across at full blast. Also, as usual after an orgasm, colors are much brighter too.

The girl takes a lick of the hot droplets collected in her palm. Grimaces in feigned disgust and wipes the cum in his hair.

And I thought it was just for peein still. But good for you! Now what about me? You don't know how to take care of a girl yet, do you?

He just gapes.

That's all right! Maybe next time, huh?

The redhead lifts herself off the boy. Staggers over to the boat. Grabs a branch, tosses it aside. Pulls another, long and heavy, over the gunnel and drops it in the water.

This is what you call hidin, huh? Are you guys dumb or what? It wouldn't't've lasted even a day here.

The boy reaches under the seat, pulls out the knot of clothes from Scales. As the girl wrestles with the other branches, he quickly undresses. Bunching up the pink hoodie and ragged skirt, he flings them into the current, where the murky water quickly spirits them away. Then he gets dressed again.

The girl grasps hold of the oar, inserts it in the pins, takes the other, fixes it in place, and turns around.

Now that's better! Like a real man.

Legs braced, they lean into the rowboat with their combined strength. The skiff slips through the whipped-up mud into the river. Keeping hold of the gunnel, up to their knees in water, the girl pushes off the boy's shoulder, climbs in, sits down. Grabs hold of his hand, steadying him till he settles in himself.

So you're sure this guy's not some pervert that kidnapped you and your brother? You can tell me.

The boy shakes his head.

You don't talk?

Little by little, they drift into the current.

You don't want to talk, or you can't? You can tell me, it's all right.

And they're in the flow. The girl holds the oars in the air.

You liked that, didn't you? Heh-heh, you're embarrassed! You don't have to be. Everybody likes it. She dips the oars in and gives a gentle pull, branches, reed bits, detritus floating past atop the dark green water. It's raining. The first light drops.

23

YOU'LL BE BACK. DRYING OUT. THE SCRAPYARD
BURIAL GROUND. ČUTANÁ, MOMS, NON-MOMS.
HOW NAPALM CAME INTO THE PICTURE.
CAMPSITE. MOCK ME ALL YOU WANT, ENJOY!
LOMOZ'S HARD SLOG.

Dad's not pickin up, says Kája and sticks his phone in his pocket.

You better go find him.

He's out fishin. He never takes his phone out fishin. Solder's there with him. And some a the other boys. Nothin'll happen!

It'd be better if you went.

We'll stop by Napie's. Then you and me gotta figure out what to do about Koryčan. Dad said so!

Bro, I don't like those Russkies.

Dad said for me to go with you. You know how furious he'd be if I turned up? Plus nobody would dare lay a finger on our dad.

Miran patiently explains the whole thing to his brother once again.

But the only response he gets from Kája is snoring, his chin slowly sinking until it drops to his chest.

Miran shrugs. After a while he turns off into the woods and stops. The path from here to Napalm's is almost imperceptible.

Miran opens the trunk, slings a pack of provisions onto his back. Rudely shakes his younger brother awake. It takes a minute. For at this very moment, Kája, teeth clenched in his sleep, is dragging that jerk Bison off his motorcycle by the hair, crushing him in a chokehold while he kicks and urinates on his bike. As he snaps awake, he lowers his fist from his brother's chin, raised with the ingrained instinct of a seasoned pub brawler.

They walk down a path through the bushes, toward the trees that tower over the river, then follow the bends along the willows to the abode of Napalm the old railwayman.

Howdy, boys! the brothers hear from overhead.

They look up. From the crotch of a tree they see a pair of feet dangling and a face peeking out. And hanging down from the tree is an enormous canvas, ablaze with colors. Peering up through the green foliage, Miran and Kája recognize the familiar, albeit algae-coated, water-warped, and unnaturally deformed face of the Virgin Mary.

Shit, what is that? Kája yelps.

That's the Holy Virgin, comes the reply. I'm dryin it out. You boys headed to Napalm's?

We are! How'd you get your hands on that, Scales?

River sent it my way! Frame's fucked, though! You boys got any bread with you?

We do!

That's good! I'll come by once it dries.

All right.

And how bout beer, you got that too?

A course! And cucumbers and peppers! Miran says, slapping his pack.

We got sausages too, Kája adds.

That's great!

So you'll come by?

I'll come by later.

A-okay.

And off they go, squishing along the sodden riverbank, the path leading them over rocks, decomposed branches, cast aside by the flood. They stride through the hushed open space of the damp forest, a chapel of creation with transparent shadow walls. Stomp! squish! stomp! squish! the circumspectly treading Miran hears Kája behind him, flogging through the mud, as usual, like a wild boar.

Here's where the beach was. A sand-and-pebble scythe jutting out into the river. He and Kája used to come here to swim. Fish for dace. Just hang out. Till they took on Solder and the others. As they grew up.

It was a long time ago now that Miran's dad took him to the most out-of-the-way spot in their territory, a vast junkyard and associated lands.

This is where your mom is laid to rest, he told him. When the boy's face began to quiver, his dad slugged him in the shoulder. Men don't cry, he said. And right here, he added, tapping a second cross sticking up beside the first, is that other one. You remember her, don't you?

Miran's cheeks flushed lightly. He remembered her all right. A true beauty. Kája's mom. It was truly something special having her around: young, slim, cheerful, easygoing. His dad ran roughshod over her. Yeah, he turned crimson red that day in the summer breeze that ruffled the nettles.

It was different everywhere else, but with the Baštas the deal was: the women walked, the children stayed.

People used to say that Ilona was Bulgarian, but nobody believed it. She didn't even stay with them long enough for Tater Tot to remember her. But there were enough other women and girls around that the little guy could always find a skirt to grab hold of. Some of them settled in with their dad in the rough little house behind the scrapyard. At one point, two beauties from Černé Voděrady had a falling out with the others and took up residence in the trailer, where the first thing they did was order a microwave. And as they say, food spurs the appetite, so the next thing you know they also wanted a shower. The women refused to back down from their demands, and they couldn't reach agreement with the scrapyard sovereign. They ended up leaving too.

Every so often, old man Bašta would go visit the crosses. The womenfolk avoided the spot. In any case, people said the real graves were elsewhere.

The brown-haired Čutaná was the woman who stayed with the Baštas the longest. Rumor was she had come to Sázava as a scout leader and deserted to the Baštas from a camp in the woods that was badly damaged by one of the floods. She was quite adept at everything she was put in charge of. Besides being able to repair any hunk of junk car you gave her, she had the boys gather forest fruits, taught them how to track game and carve small, handy totems. Together with the smaller boys she dammed up the creek, and the fish harvest was accompanied by great festivities. She even taught the boys how to fish the old-fashioned scout way, using a spear. Even the most fidgety ones made an effort for her sake, and old Bašta gaped in amazement to see his loud, rambunctious pack of boys transformed into statues as they competed to see who could stand on one leg in the rocks overlooking the water the longest without making a sound, like a heron, clutching a lethal wooden club in hand.

But eventually Čutaná shifted away from them and their father into the community of the Old Log Cabins, and though for a long time they continued to keep an eye out for her, she never showed her face again. One cabineer later told the boys that Čutaná just picked up and left one day, and rode off on the train. Maybe to the same place she'd come from, they reckoned.

So the only person who looked after the brood the whole time was Miran.

The first time they met Napalm had been right here. He and Kája used to sit around by the water, waiting for a fish to bite. Swim, laze around in the grass. When Solder got older he joined the twins, and eventually Skeeter and other boys from the area were drawn to them as well.

The day they met, Miran and Kája had just cast their bobbers when Napalm rose up like a giant out of the water before their eyes. It certainly wasn't anything they had been expecting. Wet and soggy, he scrambled up onto the bank. In those days he was a redhead, though of course at his previous station they had shaved him bald. He still had a few hairs here and there, twisting out of his skull like copper wires.

Deep-blue tattoos peeked from under his hole-riddled shorts, the words CUT HERE were inked around his neck, and blaring through the theadbare T-shirt on his chest was the audacious declaration LIES RULE THE CSSR. Skulls, women, daggers, guns, galloping horses, spiders, gallows, etc. covered his forearms, calfs, thighs, every visible surface.

What's up, boys? Any bites?

Not yet . . . boss.

Boys, I could do with a fryin pan, even a little one. And salt, make sure you don't forget.

All right.

And a bit of soap too.

All right.

But not that stinky stuff!

Okay!

He rustled off through the reeds.

They came back with boxes of fishing hooks, chosen by their dad;

bread, seasoning, jackknife; some salamis, a bottle of liquor, and also the pan . . . they got used to seeing him wandering the banks. Soon they knew where he bivouacked. Amid the tangled branches of a lightning-felled giant, on the spot where the Mnichovka Creek flowed into the Sázava.

You can run all up and down the creek and the dogs don't got a chance, the older man explained to the young boy.

Aha, said Kája, tiny eyes abulge.

They brought him a rubberized tarp. A shaving kit. Everything imaginable, their dad saw to that. Instead of his prison duds, which he buried somewhere or burned, he wore their dad's shirts and trousers. The man they called Napalm began to heal there on the banks.

Now, the two brothers turn down the path through the trees to a clearing, where the light of a fire gleams through the leaves and branches.

Richie, dressed in his usual sports coat and worn-shiny pants, with a knit cap on his head, waves, smiling widely. Napalm is fiddling with something by the firepit, the others sit around on the rocks. Kája smiles too. He likes it here, why wouldn't he? He and Miran made the trek, and all their buddies are already there, orange coveralls beaming through the woodsy dusk in solidarity.

Yep, gotta get that big gift ready, Kája says to himself. For dad. Then there's the celebration with Světla. Big days comin up! Then him and Světlana'll head out on their honeymoon, which'll probably get extended.

He's looking forward.

He whoops a raucous greeting, peeling back the branches and stepping into the clearing. The seated men holler back at the new arrivals. The brothers and a few buddies of theirs who also join in at the scrapyard from time to time. And every single one of them wears a grin. Nodding their tousled shoulder-length locks, or bobbing their shaved skulls. Their affable greetings echo through their woodland abode. Tater Tot, the baby of the family, rushes over to Miran, helps him off with his backpack, and starts digging around inside.

You bring any nuts?

To the creek with you. Scoot! Miran orders.

What about puffs?

Miran slides the plastic bottles out one by one, stacking them in the boy's arms. Put those in to cool, and watch it! . . . Tater Tot nods eagerly and everybody laughs, remembering the time Tater forgot which part of the creek he'd stashed the bottle in . . . ha-ha-ha . . . The wee lad hangs his head in shame. People say the boy's mother was the Bulgarian, but judging from his dark skin, there's no doubt she was a gypsy. Miran gives him a gentle kick to send him on his way.

What you got there, boys? Napalm inquires. The faded blue of ancient tattoos peeks from under his boilersuit, a SPARTA PRAHA scarf is nonchalantly wrapped around his neck, and a woolen cap sits perched atop his noggin. He blinks, the whites of his eyes swollen with bloodred threads.

Miran hands him the pack of provisions. Napalm dips his hand in with a smile and comes out with a loaf of bread wrapped in foil. Pulls a few pouches of seasoning from the pockets. The fish are ready now.

Whoever wants, help yourselves, says Napalm, motioning toward the fire. Now listen to what I tell you, while our beer cools off a tad.

The old geezer takes a seat by the stones around the firepit, enjoying the feel of the heat coming off them.

Now I've already told you the story of how your dad and me and your uncle Lomoz met, haven't I?

Course you have, someone peeps up, sounding a little bit whiny, a little bit annoyed.

You all, loungin around here now, were still wadin through the mushrooms, Napalm says, when the local boys were buildin up their weapons collections . . . Hey, stop yawnin, you there, what're you yawnin for? . . . Meanwhile one of the gang is stuffing his face with fish while another sharpens a stick for grilling sausage. They've heard it all before, many times. But Napalm couldn't care less.

So one day little uncle Lomoz, hidden in the cellar, cuts the stock off a German rifle and he's filin down the barrel . . . makin it shorter so it'll fit under his jacket, for roebuck and what have you . . . see, cause the Germans strung up his uncle, and his old man didn't make it out of Mauthausen, same as his other neighbors, cause y'know that was the concentration camp for folks from around here, and his old lady was a simple country girl, didn't have a clue what would happen after the war, none of em trusted in the people's rule of Communist Russia . . .

But mainly folks had gotten used to death and weapons, so little Lomoz got him some arms, for poachin, that goes without sayin, but mainly it looked like the fightin'd be goin on forever, what other kina postwar was he supposed to picture? . . . And this idea caught on with the other boys as well, and what with all the heaps of guns the Germans and Russians left behind, there was also times it was just a helluva lotta fun . . . bang and pow out in the woods . . . and so little Lomoz is down there in his basement hideout filin away, sweat pourin off of him, and suddenly he sees out the window . . . a person! And this someone says, You'll never file it down that way. Clamp it in two vices, see. The stock, that's easy, that's wood, right, but the barrel slides back and forth when you file it . . . Little Lomoz goes racin up the stairs and grabs hold of the kid at the window, another orphan, that's right, your daddy Bašta . . . and that's how they got together.

We know.

You already told us that.

We've heard it before!

Yeah, so they put together their own little gang . . . Napalm goes on, the two of them, Lomoz and Bašta, stompin around the forest, trainin themselves for combat, then old Hrozen joined up too, Pražma, and Píťa, course old man Lojda, obviously, and others.

So what about you, Uncle? asks Tater Tot, slapping a fish fillet on a slab of bread. Well done and well smoked, the way they like it.

Bon appétit, says Napalm, handing him a pouch. Black pepper, straight up.

I joined too. What is it now?

Napalm seizes hold of the coughing, moaning Tater Tot, who has his hands wrapped around his neck, and pours rum down his throat, sending him into a retching fit.

Anyone else wanna interrupt?

Uh-uhhh, comes the collective response.

So the local boys learn how to handle all those guns, keepin an eye out for Czech narks and the Red Army sergeants, who were gettin ready to leave after the war, and one day young Lomoz goes out to cut grass for the rabbits, scythe tucked in his belt, and he sees the Reds linin up with all their buggies, all their carts and horses and whatnot, so he stops along the side of the road to wave along with everyone else . . . which he never should've done . . . since one of the lieutenants spotted him . . . lieutenant from the supply train . . . laid eyes on the strapping lad and asked the mayor for assistance.

We could use a couple young men like him to mind the animals for us, drive the herd to the next district over.

By all means, nods the crowd headed by the mayor. By all means, brothers, we can help all the way to the border . . . They chose the boys deliberately, no household heads, they didn't want any fathers missing from home.

And little Lomoz agrees, figurin it's an adventure, and if he's lucky maybe he'll scare up a gun or somethin . . . along the way . . . So they headed out, right then and there . . . and uncle Lomoz didn't come back home again for twenty years. His old lady passed soon after, and he didn't have nobody else, cept his little friends, so there was nobody left to remember him, nobody to make a complaint. It wasn't so much of a big deal when people disappeared back then.

Hm, somebody says. Everyone's busy stuffing their faces. Someone brings a bottle up from the creek, apparently unconcerned that it may not be completely chilled.

So Lomoz was forced to drive the herd all the way to Russia, and ended up in a camp there, seein as he was a foreigner, not to mention they held the scythe against him as evidence, claimin he infiltrated a Red Army unit with a weapon. And after twenty some years in those awful labor camps of theirs, he traveled all over Soviet Russia, plus some other Communist countries too, till finally they let him go home, and where did he head?

We know, Napie . . .

You told us before!

Umpteen times!

Straight to the Baštas in Poříčí, right where you are now! Yep, and then we came across that tank up on the bridge.

Ah-hah!

Hm.

We know!

So you've eaten and drunk your fill. Everything taste all right?

Oh yeah!

It was all right . . .

It was excellent, declares one greasy mouth.

Then let's go, Napalm commands, and he gets up and they go rushing off into the woods. Even Richie gets up and dusts off his sports coat. The only one they're still looking out for is Solder.

24

THE JUBILEE GIFT MEGAPROJECT. A SLICE OF
LOCAL HISTORY. RESEARCH. RECONNAISSANCE
WORK MIDSTREAM. WORK ON DRY LAND.
THE RAISING. SOLDER'S PROMISE.

The tank looms over a small open space in the trees along the river.
Everyone worked their tails off to raise it from the Sázava's bottom.
Then they all took turns making the necessary repairs. Now, for the
first time, the whole collective beholds the gift in all its splendor. Soon
they'll start the engine. And not just for a test run in the bushes, through
the trees.

No. Solder and his chosen crew will drive the tank up the forest road
to the asphalt route, just a short way from U Paručky. Then, after they
show off the tank to the astonished Bašta and the assembled wedding
guests, will come the crowning touch. Solder has a live round prepared
in the launcher. The celebration will kick off with a shot from the tank.

So how did the whole idea of this gift for their dad begin?

They were lounging around the scrapyard after a fairly ordinary
workday when Richie got the idea of raising the Russian tank from the
river.

Tank?

That got the attention of the boys born and raised in the illicit auto
shop.

It'll be a victory monument to tremendous bravery and courage, said
Richie, thinking it through for the others.

I mean, it's so sad around here, said Richie. His saying so made them
all even sadder. Richie had moments like that. When the words just
flew from him. Dangling his feet off the seat he had on the porch of his
junkyard trailer, tossing back red wine.

The boys gulped at their beers.

The region is strewn with monuments, right? said Richie, lifting himself up toward the clouds of the incoming night, massing over the land like a herd of sinister bulls.

We got monuments to the fallen of World War I all over the place out here, covered with the names of heroes from local clans, including our own, isn't that right, boys?

That's right.

Plus a plaque or two for the partisans, specially in the woods out around Černé Voděrady, and the duly cared-for graves from World War II, and those little signs they put up with the names of farmers and other folks, executed under the Communists, right? said Richie, flaunting his education.

Yes, someone squeaked.

All those poor folks killed, tortured to death, missing, right?

Right!

Nothin but subjugation, right? But what about havin a Czech victory monument too, huh? Richie said, getting heated up underneath the star clusters shining wildly through the dark tangle of the cosmos.

And what would be more fitting than a tank raised from its eternal grave in the depths of the Sázava?

It was as if Richie's long-ago school days had been brought back to life. He leaped up on his seat, towering over his audience like he was lecturing from a dais.

Boys! The time for heroics has come, we need to let the country breathe! Richie flailed his arms about, hair practically on edge.

Yes, Richie spoke so fervently and beautifully that day that everyone was in raptures.

And honor your dad! And not only him! Who do you think lit the tank on fire that day in Poříčí and tipped it into the river? That's right, old Bašta here and his boys, said Richie, pointing to Lomoz and Napalm, who by that point were practically preening.

Old Lojda was in on it too! added someone.

And old man Pražma, said somebody else, remembering the one who drowned.

Sure, we honor their heroic deed and raise the tank from the bottom! Why not, right? Richie concluded as if his speech had been prepared.

But to be honest, if anyone had asked, he himself didn't quite understand what had gotten into him.

That's right! said Miran.

That's right, said Kája, seconding him.

Why not, no sweat, the others chimed in.

Let's do it! exclaimed Solder.

Yes, they were all excited. Whose dad and his buddies took out a Russian tank? Ours! It sounded good, really good. And there couldn't have been a more fitting gift in the world to give old Bašta for his coming jubilee. The idea of attaching Kája and Světlana's wedding to the date as well practically suggested itself.

Following Richie's speech, they decided to carry out the plan in secret.

They were especially careful to keep it hush-hush in front of old Bašta, carrying on with their normal work as usual. Not only did they not want to spoil the surprise. The thing about the tank was . . . there had been casualties, and not only Russkies. There was a girl. A local. If word got out, people might start poking around. Better to present them with a fait accompli.

At first Solder and Richie just sort of roamed along the riverbank with binoculars, mostly around the bridge, then they paddled this way and that, outfitted with goggles and fins, floating up and down the Sázava with sonar, patiently combing the bottom wherever local legend had it that the tank had ended up.

Naturally they took into account changes in current, as well as shifts in riverine sedimentation, mud and sand. You could walk into any dive bar around and people would tell you where the tank was. And of course plenty of folks thought it was outright fiction. But what played most into the hands of the keen investigators was the fact that the authorities had long since written off the case. As soon as the army divers brought up the dead and destroyed the equipment. Then the water swallowed it up. So the heap of scrap officially no longer existed as far as the authorities were concerned.

After conferring with Miran, who held the purse strings, Solder hired a frogman squad. And after Richie's research, he also met with several experts, for the most part history buffs, and underwent a number of valuable consultations concerning the tank's instrumentation and engine type.

Mostly they were amazed that the machine they were planning to haul up from the bottom of the Sázava was still perfectly modern. Solder quickly acquired all the latest catalogs, studying up on navigation and stabilization systems. The practical uses of the fifty-some-year-old tank were confirmed by Richie's investigations, conducted in the Municipal Library of Benešov, and of course by poking around the Internet. Finally, Richie and Solder, two luminaries possessed, selected the date of dredging.

Things moved fast from there on in. Under the cover of night, they moved the mobile crane to the spot they had picked out, and the hired frogmen slipped beneath the surface with a plop. And it came to pass.

Hands pressed to their mouths, the furious barking of village dogs in the background, the boys assembled along the riverbank gazed in awe at the streams of water flowing off the armored titan as it rose above the surface. And, hoisting the machine with massive chains by the light of the stars, they landed it in the flatbed on their very first attempt, as if guided by nature itself, the flatbed's wheels sinking noticeably under the weight.

The tank was immediately transported to Napalm's outpost, a few hundred meters distant. They had paved the road with gravel in advance. Solder left nothing to chance. He knew when it came not only to raising the tank but to its transport, he needed to think in terms of performing a miracle. And so it came to pass.

Nothing left now but to do the work that Solder and the others were used to from the scrapyard. Get a hunk of metal up and running? No big deal.

Still the preparations took months. To the constant hiss of blowtorches, Solder, Richie, and the other welding-helmeted volunteers worked at strengthening the problematic spots in the armor. The hardest part, of course, was getting the tracks back in working order, along with the control and steering mechanism, which the occupiers had either removed or destroyed.

Richie looked into the deals offered by everyone from arms conglomerates to domestic tinkerers, while Solder gritted his teeth in the face of his initial setbacks, thinking about the bombed, starving, cold-wracked Soviet engineers, who worked with the threat of advancing German troops and the gulag hanging over their heads. And it paid off.

Barbaric, primitive, and supremely efficient was how the technical handbooks described the tank. And they were right.

A thirteen-year-old could've fixed that! Solder bellowed in elation, doing a little dance with Richie on the admittedly somewhat sloppily patched seats, upholstered with blankets by the girls.

A ten-year-old could've driven that, Solder said to himself dreamily, studying the biographies of the Soviet tank commanders, who sat in the armored vehicles for the first time as illiterate orphans fleeing burned-out villages.

For live ammunition, Solder's plan was to raid the famous tank museum in Lešany. His older brother told him absolutely not.

So Solder began snooping around for sources with connections to munitions factories and armories. He settled down a bit once Richie put his network into operation, keeping an eye out for any suspicious acquisitions at army surplus stores. And once they began to stray down the various illegal paths where ammunition and tactical equipment from the Ukrainian-Russian wars was known to travel, he settled down completely. Hooking up to networks like those, reeking of crime and corruption, was just another fun adventure for the likes of Bašta's boys.

The two of them also picked up tricks and tips from the Polish TV series *Four Tankmen and a Dog*, which Richie dug up somewhere on the web and which they now spent many an evening with, loaded on grass and red wine after a day of heavy labor with soldering guns, oxyacetylene torches, milling cutters, and other tools.

And given that Richie still had errands to run all over the region, Napalm, who had proved to be a real whiz in the forest garage, ended up as Solder's right-hand man.

So it was that Solder and Napalm stood stripped to the waist under the fiery Sázava sun, grinding connecting joints.

Solder wiped the sweat from his forehead, took a slug from his bottle of beer, and glanced over at his hotshot partner, wielding a ten-kilo crowbar like it was a pigeon feather. Those studs jumped a Russian tank and took it out, unarmed, Solder thought, tearing up. Just because they felt like it.

Solder remembered his dad, who'd been buried alive in the mines. When he came out a gimp, they let him go and took everything he had.

Despite the stigma of being an ex-con, he established a thriving business, but he always had to be on the alert. Solder remembered Pražma, too, who came home from the slammer a hothead, drank like crazy, and ended up drowned. And Lomoz, who'd lived in hell ever since he was a kid, so going to prison for the tank was practically a health retreat. And Lojda, who'd already been locked up before for printing anti-Communist lampoons on clandestine printing presses. And Napalm? They broke him so badly when he was inside that he decided to risk escape and hide out in the forest.

This tank here'll be like their reward, Solder said to himself.

Just then, a cluster of sparks popped from Napalm's crowbar. Solder stepped toward him. Hey, Napie, you and me're gonna ride in that tank together!

The old man lifted his head, a breeze from the river ruffling his tousled mane. He tugged at his graying whiskers.

What's that? It slowly dawned on him. And a vision formed in his mind. The wedding guests would be ready and waiting. The whole merry crowd gathered on the lawn in front of the bordello. Bašta and the others craning their heads. Where're the boys? Where is he . . . where's Napalm? And where's the gift?

And suddenly, stunningly, the tank comes rumbling in and fires off a congratulatory shot from its barrel . . . with him, Napalm, waving and nodding from the turret.

Napalm threw his arms around Solder. They didn't give a damn about the sloshing beer. The old man in blue coveralls raised his hand, palm calloused with numerous scrapes, new and old alike, and grasped the boy's right hand in his.

Their eyes met in a long, manly gaze. In all his life, Napalm had never hoped for such glory and honor. But now it was his dream.

The two men silently got back to work.

That's the way it went.

And now a T-34 tank looms in a quiet spot among the trees a short way from the murmuring flow of the Sázava.

Napalm brings the whole pack of them over to look.

25

SANDBANK. THE APPARITION OF THE RIDERS.
BATTLE IN THE WATER. DOUBTS ABOUT THE
DEVIL. WHAT THE LITTLE GUY NEEDS . . . AND
WHICH WAY THEY'RE FLOATING. ROARING WATER.
THE COAL BARGE.

Sandbank, says the girl. That's as far as we're goin.

The rowboat's bow is stuck.

Papa has the slicker thrown over his shoulders. Bag in hand. Waves at them, hollers something. Sets off through the water toward them.

Hey, go give em a hand. I'm too fat now. It'll hold you, though.

The sand, just below the surface, locks around his ankle. Black rocks jut from the bottom, digging into the soles of his feet.

Papa stamps through the water toward them, bag in his arms. Rain falls from the sodden clouds blown in by the wind, drops of water drumming down on every side.

The girl pitches the oar onto the rocks, the boy holds it down.

Papa, stepping onto the oar, tries to grab hold of the boat, causing it to sway.

The boy lifts the bag out of Papa's arms, feeling the gunshot hole yawning under his hand. Then he hears them. Even amid the suddenly intensified downpour of rain.

Motorbikes. Up on the road. Flags aflutter, a banner declaring RIDERS OF ODIN, the riders in animal masks, someone's portrait waving proudly on their unfurled standards. The bikes spring into motion the moment the boy looks their way.

He hands the bag to the girl. Rolls into the skiff's bottom, himself not even sure how.

The cavalcade of screaming men leap from their machines, front wheels in the water. Bison is already several steps into the river, leather-gloved fists raised in anger. A few more men stamp in through the shallows behind him, splashing and spraying water. A pair of enormous wings protrudes from the head of one of them, another's face is hidden behind a sharp-beaked bird mask.

Papa and the girl are trying to shove the boat back into the current, inch by inch, wedging the oars against the black heaps jutting from the water.

Push!

A little more!

The bull-horned helmet and another bird-headed muscleman go plodding through the water like robots. The bull staggers. Tugs his foot free of the sand, but goes down. His main man tries to grab him by the shoulder, but tumbles in up to his hips himself. They flail their limbs like dung beetles, inhaling frothy impurities.

Grab hold of the oar, dude! Papa laughs.

He slams the oar down on the surface, drenching the bull man with water.

Get the hell outta here! the girl shrieks with such gusto it makes everybody's ears hum.

Papa bashes the man in the head. The harder the roughneck struggles to free himself, the deeper he sinks, such being the nature of sandbanks.

A few more brutes grind their way through the sludge while the rest of the gang stands around their bikes on the riverbank. Urging the pursuers on. Cracking jokes, whistling. With one well-aimed blow, Papa knocks the helmet off the guy's head. It vanishes under the surface, heavy as a stone. Papa hammers at the water around him, managing to land one in the birdman's chest as well.

The girl wrestles the other oar into the boat.

One more blow, the guy lands on his back and disappears into the brown, foamy water. With a tug and a jerk the skiff gives way.

And off they float.

You could've waited a little longer, sputters Papa, face ashen with rage.

What kina stupid bullshit was that?

He would've pulled you outta the boat!

They briefly tustle over the oars, then Papa slides them into the pins.

He would've drowned you, you silly goose!

He wouldn't've drowned me, he loves me!

The riverbank slowly recedes, the figures on it clustered around their metal dragonflies. The rain makes the colors appear to be flaking and peeling away.

Papa slumps back on the seat.

Whew! I thought it was the devil himself when I first spotted that guy!

Pff, hardly, says the girl.

But for fuck's sake, I mighta killed him! I really thought he was the devil.

Hey, I'm not gonna row this thing by myself!

Well, I just hope come judgment that's how they'll see it! I'd hate to roast in hell over some metalhead.

Don't worry about hell. Just worry what happens if he ever finds you.

And I didn't get a chance to change the little one's diapers!

By that point, everyone in the boat can smell it. And then it really starts to rain. The boy breaks out in goose bumps. His teeth chatter. He sticks his feet under the bag. Holds them there, feeling the warmth of his brother's body through his sneakers. Lays his hands on the bag, leans his whole body over it.

Through the trees they can see houses. Fences. Gardens and yards. They float rapidly downstream, each shaking off their fatigue. They feel the weight of the others' proximity and the all-pervading damp.

That little guy sleeps all the time, the girl observes.

I gave him a pill.

What'd you give him?

He's better off asleep.

Give him to me!

Calm down.

Give. Him. To. Me. He's gonna catch cold.

Stop movin around, you'll tip us over. And besides, he's wrapped.

He needs more than that.

Oh yeah?

He needs lotsa things.

I agree.

For instance, he needs to be changed, fed, washed, dried, moisturized, and played with. He needs all of that! You're killin him like this.

Excuse me, we are not killing him!

Then hand him over to me.

243

Wait'll we get ashore.

We're not goin ashore.

Oh no? Then where're we goin, girl?

You'll see.

Here, take this, says Papa, throwing his slicker over the girl's shoulders.

And on they float. Squatting in the wet. The boy, eyelids drooping wearily, hears the slap of the oars, feels the clingy drops on his skin.

The next time he opens his eyes, they're floating past a ravaged, dug-up section of riverbank, water streaming down the grooves in the soil as the raindrops pound the earth. Huge boulders jut from the rust-stained ground, dotted with clumps of heat-yellowed grass, stalks hanging loose in the burbling rivulets. Through the curtain of rain he can just make out the bucket of an abandoned backhoe. The outlines of mangled coal cranes take shape on the deserted banks, blood-colored corrosion and runny mud, earth's menstruation. Twisted rails go flashing past, rust-eaten minecarts locked to one another.

The skiff jostles against a tree trunk. The mighty giant, slashed with rock scars, is overgrown with moisture-imbibing sulfur shelves, some barnacle lichen here and there, like a pet with fleas.

The girl, who had been standing to get a better view, plops down on the seat under the impact, grabbing hold of Papa's hand. He wraps his arms around her and she nestles close. With the other hand, though, she points urgently downstream.

He doesn't hear her over the noise.

The roar of water rushes toward them, water crashing on water. The pounding rain had covered up the din, but now the cacophonous moil is right ahead of them.

Falls? Papa yells at the girl.

She nods.

Papa wrenches hard on the oars, trying to move the boat out of the current, but only succeeds in rippling the water's dark surface.

Coal barge, he shouts.

The boy spots a potbellied shape wedged into the riverbank amid a tangle of branches in the waters up ahead.

The girl, crouched in her slicker, keeps tight hold of the bag on her knees. Wisps of hair flare from her hood, as if there were a hidden sun reddening within.

Someone screams . . . Papa paddles furiously, but in vain . . . they go barreling straight toward the barge, another inch and they'll be crushed . . . then suddenly the current gently displaces them into softer-flowing water through a tunnel of interlacing branches, toward the vessel's stern.

A rusty stairway leads to the barge's second story. As the girl seizes hold of the handrail, the slicker drops from her shoulders and the boy catches sight of the damp red tufts bristling from her underarms. He freezes momentarily as the skiff jolts against the stairs, but recovers to help the girl wrestle the bag up the steps. Papa leaps onto the stairs behind them, flying through the air apelike, and lands so hard the entire stairway shakes.

The rowboat slips away beneath his feet like a giant old loafer, disappears in the stream. Papa lies on his back beside them. They turn to face each other in the rain.

So much for their ride.

They climb up the stairs in a knot, into the ship's belly. Papa carries the bag now, protecting the little head bulging out with his bare arm. The bullethole is getting wider. As Papa leans on the steps for support, the little boy stares out at him through the tear.

Papa swats the girl on the back to keep it moving. She could just stare and stare into those moony little eyes, those pinchable little cheeks, and his cute little nose squeezed between them, but they can't afford to stop now or they'll all slide down.

So they continue their climb up the wet stairway, Papa clutching the bag to his chest, arm wrapped around his son to keep from banging his little head against the railing. The devil only knows how many twisted bars are sticking out along the way.

The girl opens a metal door. It gives onto a ramp, which she squats right down on, followed by the others, and they go sliding down a narrow shaft, landing one on top of the other like wet sacks.

They sit amid the darkness in the belly of the barge. The floor beneath them is covered with gravel, coal grit. The roaring water down here is muffled by the ship's bottom. They can hear each other breathe. The boy blinks hard, but can't make out a thing.

Where are we? whispers Papa.

On the barge!

I know that, stupid. But where do we go now?
They'll be here soon. Gimme the bag!
Who'll be here soon?
People.
What people?
The ones that live here.
Wow! What kind of people would wanna live here.
My mom, for one.
Oh.
Just wait'll they're here. Then we'll see who's stupid.

26

WAITING FOR SOLDER. A SLICE OF MILITARY
HISTORY. MACINKA'S HORROR. KILLER FROM
THE WATER. SOLDER'S BULL'S-EYE. NAPALM:
BACK THEN ON THE BRIDGE. MIRAN'S DECISION.
MIRAN'S THE OLDEST!

Get a load a that! Napalm proudly addresses the assembled youth. And
boy, do they.

The barrel looms above the water. They gave the whole tank a fresh
coat of camouflage green, and it really looks quite threatening. The
enormous oval-shaped hull has an organic feel to it, like an animal raring to go. Just start it up and let it rip. The tracks gave them a hard time.
Looking at the undercarriage, you can imagine the terrifying crunch-
ing sound as it crushes any obstacles that stand in its path. The tor-
sion bars for the suspension are brand new, they were able to purchase
those legally.

Similarly, the fuel canisters, searchlights, armored side skirts, and
lots of other bells and whistles were easily acquired in specialized
army shops. They even managed to scrounge up an old machine gun,
couldn't do without that.

One of the Bašta brothers is missing, though. The most important
one. Miran glances about. Everyone looks around for Solder. Where
could he be?

Richie impatiently raps his knuckles against his belt. He's ready to get
started. This is one speech he prepared.

Just then, one of the twins points to the woods. Solder. Finally! As he
makes his way toward them, there is clearly something off. He's stagger-
ing, holding his hand to his mouth. Somebody chuckles. Is he sloshed?

I gotta talk to you, Solder says through his teeth, breathing into Miran's ear. His face is as white as a full moon. Miran can see he's shaking.

Not now.

Dad's dead. They killed him.

The two of them step aside. Richie, taking a breath, shoots them a "What the hell?" look, but launches into his speech.

This tank here, boys, is a tee-fifty-four. Same as a tee-thirty-four, only modified. Great Russian product with a reputation worldwide. Like the Kalashnikov or the Topol missile. This here tank not only destroyed Nazi combat vehicles, but also put the finishing touches on communism in the GDR, which was a part of Germany, boys. In nineteen fifty, this here machine established North fuckin Korea, and in fifty-six it ground the anti-Soviet uprising in Hungary to a pulp. It stood the test in Africa, when Israel attacked. And a total of six thousand three hundred of these here steel beetles steamrolled Czechoslovakia in sixty-eight, which they mighta taught ya in school. Now, we're talkin a solid machine, I mean these tanks here enforced martial law in Poland in the early eighties, and the Serbs were still runnin Yugoslavia with em in ninety-six. I googled all that for you boys at the library in Benešov, which, trust me, wasn't easy. Thank you!

Richie is rewarded with a round of loud applause.

Meanwhile, Miran is listening to how the murder happened.

It wasn't as if their dad had been alone in the encampment. Macinka had requested some time off from Monča's and had taken up cooking over at the scrapyard, partly out of a woman's natural desire to take care of men and partly because it was decent pay for a part-time job. One of the twins had been feeling faint that morning and was trying to sleep it off in the hammock. There were also a few of their buddies and some hired hands working on the cars. And being that guns attract guns, Solder happened to be out in his trailer cleaning the firearm he was planning to show off when he introduced the tank. That was when he saw their dad hobbling off toward his favorite fishing spot, rod in hand.

Solder was just about packed and ready to head out and meet the rest of them, over at Napalm's outpost.

Then he heard Macinka's terrible scream and went bounding off. He found the girl bent over the elder Bašta, who was lying in the stream. Catching sight of Solder, she lifted a bloody hand and pointed to the opposite bank. Someone was scrambling out of the water, pulling himself up by the bushes. Macinka handed Solder a big knife the killer had dropped when she startled him. Her eyes gushed tears as she sobbed that she had been bringing old Bašta a snack when a shadow slipping through the current had materialized into a man rising up out of the water. He swung the knife and ran the old man through.

Solder lifted his gaze from the current lapping at his father's corpse, raised his gun, and fired off a series of shots. The person shouldering through the overgrown hogweed on the opposite bank dropped. Then his brother from the hammock showed up along with everyone else. Someone lifted the patriarch out of the water while the rest of them dove into the river and set out for the other side.

Solder didn't waste any more time, jumping into the Fiat and racing off to give the terrible news to his other brothers.

Then he laid the open knife, its blade engraved with the name of a foreign region, into Miran's hands. It was still damp with the water that had washed away his father's blood. And now the two were listening to their little baby brother.

So our dad destroyed a tank like this? says Tater Tot in a shaky voice, standing next to the tank. It towers over him like a fairy-tale monster.

When I close my eyes, I can still see it like it was today, says Napalm, taking the floor. August sun in the sky over Poříčí. Angelus is ringin. We're moseyin along, the whole crew—Pražma, Lojda, and Bašta, your daddy—drivin the cows home from pasture. When all of a sudden, we hear this terrible rumpus. And over the bridge comes this tank here, shouts Napalm, pounding the armor with his fist. And leadin the way on a motorbike is Tab's old man, our neighbor from Pyšely, who took up with the Russians.

Boo!

Shame! somebody cries.

And one lone man strides across the bridge toward em . . . why, it's our buddy Lomoz! And, boys, you better believe, no sooner did he get home from the Russian camps and drop anchor than he spotted himself a girl, cause after all those years of misery you can bet he was horny and hot to trot, and no sooner did he find himself a girl . . . than he decides to go and mix it up with a tank? Talk about a heartbreaker! So we leave the cows on the hill and go racin down there to help . . . and we get to the bridge and see Lomoz hangin off the tank barrel like he's tryin to tear it off, and we're shakin our heads like what kina stupid shit is he tryin to pull, so we don't even bother with our neighbor on the bike . . .

and your daddy is first to jump up on the rear, I climb up behind him, and the tracks are scrapin away on the ground, tearin up the pavement, Bašta grabs a pickax the fools've got attached to the shell and starts bangin away at the fuel tank . . . I look over at Lomoz, hangin off the barrel while they spin the thing around . . . and your dad's yellin, and Lojda, who hopped up on back after him, is clingin on like a leech. He hands him a lighter . . . and your daddy whips out a copy of *Rudé právo* we were readin out in the pasture, lights it on fire, and me and Lojda jump off, just in the nick of time! . . . Your dad shoves the paper into the hole Bašta knocked in the fuel tank, and the gas bursts into flames . . . And through the cloud of smoke we see the barrel with Lomoz still hangin onto it knock the head off one of the saint statues, golden halo and all . . . And as we go rollin across the pavement . . . the people inside open the hatch and a head pops out and catches the flames full on, and now that the hatch is open the smoke and flames go rushin in and the trapped tankmen're toast . . . and Lomoz is screamin his lungs out since he's gettin scorched too . . . And no sooner does he let go of the barrel and plunk into the river . . . than the driver, who's blinded, loses control, the tank crashes through the railing, and it lands in the water too . . . Goes flyin in with a huge splash . . . yep.

And what about Pražma?! somebody yelps.

The whole time this was goin on, he was over chokin that traitor on the motorbike!

Aha!!!

And Uncle, Tater Tot pipes up after a moment of moving silence.

What is it?

So is that when Uncle Lomoz lost his eyesight?

That's right. Flames burned his eyes out. Last thing he ever saw in his life was a Russian tank.

Oooh . . .

He was one sad man when we fished him out by the weir, down in Městečko.

Aaaaah . . .

And you know why he wanted to take on a Russian tank all by himself? That girl of his was whorin around with the tankists.

Now slow down there, Napie . . . Richie lays a hand on Napalm's frame.

I mean, here Lomoz is, thinkin about the wedding, and she's gettin it on with a bunch of Russian tankmen. Can you imagine how he felt?

Napie, zip it, says Richie.

Oh well, guess he made the wrong choice. It can happen, boys. When he came back home, starved for love and affection, she took him to seventh heaven, but thing was, she had to do it all the time. Her gateway to paradise was a good solid fuck. Some girls're like that, you know.

What's that, Uncle? Tater Tot asks, eyes agog.

And that first head that peeked out and caught that wall of flames had long hair. Yep, it was her. We were all sad after that.

And Uncle?

Yeah?

What about the Czech traitor on the motorbike?

He got away. And that was the last we heard of him.

Miran senses he needs to put the whole tank thing on hold. Who killed Dad? Those two guys from Hrom's tent. The Novočeši: New Czechs! What was Kája ramblin on about back there? How when Dad dies there was gonna be a land war? He wasn't about to say one word about Dad now in front of the others. Especially not in front of Kája. He wouldn't stop at anything then. They needed a chance to think things over.

Miran bends down and picks up the black tarp that every proper tank should have in case of rain.

He steps forward, dragging the tarp behind him. Everyone is watching. He circles around the tank. Flings the tarp over the rear. Thrusts the corner of it into Solder's hand.

Miran scrambles up the machine, covering it with the tarp.

What's wrong? Napalm shouts. A murmur passes through the group.

Miran turns to face them, standing on the tank.

It's not happenin, guys. Sorry, but we won't be givin this gift today. We're buryin the tank here.

Listen, bro, you can't just . . . mutters one of the twins in shock, tearing his black knit cap from his head. The other brothers, seething in anger, clamor around Napalm. We busted our butts!

Someone hurls a pinecone at Miran and hits him square in the nose.

Miran's the oldest! Tater Tot squeals belligerently.

Kája hops up on the tank to come to his brother's aid.

Sorry, boys, but we gotta put it on hold, Miran repeats, pulling the tarp over the turret. Even Solder, the chief engineer, is willingly going along now, and everyone can see it.

What, are you scared? barks Napalm.

Listen up, says Richie, trying to smooth things over. He has a hunch something terrible has happened. Miran's right. There's no time! I mean, we're no cowards, but if the Ukrainian front . . . they got those metal flies swarmin all over the place out there!

Oh, bullshit, Napalm roars.

They ain't comin here! shouts the kid brother, flinging his cap to the grass.

Let's wait and see how it develops. We're just puttin it on hold, no big deal! says Richie in a placating voice.

Boo, boo, boo! Napalm roars again.

Richie grips him firmly by his suddenly bowed shoulders. The others look on in shock as the old geezer buckles at the knees. Is the old warrior being deserted? Not quite. Somebody hands him a bottle of rum. They gather around, patting him consolingly on the back.

Let's have a bottle, boys, says Miran. Think it through in peace and quiet. Have a seat.

The discussion doesn't last long. Napalm remains defiantly silent. When they reach agreement to bury the tank where it is and have Napalm keep a watch on it, the way he has been up to now, he just sadly nods.

The bottles have all hissed. Richie gets to his feet. Sets out toward the river. He has his assignment. He'd like to catch up to the Old Log Cabineers as soon as possible.

The others rise as well, making ready to rustle off through the grass. See ya, Napie. Bye, Uncle! . . . their calls ringing out for the briefest moment over the river and through the woods . . . and only after the orphans have made their way, one by one, down the trail do the voices of the forest birds echo through the air. A drizzle falls, the woods glistening green in the drops. The tiny little hydrophytes thriving on the waterlogged soil once more gently raise their heads from the footprints of the departing squad. And this is how it's always been. A little rain and it will be like there was never anyone here at all.

27

NAPALM'S TALK WITH THE FISHERMAN.
ON THEOLOGY. DORA? WHERE TO TAKE THE
VIRGIN. WHAT NAPALM DREAMS OF.

Napalm dejectedly trudges back to his abode, a few stone's throws away from the tank. How would he keep an eye on it if he was any farther, right?

He kicks the stones, trying to chase away the feeling of despair. The jubilation, the glory, of him riding in on the tank, the crowning touch of the wedding, how many times had he already lived it out in his dreams . . .

He notices that somehow the fire has been kindled. Scales must have blown it to life. He gorges himself on the leftovers, consuming whatever he finds.

He'd placed the dried-up picture far away from the firepit. Made darn sure of that. Flames and antique canvas don't exactly agree with each other.

But when Scales had turned up the night before, stepping into the fire's dying light out of nowhere, Napalm had a bit of a fright.

The fisherman, rolled inside the canvas, soggy and hardened with mud, was almost entirely hidden from view. Wrapped around him like a hide stripped from an animal, the picture had shrunken and molded to his body.

Howdy! said a familiar-sounding voice from inside the tube.

Evenin, Napalm said guardedly, raking the embers.

Man, I'll bet you're wonderin how I can see outta here, huh? said the voice from inside the loudly colored object, mud-splattered bare feet poking out the bottom.

Napalm was relieved. He had thought it might be a ghost. But he recognized Scales's voice. Which cheered him up a bit. As long as it was Scales's ghost, he had nothing to worry about.

There's holes in it, see? So I can see out!

All right!

I was ready to drown myself. Shit. Lost my house. And my wife! The house really got to me. But this picture here saved me.

You were drownin, huh?

I tell you, there I was drownin, breathin in water, one minute scared I was gonna croak, the next that I wouldn't, when this picture comes bobbin up under me. Saved by a sacred painting. Now that's what I call a miracle!

Huh?

Too bad the frame got smashed on the rocks! See, gone. Then the picture wrapped itself around me and protected me from the rain. Is that somethin or what? Then I'm walkin along through the dark and I see your fire through the holes. Nice, right?

Are you hungry?

I am! What you got?

Got fish.

Any bread?

Bite or two.

Sounds good.

Scales bent forward, sliding the tube off over his head. He laid it on the ground nearby and took a seat beside his friend. Accepted a hand-rolled cigarette, lit it with a twig, and stretched his legs out toward the blaze, luxuriating in the feeling of bliss.

Napalm tries to get the tank out of his head. Back when they had stormed the tank, they had been fearless, young. Scarily young, didn't give a shit about anything. Now all he was doing was getting old, and soon he'd be in the ground. That tank was what had made him the man who everyone knew today.

Napalm watches Scales stuff his face. Takes out his tobacco, waits politely for his guest to finish feeding himself. Then rolls them both a smoke.

Boys were here, says Napalm. Bašta's crew. Whole army of em.

I seen em when I was dryin out the picture in a tree, says Scales. So they're gone now?

Yeah. Where you headed next?

Chlum. Take the Virgin to Black Lukáš. By the way, you did time with him. How'd he get that nickname, Black?

No reason, just for kicks. But that painting's all spattered in mud. And you made holes in it!

It's miraculous, my friend.

Listen, Scaley, I know you don't hide the fact you're religious. But I live in the woods, and I ain't good for shit anymore, but when it comes to God I got my own opinion.

Don't matter to him, Napie. One way or the other.

Look, you don't need to lecture me, Scales. Besides, I'm older than you are.

Yeah, yeah, you'll be outta here soon.

Least I'll have peace and quiet.

You sure about that? You really think?

Don't piss me off, Scales. I'm pissed enough with life as it is.

You know sumpin better?

Don't piss me off, I told you!

Listen, after death you're in the dark, like we'll be here in a while. Even in the dark you can still hear the wind fart in the grass or the blindworms crawlin around, and what do you think that is? You donno? That's God talkin. Straight up!

Huh, I never heard that before. Just the yowlin and squealin when a male muskrat climbs on a female, and they're slappin around out there, livin it up.

Well, there you go.

I'll be damned. That never occurred to me in my life.

Well, that's it.

Listen, though, Scales, what about you? You gonna go runnin around the woods rolled up in a painting? Now don't get stupid on me. Old Máťa, you know what a tough guy he was, till he got a sniff of those church pictures. Shit. All that paint, those old nasty smells or I don't know what whosit's cunt, but it drove him right round the bend. Everybody knows that. And look at the woman he had! You remember Růženka, right?

That little gal?

Yeah, she was little, but you could live in that thing of hers, shit.

Růženka, yeah.

Well, he ditched her, long with everything else. Hot mama like that!

Matter of fact, I'm lookin for a woman myself. Name is Dora. You know her?

Beats me.

Either I find her or not. We'll see after that.

Look, Scalester, I got this bottle of rum. Bašta boys left it here for me. So I wouldn't be so sad about the tank. Ah well!

Let's drink! But why're you sad?

All the work I put into that tank. I was so excited to fire it off!

The heck're you talkin about?

Ah, you wouldn't understand. I just wanted to ride in that fuckin tank at least once, for fuck's sake! Solder promised!

Napie, you're outta your mind. And you're not even drunk. I'm gonna head out with the Virgin in the mornin. Maybe even float on her a ways. Why not! Least then I'll find out if she's really miraculous. Come up to Chlum and see us.

Sonuvabitch, I can't tell you how many times I've dreamed of ridin in that tank!

Shit, you're like a little kid.

I took that Russkie tank *out*!

No more drinks for you, Napie! Better get some sleep. Maybe you'll dream you're in the tank again, says Scales, suppressing a laugh.

And come daybreak, both he and the painting are gone without a trace.

28

HYGIENE ONBOARD SHIP. CAPTAIN LOJDA.
GORGEOUS FUR. THE STORY OF THE OLD LOG
CABINS. BOOZE COLONY. MÁŤA AND WHAT HE LEFT
BEHIND. MÁŤA AND THE MAN WITH THE PANS.

Lost in the darkness of the coal ship's womb, they cower under the blows. Someone's feet are stomping across the metal sheets above them.

There must be another set of stairs leading into the darkness; they can see the glow, the flickering glow of a candle. They look around at each other, establishing eye contact . . . Papa, every muscle tense, presses the bag to his chest as the boy crawls toward him, taking in his papa's tang amid the wet, and out of the gloom a shadow emerges, taking shape as a man in a sports coat, it was him tramping around up there a moment ago.

Richie! Světlana launches up out of her squat toward him. She rolls around in his arms. Richie lifts a candle over his head. Ikea, thick chunky log of a thing, for romantics. He digs a flashlight out of his pocket, hands it to her switched on. The soot and coal dust they've kicked up floats in the air around them as they stand, coughing, amid the feeble light.

Hey, Richie! I came to invite everyone to the wedding! Where's the captain?

You guys're soaked, huh? You can dry out up top, c'mon!

The girl sets off with the others in tow, treading cautiously through the depths of the ship, following the cone of light . . . as they climb the spiral stairs, the boy glances up at the girl's firm, meaty rear end, water dripping from her slicker . . . they press on toward the inviting warmth.

In a dark, narrow corridor the girl grips hold of a door handle, opens. A cabin. They all crowd in behind her.

A stove. Prehistoric, iron, and burning hot. A poker, coal scuttles. The visitors, hissing in pain from their scrapes and bruises, huddle around the stove. Warmth radiates too from bulbs along the walls, covered in paper shades decorated with squiggles. Hanging from their cords, the Chinese lanterns sway and bump.

Next to the stove is a newish-looking shower stall. Sliding open the plastic door, a mighty naked hulk of a man, more giant than human, eyes the unexpected callers. Bearded and shaggy, his gray-haired bushy chest is sprinkled with black flecks, leading down his belly to the shadowy gray of his crotch from which his privates hang. He stands in a cloud of steam. The reflections of the stove's dancing flames skipping across the white exterior of the stall only serve to enhance his intimidating appearance.

Stacks of books, heaps of newspapers and documents, spill across the floor amid the gloom around the rumpled bed . . . Papa, moved perhaps by the volume of erudition, gasps.

The man stares brazenly back at his unannounced company. Using a purple washcloth, he wipes the drops from his arms and pats down his hearty chest, dabbing at his skin as if arranging himself into place. The top of his head brushes against the shower stall roof. He swipes at the showerhead with his paw, turning it off. Focuses in on his visitors, taking a closer look.

Světluška, my child!

She leaps into his arms, the slicker sliding off her. What does she care if it lies in a puddle, it's soaked through as it is.

The naked man picks her up off the ground, ignoring her squeals, showering her with kisses. No sooner is she back on her feet than the girl rushes over to Papa, wrests the bag out of his hands, and drags the little boy over into a nest of blankets.

Sit down, folks, make yourselves comfortable, says Lojda.

He steps out of the cloud of steam, and as he sneaks past, slowly drawing a red blanket off the bed to cover himself, they see that he's an old geezer.

The power of his upper arms and thighs is collapsing into the sagginess of old age. Spots cover his hands and chest. The skin of his neck, scarred with wrinkles, hangs limp like a wet cloth.

The boy unconsciously mimics his papa's movements. Just like him, rubbing his hands over the stove and stomping his feet. He watches in fascination as their shadows mesh on the wall.

What comes next amazes him even more.

As the girl lays his brother, unpacked and naked, onto the blankets, the boy sees there are tendrils of flesh covering the little boy's teeth, as if they'd just pushed their way out.

Face twisted into a smile, the little one lolls on his back. He extends his moisture-swollen arms, little legs like rolling pins, skin blanched, tightening and contracting over his narrow bones. He grins toothily, drooling. The joy practically flares out of him, fusing with the warmth of the stove. Then suddenly, with an almost imperceptible movement, he rises up on all fours. Lavished with attention from the captivated on-lookers, the squirt props himself up on the blankets like an enormous human flea.

The boy, quite confused, glances down at his own scrawny legs. They tremble, even in spite of the warmth rising up through them like a plant.

The stove is glowing hot.

Rusty hair flying in every direction, the girl washes off the child, keep-ing a firm hold on him, till some internal spark, likely ignited by the heat, propels the little demon into action, slithering out of her arms.

But the redhead knows how to handle him!

Next thing you know, she's pulling up a washtub, squirting a gener-ous dollop of Caribic Energy liquid soap onto a sponge she scared up, dousing the restive pup in a rain of Intim Beauty body spray, sloshing the babe around in the tub, and perfuming him with a rich assortment of other products.

Clearly she is well acquainted with the space they're in.

She unearths a few more hygiene items from the corners of the room, some of them almost luxurious-seeming.

Even as the moisture evaporates from her own clothes, enveloping her in a robe of steam like she was some water priestess, the redhead doesn't give a damn about herself, absorbed in her loving caresses of the little guy.

And Lojda? He towers over them in his red chieftain's blanket, taking part in the cleansing with the occasional reassuring grunt like a barbar-ian king, calmed after his own purifying bathing ritual, attention trans-fixed by the pietà.

Jesus and Mary, look at the schlong on that tot! he says. How old is he?

Hello, Papa says.

Well, hullo! I recognized you right away. You me?

The same, Papa nods.

Lojda moves to the stove, where the weary trio are warming themselves: Papa, his boy, pressed to his side, and Richie too. They stand holding their palms to the heat.

People told me bout you.

Yeah?

Made more of yourself than anyone else in the class. Not that you had a lot of competition.

Heh-heh.

No but seriously. Did you really do plays in Italy? Holland? I heard you were even in Oslo. People saw you on TV at the station in Čerčany.

Yeah?

I saw Tab! I get reports from folks every now and then. But then came the real news: Tabby and the boys're here on holidays!

That's right!

So you're famous. I'm impressed. Saw the world, tasted freedom, made a name for yourself. How many folks can say that? My hat's off to you!

Ah, jeez, I mean . . .

The hell're you wearin, you clown? That T-shirt your way of playin a Russian sailor? Or is that your Popeye disguise?

How long's it been since we saw each other anyway, teacher?

Thirty years. I was mister teacher to you in those days.

Lojda steps to the bed, reaches out a paw, attaches it to the girl's behind, caresses it, tenderly and earnestly. She stretches up to the leathery canopy of his hand, then spies the pair at the stove.

Stop that!

Fur's done, says the old geezer, kicking aside the slicker tangled up in his feet. He recedes into the gloom, comes out again with something hanging from his hand.

Now I'm givin it to you.

When she stands up, even with the heat from the stove, it's like another lamp turning on in the room.

She's blushing.

I used to give her a fur for each trick, explains the old man. And I hunt the old-fashioned way, live traps only.

He tosses the fur coat over the girl's shoulders. With a dip of the arms and a shrug of the shoulders she slips it on, the queen, turning a circle in front of them.

Caught the last fella not too long ago and sewed it onto the hood. Does it fit?

She flips the hood up over her head. Turns in a circle like a short, curvy nun.

It'll remind you of the human warmth we used to spark, fuckin out here in the wet and desolation, isn't that right, baby doll.

Mm-hm.

I'd just hunt, skin, and sew, killin time till you showed up. Just glad I got it done, can't see for shit anymore. Ruined my eyes readin, y'know?

I know, she nodded.

Those aren't beavers, are they? Papa asks. Those're nutria, right?

Muskrats too, says Lojda.

Whatever, says Světlana.

She spins again in the glow of the stove's flames, wriggles in the bulbs' shine, dances in the lanterns' blaze. Not a seam shows, the shaggy garment fits perfectly. Papa and the boy stare, knowing the hands that made that fur coat have kneaded every inch of her body. The buttons on it are made out of colored plastic bottle-tops.

My little Světlana always came back to me from all her travels, like a bedraggled little kitten, isn't that right?

That's right.

It's always been my goal to have mistresses so young that I won't be around by the time their beauty fades, the old-timer shares with them.

Papa nods.

Now she's gettin married, announces the old man, raising his voice.

Is that right? Papa says.

And not only that but she's pregnant!

Well, teacher, we really appreciate havin the chance to warm ourselves up here with you. Thank you so much! But we've gotta get goin now. Could you tell us where we are exactly?

Where you are, my boy? On an anchored boat. Right here.

And which direction is Městečko? That's where we need to go.

Can you walk on water, Tab?

I figured me and the boy'd give it a try. We could leave the little one here awhile. What do you think, teacher? He seems to get on well with Světla.

I could use the older one as a cabin boy. You can take the little one.

Right. We'll just have a bite to eat, if you've got anything, and then head out.

Goddammitall, Tab, relax! All you ever think of's yourself. Wedding's a pretty important thing in a young girl's life, don't you think? You're doin just fine for yourself, the old geezer says.

Really?

Don't you doubt it! Folks know who you are, know bout your art. And besides, you're a father. There's people here stuck in the same place their whole lives. Never did shit. My congratulations to you.

But now I'm just totally fucked and full of shit, aren't I, teach?

Now don't you go hangin your head on me!

My family and me got on this crazy ride and I just can't make it stop.

C'mon now, it can't be as bad as all that!

Sonuvabitch! Papa shrieks. I guess it's me!

The main thing is not to scare your boy. Don't want to do that.

Papa breathes in, seemingly about to let loose, then instead furtively wipes away the tear that wells in his eye, rubbing it into his beard where it can't be seen. One tear, that's it.

Children are a joy, Tab. Nature has been generous to you. But one thing I can't get outta my head. Where did you say you were goin?

Městečko. Monča's there, y'know. She can take care of the boys. So I can get to work.

Then what?

You must have a boat here, right?

So what'd you decide on? What's your work gonna be about?

I'll tell you, teach. The things I've been through, I'm fuckin pissed. It's just pourin outta me. I gotta write.

Yeah, that's understandable, Lojda nods. At least let the children warm up, though. Let em rest. This boy can't stop shakin. And the little one? You sure Monča's gonna want him too?

She's fine with it, Papa snaps.

All right, you'll see. So you all're hungry, huh?

Richie comes dashing up from the bowels of the ship, hands full of plastic bowls and plates. Lays down a basket of bread, then with a wink some sort of historic preserves. The boy stuffs himself to the point he practically faints.

Last but not least, Richie brings in a huge pan, gripping it proudly by its elaborately carved handle, then proceeds to dish out a mound of noodles, till not a one is left. And every other second, the old geezer slips the boy a radish, a piece of kohlrabi, a breadcrumb-coated goose neck . . .

They have an abundance of everything, old Lojda says with obvious satisfaction, explaining that all it takes is Richie stopping by a few convenience stores from time to time whose friendly owners are not only glad to get rid of their expired foodstuffs, but even toss in a few outright delicacies, especially when every now and then they get something in return, since occasionally the river washes up some interesting finds, such as for example these sets of dishes from the camp that got flooded out.

Of course, they live differently on the barge than they would have in their original destination, the Old Log Cabins.

So what happened? inquires Papa, licking his umpteenth plate.

Old Log Cabins are gonna be torn out. They're fillin in the furrow already.

And what's gonna be there instead?

Swan Lake it'll be called. A giant skating rink. It isn't far from Prague, so they're puttin in an underground line straight from the airport.

Someone'll make a damn nice profit outta that, says Papa.

Yep!

So you all came from down there, is that it?

Well, I brought some folks here, to the barge. Course it's miserable here, ground all dug up from the mines, so it'll be a while till they get it filled in. Some of my folks're stayin in caves. But the sicknesses started comin soon as the booze biz collapsed.

What, huh? Papa says with his mouth full.

Yeah, that's how come we didn't even tell our families we were leavin. Bein ashamed was part of it too. And Richie here kept his mouth shut. What happened was our guys had a deal with the bottlers to sell the booze direct to pubs, snack bars, any place with a table set up along the river, train stations, what have you, that booze is crazy cheap. Course I don't approve of how many of those sorry cripples ended up blind. I got my own stuff to drink. Care for a drop?

I suppose a drop wouldn't hurt, says Papa, brightening up.

Richie places cups at everybody's feet, tips a dark liquid into them out of a plastic bottle. He hesitates before deciding not to give one to the boy.

Světlana takes a seat. Leans against the old man's shoulder. The pleasing smell of her crimson hair hovers over the group. She raises her hand with a glass in the air, Richie is there in the blink of an eye to fill it with a smile.

We got people paralyzed, blind, deaf, even dead. Some of the folks that came with me did it cause they were pissed off they were taking em to the hospitals.

Now that's what I call a mess, Papa says. He gets to his feet. Well, teacher, it's been nice seein you again after all these years. Thank you for your hospitality.

Just wait a sec, relax a little, let your sons get some rest. I'll tell you a story bout someone I know.

As Papa stubbornly refuses to take the hint, the old geezer first gently lays a hand on his leg, then covers his knee with his mitt and, quite brutally, forces him down.

Richie is right there to slip a pillow behind Papa's back. It's quite pretty actually, embroidered. There you go. He leans back in the chair.

Now he's in the Kingdom of God. Departed, as they say. But this pal of mine, Máťa Píťa, he used to run all over the place around here. There was nobody he didn't visit, have a sit with. He liked to talk.

Mmm, came the reply from the pillow.

Smiley, exuberant, basically just a helluva guy. Women loved him. He'd even stop and say hello to a worthless old granny, why not? Painted funny scenes on the walls in the pubs, so people felt good in there. Some of em busted his chops, sayin he should paint the hospice! But he went and shut himself up in a cabin. Sat and wrote in there is all I know. I was curious. Not the locals. To them if you read it makes you an asshole, since you're not doin anything. So he kept it quiet. Was a time he did pretty well for himself, paintin shop signs and stuff. Picked it up from lookin at churches, all those paintings they got in there.

Church paintings, huh? Pictures?

I think it was those churches put the thought of writin in his head. Maybe he suddenly got religious? Never used to do anything worse than drinkin and foolin around with Růžena. That's what made him so much fun! But I guess he was religious after all. Heavy stuff, this God business.

Mm.

How bout you, Tab?

Hey, if there is a God, he doesn't care if you believe or not.

Well, yeah, but you'd be better off.

Well, yeah.

I stopped by to see him a few times over the winter. Y'know, always brought something by. A sausage, can of sardines, a lemon. He had hundreds of pages covered in words. Where'd he get the paper and pens? From the Vietnamese? But the whole thing turned out bad, ah well.

How so?

Listen, people round here tell all sortsa stories about how Máťa Píťa met his end, but none of em are true. He drowned in the creek.

So he drowned, huh?

But that panman's somehow mixed up in it!

Who?

They found footprints. And the panman even said so! Up there in the pub U Franze.

How so?

I can still see it when I close my eyes. Someone knockin on the window at Máťa's cabin, all numb with cold and askin for a cup of warm tea. Normal enough, isn't it? No big deal, right? But who is this guy? Well, nobody special, not even from these parts. Makes a livin sellin pans. Carries around a load of shiny dishes on his back, goin round secluded huts even in the dead of winter, knockin on cottage doors long as there's smoke comin out of em, beatin a path all up and down the river. He knows when someone comes knockin on the door in cold like that, folks are glad to invite em in, more like a visit than business. Have a cuppa tea, little nip of course. And why not buy something too? His prices can't be beat, and when they get a load of the pack on his back . . . now that's honest, manly work for you, right? . . . in this day and age! . . . man feedin his family like that, how can he be a bad guy?

So he went to Máťa's?

That's what I'm tellin you! Maybe he got lost and it was just a mistake. Hard to be sure at this point what it was awakened that strange desire. Hard to say how he hatched the idea of swipin Máťa's manuscript. What got into him? Did Máťa say somethin funny? Bait the man somehow? Tell him the manuscript was valuable? Or say somethin that spooked the man? Maybe Máťa asked him to take the manuscript and destroy it? Well, nobody knows. In the old days, people would've said the pan seller was tempted to theft by the devil himself. If it even was theft. Only thing certain is he left Máťa's cabin by the light of dawn with the manuscript in his pack.

Oh, shit! Really? And then what?

Well, he fell through the ice. Luckily, close to shore. He crawled along the bed of Šmejkalka Creek and up the snow-covered slope to Senohraby. They say when he staggered into the train station pub, he didn't know if he was alive or dead, and didn't care. He couldn't get a word out. The girls in the kitchen gave him a steam bath and brought him back around. But when he broke through the ice, he lost everything on him. It wasn't just his pans that ended up on the bottom. He lost all Máťa's papers too. Left em there in the water.

But what about Máťa?

Most likely what happened was the man got up early, while Máťa was still asleep, packed up the manuscript, and went along his way. And our Máťa? He probably set out to track him down, chasin after him like a blurry vision. And it ended up bein fatal.

The old man falls silent.

There, there, Papa says, patting him on the shoulder.

The girl strokes the old-timer's back. The little boy is still on her lap. She gives him a smile. Just the tiniest grin.

Are we ready to go? she whispers.

The boy nods.

Let's go and see Mom, okay?

29

MIROŠOVICE. TŘEŠEŇ AND HIS MOMMY. WHAT
POSSESSED MÁŤA. GATHERING ON THE BANK OF
THE SÁZAVA. A MEETING WITH THE PRESIDENT.
KORY'S OPINION. KORY IS AMAZED.

That Kája is one lucky guy. Falls asleep the second he gets in the car.
And has a dream that puts his beloved back in his arms. The young hulk
smiles in bliss.

Miran, meanwhile, scowls and frets, eyes glued to the road. Dad's dead.
What about the wedding, what about the rest? What'll happen now?

He shakes his head, wishing he had Monča there to confide in, to lay
his head in the curly-haired wedge below the vault of her tummy, he'd
like to do that most of all. But Dad had given them a job to do—for the
last time in his life, Miran realizes with a whimper—and they were going to finish it. For their dad's sake, if nothing else.

As Kája embraces the lust-spattered Světlana in his sleep, the sensu-
ous dream flushing his face purple, Miran clutches the steering wheel,
knuckles white with rage, steering the predacious sedan through a bend
here, a bend there, tires squealing, and here they are: Mirošovice.

They have a meeting with Koryčan in the local soccer pub. Right next
to the highway underpass, which separates the playing field and the
pub from Pike's Pond—Štičák, as it's affectionately known—and the ad-
jacent meadows.

The playing field is in immaculate shape, neat and tidy with well-
trimmed grass and regulation white-painted goals, the pride of the
village, ready and waiting for players at any time. But it's more than
just that.

Amid all the homes, cottages, huts, the roar of traffic from the D1,
amid all the people's trudging and grinding, the playing field alone

looks and feels constant and lasting. In fact it has something of a Brahmanic tranquility to it. Yes, it is an oasis, the true heart of the village.

Their neighbors, for example across the highway in Hrusice, have one just like it. And of course there are screaming youngsters running around playing fields in Senohraby, Světice . . . and elsewhere, little girls practicing with hoops, local championships being held.

The field is always carefully tended. A sacred space no one ever desecrates with trash or cigarette butts. For some bums with bottles to rendezvous here, even late at night, is out of the question. In the event that some crackpot, unconcerned with sparing either the property or the lives of his fellow citizens, were to take it into his head to start a fire on the field, it could only be seen as a clear attempt at suicide. Any such thing is, frankly, beyond imagination.

Compared to Hrusice or Senohraby, Mirošovice also boasts smaller bleachers. For locals there's a section marked FAN CLUB that fits twenty or thirty loudmouthed rowdies. In the pub you can purchase enthusiast coasters, cheer-em-on trumpets, and SK Mirošovice T-shirts. You won't find them anywhere else. Over the tap they have the logo of their model, Sparta Praha, a club for lovers of ancient tradition and the world's most hard-core soccer warriors.

A large part of the pub consists of a wood-roofed garden with a perfect view of the field and a sign designating it SMOKERS ONLY.

Venda Třešeň is sitting there now. He nods his puffy head, cheeks permanently red with drink. Next to him squats Koryčan. Kory is a big man. Coveralls, black T-shirt, baseball cap, rubber boots. And there's someone else too. A little old lady in a gray nylon jacket, half-lying, half sitting on a wooden bench. Eyes closed, she sucks from a plastic bottle through a straw. A few tables away, a group of men sits playing cards. Koryčan, the debtor, pours a beer down his throat. He's got more than a few in him. Same as Třešeň.

There's no action at the moment on the pitch behind their backs. The locals on the other side of the wire fence that separates their gardens from the playing field gather together the freshly mown grass, pitchforks, rakes flashing against the skyline as they toss the grass onto large tarpaulins, which they then dump into the bed of a truck. Heaps of old grass, an assortment of cuttings and lopped-off branches, twist in the heat of a fire. Dark smoke rises upward, feeding the sky, a sacrifice.

Kája and Miran step out of the black sedan, slam the doors, and head straight toward them.

Venda Třešeň gives them a nod. Whoops at the brothers, grinning from ear to ear. Třešeň—why do they call him Cherry? Because of his soused-red face and because he passes himself off as a Communist. Even has a COMMUNIST PARTY OF MIROŠOVICE sign up on the outside of his little house. The longtime liars, thieves, and murderers of the Party had added a pair of juicy cherries to their logo back in '94, as a symbol of the neighborly garden thievery now so common in the country.

Have a seat, boys, meet my ma. Cherry pats the little old lady on the shoulder. She sits up straight, gawking at the newcomers.

Ten crowns, she barks, holding her palm out to Miran.

Excuse me, please? Miran asks.

And don't shit too long, ya big lunk.

She keeps shoving her hand in front of Miran's face.

Guess she thinks you look bloated, dude! Relax, breathe out, Cherry tells the grim-faced Miran. My mom used to staff the crappers at the Main Station in Prague, he explains, wrapping his hands around her arm and pressing it down to the bench.

Listen, gravediggers, I'm not givin your dad nothin, Koryčan says, entering the debate. He rises to his feet, towering over the table. Big as he is, though, he's not as big as the brothers.

Dude, that plan for a private carcass dump? I don't know what your dad's got for brains, but boys, come on, spits Koryčan.

You borrowed, you pay, says Miran. Simple as that.

Old Bašta's not gettin jack from me, Koryčan declares. He sways briefly, then sits back down.

Miran studies the tiny, disheveled old lady in her nylon jacket pulled over a stained tracksuit. The nicotine-stained mustache underneath her sharp snub nose, the wrinkles almost pulsing in her aged and shriveled face, and in every bit of her body, fading away beneath her clothes.

Miran takes a seat. But Kája remains standing. He's built like a bulldozer, as already mentioned. But in all seriousness, few people can visualize just how much his frame darkens the horizon in the Mirošovice woodshed.

Get this, guys, Cherry heehaws. They got young tarts workin the johns at the Main Station now. Toilet attendants, they call em. Went and sacked my mom in the prime of her old age! That's no good, is it, Momma?

Nope. Now they got the young fillies in there, the men get hard and it takes em longer to urinate, see? Now they got lines.

And check this out, guys, these toilet attendants wear uniforms made by Louie Vatahn, that fashion company that dresses the Pope. Got all these little pockets on there for all their brushes and scrubbers, only slick like, so you can see their tits, but not too much, like stewardesses, right? My ma's too old for that.

We used to dress how we wanted, the old lady interjects. And there were lines for the ladies' room, not the gents'. Things're all upside down now.

You guys see what I mean? My ma ended up sick. Here she was hopin to get another glimpse of the president, and instead, whoosh, off to the hospice, Momma, isn't that right?

But the old gal's not ready to throw in the towel yet, says Koryčan. Not as long as she's still chipper!

They got turnstiles there now, the old woman gripes.

That's right, you gotta go through a turnstile like they make you do at the border. It's so impersonal. Wouldn't shit there now if you paid me.

Turnstiles! How's that make any sense? There's a slight cracking noise from the floorboards as the woman stomps the ground.

You put your time in, Ma. You earned every heller.

And the cast a characters nowadays! the little old lady laments. Black dicks, brown dicks, at the Main Station! Terrible people! Strange, foreign people! She nearly bursts into tears.

Easy now, Mommy love, just relax.

Those young sluts couldn't care less, but I'm Communist old school! Czech lands for Czechs, I say, God forgive me!

That's right, Mommy hon, don't you worry. You'll go to the Good Shepherd and get all the rest you need after a lifetime of hard work.

I'm tellin you, our folks, when a man comes to the toilet, takes a pee, takes a poo, long as he isn't crocked, he's shy and polite, lays down his coin. But nowadays? Dicks, nothin but dicks, all day long, black, huge, swollen, the old lady rants.

There there, Mommy dear.

I'll go to the Good Shepherd, if that's what you think is best, honey-bun. I don't wanna take up space, you know that.

You'll be better off there, Mommy darling. I promise I'll come see you.

I know, sweetie. It'll be fine.

Mommy love.

So tell me, they got TV there in that hopsice?

Course they do.

My sweet little boy, the little old lady says, wriggling under Cherry's elbow.

Koryčan interrupts the family idyll. Scuse me, ma'am, but could you tell us how you met the president? What did he say? Folks, Koryčan announces, turning to the table of cardplayers, this lady here spoke to the president, our very own Mr. Zeman!

Just hush yer mouth a minute, someone says between the slap of cards.

But, guys, this is important stuff!

Shut cher trap, Kory . . . slap smack slap, comes the sound from the players' table.

Don't forget that you promised to take me to Hrusice, sweetie, the little old lady whines from under the drunkard's elbow. I wanna go one last time to U Sejků and see the picture of Mikeš, that blunderbuss wayfaring feline of ours that my Máťa Píťa painted up there on the wall.

But what about the president, Mother? rumbles Koryčan. Before he can even finish his sentence, the little old lady unfolds herself from underneath his elbow, snatches up a plastic bottle, tips it down her throat, and shrieks so loud the spit comes sailing out her mouth.

Yeah! And who do you think painted that puss in boots with a walkin stick and a cap? A la master Josef Lada? None other than your daddy, Venoušek: our very own long-legged Máťa Píťa!

Go ahead and set the record straight, Mother, but after that do you promise to tell the story about the president? Koryčan pleads. Meanwhile Cherry sits jaw-dropped.

So, Máťa Píťa Longleg back then had a deal with the folks ran U Sejků in Hrusice that he'd paint the pub with pictures from the life of Mikeš the Tomcat in exchange for drinks, like old Rembrantle used to do. Then he up and stopped drinkin. But why? We were happy. Then he got faith. Said it wasn't enough to just paint what he saw. But why, for God's sake? I was a good wife. Then all of a sudden he starts hangin around in churches! Goes runnin out of U Sejků to St. Václav's, then runs off to Mnichovice, Sts. Jakub and Filip, they got those scary old paintings of bulls and eagles there, it was him that dug em up. Drew the neighbors' animals into Nativity scenes. Then he ran all the way down to Poříčí to study up on our very own Virgin on the Mount. Those type of distances were nothin for him. Longleg, that's how he got the name! Course it wasn't just his legs that was long. You little puppies got nothin on my sweet Mr. P!

Everyone pauses a moment. The little old lady sheds a tear, knocks back a shot from somebody's glass. Takes a breath and launches back in.

So the folks in Hrusice went lookin round the churches for him, since he hadn't finished the job in their pub, and meanwhile he was off somewhere sittin in a pew, smellin of flowers and candles, half-tormented to death from thinkin. And what was he chewin over? Well, he'd made up his mind to treat U Sejků like a sacred image, which meant he wanted to do the faces of the heroes in the tomcat stories, all the neighbors and goats and water sprites and boys and grannies, with the nobility of spirit that the martyrs of old possessed. That's what he confided in me, seein as I was his wife and all.

So I said, Fine, but first you better give Mikeš some proper paws. Way he looks right now, all the kids that come're scared of him! That was my advice. And folks in Hrusice felt the same. They wanted Máťa Píťa to finish up soon as possible, so parents'd bring their kids to the pub to see Mikeš the Tomcat. Tourists from all the way in Prague. Brno even! Cause I mean, every real Czech knows that book. Moravians, Silesians, Slovaks too! Just like all a you, the grandam sputters.

That's right! Kája exclaims.

Absolutely, Miran nods.

How could we not? Koryčan grins.

You used to read it to me, Momma! Cherry says, clapping his hands.

Way Máťa Píťa explained it to me, the adventures of Mikeš the Tomcat were like a modern-day bible, where this stupid little cat, which'd normally end up mangy and probably stoned to death, passes himself off as Czech, and even starts to speak Czech, so he's one of us, capeesh?

Yes, ma'am, babbles Koryčan.

And just like Josef Lada, who Máťa Píťa took his inspiration from, drew our sacred soldier Švejk, Máťa Píťa drew Mikeš the talking tomcat who gets stolen by the gypsies, and that little slut Micinka from Světice tries to bang him, and practically every stranger he meets along the way tries to do him harm, but Mikeš, he gets through it all, lands a job in the circus, where else, bein a born prankster, and gets to travel and see the world. And on top of all that, he helps his friends Pašík the pig and Bobeš the goat bring up his successor, the holy terror Nácíček, aka little Nazi, and a course some people claim otherwise, Oh no, that's just short for Ignác! but we all know he was a fashy, right?

Nácíček, wow, someone chuckles, and others listening in from the surrounding tables open their mouths wide in a round of mirthful laughter.

See, that was still before World War II, and Mikeš was smart, since nobody knew which way the fortunes a war would turn, so it was damn handy havin at least one fashy in the family. The rest of em were good Czechs, though, I swear! The goat and the pig and the water sprite and all the gang! Anyways, that's how Máťa explained it to me, and I held my tongue so he wouldn't bust me in the mouth, since after all he was my hubby.

Sensible on your part.

Beatin a woman's like fertilizin a field . . .

Well, so Mikeš the Tomcat returned home from the world a rich man and spread his wealth among his neighbors, and that's the happy ending. The hepáč, they call it down at the Main Station nowadays, when everything comes out all right.

So what about the president? What'd he tell you? What was it like? Koryčan insists.

Wait, Momma, so I'm Píťa's? Cherry says softly into the little old lady's ear.

But if you wanna know how it all turned out, she continues, what Máťa Píťa put on the walls a that pub wasn't your average pictures.

Oh no? says Koryčan.

No. In fact the whole thing ended up pretty strange.

Really?

Yeah, it was a mess. U Sejků had a grand opening to unveil the paintings, with the Ministry of Tourism, and the Department for the Rescue of the Czech Countryside, and all these bigwigs from the government, and it was awful. Máťa insisted on keepin the pictures behind a curtain, and everyone was in shock when he pulled it back, specially Bishop Duka and the other church dignitaries!

What?

You were still little boys back then, but the local paper in Hrusice said it was a scandal. All the water sprites and dogs had halos painted over their heads, lookin pleadingly up at the sky, hands, paws, and cloven hooves clasped, and instead a Pašík the roly-poly pig that we all know and love, he was all fasted out, ribs pokin through his skin, and Bobeš the goat had this ancient beard, and even with the halo on him people said he looked like a Hebe, and to top it all off, Mikeš the world traveler was painted as a black cat, which is what he is in the book a course, except when you see the picture he looks like he's a gypsy, or, pardon my French, a total nigger.

What? shouts Koryčan.

Another ring of beers lands with a thud on the table in front of them.

And little Nácíček wasn't even there, says the storyteller. She slams her elderly fist down in a puddle of beer, paying no heed to the spray.

Not there?

No way!

What?!

That's right. Maťa insisted. He acted like there wasn't any Nazi in the book at all.

Oho! gasps one of the bunch.

Can you even do that? says somebody else.

So what happened next? someone inquires.

Well, says the old woman, bowing her head to the table. They painted it over. I don't even like goin there now.

Ha!

Boy, that's some memory you got on you, ma'am.

Mommy dear? asks Cherry.

What is it, hon?

I never knew the famous Máťa Píťa was actually my dad. That's so cool!

Honestly, hon, to tell the truth . . . who can really remember it all. I mean, it's been years.

Well, sonuvabitch, was he my father or wasn't he, dammit!

Honey, don't get angry, stop acting like a little boy.

I guess you're right, Mom, what does it matter?

That's the attitude, son.

Kája nudges his brother's back with his knees, eager for action. But Miran gestures toward the little old lady, as if to say it would be embarrassing to cause any discord in her presence. He appears to possess the patience of a king.

Koryčan prattles on in their direction.

Look, boys, I got a good job, I'm a cook. I make decent money. But I got cancer. In my throat. I was hopin to live to see fifty. And if I had, I woulda thrown a huge bash at the Distillery down by the water!

Hey, now don't get emotional on us!

Beer flowin nonstop, I swear! Whatever you want on the table, you got it. I'm a cook at the Good Shepherd hospice. Listen, cutlets. Fish, obviously. Fried cheese. Whatever anyone wants! We'd get riproarin drunk, I swear!

Niiice, says Cherry.

Man's gotta get drunk sometimes, am I right? says Koryčan, dumping a shot of peppermint liqueur into his beer.

Man doesn't gotta do shit. It's everyone else gotta do it, says someone by way of enlightenment.

And you know what, boys? I don't even care I won't live to fifty. I'd just like to leave enough cash behind so you can enjoy yourselves. Burn the dead, roll the living up to the spread, am I right?

You're a good guy, says Cherry. I'm sure they can cure you. You'll outlive us all yet. Get over here, bro!

The two men hug, a genuine manly tear sliding out from under Cherry's swollen eyelids into Koryčan's stubble. They don't stop grinning, though, not that.

But your old man's not gettin shit outta me! I won't give so much as a booger for that burial ground of his! I wanna be scattered. You can handle that, buddy, right?

Settle up with the boys, Cherry says in a squeaky voice.

The doctors ask me, Where do you work? At the hospice of the Good Shepherd, I tell em. They laugh, So you're good to go! That's doctors nowadays for ya.

You gotta be kiddin, Miran says to the next ring of beers and circle of shots the waitress slams down on the table.

I wanna be scattered! Is your old man plannin ovens at that burial ground of his? You plannin to do cremations there? Huh?

No, just the usual, in the ground.

You see? You just want to keep people down. Even when they're dead. You're mafia, Miran. You too, Kája. How many times did I rock you on my knees, singin, Fa la la la la, la la la la? Too many even to count.

Same rules go for everyone.

Yeah, don't mess things up for us here, Kája adds.

They knew every excuse in the book. Oh, now the gentleman wants to be cremated! All of a sudden.

But I'm not scared of you, boys. In fact, I think I'll have a shot.

He promptly downs a drink.

Look, boys, I don't envy you your lives. The Icelandicization of Europe. A mosque over here, then a mosque over there . . .

Huh?

Shit, we're bein flooded with em, bandy-legged Islamists, says Kory. They don't even work, what with prayin five times a day and washin themselves all the time, from their beard down to their toes. So when're they sposta work? Not to mention they're gonna kill every one of you, far as I can see. Glad I won't be around for that!

Just like the president! the little old lady squeaks. When the president sailed his boat up to the Distillery, he was steerin by faith, I'm serious, floatin across the water . . .

Oh, finally! Koryčan shouts.

. . . solid and majestic, all of us women gathered along the banks on both sides were throwin him kisses with our eyes. All he had on was a life ring, which as a head of state he has to have, and a pair of swimmin trunks. Lord, you wouldn't believe the hilarious suit he had on, the little old lady says, clapping her hands. Talk about a Goliath!

So there weren't any men there, Mom? asks Cherry.

Don't interrupt, boy.

Yeah, for real, dude, be quiet. And you too over there, Koryčan says to the gambling table. Somebody nails him with a coaster in the eye.

There was a solid crowd of us there at the Distillery. Down under Zlenice Castle. Where Hus used to preach! And I tell you, President Zeman knew what we were all thinkin, cause first thing he does is shout out: Folks, not to worry! These refugees tryin to get in are nothin but terrorists and we won't have it! Then he put this towel on his head like he was a Muslim terrorist, and we laughed so hard! Jesus and Mary! I'm a Communist just like our president is, but I love the truth, and that darn near tore my heart out.

Mommy, careful, your heart!

Oh, sweetie, that was ages ago! So here's our president in swim trunks, a real person, like Dubček back in the day, and he's tellin the truth.

Which Duce was that, Mom?

Our President Zeman's been on trips to Russia and China. He's a real someone. What did Master Hus know about the Chinese? Jackshit, pardon my French. Our president is much more powerful than he ever was. And the Sázava's quietly flowin behind the president's back and I guess all that moisture from the river must've got into my eyes. And it wasn't just in my eyes, I mean I'm tellin you, he is majestic, he's a real man, our president. And the way he eats! Then he walks right up to me and says: How're you doin?

Wait, Ma, for real?

Here it comes . . . Koryčan blurts through his teeth.

And I told him everything. Right there, in front of everyone, I gave the president a report on the Main Station. About the bedlam in the toilets and the big, black dicks comin in all the time, the veiny Arab giant black cocks on all those subversives comin in to *our* Europe . . . and the sandwich bags they steal from us pilin up in front of the toilets . . . and nobody laughed!

It's no wonder, ma'am, says Kory. No wonder!

And the president didn't even crack a smile. Just scowled. Nodded his head. Some drops of water trickled off his mighty chest onto me! All the women were jealous!

So what happened next?

So the president said, Folks, this is no laughing matter. Our indigent Czech goes to pee in the bushes, which proves this isn't about some poor unfortunate refugees, but terrorists equipped with money for turnstiles and all sorts of elaborate logistics, and the Main Station in Prague, oh, just a moment . . . and he reached into his trunks and pulled out a tiny phone and said, Privet, molodyets, kak u tebya . . . then proceeded to engage in a lively conversation . . .

Shit, someone says.

He knows Chinese too, Cherry says breathlessly.

So I've just spoken to President Putin, our president informed us as the sun dried the drops on his shaggy-haired chest . . . and it seems he has a similar problem. He told me about those cunts who desecrated his Orthodox cathedral on the main square in Moscow, dancing and chanting against him.

Oh shit, a cathedral? someone shouted.

That is a serious no-no!

So what happened next, Mom?

Well, then the president said not to worry, he and the president would take care of everything.

Aha!

How?!

Yeah, Mom, how?

Well, I see you boys sat on your ears in school. Pardon my French, but you're what we'd call dunces from the Havel days. There's a pretty straightforward way to handle these sorts of things.

And what's that, Ma?

Well, any cunts or pricks that act up here at home, lock em up or kill em, and as far as the ones outside the border, just don't let em in.

Oh, right.

So then what, Ma?

Then President Zeman gave us a speech about the future of our country.

Holy crap!

Keep talkin . . . and have another snort!

The president drew a circle around the Distillery with his hand—the pool in the Sázava with the window sellin beer and sausages and all, and the sunbathing and frolicking and summertime lounging at the foot of the old watch castle—and he said, This is the future of the Czech lands.

Huh?

What'd he mean by that, Mom?

Boys, gimme a hand . . . and supported by the men's willing arms, the old granny climbs up on the table, gingerly at first, but once she is standing firmly on top her voice is loud and confident.

Heads turn among the company gathered in the garden restaurant, initially in amusement, but soon in astonishment and delight.

President Zeman said we had nothing to fear, for he and the Chinese and Russian presidents had decided our marvelous Czech land, protected from undesirable aliens, would be transformed into a paradise, the little old lady declares.

There'll be no shooting range here, thank heavens! rejoices the little old lady, stomping her foot on the table, and no tankodrome, hallelujah! she cries. No concentration camp and no sweatshop, hip hip hooray! But any filthy-rich Chinks and Russkies who want are welcome to come here on their kanikuly and prázdniky, and there'll be lotsa grill bars, ski parks, pigeon houses, relaxation centers, and arcades and casinos too, the old lady gushes, her voice now falling off a bit. But still she stands above them all, taking in the applause and the whistles urging her on from every corner.

So why did I come floating down to see you folks here on the banks of our glorious Sázava River? the little old lady says, imitating the president. Cupping her withered hands around her leathery lips, she shouts: Because you've already begun building that peaceful tourist paradise! Right here, in the beloved cradle of Czech culture made famous far and wide by Josef One-eye Lada. Diligently building, diligently preparing ourselves for the throngs of nonhostiles. You know, folks, everyone already loves Krteček, the little mole, our country's cartoon mascot. Now it's time to lift up Mikeš, our very own cunning Czech cat, and this gorgeous Czech landscape here. Hoorah! the old lady shouts, quickly adding: That was the crowd. She then takes a bow and hops off the table, Miran and Kája catching her just in the nick of time.

Mom, that was great!

Keep talkin, keep talkin . . . Koryčan says, bouncing up and down on the bench.

He is one clever man, that president, boys, the little old lady wheezes, now talking just to them.

There's gonna be reigns of terror and tsunamis and terrible wars, but the Chinks and the Russkies, the military commanders and captains of industry, they won't let us go under! They'll be usin our river basin here for recreation, right? So our president is urgin us to sign up our kids for courses in hotel management, guide services, languages, and footmanship. Good idea, right? Course I'm not plannin on havin any more children myself, so it's up to you, boys.

Golly, ma'am, I'm not sure if I . . .

Whoa!

So how did you remember all that, Mother?

I remembered it because I love our president.

Miran waits a moment for the old woman's words to sink into the darkness and float away, then slugs Koryčan in the shoulder, saying, Come outside.

Fuck off, Miran. What my mom just said here floored me. I don't even wanna die anymore. Not when the president's got a plan like that! The brains on that guy.

Hey, if you don't have the cash, you don't have it. But you can't tell me you won't pay our dad.

Oh, I got it all right! I got the cash, but your pop can go fuck himself. And the both of you too!

That cremation stuff is bullshit, says Miran. I mean, nothin against your customs, but that's just bullshit.

You mafia motherfuckers think you can outslick Sázava, but you can go to hell. I'm the president's friend now. I wrote him a petition and he's gonna receive me at the Castle in Prague.

Koryčan gets up and folds his arms.

And why is the president gonna receive me? Because my petition says how we're gonna sort things out with the refugees and their murdering, raping gangs. Now quiet, everyone! Koryčan bellows.

Over there, he says, pointing past the table of cardplayers to the soccer field where the goals shine white in the dusk. We'll line em up right over there. Soon as they get off the boat. And fire! Bra-ta-ta-tat! No mercy! Men, women, even those little suckers they use to get our sympathy. One machine gun squad's all it takes. Or not even machine guns. Why bother? Hunting rifles, whatever folks've got'll do the trick. Leave the army out of it. Militia. Let the president keep his hands clean! Main thing is to get pictures and clips! Then our young ones can put it up on YouTyoub in response to those beheading videos of theirs, so anyone plannin to come our way can find out how their spies ended up on the soccer pitch in Mirošovice. We can dig pits under the stands. Anyone got a shovel? Who's got a gun at home, huh?

Another coaster comes flying from the cardplayers' table and hits Koryčan in the ear.

Ah, shut cher trap, Kory . . . you're worse'n the radio.

Don't disturb the game . . .

You are one bloodthirsty motherfucker, shit, Cherry says, shaking his head. The old woman seems to have fallen asleep on his lap. She really does look like a baby bird. So tiny and light.

Momma? Mom? Cherry shakes her.

What is it, son? Are we leavin now?

I'm not sure how to tell you this, Momma, but . . . look, Kory's an expert. It sounds like you're gonna have to wait a while for the hospice, kay?

So I can stay with you till then?

Well, no, Momma, but there's something I thought of. So you can have peace and privacy. Listen, waitress, you know what? Give us some more of those Fernets here, yeah? Make em doubles!

They drag him outside, arm twisted behind his back. The drinkers at the tap step aside to let them pass.

As soon as they get him out onto the road, Kája kicks him off the asphalt into the bushes. The lights from the cars flying by on the highway overhead burn through the darkness as a gust of cool air blows off the pond.

Kája takes hold of Koryčan by the arm and drags him back to his feet. Kory tries to resist. He always did have courage. His face is battered, skin shredded, blood flowing from his mouth, one ear puffy and red as a piece of meat.

Don't be stupid, Kája tells him. It'll only make it worse.

Koryčan shakes his head. Kája slugs him in the head from the side. Kory sinks to all fours and stays kneeling like that awhile, propped up on his hands, staring at the two brothers.

Just don't kick him, Miran says.

Koryčan stands again. Stupid pricks, he says, flailing his fists in front of him.

Look, next time you hit the ground, I finish you off with my boots. I don't care what my brother says.

I ain't scared a you. Koryčan spits blood.

That blood is from your lips, says Kája. Nothin from inside. Yet.

Koryčan takes a swing, so Kája punches him right in his swollen ear.

Koryčan lets out a howl, reaches a hand into the pocket of his coveralls, pulls out a gun, fires. There's a flash of light, a sharp smell, and Miran drops to the ground with a hole in his chest. He didn't even aim. None of them was expecting this. Even Kory looks surprised.

Told you I was armed, he snuffles. Backs away, turns, and scurries off into the night.

30

VENDA'S PROPOSAL. UNDER THE BRIDGE AND
BEYOND. RŮŽENKA AND THE MOON, ITS FACE.
AND EVEN FURTHER BEYOND.

Venda Třešeň and his mom are left alone in the pub.

They finish off their Fernets, the old lady tipping back her glass and
licking out the last drops with her tongue.

Now that those're done, are you takin me back to your place, hon?

I thought we'd have another round!

Fine, sweetie, whatever you want. And then where will I go?

Actually, you know, I was thinkin of Bečka's shanty. You can stay there.
For now! You'll have a garden, I'll put in a telly. What more do you need?

Boy, are you out of your wits? What garden, the place is a trash dump!
It's a shack in the fields. Not a soul around.

I'll get you a cat.

Ground is all soggy and wet, stinks to high heaven.

Thing is, there's a wait for the hospice, Momma, see? And you're still
spry as ever.

What about Bečka? He was already old when I was young.

Yeah, well he just died.

Oh, I see!

Be right back. Gotta pee again. Prostate, you know! That's one thing
you don't have to worry about.

The old woman flinches as a tray lands on the table with another
round of shots. As soon as the urinal door swings shut behind her son,
she takes a little sip and feels her spirits lift as the warmth flows down
her throat. She rolls up her jacket sleeve, stares at the sticks of her
arms, skin flapping loose.

I'm so old I got old age behind me and still, here I am. Tell you one thing, I don't want to be trouble, no sir. But who knows when my day'll come.

She finishes what's left of her drink and drains her son's shot as well. Slides the bench back from the table and gets down on all fours. She makes her way toward the door, crawling like a lizard. Languid but exhilarated by the sudden swell of drunkenness. That was how it had always been. That beautiful feeling of warmth and a spinning head. And when the spinning stopped, tremors and emptiness. She pats her jacket pocket where she keeps a plastic bottle in reserve. Half full. Just enough. Warmth aplenty. Once that melted away, life reappeared, naked and terrible.

She crawls under the cardplayers' table.

Jesus, she is piss drunk. Hey, lady, one of them says, expressing his concern. He slaps down his cards, gets up, lifts her off the floor, and sets her on her feet. Not that he isn't good-natured about it. "Cigarette in the teeth, a flattened cap, all that's missing are the stripes on his back" . . . she suddenly remembers the dance song. There were men everywhere in those days. That was the best.

Looks like Cejn's caught himself a lady friend!

Always knew he was into the mature types, heh heh heh!

Hey, fellas, I'm Růženka, she says, leaning on the man's arm, staring into the face of the driver or woodsman or whatever he is.

Think you can make it the rest of the way? he asks, his smell washing over her. That man smell. Plus rum and cigarettes. Sweat.

What a fine man you are, Růženka chirps.

He wraps his arms around her, gently lifting her from the floor. As she straightens up, she runs a hand down his chest. She was tiny, men liked that, and almost every man was a giant to her, which was also good. She shuffles out the door, buoyed by his touch. He may be gone, but she can still see him when she closes her eyes.

Růženka plonks down again on the asphalt in front of the pub. Two drunks brawl in the bushes while a third man looks on.

She shambles off under the overpass, once again on two feet. The cool air is redolent of fish. Collapsing into the grass, she crawls toward the sparkling water. The inner warmth is gone, though. She can feel all the sourness bubbling up from the depths. She takes a drink, stuffing the anxiety back down. Peeks at the bottle to see how much is left. I can make it, she says to herself. I'll crawl through the grass like a big black bug. Máťa was my snuggle bug, the biggest snuggle bug of all, I always felt best with him. She crawls her way to the water. Pike's Pond isn't exactly huge.

Hey, now that's a moon, Růženka snickers. It reminds her of a smiling face. None other than that of her very own Máťa Píťa.

And she's right. As the moon hangs there, imprinted on the water, a fish shoots up from the surface, then lands again with a slap.

I don't care if it's you or just my magination, she tells the moon or Máťa. I still got a nip and that'll do. So quick, before the warmth is gone. And it's easy as can be. Růženka downs what little's left and plops beneath the surface.

31

THEY MEET SKEETER. UNFORTUNATE IN THE CAVE.
AUNT MY GOODNESS. LOJDA'S PLACE. STADIUM,
MORE LIKE A SOCCER FIELD. PRODIGIOUS LOVE.
WHAT LOJDA PUT DOWN ON PAPER. WHAT MÁŤA
LEFT BEHIND. WILL YOU HELP ME?

They're going to see Mom?

Is that what she said?

The redhead takes the boy by the hand, to keep him from wandering. Richie carries the little nipper wrapped in a blanket. They grope their way through the coal ship's bowels, crates heaped on all sides, machine parts poking out through the worm-eaten walls. Frayed plastic bags dangle and flap. They stumble out of the chemical stink. The sun hits them hard as they step outside. The heat is stifling as they cross the wooden gangplank, fixed in place with rusty nails, over the water. To their left bristles a jungle of reeds. Tall stalks, sunk fast in the stagnant waters, swaying in the wind.

They jump down from the gangway into the shabby grass. Stretching out before them is a beach bounded by hills, rocky outcrops, and walls of slate. They crunch through the sand past shacks, rickety huts, tents.

He's really heavy for such a little boy, Richie mutters in an aggrieved tone of voice. He must have been bent over inside the ship. Now, with his back unrolled, it's clear again he's a beanpole.

Guess you'd make a shit dad then!

I never promised you anything, he giggles.

Heading toward the rocky hills, they stride along the sandy beach, dotted with islands of dirt where hogweed and twisted shrubs have taken hold. The line of shacks and tents continues.

Where you goin? inquires a bewitching apparition, more imaginary event than human being. It grinds its behind against the wall of a nesting box stuck in the sand, swollen glands of its spotted craw puffing its neck so badly the boy squeezes shut his eyes so as not to see. He trails the girl through the campground like a speechless puppet. Her warm palm gives him trust in whatever move comes next. To those they pass the boy may seem not even to possess a brain. They make their way past mud pits filled with bulrush and sedge growing up through the muddy water.

Ow, the stinker bit me! Richie cries.

Get the hell out. I washed him. I know for a fact he doesn't stink.

Richie points to a drop of blood quivering on his fingertip.

Passing a pyramid of plenty, they catch sight of a tiny fellow in house slippers with hairy legs, rummaging through cans of food and a heap of plastic bags. He's dressed in briefs and a T-shirt several sizes too large, as though he had stripped the clothes off a giant after a battle in the swamp.

Skeeter, what're you doin here? Richie yelps.

I live here, shit, frowns the runt. I'm good!

Wow, look at you, shit, laughs Richie.

You ain't preachin to the kids from the dais anymore either, huh? They threw your ass out. Forget me, shit, look at you!

Richie grumbles some nonresponse and, burdened by the strange child, carries on toward the gloomy hills that overlook the valley. His companions hurry after him. As they leave behind the huts and tents, walls of black slate rise up on either side, threaded with cords of lime-stone slimy like snot. Cave mouths breath out sulphurous steam and salty, viscous moisture. Now the small, busty redhead takes the lead as they make their way around boulders, skidding over the hard rocky ground peppered with clusters of dwarf thistles.

Until they reach the lagoon.

The handful of planks and beams that people lugged in when they still had the strength have been replaced by a small bridge over the giant-sized pool of stinking mud known as the lagoon.

Let's go, commands Světlana. Anyone scared, just keep your mouth shut!

She steps out first over the depths, putting a lid on the boy's fears. Then Richie stomps out onto the boards and makes his way across. The girl runs for it, belly bouncing up and down, yeah, there's a bit of a spring to her step, he can see it as he catches her, braking her landing, safe again on the rocks.

Covering the mouth of the cave is a plastic curtain. She rolls it back, slips inside. One step, two, and they find themselves in a darkness thinned by the glow of a fire, surrounded by an assembly of tightly clustered backs.

The boy weaves his way through the gathering after the redhead. He can't make out the words in the whispers of the shadows, paying attention lest he step on a hand or kick somebody. A few people shuffle along the walls. Richie pants for breath at his back.

A woman appears before them, spat out of the gloom. Short and fat, in a black dress, scarf, an ear pierced with two earrings.

Auntie!

Světlana!

They embrace, filling the darkened space with the gushing warmth of female welcomes and instantly ensuing chatter.

Auntie, you look terrific!

Come, lemme have a look at you, girl!

Where is she? Where's Mom?

Oh, I just gave her some porridge, her poor little legs are so weak she can barely stand.

So how've you been, Auntie?

Never mind me, aren't you the beauty now!

She reaches out a hand to feel the life budding within the young lass.

Auntie? Where is she?

The older woman guides them through the rocks, across a dip where water trickles down the walls, sparkling in the firelight, while the beam of the redhead's flashlight plays over moldered rock and wobbly stones split with cracks and carved with black fissures.

The bed is just around the bend.

The boy hops eagerly along behind the women, rising up on his toes.

The little old lady lies on her back. She is absolutely diminutive. Pointy-faced, eyes closed over her hook of a nose. Face wrinkled and diseased, fatty neck covered in spots.

Světlana lets out a sob. And, supporting her pregnant belly, takes a seat. She lifts the plastic bowl lying beside the old woman and practically buries her face in it.

Mom? What do they feed you here? Are you getting plenty of everything?

Your mum's doing pretty well! Ask me, all she needs is some proper medical treatment. After that, she'll be spry as a cricket, you'll see!

I donno bout that, says the girl.

It came over her while we were out gathering wood. There we were, stackin it up, when all of a sudden she collapsed, and ever since, all she does is sleep. Just sleeps all the time. Says she doesn't want to go to the hospital, though. She wants to go to Chlum. Talk it over with Richie here.

All the way to Chlum? So far? I donno.

I donno either, the woman reflects.

You think it's all right that she sleeps so much?

Yeah, the woman opines.

The truth is, I came here to invite you.

Invite me?

You, Mom, everyone! To the salon. The bridal salon in Městečko, that's where my wedding'll be.

Congratulations, girl! That's wonderful!

Thanks!

He still treat you right?

You better believe it!

My man Pražma used to treat me right too! The stories I could tell you! But honestly, girl, I donno if we'll make it. Less your mom gets better by then. No way to know.

You're right about that, Auntie!

Hey, Richie, you got enough gas?

You bet!

He tugs on the boy's elbow. The boy, seeing Světlana's mom, clutches hold of the rocky wall. And falls completely to pieces. If it wasn't for Richie, he would sink right into the rock. But that skinny fellow's got some strength in him! He holds the baby with one hand, while his wandering paw wraps around the boy.

Richie's the only one here with a way to get from A to B, you know? Keeps it hidden. Don't you, Richie? Světlana's aunt says proddingly.

He feels queasy. We're goin outside, he announces.

They make their way through the cluster around the fire, through the sticky, foul-smelling haze. A wide-eyed old geezer, face ridden with pustules, snatches at the boy. Richie knocks the rag of a man into the corner, atop another decomposing mess.

Arms flail at them from the nests in the ground, the wraiths at their feet grunting open-mouthed, jabbering unintelligibly.

Somebody snatches at Richie again. He is so appalled this time, not even a flake of compassion arises in his mind as he tears himself from their grasp.

There's too many of em, says Richie. Ya can't breathe in here.

They finally make their way back to the plastic at the opening.

I thought I was gonna leave you guys here. But I can't.

The boy lifts the plastic sheet and slips outside.

Richie emerges with his load right behind him. They take a deep breath.

The plastic flaps behind them.

She'll make it outta there, she'll be here soon! Světlana and Aunt My Goodness both! Don't you worry bout them!

That's the piss of it too, Richie adds after a moment. That old lady there's not even her mom. Shit, you know what Světlana's been through?

He shakes his head, still breathing deeply.

They found her on a train when she was a baby. The Prague–Benešov express. In the john, if you can believe it! Apparently all she had on was a pink baby cap and pink socks, y'know, girl and all. That's why some of the guys call her Fast Train, ha-ha-ha!

The boy looks up at the tall man. His little brother is still wrapped in the blanket up to his ears.

Fast Train! But don't tell anyone I told ya, kay? Richie laughs. Let's skedaddle, c'mon.

So off they move. It's faster going down the rocks than it was climbing up.

Hey, what're you doin? Richie hollers over the boy's shoulder. Skeeter the runt is going at the plank bridge with a pickax. He pries loose a board as another already floats in the lagoon.

C'mon over! he calls out to them.

Are you crazy? Světlana's up there with her mom!

They somehow make it across, Richie first, clutching the little nipper in his arms.

We'll shout out to her, says Skeeter.

Skeeter and Richie curl their palms into the shape of a cone and scream at the top of their lungs, launching Světlana's name into the wall of fissured slate. They scream so loud the rock practically shakes. Just to be safe, they cover the boy's ears.

Then Richie gives him a slug in the shoulder.

Now we're all gonna scream, okay? To get the girl to come out, okay? Scream as hard as you can!

And once again the men cry out into the core of the earth.

The boy feels a shaking under his feet, cups his hands to his mouth, they scream.

And again the earth slides beneath his feet.

She'll come out, you'll see, says Skeeter.

I'm not so sure, says Richie. I think there's somebody here who's not callin her.

He slugs the boy again. Lightly.

Don't harass him, Skeeter says.

They scream again.

The top layer of one of the slate rocks tips up, slides forward, breaks loose from the mass, and tumbles into the lagoon with a thunderous crash and a spray of mud.

Skeeter tosses away the pickax and makes a run for it.

Richie and the boy follow right behind.

They sail down the same paths they ran up earlier, the boy catching a whiff of Světlana's breath, touching the trace of a droplet of sweat soaked into the boulders, spotting a hair that fell from her rust-colored mane as they hopped from rock to rock. Then they see the first tents and shacks. And finally they slow down, bent at the waist gasping for breath after their mad dash.

There's a wind blowing down from the hills now.

I was fixin to make a raft out of those planks, says the runt.

What would ya want a raft for? Richie inquires.

I was thinkin I'd float away.

Where to?

Up my ass, hell, who cares. Hey, you hear that?

Amid the tangle of shacks and tents, amid the makeshift dwelling's blankets of trash, there is movement happening. They hear shrieks and cries. The plowed wasteland, bounded by the shaky rocks and the flowing mass of water with the silhouette of the coal barge lodged among the reeds, by way of some magical incantation risen from the breath of the rocks, is swarming to life.

The booze colony's inhabitants emerge from their tents, huts, and shacks, joining in with the clamoring group slogging up from the river. They tread heavily under their burdens, in some places sinking into the ancient mud beneath the weight, in others dragging their loads through the sand.

The strong wind kicks up dust in gusts.

Look what they're carryin! says Skeeter, shielding his eyes with his palm.

More like who, Richie says.

They pick up the pace.

He hurries after them.

The glow from the stove is no longer so noticeably all-embracing. Either that or Papa has gotten used to the radiant heat weighing down on his arms, slackened trunk, and head. He has ceased fidgeting around on the cushions. Floating on the warm air, the paper lanterns dance over their heads like fairground balloons. In spite of the scratches strewn across its surface, especially at the level of the coal scuttles, the still-lily-white shower stall serves as a gentle reminder of modern times.

The two men have settled comfortably into discussion. The old man has even crawled into bed. Surrounded by heaps of books, he sits facing Papa, his giant-sized body wedged in place with pillows.

So you say you want to write, young man. What about all this we already have?

The captain points to the stacks of books, titles covered in dust, soot, to the towers of books topped with mugs full of grounds, dishrag-draped ashtrays, and open folios, with the underlinings and strikethroughs in their worn pages visible even despite the low light of the cabin.

I couldn't care less about that!

Lojda nods.

You know what, teacher? If they hadn't kicked me outta school, I never would've seen the world! So thanks!

Saw the world, huh? Lojda grins. Had a good time? You sure it wasn't a waste?

Huh? What?

Look, you were out there walkin the boards, livin off of grants, milkin arts institutions for funds like Romulus and Remus suckin at the she-wolf's tit. Made a decent career for yourself, for real. So why'd you come back here? Couldn't take the competition, huh?

What?

You want to write? Then write, for fuck's sake, what's holdin you back?

Some fun you are, mumbles Papa.

When it came to freedom, you blew it, boys, yep. You say you came back for old Hrozen's inheritance, but you forgot to get married. Well, that's just great.

I hate to tell you, teach, but you've gotten pretty run-down.

You know anyone who's not gettin older?

You sit here talkin about fuckin that little girl and goin on about the past, but you were the one who turned me in. I was seventeen.

That's right. So you still aren't over it?

Narks showed up, slapped me around right there in the principal's office, and whoosh, off to jail. Me versus the whole Soviet Union at seventeen. You have any idea what that felt like?

And do you have any idea why I turned you in, you bungler? We had mimeographs down there in the cellar of the school. The whole teaching staff was in on it.

Oh!

Your youthful carelessness put us at risk. And what happened to you? You got knocked around a bit, got famous. Now you're an underground legend to infatuated teenage girls.

Uh-huh, and you're still the winner, is that it, teach? You were a snitch!

It's called playin both sides, boy. The second time they stuck it to me all the harder. "Rat in the Schools," the papers wrote. But after my second bid, I found a foothold in the Old Log Cabins, which was perfect. Sometimes you get lucky.

So what're you doin here on a coal ship, you old windbag?

Waitin for death. I'm serious!

Won't be long now, sorry!

Gettin old isn't for sissies.

Riiight!

Far as that lady cop you knocked in the water. Just do the time. Maybe you'll get some writin done. Prisons these days're comfy, not like the ones we had. You got all sorts of therapies in there. They'll let you jot a line or two.

I was also thinkin that, Papa nods.

But after briefly and clearly informing Lojda that in order to write he needs alcohol, a great deal of it, and unlimited quantities of tobacco, the old man no longer insists.

I'm gonna park the boys with Monča, then move on down the line.

You mean the road as existential escape? said Lojda. I too believe travel's the cure for existential anxiety. The never-ending journey. Only I'm already dyin. Fuck it, ah well!

I really am sorry, teach!

I remember you as a little boy. Little dissident, hair flappin. So what've you done with these twenty-five years of freedom we've had so far?

What do you mean?

You're old now. Don't you feel stupid? The only thing you've managed to achieve in that freedom is old age. It's you and people like you that'll benefit most from the Russkies.

What the hell're you talkin about? This isn't Ukraine.

People like you'll end up prayin for Putin to invade. Put an end to your irrelevance. You need violence! You need the Russkies to cover up your pathetic fate, the mess you've made of your lives.

What the hell're you talkin about?

What's better, Tabby? Hidin out in a cellar writin poems, fightin for freedom, takin a few slaps now and then, and bein famous? Or goin to work every mornin, payin your bills, and bein absolutely irrelevant?

Oh, now, c'mon . . .

And on top of it all, subject to global competition?

Blah blah blah!

You and your lot went runnin all over the world when Havel was in charge, and what did it get you, you chump? Nothin, huh.

Oh, c'mon, teach . . .

Just shut your mouth a minute. Sure, the Russians are spreadin conflagration and ruin. But that's what's savin us. From a so-called normal life, filled with all the crap that comes along with freedom. Uncertainty and antidepressants, most of all. The Russians're strappin on the night rider's ghoulish helmet and givin you the chance of your life to fight for freedom, you baboon! Martyrdom, that's their thing! Get it?

Hey, teach. You mind if I have a bit more to drink?

The Russians are like nature, they can't be stopped. The horsemen of Belial are on the move again—it's the only thing they know. Afghanistan, Chechnya, that's all forgotten now. The day before yesterday Georgia, yesterday the Crimea, today Syria, tomorrow Ukraine, after that the Baltics, Poland, the usual. Next thing you know they'll be back here, and Cossack horses'll drink from the Sázava again. Who's gonna stop em?

Heck if I know.

But the main thing is to admit, deep down in that black heart of yours, that you're glad to be a paleface, you punk little dissident.

Scuse me?

It's been written that the nations will overflow from tempestuous waters into a pool, causing it to ripple. You know how many niggers stayed here in our country from that wave of refugees?

How many?

Not a one. We hit the jackpot, huh? What do you say to that, Mr. Human Rights Crusader?

I could use another swig.

That's right, and the main thing is, with bombs fallin everywhere there's nowhere left to emigrate. You got nowhere left to run to, nowhere to hide, you actor.

I protest!

Sure, protest to your heart's content. No one's gonna lock you up for some silly samizdat anymore. Forget that. That was paradise back then. Slaps and cages for a few little poems? Shit, talk about your twentieth-century romanticism. You miss it, buddy, don't you?

Oh, c'mon.

Course, a moderate protest like that, it'll be harmless entertainment. They'll have a special channel for it on TV, monitored and regulated. Don't worry, I'm sure they'll take your hackneyed ass.

I protest, dammit!

Oh sure, there'll be a couple a loudmouths. By now, I'd say, that's an anthropological constant. But you know what Alexievich said? In Russia they wouldn't fill more than a stadium! Probably a decent-sized one too, but here in this country, a little soccer field oughta be enough to hold the dissidents, like that one that they play on in Hrusice, or that little one over in Senohraby, that'd do.

I didn't know you were so in love with the Russkies.

I hate em. But that's just the way it is.

Not true!

True.

Not true.

Just calm down. In the end it doesn't matter, Tab.

You're right, teach.

Burrowed into his blanket, Lojda notes the tremor that shakes his visitor's fingers as he refills his glass. The gulp quiets it.

The two men, now smiling again, reconcile with a glance. The guest praises the cabin. The tastefulness of the furniture. The comfort of the bed. He also mentions the excellent cuisine. The captain practically undulates in delight. They both lean back, stove glowing.

I just don't have the strength anymore, says Lojda. It left me with Světlana.

Sorry to hear.

But she's gotta get out in the world! She can't just hang around here all the time like a stray bitch. She's lived her life to the fullest, I'd say, gone through all her girlish adventures. Even got a tummy now.

I noticed—nice!

And a man to go with it, good one. He'll see to things from here on out. She's a clever one, she'll make it work. And what else is there? But what's in store for me? Unfortunately, Tab, that's a matter of some importance to me.

Oh yeah?

I don't want it to last long, and I really don't want it to hurt.

You and everyone else . . .

It's great you stopped by, Tab. Shall we have another drop?

Absolutely!

The old man fills their cups to the brim and gropes around in the cushions of the divan. He fishes out a pipe, packs it with a few indistinct bits, gazes into Papa's widened eyes, evidently pleased at the vision of what is to come.

Tell me, Tab, it ever dawn on you that booze and drugs're distributed by the devil?

The thought has occurred to me.

The young men I've seen—high-spirited, boisterous, arms made for wrapping around a woman, transformed into sobbing wrecks. That's drugs for you.

Oh, c'mon . . .

Thank god I'm quittin, though, the old man says, coughing. Ignited pipe clenched in his lips, he gasps for breath, inhaling until his cough turns to quietly burbling laughter.

Suddenly he stands, the red chieftain's blanket flowing down from his shoulders. Thrusting out his arms, he dangles them in the air, dried black scabs dotting his long-fingered hands. He rasps.

Has it ever happened to you, Tab, that you got up after making love and found yourself in the light? And the light surrounded you even walking down a gray street or in the midst of a wild forest with rotten, worm-eaten stumps? That after making love the world was more beautiful and all the colors were sharp and clear?

Now that's some fag talk there.

That's what happened to me every time I made love with that girl.

Yeah? Seriously?

Yeah, I experienced the fullness of the human touch that is love.

Come off it, teach. You're just talkin about fucking now. You just mean sex.

But I figured out there's an even greater love! the old geezer cries.

That's still just a physiological reaction, though. Serotonin, oxytocins, all that. The menstrual cycle plays a role too. We learned that in high school science!

And man said to God, you gave me a woman to stand by me. But she took the apple from the tree. And that's how this whole hullabaloo, this whole rat's nest, got started! says Lojda.

Slowly, bit by bit, he folds himself back together, sits down, and sprawls across the pillows.

But on the other hand, with a woman you see the light, you said. Papa grins.

Nice little chat we're havin, huh, Tab? You know what? I'm pourin you one more. Yep, you'll be an old codger too. Nothin you can do about it!

Now c'mon, teach . . .

You knew me as a boy. You kids used to shake inside the classroom when I yelled out in the yard. And now?

Oh, c'mon, it'll be fine.

No, it won't! And the main thing I been rackin my brains about lately, Tab, is whether God's here in the world, with us, or whether he's out there.

Seems reasonable. What else're you gonna do once your piece of ass up and walks away? You're lonely, Cap, that's all.

Never mind that. I think I've finally grasped the true nature of evil and suffering. And seriously, it's a fantastic relief.

Really? Lay it on me!

God created everything, but then he backed off, right? To let things run their course. But he stayed here as love. Not ordinary love, like when we fuck. But divine love!

Sure, why not?

He stayed here as love with the force of a supernova of three billion multiorgasms! But it's the kind of love that you can't get to till you need it.

Sounds good to me . . .

But in the beginning, apparently right that very first Sunday, God backed off. He renounced his power in order to permit an existence that isn't possible without evil, the old man says, swinging his barrel-like arms again with their mighty paws at the end.

It isn't?

No! If he allowed only good to grow, it'd interrupt the whole cycle, all movement. In short, life. Would you want that? Is that what you'd want, Tabby? Shit, are you even sane?

You were talkin about the light. Your girl left you and right away you go outta your mind? Givin her a fur for a screw like you were some pasha or somethin. You gave yourself away with that one, you old perv. But she's gonna leave you anyways, right? And then what'll you do?

Sit around and talk with potatoheads like you.

Bullshit, old man. You'll rot to pieces here. Either that or you'll croak somewhere in some ditch, or freeze to death drunk in the woods. I can totally see it.

You know, that might not actually be so bad, right?

I guess not.

How many times've I told myself I'd rather walk into the water than spend my last days jabberin away in some hospice. Kill myself, you hear! But will I have the strength?

Oh, so that's what this is about . . .

That's right. The question isn't whether or not. The question is how and when.

I guess so! In your case . . .

What do you think, Tabby? Does God create the darkness?

Huh?

C'mon, use your brain a little! Does God create evil and destruction?

I sure hope not!

Lojda produces a tiny piece of paper from somewhere and lifts it to his eyes. Or was he clutching it in his mitt the whole time? He clears his throat. Holds the paper up to his eyes and reads.

"I am the Lord, and there is no other. I form the light and create darkness, I make peace and create evil, I the Lord do all these things."

What? Create evil? Is that what it really says? You sure you didn't make that up? Maybe your brain's already fucked and you made it up, all sad and lonely out here on your straw mattress?

No. He creates evil. Why is your face so red all of a sudden, Tab? Is it the drink? Go ahead and have another. I think I'll pass. Or are you scared?

What should I be scared for? You said the rum was pure! You told me the booze wasn't tainted!

Look, Tab, don't be frightened. Use your wits. If God created evil, he's also the master of evil, so I'd say he can turn it into good at any time. Think logically.

Okay.

Or at least hope so!

Hope that there's hope?

Yes.

Cock-suckin sonuvabitch!

What's wrong? Hope's not your cup of tea, I see . . .

It's just that it's always the same thing, for fuck's sake: "The whole thing's a nightmare, but there's hope." You can all take your hope and shove it up your asses!

But there is hope! Really, Tab. Nothin you can do about it.

Thanks for everything, Cap! But me and the boys're gonna be packin up and on our way.

Don't go along the river. There's roadblocks there. Stick with Richie if you want to get out. He's got a cycle stashed.

Aha! Well, all right then.

Before you go, though, there's somethin I wanna give you. Seein as you're leavin.

Deal. What is it?

The old man fumbles around in the space between the divan and the wall, then lifts out a plastic bag. With the logo of a department store. Crammed full of sheets of paper.

The pages're covered in writing all the way to the edge, says Lojda, sliding the bag across the floor to Papa with his foot.

Papa dips his hands into the bag.

I fished it out of the ice. And dried it. That's what Máťa wrote down. That's his book.

How is it? Papa asks.

It's amazing, says Lojda. Amazing.

What's it about?

Máťa Píťa got a peek at God's plan's how I'd put it.

All right! But what's it about?

It's about evil.

Are the pages numbered?

Of course. Will you take it?

Yeah, I'll take it, says Papa, drumming his fingers on the manuscript's soft cover.

Thanks.

Mm-hm.

Listen, Tab, though! What about me? I'd like my ending to be better. I took care of my people best I could, but they're all droppin off. You'll see when you go out there. Some might say the situation calls for a miracle. But you know what? I don't think so. Things here've run their course, this branch here is rotten. It happens.

Ah well!

Help me. Then after that, grab the boys and run for it!

Mm, mm.

Will you help me?

Yeah. I guess so.

I don't have the strength anymore, Tab. Look. My body's changin.

From the rumpled blanket the old man raises an arm covered in crusty black boils, lifts the branch with its gnarl of an elbow, skin hanging off of it; tries to stretch his arm over his head, but it won't reach.

32

WHO AND WHAT THEY FISHED OUT. ATTACK. MOUNTAIN'S END. RICHIE'S HIDDEN TREASURE. DISCOVERY IN THE CAPTAIN'S CABIN. ON THE RAFT.

The wind, gliding down from the hills, whistles through the rocks, lifting up sand and dust and flinging them against the tents by the fistful, buffeting them, tearing away the plastic sheets that serve as makeshift dividers.

Skeeter leads them through the tangle of huts, leaping firepits, stomping through the ashes, sending stones and ash alike flying from the sand.

The boy sticks close to his little brother, the human bundle still firmly in Richie's arms, now fidgeting, puffing up, the little guy jerks and twitches, head bobbling on Richie's shoulder as they hurry through the tents.

The next thing he knows they are on the riverbank. The rustling of the reeds bent by the wind around the boat hums in their ears like a song.

The excruciating sounds coming down from the rocks are absorbed into the wind, into the rattling of the reeds. But the screeching from the hills is soon lost amid the uproar and turmoil as everybody crowds around the man fished from the water.

Skeeter, Richie and his load, the boy trailing behind, navigate through the summer throng . . . tattooed men in tank tops and boxers, two or three girls prancing about, whinnying at the affable obscenities that stream from the mouths of Poříčí's womenfolk, matrons in various stages of bulbousness decked out in bathrobes and tracksuits. Barely cognizant small fry nuzzle close to their skirts and chopping-block legs, their shielding arms with palms outstretched for playful slapping.

Meanwhile the people dragging the man from the water lay him down on the sand. And try to resuscitate him. The boy blinks at Richie's back as inside his weary head it dawns on him who it is.

There is a scramble to find the captain. Rocks and stones pelt the ship's tin flanks, the cabin windows. The barge sits before them, squatting heavily amid the sand and the swamp.

Hey, Looojdaaa!

Yoo-hoo, Captain!

We just fished Macek out!

Amid the jolly, laid-back atmosphere, the plastic bottles make their way hand to hand through the rippling crowd. Everybody wants a chance to drink to the discovery.

Guy ran the falls, respect!

And look what he did it on, too!

They nearly trampled the tube. Covered by a snarl of grass with muck and detritus clinging to it, the sacred painting lies in the sand next to Scales. He suddenly sits up. Water spews from his mouth.

The wind intensifies to a hair-whipping level, foretelling the coming darkness of dusk, if not something even a smidgen more apocalyptic.

The boy stares at the figure in soaked rags, battered half to death by the current. The familiar grizzled face, the head of limp hair, now snarled with clumps of algae and a length of nylon fishing line.

Scales, attempting to stand, drops on all fours. A green mush plops from his mouth.

Wakey-wakey, Scales!

Watch it, folks!

Jesus and Mary, over there!

Will you look at that . . .

They stand on the rocks above. Like a horde of ancient warriors risen from the slate, sulfur, and mists. Helmets. Horned and winged. Hairy wolf heads with glittering bits of glass inset in place of eyes. The flap of varicolored banners in the wind. The flowing chieftains' manes on the riders who have removed their helmets to cool their brutish skulls in advance of the attack.

The crowd on the beach stiffens in mass shock.

DISPERSE THIS RABBLE! cries the sharp voice of the lead rider, a man in a horned helmet.

Amid the burst of gusting wind, the revving of engines sounds not unlike the groaning of the rocks' innards, scraping against each other since the dawn of the ages.

The saddled warriors are not alone. A platoon of light-armored infantry stands with them on the rocks. Jumping out from behind the riders' backs with cords and ropes, they fix their lassos over protrusions in the rock and, twirling like worms at the end of their lines, lower themselves, knot by knot, down along the slate walls, then leap off into the mouths of the caves.

The militia's here!

Lojdaaa!

Ruuunnn!

A line of foot soldiers forms at the foot of the rocks. Someone plunks into the lagoon, but a pool of water isn't enough to stop the attacking cloud as the rock ninjas rush forward, tonfas, bars, and bats, lashed to their backs during the descent, now clutched in their hands . . . here they come . . . kicking down tents, slashing and ripping at fabric and plastic . . . A gangly bruiser in an SK Mirošovice jersey scatters the glowing coals with a kick . . . A handful of residents in varying states of wretchedness dodge the incoming wave of assault, driving anyone who didn't take part in the riverside festivities toward the water . . . Just then the boy catches sight of his papa over Richie's shoulder.

Standing on the gangway, he is shrouded in a red blanket. Angry spikes of light quiver in his eyes as he blinks off the gloom of the coal ship's bowels, clutching a stuffed plastic bag in his hand. He flings the bag skyward, then punts it over the the gangway ropes. Sheets of paper flutter out of the bag and are swallowed up by the water.

Papa leaps from the bridge, joining the bag's contents. The warriors dash to surround the ship from behind Richie's back, racing down the barely perceptible path, reeds crackling, snapping . . . and suddenly, with a startling boom, the slate wall collapses under the barbarians' feet. The main slabs, tall as a two-story house, split mid-topple, crushing the limestone to splinters and burying the invaders.

No sooner has the deafening roar come to a stop than the hulking man in the soccer jersey sprints onto the trail, shrieking and brandishing a bat . . . he takes a swing at Papa, who deflects the blow with his blanket . . . Richie gives a faint cry as Papa yanks the bat from the hands of his attacker, flips it on its axis, and whack . . . comes down on the big man's back with all his might, snapping his spine. Papa's pursuer sinks to his knees and drops headfirst into the wet.

Richie sets the little boy on the ground. As he and Papa grab the man by his arms and legs, lifting him up, Skeeter takes a running start and kicks the guy in the head. The stalks barely ripple as he comes barreling through the reeds. That's how small he is.

He helps them roll the guy into the swamp.

They take their time after that. Papa ties the blanket around his waist, clutches the little boy to his chest. And off they go. They only come to a stop when they hear the sounds of impact. They peer through the stalks.

As the last boulders tumble into the valley with a crash, they hear faint shouts. Flames flicker among the huts. A cloud of dust rises.

Shit, lookit that! Skeeter shouts. Just like in *Mackenna's Gold!*

Guys, was that Scales lyin there? Was that him? Did you see? Papa asks.

Richie urges them onward. Stretches out his arms, which have probably fallen asleep. His fingers on both hands are trembling as he takes his first step.

The others set out behind him.

The boy and his father bring up the rear. Papa runs his free hand over the boy's ribs, gives him a slap on the shoulder.

Still all in one piece?

Every now and then one of them turns to look back. The cloud of grit, all that stirred-up rock dust, is settling into the blackness of dusk.

They keep walking.

Then, without warning, Richie stops. Pulls something out of the reeds. A piece of mesh, the wires intertwined with reeds. He lifts the screen and behold! The fugitives can't believe their eyes. Here in the swamp, to their surprise, they have stumbled across a relative of the crushed vehicles they just left behind. A motorcycle. With a sidecar. And there's even a cart, a trailer.

Weren't expectin that, huh? My bike!

Fantastic, says Papa, patting Richie on the shoulder.

Skeeter runs his fingers over a rusty plate screwed to the fuel tank. MOTOCROSS POŘÍČÍ N. S., he says, sounding out the words, then laughs his head off.

Shit, where'd you get that hunk a junk? You swipe it from the trash dump?

It runs, asshole, Richie says.

Papa stares as if frozen. Runs a finger over the peeling, rusty plate. Taps the tiny logo in the corner. Then takes a breath.

So for real was it Scales they fished out? Yeah? Did you see him?

Absolutely, the two men confirm.

Papa squats down, arranges the red blanket on the driest-looking patch of turf within sight, lays the wrapped child on top of it. Straightens up.

I'm goin to get him, he says, and disappears into the reeds. They almost can't hear him. And can't see him at all. The reeds, stirring in the evening breeze, rise higher even than Richie's head. And he's a tall one.

My Goodness pushes off from the ship's flank with a broom, leaning in till the handle creaks. The expectant mother remains squatting down, playing it safe.

A veteran pirate, My Goodness keeps a lookout for floating branches and tree trunks, shoving the lumber on which the two women crouch away from the rocks, steering them into the current. The massive earrings creasing her ear glitter in the darkness, but nobody sees them, they slipped through. And now they are floating. Nestled together.

Torn loose from the coal barge by a boulder, the gangplank they're using now as a raft was put in their path by the Poříčí Virgin, there's just no other way. Bit by bit, they pull themselves back together in the wake of the frenzy.

They crept their way through the camp to escape, stealing past the flattened huts, scattered tents, stone smithereens everywhere from the downpour of rock, people lying about unmoving or battered all up and down, sighing and groaning . . . They snuck past the fire where the devastated booze colony residents huddled together, guarded by men in tracksuits barking into their phones, then slipped inside the ship.

And there . . . Lojda lying on the floor. The redhead, who had the key to the cabin door, squatted down to him. My Goodness knelt down alongside. Světlana covered him with kisses, My Goodness too. They sobbed as they made a cross on his forehead, sobbing as quietly as they could.

And then they came for them, the savage idiotic fucks, stomping all over the ship.

Světlana grabbed the fur, My Goodness scooped up the food, and the only thing that rattled her was who had scraped out the stove, scattered hot coals across the floor, and tossed them on the captain's bed, still smoldering? Or had Lojda gone into convulsions in the end and somehow done it himself? She didn't bring it up with her young companion when she roused her from her sobbing. Who knew what had happened.

They hid in the broom closet, and as the tracksuit mob swarmed through the cabin, turning everything upside down, the metal door slammed shut on them all by itself.

Must be hotter than hell in there now, My Goodness thinks as they drift down the river. Let em roast to death. I got my niece here still sobbin away.

Quit your mooin! You gotta take care of that tummy!

I had no idea I'd cry like that. I mean, he was super old anyway, right?

It suddenly dawns on My Goodness. Lojda is dead. She plops to the floor, still gripping the broom. Then suddenly breaks out in goosebumps all over, back, thighs, even the back of her neck.

I loved him too, y'know.

I think I'm gonna start bawlin again!

Silly girl. I got reason to bawl myself. He was one of my first, and you don't see me cryin, do you?

Now don't get mad, Auntie, but it's easier to get over a man when you shagged him thirty years ago. The captain and me, we were so in love! She sighs. He gave me this fur.

Světlana, look out, rock!

Twirling the broom like a samurai sword through her veil of tears, the girl pushes off just in time.

By the way, did you see his neck? All red like that? My Goodness says. I mean, if there was some humungous snake that lived here in the swamp and it slithered in there and strangled the captain, well, that'd be one thing, but there's nothin like that around here!

There isn't, is there?

You kiddin me?

Lucky for us then.

That's right!

Ah well, Světlana sighs.

So how bout your boy?

Kája's a good one.

Helluva hothead.

But he loves me.

That's good. For now! But I hate to break it to you, you're gonna be stuck at home, kids up the wazoo. He'll stretch you out, then go off and find himself another cow, young and well rested. What happened to me can happen to you. Look out, rock!

Světlana poles them away from the rock, sculling them into the flow with the broom.

I'd kill him.

Oh bullshit, why would you wanna do that?

With me and Kája it's different.

That's what every girl thinks. When we're young and pretty like you! You think us womenfolk might cook somethin up together, try to help each other out? You kiddin? Truth is, we're not even friends.

Stop tryin to scare me all the time!

I know, you're a good-natured soul, happy. I hope you stay that way. Your week's just about over, isn't it? Don't hump your way through your beautiful years, I always say.

Světlana just plunges her broom in the water, offering no reply.

Ai-yi-yi, that Lojda of ours, he always was a good one. I'll never forget him, I swear.

I swear to you too! Světlana says.

Just hold tight to that broomstick or we're gonna drown!

Are we takin the river all the way to Městečko?

You kiddin? To Richie's hideout is all. What's wrong? What is it now? My Goodness yelps as the girl suddenly lets out a screech.

She kneels, then drops to a sitting position, her rounded belly sticking out, sobbing from the depths of her soul, a moon-silvered tuft of hair falling into her eyes.

What're you on about now?

My mom!

Yeah, poor gal. Maybe she'll dig her way outta there somehow, maybe they'll dig her out.

Don't gimme that crap, Světlana says.

Neither woman says a word. Not for long.

I'll tell you one thing, though: There's nobody else with a tombstone like my mom's!

Save your energy, hon!

She's got a whole mountain on top of her!

Look, they'll be sendin in a rescue crew, the best doctors in the region, helicopters, paramedics, you'll see.

Ai-yi-yi-yi-yi-yi, mommy, my dear mommy, I came all the way here to invite you! And now she's got a tombstone of black slate, ai-yi-yi-yi.

There, there now. Think of the little one!

Yeah, yeah.

Listen, Světlana . . .

Mm-hm?

I know it's an awful thing to say. But at least it happened fast! Fast, just like she wanted, you know?

What do you mean?

So she wouldn't end up in the hospital! Uh-uh, not your mom! She liked havin her fresh air, high-spirited folks around, jeez-o-pete, you kiddin? Goin off to lie in a bed in some room with a bunch of goners?

You think?

Your mama, bless her golden heart, she made me swear up and down, no dead meat chamber no matter what! Never! "My Goodness, now you swear to me, or you won't ever pig out or get laid again, you old chatterbox, swear it!"

Seriously? She said that?

Yeah, she said that to me, her friend. Guess she realized she wasn't the youngest anymore.

Seriously? Just like that?

Just like that, and girl, you should be happy she got what she wanted.

Yeah, I guess . . .

At least you and your mom got to see each other, right? Some aren't even that lucky!

That's true.

There, you see!

Auntie, look! Světlana squeals.

The unexpected oval shape billowing the riverside reeds reminds her of a bloated serpent. The two women scream.

A man is standing in the reeds by the thing. Waving at them.

33

MONČA . . . GUARDIAN OF THE SALON. STOOKING
A PERSON. THE ARRIVAL OF THE PIOUS FLOCK.
LUKÁŠ AND LOMOZ. THAT INSTINCT AGAIN.
HELLHOUSE. SO WHAT? IN THE BUSHES.

A few hours after Kája burst into the house of pleasure with Miran's corpse, Monča is still drying her tears. Kája left the bloodstained Beemer in the fields and lugged his brother there on his back.

When in that first, merciless moment she laid eyes on his lifeless body, she thought her heart had died. But it had not. Now the terrible night had barely passed and here she was, gently resting her hands on her swollen belly, consoling Kája. So great was his distress that he just lay there, gnawed by pain, on the bed that was to have served as nuptial couch.

Meanwhile the female residents of the house, frozen in shock, sought each other out through the night, attempting, in girlish fashion, a reset, sobbing, snuggling, speaking in whispers.

The bridal salon yawns empty, the girls guarding the entrance. In a fancy cage in the hallway leading to the salon, a gorgeous canary spreads its wings, provoking waves of keen agitation in Baltie, the coal-black tomcat. It almost seems the bird is doing so intentionally. The polished door handles shine throughout the house, the windows washed, floors clean, stairs scrubbed. After a major washing and dusting and ironing, the girls' beds of sin are all freshly made, the vases on the tables and nightstands in every corner filled with gorgeous bouquets.

And a teddy bear forgotten on the sideboard in the bridal salon, the only knight guarding the waves of grief, helplessly fixes his glassy eyes on all the furbished splendor.

The scent of flowers, faint but intoxicating, reaches Monča sitting with the deceased on the bed in her guardhouse.

Kája stretches out Miran's arms and legs, fending off the rigor mortis that causes the muscles of the dead to stiffen and contract.

It was supposed to be Kája's last day as a bachelor, but now, tears in his eyes, he is burying his brother's bullet-pierced shirt, his jeans and belt and cotton-embroidered hoodie, underneath the bed. And what of Monča? Proud, short-tempered, jealous and fierce, but always generous and solicitous. What would she do now? And what about the baby?

They should report the murder. But they don't want that. No, they don't want any outsiders involved. Besides, all of the relevant officials inclined toward the family are already invited for the wedding ceremony.

In the end, it is Monča who comforts the weeping hulk. Protected by Miran, Kája himself was unable to protect him. But who ever heard of younger brothers protecting their older brothers?

The early birds Janinka and Vendulka come walking in. Naturally they offer their warm, friendly cunts to Kája. But he shakes his head, fists still crushing the tears that gush from his eyes.

So they help Monča instead. Washing out the wound, trembling fingers in dishwashing gloves picking out the shreds of flesh, tossing them in a bucket, washing away the drips and clumps of dried blood. Miran's pale, sunken face appears chalked on through the thicket of tattoos. The girls avert their gaze. In death, he looks like a soulless dummy. Even the fact that, as Janinka whispers, he reminds them a tiny bit of the spear-pierced Jesus is no help.

Once washed, they cover him up. At first with a fuzzy blanket, but then that strikes them as wrong, so instead they take a clean pillowcase and cover his face with that.

Just then comes a soft knock at the door. Perhaps the visitor chose not to ring the bell in view of the early hour.

In fact, the dawn has caught many a visitor in front of the house. None of the men in the group heading up to Chlum with Lukáš have any intention of missing the celebrated wedding day.

They sit run-down on the benches outside, covering the wet from an overnight shower and the morning dew with their raincoats, while the bearers of the wooden Savior park at the gazebo in front of the still-sleeping bordello. And if anyone still turns up their nose at the evident sinfulness of the place, the unpleasant smell of the cesspit will hit them right in the nostrils. Which tends to happen around cesspools after a rain.

The state of the cesspit has been keeping Lomoz up at night. Besides, he also has a more sensitive nose than everyone else.

He spent all evening walling it in, even mixed up some fresh mortar in the morning, before daybreak, but he couldn't pull it off.

Lately he's been dropping things all too often. The weakness that came over him and knocked the trowel out of his hands before he could complete the job is a sign, as far as he's concerned.

And he intends to settle it once and for all.

He's going to kill himself.

Truth is, he had been expecting this moment. He was still the same unyielding, unbreakable man-mountain Lomoz, but he was alert to the signs, and now that he realized the time had come, it was actually a relief.

He sits in the bridal salon with a pot of tea, his level of privilege such that he even takes out a tray of wedding pastries to sample. He pours a cup of refreshing tea for Lukáš, the legendary builder of Chlum himself.

They keep their voices low, out of consideration for the slumbering whores.

You live your life, day in day out, and it doesn't ever look like it's really gonna end, says Lomoz.

Splotches of black paint, flakes of mortar, cling all over his arms and hands, calling to mind nothing so much as the limbs of a forest giant.

How do you know it'll end? You only know there's people that were with you, then they're not. You see, the conscious mind can't accept its own nonexistence, the albino man elucidates, fidgeting in his chair.

How do you know?

A man said so.

Yeah yeah. You know how many men I've seen kick the bucket, Lukie? Not a soul around can match me when it comes to that, y'know.

I can vouch for you there.

How many of em I outlived, even when I was just a boy. Frozen to death in the snow, gunned down, you name it.

Everyone knows the story about you and that Russian herd, back when you were a boy, and how that whole thing turned out.

313

And y'know, I still don't believe it myself? That it could end.

Yeah, I get you.

More tea? Touch of sugar?

Sure, if I can, I'll take a cube.

Like your life sweet, huh, Lukáš? You little angel you.

When I can.

Help yourself. I might knock somethin over! Girls've got things all set up here.

You're mad, Lomoz, that's all. I know you're angry, but you shouldn't be.

It worked up to a point, but not anymore.

Life is good.

You're buildin yourself a church, great. Why bother? It's gonna take you forever with that bunch of potatoheads you got!

It's a good spot, Chlum.

I was sposta wall in that cesspit, and I can't even do the work anymore. You smell that stink? Back, hands, noggin, all crippled. And here I was braggin to Kája just the other day! I just want nice things for him and Světla, that's what matters.

Right, you need to be with them.

Well, I don't plan to ruin it for em. I'm takin off. Everyone knows I disappear from time to time, specially Monča. And if I don't come back? By then they'll be wed and the whole thing'll be over.

Give yourself a breather. It's your God-given right.

Can't wall in that fuckin pit. I ain't worth shit anymore, fuckin hell.

Sure, you're a believer, but what about me? That's not my thing.

I know. Person's gotta be built for it. Otherwise it just doesn't work!

Ain't that the truth? Hey, Lukie, any of the boys in that crew of yours masons? I got the mortar all mixed and ready to go. So it won't stink up the big day for the young ones.

Give yourself a rest, Lomie! Take it easy.

Everyone's rackin their brains wonderin why you're buildin a church up on Chlum. So how come?

It's a good spot. The kinda place where anyone can come. I like it there.

Help yourself to another cube, Lukie. I can feel you squirmin from here.

Great, thanks! Can I have two?

Course. The girls've also got some lemon around here somewhere. Case you got a cold comin on. You like lemon?

This is fine, thanks.

They did the shoppin, the cookin, brought home the flowers, spent the whole day cleanin. They've been runnin around like chickens with their heads cut off.

They're good girls all right.

So listen, I heard that church of yours got broken into! All smashed up! It's not that bad. A couple bags of cement'll do the trick.

Man, I fucked up that cesspool, I can hardly lift a brick, and they reported last night on Sázavan that that nurse from Rumburk was not guilty. Y'know, that one with the potassium? That did me in.

What're you talkin about?

I thought she was helpin the old and the weak. But nope! D'you hear about that, Lukáš? Up there on Chlum?

No, I didn't.

Potassium, man. I said to myself, Aha!

Hm.

The biggest problem is, you gotta do it before your instinct for self-preservation kicks in. That's what I wanna prevent. At all costs! I know where that instinct comes from, too. Nobody knows it better than me.

Do what?

Kill myself. What are you, stupid?

Look, Lomie, don't do it.

You say, leave it to God or some such crock, but I'm not doin that. So don't ask me to.

Oh, come on . . .

Spare me the priestly speeches. You're an old jailbird yourself. You just happened to find yourself a side gig. Hey, I know what that's like. I was no different, heh-heh.

Oh, come on now!

Heh-heh-heh! You sure know how to set things up for yourself, Lukie, yes sir! People follow you. And they don't ask for receipts, do they?

You're mistaken, Lomie. I think I'll take a drop of that lemon after all. The girls put it here, on the sideboard.

Fine, Lukáš, then tell me, how bout the old-timers and old bags sittin around on their asses, just lyin around, waitin to die. No one can stand em! God's got no idea what it's like bein such a sack a shit. And the old folks? Still chasin around after every sweet thing, lookin for a breeze at every turn, well, shit! But to normal people they're gross. And I'm not even talkin about the way they shit their pants.

Come on, Lomoz. It doesn't have to be that way.

Back when I could still see, I saw em. The old people. But I never thought one day I might be just like them. Now I do. And I ignored em. They were like insects to me.

I'm sure that's not true, Lomie!

And you know who to blame that we're disgusted? It's all the fault of that bastard instinct for self-preservation. You might not want it, but the instinct sure does!

Look, Lomie . . .

Shit, I'll promise you one thing. I'm gonna fight that self-preservation instinct with every last drop a life in me.

Take it easy.

I'm gonna have it out with him like a man. There's no one can take me down, shit!

Oh, no doubt. That's for sure!

Hey, Lukie, you mind leanin over and grabbin us a drop off the sideboard? Right there, behind the cups. Girls got it all lined up.

Okay, but just a little. It's still morning.

We're big men, we can have a big drink. Girls got some rolls there too, poppy seed. Take that too, if you want.

All right.

Those girls a mine, Lukáš, all perfumed up, here in their rooms, I don't want to gross em out, get it? If I were to keep on livin, I can guarantee they'd be disgusted. Might even be in a week! I already got a flappy old neck as it is.

Don't be silly, Lomie. They love you.

First they sleep with you thinkin you'll do em nice. Not that they feel like they have to, not at all. For money or love, it's all good. They're havin fun. But as soon as pity comes into the picture, man, fuck that, know what I mean?

There's other things besides sex.

Help yourself! You know, the girls don't buy that cheap rotgut, uh-uh,

Monča would chase em right out the door! Nothin but the good stuff. How bout those rolls, tasty or what?

Super tasty!

Have some more! Our girls're always countin calories. Hell, I remember workers countin calories to survive.

Yeah, oh yeah. Times're different!

You said it! They'd beat you to death out there for a couple calories. But who's keepin track of calories when it's a wedding, right?

Absolutely.

So anyway, you and that church. No question in your mind that it's a place of God, as they say, is that it?

That's right.

It just came to you, like that, huh?

That's right.

Say, Lukáš, do you know how old I am?

No, I don't!

Me neither, but it's goin on ninety. Maybe more like ninety-five. Somethin like that.

Whoa!

Or is it eighty-five?

Listen, you know you can always come join us. People appreciate you.

Oh yeah?

Everybody likes talkin to you, c'mon, you're a clever guy. You know tricks the young ones don't.

I can't even hold a trowel anymore! I'm tellin you, today I broke it for good. Mixed up some mortar, did a little wallin, and boom, done.

Look, just come on by. People'll be happy. I'll be happy.

What if I can't walk anymore? It happens, y'know, to quite a few.

So we'll carry you, no big deal.

I'm touched to hear it, Lukáš. So you really believe, huh, holy man? You pray and everything? You can tell me.

I do, yeah. Yes.

You went and built a henhouse up there on Chlum, and now you're cock of the walk, huh? So that's it. You're the same as everyone else.

I guess so. But I didn't used to be. I was awful.

Oh, spare me. Where I come from, they were a dime a dozen. Nothin but awful killers, people here don't have a clue! I may not know about God, but I know plenty about the devil. Even know his name.

So what is it?

Same as mine.

Huh?

Surprised, are you, Lukáš?

Wherever there's people, the devil is there.

But whoever says there has to be a God if there's a devil is a fool. It doesn't even out like that. It's worse. Sorry to say.

Now you got me confused. And how come you're bein so hard on yourself?

Girls baked all these rolls for the wedding. Delicious, right? They baked all night, I think. I could hear their sneaky shaggin.

Ha ha ha!

I like talkin with you. One more to fill the other leg. Before I hit the road.

You're the boss.

Well, I won't live long enough to see the next crop of girls, I can tell you that. I knew their moms and aunts, before they got hitched or drank themselves to death, or both. Some of em're okay and have kids with their husbands or what have you.

That's the way it goes.

So I became the devil in this building in camp that became a living hell.

They tortured you there, huh? Nasty times. But that was all years ago now!

If it happened once, it'll happen again. How bout Chlum? How strong is it? That Chlum of yours'll save you, huh.

Like I said, you're welcome to drop by!

First the guards show you how to knock somebody's teeth out. Then you do it yourself, and once you realize what's goin on, you do it gladly, less you want somebody else doin it to you.

Puh!

Listen, two guys in a ring floggin each other with canes, two buddies, but that's just the beginnin. Picture this: you pick some guys you know, and they gotta flog each other and you're in the driver's seat, you're in charge. And now they're skinned to the bone, barely still on their feet, and they're beggin you, but you don't give in. Cause if you do, you're next. And then you gotta pick the next guy and think up a torture for him. So tell me, Lukáš, who would you start with first? And I warn you, soon as you run outta people, it's your turn out there.

Listen, Lomoz, I got nothin but respect for you. Those camps out there in Siberia must've been unbearable.

Yah!

Next to that, what we had here was a walk in the park! Minkovice, Valdice . . . in our prisons you had to watch your ass, but I know it was nothin compared to the slog you went through!

You kina got used to them torturin if they needed to find somethin out or break somebody. In that building, though, they tortured just for the hell of it, nonstop, day and night, accordin to strict principles, on a slidin scale, like the calories. Comrades had a regular research project goin on. Out there in Pitești.

Puh! That's just awful!

Either you tortured other folks, or they'd torture you. Knife, stick, fire, whatever. People went deaf and blind, they were so beat up. The screams alone were enough to make you deaf, so we had to plug our ears with corks. It was no joke! You had to make sure your guy was almost finished off, but stop in time so he wanted to die but he was still alive. Get it? To keep the whole thing goin.

Jesus and Mary!

Almost nobody made it, I'll tell you that much. From the ones of us that didn't balk and went ahead with the torture. They couldn't take it. Committed suicide. Stopped eatin and starved to death, or snuck out of the building and froze somewhere in secret. Their instinct just snapped. I guess that's why you think people're basically good, huh?

That's right! I do.

Well, they aren't.

They are!

I made it, though, fuckin A! Me, the only one. Out of all of em.

You?

Yeah. Two years I worked there, and not one person stuck it out. Poor souls took me for an actual devil. It wasn't just professors and brainiacs in there. There was also folks from villages, some of em pretty religious a course. It was them called me that. The devil. Pitești devil, they called me in that Romanian lingo a theirs.

That's horrific.

It's true all I had left by then was a pair of boots, a warm fur coat—nice one—set a keys to the guardhouse and the pantry. But then Stalin died. Hm, I said to myself. Wonder what's gonna happen to me?

And?

Nothin. Whole thing got swept under the rug. I thought they'd kill me, but nope. Everyone was already dead, so nobody knew a thing. I got lucky.

And then?

Then I shuttled round various posts. It was rough there too, but not as rough.

Mm-hm, mm-hm.

You can google it. Name of the prison's online. Wasn't that long ago, really.

I think I'll pass.

Seriously, you should look it up. Pitești Prison's the name of that cutthroat fuckin whorehouse. And you know how I got from the Union to Bessarabia or whatever bumfuck region it was? And how I got back to the Union?

How would I know? Let's hear it!

Nah, what's the use.

Hm!

The things I lived through, no one else on earth has ever seen.

God bless you, man!

But that's what I don't get. I mean, he's been blessin me this whole time! All those folks tortured to death, hundreds, not to mention their families . . . and here I been all these years, surrounded by sweet young things, good drinks, good food, much as I want. I go round makin home repairs, wherever I go folks're glad to see me. I'm in paradise. I mean, it's like fantasyland! How is that even possible?

I donno.

Thanks for sayin that, Lukáš!

What for?

Cause I donno either. Look, the main thing is for the young ones to have a nice first day together! I admire people gettin married like it was nothin. I don't intend to spoil it for em. You're not thinkin you're gonna try and hold me back now, Lukáš, are you?

But . . .

But what? You're about to ask me if I regret it, aren't cha? If I'm sorry? Yeah, I am. Every day, long as I'm not piss drunk or with a girl . . . more like in a girl, heh-heh. And sometimes even if I am. So what?

So what?

So nothin! Thanks for the priestifyin questions. Hey, and if Monča asks, I just stepped out for a breath of fresh air, okay?

Okay. You can count on me.

Or you still think I should come and join you on Chlum? Even after what I told you?

You can come if you want. You bet.

Nah, fuck that, just kiddin! That's the last place I want to go. Take care, buddy.

Take care . . .

I wish you all the best, Lukáš. I mean it!

Same to you!

Bones cracking, the blind man straightens up, thrusts his hand un-erringly through the cups into the sideboard, snatches the opened bot-tle and drops it into his boilersuit pocket. Then he ambles his way down the stairs, stomp stomp stomp, his workboots sounding a wakeup call for anyone who might still be asleep.

Outside, plunged into the still-cool morning air, condensing little by little with the rising sun, he affably responds to the inquiries of the horde seated around the entrance, asking whether or not Monča is awake. And the girls? He amiably replies that they have yet to pry them-selves out of bed.

Lomoz shakes their hands as one by one they slap them into his out-stretched paw, and wishes them all good health, what else . . . then dis-appears behind the fence.

And as the shots and tea hit bottom, the blind man, believing him-self to be hidden behind one of Monča's rose bushes, unzips, grips him-self, and proceeds to sprinkle the burgeoning day with the contents of his bladder.

A lady neighbor cries, Get outta here, there's kids around! . . . and, to general laughter, accompanied by a brief round of applause from one joker, albeit subdued out of respect for Lomoz's age and blindness, he politely walks a few steps away.

He now ascertains by touch the presence of a thick bush, the thorns that would injure a finer skin to him nothing more than a slight tickle. Hiding his pride and joy from working eyes, Lomoz smiles, a delectable rush of arousing moments flashing through his mind. How many times has he taken it out inside this house? He recalls with every fiber of his being the tenderness accumulated over millions of fleeting and exuberant coital movements, resting in each other's arms as the reciprocal movements subside . . . is this really my last time here? All right, then! Hell, why not?

To his astonishment, he shivers, dread running down his spine.

But he shakes himself off, zips up.

And walks off, entirely steady now, through the still-quiet village. The path stretches along the water, past the linden trees shedding blossoms in the scorching summer heat. He treads across the carpet of soft fallen flowers, and as the trail turns he heads uphill, away from Městečko.

34

SITTING AROUND THE FISHERMAN. A BANQUET.
ON THE VIRGIN. THE TATTOOED BOY AGAIN—
A LESSON IN HUMANISM. AND THE CAVALCADE
SALLIES FORTH. PRAŽMA. I RESPECT OLD FOLKS,
BUT . . . BITTEN BREAST.

When Papa rises up out of the reeds, he insists that the women take only him and the piece of junk onto their raft.

But My Goodness is furious.

Toss that thing in the water, we're not leavin a person here! Where's your common sense?

I'm afraid we can't help him now anyway!

It's Scales, you oaf!

So the women take them both. With difficulty, but they manage.

My Goodness bites her fist after they land at Richie's moto-hideout and Papa carefully unrolls the painting, spreads it out on the driest patch of mud he can find, and weighs down the corners with stones.

She's crossed herself under the painting many thousands of times in her home church, and she does so again now, under a sky with birds flying overhead, in a landscape open wide to escape.

On your knees, girl, this minute. Forget the wet, you're soaked as is. The Virgin washed up here for you!

All right, Auntie, all right.

Mary, mother of Jesus, is one of the most powerful beings in the universe, gibbers My Goodness. She's queen of the angels and she'll never forsake you, and that's the truth, so remember it, Světla!

Yeah, yeah, says the full-bellied girl, swaying a little and yawning.

The number of times I walked up that hill to her when Pražma got all steamed up that we didn't have a baby yet.

Oh yeah?

He was furious, it was always my fault, we went at it like rabbits, but then Zděnina was born and I was so happy.

Papa, Skeeter, and Richie together lift Scales from the raft and drag him through the muck. The boy holds his feet, doing his best to avoid looking into the drowned man's face.

Using her hands to help herself up, the girl gets to her feet. Gives the boy a nice smile in greeting. Trailing her fur through the wet grass, she pads her way to the red blanket, scoops up the swaddled boy, stands him up on her lap, and together they peer off into the grass. What's that creepin around in there?

The men finally succeed in moving Scales. Gangplank groaning under his weight, up to their knees in water. They set him down.

Daybreak, huh, Papa says to the boy. You get any rest? That's good, we gotta keep goin. How bout your brother? Not makin a fuss, is he? Wash that off, he says, pointing at the green splatters on the boy's calves from rubbing against the dead man's mouth.

The boy slips off his track pants and T-shirt, steps into the water. Breaks off a reed, wipes at the phlegm. Lets it wash away with the current.

Richie steps up from behind, slaps the boy on the neck.

This is mud, that's a scab . . . he says, poking the boy with his finger. It tickles.

They soak in the water, which flows lazily, gently.

Hey look, says Richie, showing him a stone plucked from the bottom. Look at what all lives in this river. He thrusts the rock under the boy's nose, the grooves in its surface wriggling with snails.

Lemme get a look at ya! He pauses a moment, then: You'd look good in jeans, Richie says conclusively. Black, or blue, whatta ya think? You should have both. Not just track pants.

As the boy moves into deeper water, the long gash on his thigh, all the little scratches and scrapes, sting at first.

I heard you been goin around in girls' clothes. How come? I mean, nobody cares when girls wear their hair short and dress in leather jackets and boots, why not. But boys walkin around in skirts and pink dresses? Different story! It's unfair, don't ya think?

He squeezes the boy's shoulder. Slips his fingers into the hollow over his collarbone. The boy flinches.

I've known lotsa boys like you, y'know. Stubborn. You'll talk when you're ready, right? When you feel like it's worth it, you'll say somethin.

Hey, you guys! Skeeter calls, rising up from the reedbank. Come over here!

Richie and the boy walk over to find Skeeter bent over Scales, feeling around, hands busily at work.

A second later he raises his hand, they glimpse the flash of a fish belly. He's come up with a whopper.

Thing was flappin around his pocket, mouth still movin and everything, Skeeter explains.

He brandishes a frog knife over the giant carp. Flicks a lighter under a heap of dry leaves that he gathered up, and a second later he clambers up on the riverbank again, dragging flat stones out of the water. He scrapes the bugs off the rocks with a twig.

Meanwhile, Papa and Richie contemplate the motorbike. Who'll sit in the sidecar, or should they secure the painting in there? They hash it out.

Which way to Městečko? Papa asks.

Thatta way, Richie points.

And how far?

Depends how ya go.

The sun overhead is beating down by this point.

Richie keeps a little plastic canister from Billa in his hideout. Filled with water. Also a plastic bottle of wine. Two liters.

The fisherman's face is still firm. But it has taken on a green tinge, from the mud and mush brought up from his stomach. His hair is pasted to his temples, the pale whites of his eyes shine from under his half-closed eyelids. The corners of his mouth are twisted, his darkened tongue has sunk behind his teeth.

My Goodness drops a bandanna or kerchief over his face, some sort of small scarf she happens to have with her.

I'm just glad we didn't leave you back in the mud all by your lonesome. Least you're with friends now, right, My Goodness says, glancing over at Papa.

Světlana spreads the red blanket over a piece of wood. Plops down and sits perched on top, holding the little one. Everyone admires how good and well behaved he is, as if he weren't even a child. Světlana undoes the plastic strap, opens up the fur.

He was always such a good-hearted guy, Scales. Anyone could come and see him, he'd talk with anyone. You don't find folks like that anymore nowadays, My Goodness says, wiping away the tears with her palm.

That's a fact! says Skeeter.

Treated me and the boys like kings, says Papa.

Somethin strange about it, though, says Skeeter.

Everything's strange, son, says My Goodness.

But I mean he was still alive. He could still stand, back there on the beach, says Skeeter. He stares at Papa. How'd you get him outta there?

Dragged him through the swamp and the wet. Those fuckers were runnin all over the place, Papa quickly answers. Maybe he smacked his head in a puddle? I donno, there were fires burnin, but I couldn't see shit. Then by the time I came back for the picture, says Papa, waving his hands . . . his soul had up and left. I'll tell you folks, was I ever glad when those ladies came floatin by!

Thank the stars you saved the Virgin! My Goodness declares into the sudden silence.

He was cryin and pukin all over the beach, green shit comin out of him, but I figure he must of had water on the brain already by then. There was no helpin him, Skeeter reflects.

Exactly! says Papa.

If that's how it was, then that's how it was, Skeeter nods. He flips the fillets on the hot stones using a twig and his knife.

And what about me? I've known him since I was a little girl, Světlana says, wiping her eyes. Scales was like an uncle to me.

They all look at Scales. Then into the fire. It's a pretty little fire, now that the sun has come out.

Nothin we can do now, folks, says Skeeter. First batch is up! Richie?

Heh?

Got any bread?

Nope, no bread!

Sheesh, I must have a hole in the head, says My Goodness, slapping her forehead. She leaps up, zips open her track top, rolls up her hoodie, gives a little jiggle, breasts bouncing on her belly. What's the old earring up to now? And down it pours, all over the grass. Radishes, onions, cauliflowers, even a length of klobása she was keeping warm in there. And a loaf of sliced bread in foil.

Folks, sobs My Goodness, all choked up again, this here's courtesy of the captain's cabin! Světla, hon! I don't even have words! We can talk later, kay?

The redhead nods. They all stuff themselves in silence. At least Richie has salt.

Still plenty of fish too.

And wine?

More than enough. They gargle it down. Little by little, basking in the sun. The bottle seems practically bottomless. Meanwhile the stack of fish fillets piles up.

There's no end to it, My Goodness says dreamily.

I guess all this misery's shrunken our stomachs, Skeeter conjectures.

They wipe their greasy fingers on the driest patches of grass.

Don't be shy, girl. Remember, you're eatin for two now, My Goodness tells Světlana. But she doesn't need to be told twice.

The men gaze with pleasure on her bulging tummy and the tips of her nipples, threatening to tear right through her thin little T-shirt. Even the boy stares. She knows they're staring and couldn't care less.

I've been cravin fish all the time lately!

Really?

I mean, I get all sorts of cravings, but mostly for fish!

All right, just be careful of the bones.

The boy picks out the whitest bits of fish for his little brother, wrapped in the red blanket, enthroned on Světlana's lap like a miniature king. Before feeding him a piece, he pulls the bloody pacifier out of the half-pint's mouth. Crushed in his tiny fists, the small boy clutches a mishmash of grass-dwellers. Meal beetles, grasshoppers, whatever swarming creepy-crawling thing he could lay hands on. He gets as much tender fish meat as he wants, and still wants more.

So how're they going to move on from there?

Richie explains.

He and his motorcycle will lead the cavalcade. Skeeter will hold on to him from behind. Papa will ride in the cart, guarding the painting.

With his boy. And the ladies? They can fit comfortably in the sidecar with the little one. The inside is all nice and soft. Which is good for Světlana!

Well, all right then!

They roll the Virgin up again, still barely dry. The paint crumbles a little. Nothing they can do about that, though.

Richie and Papa get the Virgin settled in, while the women, little one snuggled against the redhead's breasts, clamber into the sidecar.

They send the boy to clean up camp.

Wouldn't want to leave any leftovers by the body. Not with all the blowflies around. Once they report the death to the proper officials and the folks from Městečko come to collect the remains, they want them to think well of them.

They turn for one last look at Scales. It's sad. Him lying there like that.

The boy hurls the flat stones back into the water. Grabs a piece of wood and nudges the charred twigs and ash into the current. Covers the firepit over with sod. Gathers up the peeled-open fish carcass.

How many times has he camped like this before? With Papa. And Mama. He can feel the hole of her absence. Filled with scraps of conversation, incidents whirling about. Floating up from his memory.

And suddenly he sees them. And freezes.

A woman squatting in the reeds on her haunches. The reeds bending in the wind, or with her movements. A boy stands a step in front. His darkened face tattooed with dots darker than his skin. That's how he recognizes the boy. The one he gave the donuts to. How did they get here? What business is it of mine? he thinks. He lays the fish in the grass. In front of the other boy. And scampers off.

He doesn't come to a stop till he reaches the motorbike. When he turns around, all he sees is the bank of reeds shining brown through the water.

Richie walks around the cart, kicking the tires.

All good? Can we go?

The boy nods.

What's got you so spooked? Climb in.

The boy grabs the side of the cart, pushes off the tire. Swings up and in.

Saw them roamin around back there, huh? Skeeter spotted em too. They aren't gypsies, are they? Anyway, no skin off our backs.

Papa sits in the cart on a heap of rags, empty sacks. Keeping a grip on the rolled-up painting with both hands. They have it secured standing up with ropes and cords.

The boy tries to figure out how to help. Squats down by his papa.

My Goodness holds the little nipper on her lap, but he scrambles over to Světlana. Leans his head against the redhead's breast, smiling. Occasionally gives a quiet purr. Apparently taking pleasure in the burbling conversation.

Maybe you shouldn't of looked at that drowned man so many times!

How can you say that, Auntie? I owe him my life. I went to the pond with my mom one day. She forgot I was there, or dozed off in the grass. So I go chasing off after a cabbage white, those fluttering wings were all I could see, and whoopsy-daisy! I tumbled right in the pond! If it wasn't for Uncle Scales, I would've been dead.

He looked so awful, though! I'm just thinkin of your baby.

I remember how kind he was, though. That's good for my little one, don't you think?

He reminded me of Pražma, y'know?

I know, Auntie. I know.

The way he was all puffed up and bloated. I didn't wanna tell you, but his stomach burst. I'm not gonna go into it, seein as you're expectin and all, but he had lumps comin out of him in the fridge down at the station house. I says to him, That's the last time you cause me grief, you piece a shit.

Oh, Auntie, no!

He got drunk as a skunk at the Distillery during that high water that ground him up against the rocks, then swept him under the weir in Čtyřkoly, yep! You call that a life? With him? How many of em got locked up, and he was the only crotchety one. Always in a rage. And then this. So there you have it. You say your Kája's a good one, though?

He's great!

Well, my Pražma used to be good too. The way we loved each other, girl? Used to go dancin all the time.

That's so nice!

If only he didn't drink so much! But still it worked. I donno where it all went wrong. By then we'd had Zdĕnka already.

Aw, I'm really lookin forward to that.

After that it was nothin but fights. How come? Beats me. By then Zdĕnka'd already cut and run, she was long gone. I don't even wanna know if he, whatchamacallit—traumatized her.

Auntie!

Well, I was no saint either, not by far! It's impossible with a man like that in the house. If only he'd been around at least.

Hm!

Then he told me he was leavin.

How come?

That's what I asked. No reason, he says. You're just old.

What?

Yeah, that's exactly what I said. What?

And what'd he say?

Nothin you can do, he said, just the way it is. You used to smell of pussy and milk and bein with you was always a laugh. Now you're just old. You stink like your mother.

I mean!

I don't wanna tell you what to do, now that you're havin a baby and all, but that's men for you.

Hm.

What foolishness is he gettin up to now?

The little nipper greedily attaches himself to the girl. Pawing at her relentlessly.

Svĕtlana?

Mm-hm.

Don't be a scowler. You don't want him inheriting it!

Mm-hm.

Don't tell me you're cryin now? Oh, c'mon!

Now I'm gonna have a little one. And Kája and me love each other!

Well, good for you, girl.

And my mom loved me. She loved me a lot!

Svĕtlana, hon, course she did!

And there's somethin else I wanna say, Auntie.

Go ahead, girl. What is it?

Listen, I respect old folks, but when they talk crap, I tell em, all right? So shut up for a minute, all right?

Owww, Světlana yelps, jumping up so abruptly the little one's head rebounds.

Howling in pain, Světlana tears off her T-shirt, wiping away the drops of blood from her freshly bitten breast, leaning half-naked out of the sidecar. As they bump along the turf, her wailing peters out amid the chuckles of the men, and Richie brakes the bike to a halt.

Papa pushes off the sideboard, hops out of the cart.

I will slap you silly, you pipsqueak! My Goodness yells, raising a hand at the little one's head.

Nobody's ever hit him yet . . .

You little bulldog!

. . . and that's how it's gonna stay, says Papa, grabbing hold of his son and lifting him off Světlana's lap.

Get that little tick outta here! He chewed clean through her breast!

Nobody's ever beaten him cause it's no use, Papa explains, clasping the little boy under his arm. He climbs back over the sideboard and settles onto the sacks again.

Světlana too retakes her seat.

Are we good now, yeah? says Richie, turning to them. He giggles into his palm.

A few drops landed on them. But only very light.

And the cavalcade once again sallies forth.

35

VENCA BAJER. DEFECTIVE POOCH.
MORE CINEMATOGRAPHY. LOMOZ'S BET.
CROSSBOW VERSUS PINECONE. REQUEST FOR
WALNUT SCHNAPPS. INTO THE CAVE.

Leaving the village below, Lomoz scrambles up the trail to Lebka, clutching hold of stunted trees to steady himself as he goes. Scarlet and deep blue clumps of grass bend in the wind. A viper flits past, causing him to pound the trail with his boots. His heart rings inside his chest, breathing, expanding.

The rock towers over the hillsides and woods, totally bare. Were someone to look down on it from above, it might remind them of a skull. Which is probably why the locals call it Lebka.

In the area around Lomoz's cave, really more of a hollow, a den, its bottom lined with foliage, new leaves deposited on top by gusts of wind, he has the distance stepped off to every stump, a mental map of every stone.

The idea that he would come to rest, as he always solemnly said to himself, and pictured in detail many times, had emerged in his mind with no fear attached. No doubt, no throbbing temples or pulse in the ears, no tension at all. It came almost as a comfort.

Until today.

He hadn't expected he would be shaking.

It's not that I'm afraid. That's the weakening comin on. I gotta be fast, though, before it can work its way into me.

Feeling his way along the rock with his palms, he climbs into the hollow, sits beneath the overhang.

This is it, this is where I'll take myself out.

First I'll have a drink. A drink'll fire up the heat, make me nice and cozy. Yeah, feelin good now.

He checks how much is in the bottle, tilting it to hear the fizz, the liquid sloshing back and forth.

Main thing is, make sure there's enough. So I don't get hit with cravings for another bottle and go flyin back down the hill like a jackass. It could easily happen! And to make matters worse, I might trip somewhere and injure myself.

He pulls out a knife, an oiled-up jackknife, nice and sharp, like every craftsman should have.

The drink flows in, all cozy and warm, then vice versa the blood streams out.

And that calms you down too, doesn't it.

So what about after?

Probably nothin. Won't be shit there. Probly dark. Either way, I won't be there.

The girls and me had us some fun. That time I had Denisa with the pretty young tits upstairs. That time Zděnka laughed so hard we almost couldn't do it. Or that one who purred like a kitty and always wanted more. Jesus, that was beautiful.

Better take myself out now. While I got all these riches rollin around my head.

While I still got my wits about me.

He pushes up his sleeve, pats one of the long veins in his arm, more like a rope, with the tip of the knife. That's the one he's chosen. He'll also slice through the artery, obviously. A breeze flutters through the leaves overhead and all around. There are pine trees there too. A crackle sounds somewhere amid the pinecones; a fallen branch, corroded and dried by the sun.

He cuts himself. Just a tiny bit. But he knows he's got to bear down hard, clear through to the bone, slash, in a single stroke. How many times he's pictured it. And how many times he's seen the twitch of bleeding, hurting flesh.

But he keeps flinching away.

I can't do it. What's goin on?

Fuck me, not this. I still got some pep in me.

Or had it already started. The weakening. I'm losin myself.

He takes a swig, pauses. So as not to lose the strength of the compress due to the drink, descending over his body and mind like a cloud of paradise, propelling him into a state of bliss.

Now it should work.

Yeah, just a flick, that's it.

He hears the cracking again. In the brush. Can't be a deer. Wild boar?

That's all I need now is some bitch wild pig to ruin it for me. My whole life I been lucky. And now I can't catch a break.

A huge dog comes bursting through the underbrush, lumbers over to Lomoz's promontory with a slow, hunched gait. Bandaged paws, one front, one rear. Floppy ears, skinny hips, sits, shaking all over and whining. Barks shrilly, twice, announcing itself.

What is it, doggie? Lomoz says. Do you know me?

Someone is forcing their way through the bushes, trampling branches, panting for breath.

Who's there? hollers Lomoz. Hiding the knife in his pocket and struggling to his feet, he rises up before the intruder like a man of leaves.

It's a young guy. Sweat-soaked T-shirt, shorts, wielding a crossbow. Bolt cocked and ready.

The big dog limps toward him, tongue hanging out, threads of saliva dripping from its maw.

Jeeeesus, what're you doin here? Want some help?

He hides the weapon behind his back. Then relaxes, lowering the crossbow to his side, bolt tip to the grass.

And what're you doin here?

Just out and about.

Lomoz is trembling. His legs are trembling. Just like the dog's. His hands are trembling too. Blood drips off of him.

What devil brings you out here, boy? What's wrong with that mutt?

Quite a scratch you got on your arm!

It's nothin.

Lomoz tips the bottle to his lips, sucks and swallows.

Now I've gone and finished it, you twit. That's your fault!

I got my own. Care for a taste?

The old man nearly runs into the crossbow as the young man thrusts the flask into his groping hand.

Goddam, that's walnut schnapps, isn't it?

My dad's. Don't drink no other.

What's wrong with that mutt?

I know you won't tell on me, Mr. Lomoz. He gets runnin all right once he's on the trail of meat. Paws are beat to hell is all.

Pooch like that oughta be snuggled up in the doghouse. What's your name?

I'm Venca. It's just we got more dogs than we know what to do with, Mr. Lomoz. They run, fine. They don't, that's fine too.

That's a cruel way to treat your dogs, boy.

Nah, nothin to fret about.

Tuggin a defect mutt through the woods, kina nonsense is that?

We been runnin since mornin and he's still fine.

Bullshit, I can hear his ass draggin. And listen to him whine, poor thing. You got no sense, seems to me.

My dad'd never put up with him. Hopefully he'll perk up. I put pads on him, bandaged him up. Dope for the pain. He's my best one.

Maybe. But he shouldn't be runnin.

Stupid tree smashed him up.

Oh yeah?

That tree at the fairground that fell. Right on his paws. If it'd come down on his back, he'd a been a goner.

Oh yeah!

Whole heap of people got crushed, but not me.

Lucky for you.

I'm not much one for fairs. Woods're more my thing.

Oh, I know that, you poachin thief! I know you Bajers well.

Don't tell anyone I'm out here runnin with this crossbow.

Give it here!

Careful, better I hold it.

Sharp, the old man observes, testing the tip with his thumb. Got a stock like a rifle, huh. What's this?

That's the trigger there, Mr. Lomoz. I squeeze, arrow shoots, bull's-eye. I always hit my mark.

Stop callin me mister, for fuck's sake.

Okay!

So you never miss?

Course not.

You're a regular Winnetou, boy!

Huh?

Crossbows! I know them! They had em in that movie about Žižka, where at the end they kill that lady they both wanted.

What?

Those two Hussites, cripes!

Right. Knights had em too.

Fuck the knights. You Bajers're out here runnin the woods with crossbows. Even killed a calf, heard tell. I know bout that unlawful slaughter. You Bajers been stealin! Bašta boys're gonna come down hard on you, you'll see!

Fuck the Baštas!

Torturin dogs and baby cows, you're gonna pay.

Hey, what's the problem?

So you see I know all about you. Drop the squabbles. Can you do an old man a favor?

What's that?

Let's make a bet, Venca, whadda you say? You know *The Magnificent Seven*?

My dad loves that flick.

Right, so this one guy, cool as a cucumber, all he's got is a knife. He goes up against a cowboy with a gun. Tell you what. We put five meters between us, you and me. You think you can hit me?

Hell yes!

All right then. I'll throw a knife, and if I don't put my blade through your heart, you put a bullet in mine. Deal?

This is crazy.

You scared, boy?

Pops, c'mon, drop it!

I can tell where you are from your voice. The old man energetically steps off the distance, kicking rocks and pinecones out of his path as he strides, one, two . . . five meters, he announces amid a cloud of dust. He's almost all the way back in the hollow. He feels around the rock wall. Turns to face the crossbowman.

Venca?

Yeah?

Look, if you're scared, I won't throw the knife. I don't want to hurt you, really! I'll use a pinecone and you use the crossbow, okay? Ready?

The old man bends down, fumbles around in the needles, snatches up a pinecone.

The young man, big dog at his feet, doesn't move. He grips the crossbow, barb pointing at the ground, eyes wide, jaw dropped in amazement.

Say somethin, Lomoz says, pinecone in hand.

Like what?

The old man swings his arm, the pinecone sails through the air, biffs young Bajer in the center of the forehead. He groans in pain, the big dog howls.

Get me back now, c'mon!

Ow, fuck, I got a bump!

Shut up and shoot me!

You've been out in the sun too long, Pops. Enough with the pinecones, for fuck's sake!

Venca Bajer is a thieving fuck, a poacher just like his old man. Not only that but you're chickenshit!

C'mon, we can go back down together.

Think about it! You're a hunter. Anybody that hunts has gotta wonder what it'd be like to hunt down a man, right? If they had the chance. I used to be a boy too, don't forget! Chasin around the woods, thinkin about war. Wonderin, would I stand the test? So shoot me. Then you know you'll stand the test every time.

Pops, cut it out.

I may not have eyes, but I still got a tongue. If I talk, you Bajers're goin to jail. But I can also keep my mouth shut. Think on it!

What the fuck do you want from me?

I told you what I want. Shoot me. And go fuck yourself while you're at it.

Pops, c'mon . . .

Nobody'll find me here. You can cover me up. It's a cinch.

You're outta your mind!

I'm not outta shit. Matter of fact I'm right in it!

Why're you doin this, Pops?

Cause you piss me off, you chickenshit. Do what I tell you.

No.

Kill me.

No!

Know what? says the old man, tucked into his hollow in a wedge in the rock. I'm feelin kina queasy.

I'm not surprised!

Forgive me, boy.

Christ, Pops, I'm sorry bout this whole thing. You gave me a scare.

Could you do me a favor?

What's that?

Leave me the walnut schnapps, yeah? Could you do me that favor?

Venca takes a few steps forward and slaps the flask into Lomoz's hand.

Anythin else you need?

Go on now, junior.

I'll stop by Monča's and tell her you're here! I'll just say you were out in the sun too long.

Look, I'm fine. Just gonna lay down a while.

I'll stop by there anyway!

Do what you want.

Leavin you here like this, I donno. I'm afraid you might do somethin.

Go on and get outta here, boy.

Aright, I'm goin.

The crossbowman whistles to his dog and Lomoz hears his firm footsteps over the needles, accompanied by the soft, irregular beat of canine paws.

Tilting back his head, he feels a sudden gust of wind scrape his face, bits of pine needle, dust particles, fine grit grating his cheeks, as if the stone cradle had already borne him away.

He props himself up on his elbow.

Hey! Venca!

The footsteps stop.

Pops?

Hey, your dad was right!

Oh yeah?

That dog a yours isn't worth shit.

I know that!

Get goin already!

You sure there's nothin you need?

I got everythin!

Aright then, I'm goin.

36

NAPALM TORN FROM A DREAM. ARRIVAL OF
THE CAVALCADE. THE IDOL'S IMPERFECTION.
LOST BROTHER. HANDCUFFS. ROAD CLOSURE.
THE LOVERS—INQUISITIVE SVĚTLANA. TINY KING.
APPARITION THROUGH THE SHRUBS.

Napalm is having a dream. In his dream he is inside a tank, its dusky interior throbbing with the danger of live ammunition, but he welcomes the tension of combat. How many times now has he sat alone by the fire, sounding out the words of the handbook *Leading a Tank Unit*, drunk at the prospect of having it actually happen . . . In his dream, they approach the bordello, old man Bašta standing on the stone front steps, smiling at the tank parade, the girls smiling and applauding as Napalm, in the style of the legendary tank fighters, just smiles thinly, waving to the crowd . . . at which point he wakes into a milky mist drifting up from the river in clumps.

He feels cold, having fallen asleep by the fire after polishing off the bottle that he started on with Scales. Chafed by the view of the parked tank, Napalm fell asleep twisted into a knot, hair stinking sourly of dead coals, clothes daubed with bits of fish . . . He opens his eyes and sees Solder.

Get up, we're goin, Solder hisses. He flings a tank helmet at Napalm's feet. And the bundle of clothes Napalm catches in flight? A camouflage suit. Pants and a jacket.

And only now does Napalm notice that framing Solder's youthful face is the helmet of a tank warrior. He too is outfitted in camouflage, and he's not alone. Trembling in the cold at his side is little Tater Tot. On his head, instead of a helmet, he wears a knit cap.

Napalm lies back down in order to savor his dream. In this version of the dream, they'll be riding in the tank from the beginning, and he's looking forward to it.

Solder gives him a boot in the side. Then another. Tater Tot lets loose a fearful shriek. Nothing dreamy about it. It isn't until Solder inserts a new bottle of rum into the incensed old man's hands as a liquid offering that Napalm believes it's real.

So we're goin? he asks eagerly.

Yeah! the brothers shout.

Napalm bounds to his feet like a deer, and, huddling together, the old man, young man, and boy jump up and down, pounding one another on the back. Braying, hooting with laughter. Napalm is sucking down the rum for all he's worth. Solder, as befits the driver of a tank, imbibes at a more measured pace.

He's had enough to drink as it is. Didn't sleep the night before. Left the Fiat out in front of the bordello. Neither Miran nor Kája was answering the phone. All the better. He would show off the tank to whoever showed up. Now that their dad had died, there wouldn't be a wedding. Instead all the food the girls had prepared would be gobbled up at the funeral feast.

Tater Tot realized what was going on as soon as he saw his older brother taking the helmet and camouflage suit in the dark of night. He didn't even have to beg that much. Napalm would lord it over everyone from the turret, Solder would drive. They just needed someone to keep watch over the carriage with the live munition. The last thing they wanted was to fire it off by mistake! Tater Tot's duty was clear. Protect the ammo with his body.

Solder had gotten a good look at the bald, tattooed sonuvabitch who murdered their dad. He didn't recognize him. But it was no coincidence. Someone was out to get them. In which case having a tank wouldn't hurt. Let Tater Tot get some practice in.

The next thing he knows, the three of them are racing toward the tank. Solder in youthful bounds, Tater Tot scooting along right behind, and Napalm, more slowly but doggedly, hustling along on his gawky bones, bringing up the rear.

The sun works its way up over the bordello, not yet scorching, lending the day a pleasant shine. The breeze from the river skims along the village's red rooftops, sweeping dust away, lifting skirts, gliding over sun-browned cheeks, cool and gratifying.

Richie parks the motorbike by the front door. Next to the battered Fiat. Papa and the boy remain squatting in the cart, guarding the tube, taking in their surroundings. Skeeter and Richie exchange boisterous greetings with their friends from the flock, with the numerous new arrivals from Městečko and the surroundings. My Goodness helps Světlana out of the sidecar and vice versa.

The riders from the cavalcade, however, are soon astonished to find their playful, festive exuberance met with nothing but sad, gloomy faces. Everyone there now knows the dreadful news of Miran's passing. So, obviously, there are no pre-wedding festivities underway.

A flock of people are gathered around the gazebo where Monča's girls are bringing out pots of tea, platters of wedding strudel, and dishes heaped with jam-filled buns.

The sooner the better, I guess, huh, the pale, tearful Zděnka says to Janinka as the dishes and platters empty in the blink of an eye. The sun reflects off the stud in her navel, her bosom plainly visible through her camisole top. Confused as she was by the turn of events, she mistakenly donned her whoring garb.

Světlana, barely out of the sidecar before she was crushed to learn the awful news, sits plopped on her fur on the ground by the gazebo.

The sturdy woman who is also in charge of distributing the spread walks around with her blouse unbuttoned, holding a baby suckling at her breast. She thrusts a mug of sweet tea into Světlana's hand.

Without asking, she adds a slice of lemon.

Thanks, Dora, snivels Světlana, and also without asking offers My Goodness a sip. She too stares at the goings-on around her, totally done in.

I thought there'd be cutlets, a fellow says to Dora sadly.

There might still be, she replies.

No worries, says the man. There's plenty of food as is.

You're right there.

It does stink a bit, though.

You'll get used to it.

You think?

I did.

I'll wait for Zděnina and then I guess we'll head up to Chlum. How bout you? says My Goodness, handing back the mug.

We'll see. I gotta talk it over with Kája.

That little vampire bite you bad? My Goodness asks.

Světlana shakes her head.

You think it won't hurt when it's your own, but you'll see. You don't have a clue yet what a woman's gotta put up with. Had a heck of a week, though, huh? Yep, I was no different. Now what about the wedding, though?

Auntie, that's awful! I loved Miran!

Good Lord, the things old Bašta's lived to see! Well, always did walk around with his snout too high for me, poor bastard. Not surprised he hasn't shown his face yet. Talk about a screwed-up birthday.

Jesus and Mary, Auntie, what about Monča! And her baby?

What about you? Least now Kája'll behave himself. How many times've I said, those Baštas' shady dealings're gonna come back to haunt them, and here we are!

Kája's inside with his brother. Where else would he be?

I'll tell you, girl, the world right now is seriously up shit's creek. Miran dead! Who'd of guessed? Want a bun?

Skeeter, completing his reconnaissance of the tidbits in the gazebo, stashes a hunk of strudel up his T-shirt and goes to hang out by the rosebushes, but soon finds himself goggling at the statue of the Savior. The bearers have taken him off the litter and leaned him against a wall.

They trade a few words back and forth, and when Skeeter obligingly promises to watch the wooden idol for them, they go running off to get in line for a fresh batch of delectables. Skeeter wastes no time waving to Richie.

Hey, lookit what I'm guardin here!

Hey, Skeet. You goin up to Chlum afterwards too?

I donno. Think they got anything there? What could they have? How bout this, says Skeeter, jabbing the wooden Savior in the chest. How much you think this is worth?

Richie runs a finger over the carved, puckered robe, touching the protruding ribs and staring into the Savior's eyes, the pupils sandpapered smooth. He stares at the rigid head, towering over him, a tall man.

Shit, I think it's worthless, Skeeter goes on. Járin carved the whole thing while he was servin his sentence. He had all kindsa time. Still, you ask me, there's Christs out there look a lot worse than Járin's.

The ones they got in churches, though, Skeet, are all rubbed down from people's prayers. They're old. That's why they're worth somethin. Maybe in a thousand years this one'll be worth crazy millions.

Oh, sooner than that, for sure!

Listen, Skeet, this isn't old. That Virgin we got rolled up back there, now that thing's old. That's the real deal, that's worth somethin.

Shit, Richie, that picture's damaged. Scales messed it up. And the frame is history.

But it's authentic. Why do you think Tab wants it so bad? That thing's worth millions. Not this.

You think? Well, you're the one with the education. And what good'd it do ya? Guess you got a little handsy, put your mitts where you shouldn't of, and they kicked you out, heh-heh-heh-heh!

Shut up, Skeet.

Listen, I'm a redhead, so no woman ever wanted me. But I'd never sink as low as you, Richie. Never!

Just then Skeeter, taking a mighty leap, clenches his fist and whacks a blowfly that's landed on the Savior, pasting it on but good. Then, just for good measure, he grinds it into the wound in the Savior's side with his index finger. He gets a kick out of watching the fly wiggle its tiny legs.

Ow, shit! he cries a moment later, showing his blackened pointer. Bruised my finger.

Divine retribution, dude.

Ah, b.s., it's just bad luck. And when someone's got bad luck, they can even catch their dick on a nail in someone's pussy. Or in your case, up their ass!

What're you up to over there? A woman's thunderous voice chimes in as she steps out of line and heads toward them. She's been sizing them up for a while.

Oh, nothin, says Skeeter. Just keepin a watch on Lojza here.

That's not Lojza. That's Jesus Christ, the Son of God!

Same difference to you, Mom, Skeeter grins.

I'm not your mom, you reject.

Whew! I got lucky there.

So you're on the bearers' roster, huh? I'm gonna go ask Lukáš, says the matron, rustling off.

Hey, let's get outta here!

343

Where to?

Check out the painting. We'll see after that.

The boy stops by to pick them up after navigating the line for food. He takes a nibble or two, but mainly he's looking around for Světlana. Was that her he spotted through the gazebo, through all the people milling about or sitting in clusters absorbed in debate? He'll find her later on.

Young Tab. What do you want? snaps Skeeter. I spose your pop is lookin for us?

Did ya get a bite to eat at least? Richie asks with concern. Then the two of them hurry after the boy, slipping past the line.

Světlana leads Kája by the hand. She snatched him up the moment he set foot outside the house. The sun is overhead, it's warm. Her fur is balled up under her arm.

Lemme see. Wow, it's heavy, says Kája, swinging the fur over his shoulder.

They walk past the beds of roses, leaving the bordello through the main entrance.

Kája, still broken up by the disaster, walks hunched over, as if he were hauling the sun around on his back.

Světlana suddenly stops Kája short—he almost stepped into the road. A pickup truck drives between the lovers and the pilgrims, its bed heaped with yellow road barricades. Zooming in after the pickup is a police car, followed by the motorcycle cops that assist with every road closure.

Světlana steers them twisting through the village streets, stepping over puddles, sashaying along fences, past gardens, greenhouses, lawn pools, and garden huts belonging to all manner of kind, ordinary, friendly folk, the scent of cooking wafting from the homes' open windows. The flower beds still glisten with the last spring shower, while elsewhere bushes are watered with sprinklers.

Světlana, heeey, ciao! calls a rosy-cheeked girl from behind a fence. Ciao!

Bad luck, huh? Second time round's a winner. Guaranteed. Kája, condolences!

Thanks!

They pass beehives, hutches of munching rabbits. Lost in a yogic trance, staring blankly in front of her, Světlana responds to the greetings of a young lass taking out her empty bottles. As she expresses her condolences, tossing one bottle after the next into the container, Světlana can't hear a word amid the sound of breaking glass. The couple then moves along, Kája pattering at the side of the mother-to-be, listening attentively.

I still think it'd be good if you were home more, Světlana says. What with the baby and all.

Oh, for sure. Is it a boy?

I donno. Besides, why would you wanna go out anyway, once you've got him at home, right?

And you.

That's right, Světlana murmurs. Stopping Kája in front of a puddle, she cradles her tummy and stomps her foot down, spraying water everywhere.

What the hell!

Hey, are you gonna leave me when I get old?

What the hell! I'm gonna be old too, aren't I?

The girl nods, they walk on.

So you wanna go up to Chlum with the others?

I don't care.

Me neither.

Papa settles his little son into the cart.

The tiny boy rests on his back atop the red blanket, eyes roaming over the painting, the chipped colors, fastened to the sides of the cart with ropes and cords, curled into a huge roll.

Papa paces back and forth in front of the door to Monča's house. Makes the rounds of the clusters of discussion. Returns to the dirt bike and peeks inside the Fiat as well.

The front door opens and Lukáš steps out. His tall figure is overshadowed for a moment by the glare of the sun itself. Striding away from the brothel door, his shaved head seems to glow, the rays of sunlight catching his white eyelashes, silvering the manly hairs that cover his arms and neck.

Those who are sitting slowly rise to their feet. The women shake out the blankets and hunt around for their young ones. As Black Lukáš walks past, everyone who is already standing turns and follows him. Past the gazebo and beyond.

Hey, that's Richie's cart, Skeeter whispers to Papa's back.

I know what barn it's stolen from, Papa says, giving the bike a smack.

So what'll you give us for it? Skeeter asks. You gonna give us that painting, right?

Skeeter swings into the cart and starts to jiggle the ropes, trying to shake the tube loose. Richie leaps to his aid.

Don't be stupid, he says to Skeeter's back. We need the cart. How else're you gonna move it?

That little car'd be better, his accomplice says, continuing to loosen the ropes.

But it doesn't fit in the Fiat, Richie objects.

It fits. You'll see. We'll flatten her out somehow.

Suddenly the movement of the flock, as it detours around the sea of Monča's rosebushes, is brought to a stop by an incoming vehicle. Skeeter is first to spot the police car. He stops tugging at the ropes and seems almost to merge with the tube.

The car comes to a stop on the front lawn of the bordello. A female officer with her head wrapped in bandages springs from the car and makes a beeline for the house. The other cops follow her at a more leisurely pace.

The lady cop walks up to Papa and snaps a pair of handcuffs on his wrists.

I believe we've met, no?

She yanks at the handcuffs.

Papa hisses in pain. The boy rushes to his side, grasping hold of one of his fettered hands.

He hisses even more.

Lousy bastard, the bandaged cop blurts in Papa's face. I've got a concussion, you pig. How come you hit me? How come you drove away from that bridge? How come you didn't report it!

I thought you were dead! They made me believe I killed you! So they could get my car, the pigs!

A male cop, looming behind the steamed-up officer like a uniformed wall, turns to the members of the flock's rear guard, who have brought their pilgrimage to a halt and are now curiously peering at them from behind the roses.

Move along! the cop hollers. It'll be better for everyone!

You lowlife. The lady cop grins right up in Papa's face, so close the wart on her chin is almost pressing against him. We're gonna lock you up and let you rot in jail.

Papa casts a quick glance over her shoulder. At the dirt bike, the cart with the tube tied down inside. And the Fiat. And only a truly sensitive person right now would sense the warmth as the possible scenarios of escape flash through his overheated mind.

Jarča, are you nuts? Monča opens the door, arms folded on her belly, looking completely pale. Hair helter-skelter, strands hanging loose around her shoulders.

Monča, my sincere condolences, says the bandaged cop.

Release that man immediately, he's my guest. Monča looks Papa up and down, noticing his cocked nose, his panic-stricken eyes. Her gaze slides from his spattered shorts to his striped T-shirt, then comes to rest on the handcuffs.

Now Monča, I warn you, don't go tryin to obstruct justice. You know how much I liked Miran. This man here's suspected of murder!

No, he's not, Jaruna. The hell're you talkin about.

Just calm down, Monča.

You calm down, Jaruna. That uniform never did suit you. Looks like you got injured. What happened? Hit your head, did ja? Slip and fall?

Papa and Monča give each other a look, cracking smiles.

My condolences, Moni.

Thanks, Monča nods, and all of a sudden the girls' frizzy heads pop up around her like dandelions. They hold and soothe their commander, the girls risen up from the depths of the house. Janinka throws some plaid something or other over her shoulders, some blanket or what have you. The attractively colored item contrasts with Monča's pallor.

They'll be by for him in a jiff, the lady cop informs them. Mourning's mourning, but there's hygiene standards, y'know. Miran's dad is all squared away, pardon my sayin so. And our boys are out combin the district for young Solder. He's been foolin around with a gun. Don't suppose you'd know where he is?

Oh my god, a baby, Macinka squeals, leaping down from the stairs and racing to the cart. He is sooooo cuuute!

As she lifts the little nipper, he goes straight for her breast.

He's hungry, announces Macinka. In the blink of an eye they're on top of the cart, the other girls gathered around, encircling the little boy like a living, multicolored bouquet, the girls' faces in place of velvety-soft petals.

Hope you don't mind I brought my boys, Monča. You can find room for em, right? Papa asks.

They can study to be pimps, sneers the lady cop's backup.

But just then they all turn to look, as the hubbub from the roses is growing louder. The worshipers at the front of the flock, led by Lukáš, who instructed the Christ-bearers to mount the idol on the litter, have already gone ahead, but the lazier, slow-moving ones, disconcerted moreover by the police intervention, are returning to the bordello. They drop snide comments, faces plastered with smirks, offering bits of ironic advice that would be better left unheard.

Monča, stop them. The cops're sealing off the house!

You stop em, Jaruna. What's this for, anyway? We don't owe anyone a thing!

Suddenly someone elbows their way through the crowd. A monumental grizzled man with a nose like a beak. Garbed in a tracksuit, head bandaged, he leans on a cane. To judge from his bowed posture he would seem to be injured, yet he slips through the assemblage with ease. Trampling Monča's flower beds without the slightest hint of shame, he untangles himself from the rose thorns. And here he is, in front of them.

Braht moy, what this! cries Ivan, tugging at Papa's handcuffs perhaps a tad unsparingly.

He turns to the lady cop, gaping at him through her bandages.

The two of them, with their gauze-wrapped heads, look like walk-ons in a public service ad about cripples on a date.

Járunka, I beg! Járunka, you and I meet before, Ivan grins. I am first reported this house to police, he says, turning to the others as if they had asked.

The lady cop raises a hand to her cap, salutes the burly, loudmouthed gimp, and then, at his behest, unlocks the cuffs with a key that appears out of nowhere.

Good. Ranks in Russian police will be above ranks in Czech police. New decree of President Zeman! Járunka, well done, smiles Ivan.

The next thing anyone knows, he's barging into the house. Pushing Papa ahead of him, past Monča, who doesn't have time to so much as neigh, and squeezing Papa through the clutch of girls into the hallway.

Monča takes a breath and lets fly. For the most part dirty words coarsened with defiance. The two cops have their hands full reining her in, but they manage. The boy lunges toward the house, but the big cop on the front step just spreads his arms across the doorway and laughs.

Finally Monča strides through the door and angrily slams it behind her.

The girls stay where they are. Around the cart. Surrounding the tiny king. They've stripped off his smelly rompers, along with his sweat-soaked, crusty Donald Duck T-shirt and his little socklets from Hungary: all that now lies at their feet. The little jot smiles, revealing his teeth, his tiny body exposed to the sun and the breeze. He is pampered, cuddled, tended to, admired. Using a perfumed handkerchief, Janinka gently rubs his skin clean of the more deeply seated filth.

Vendulka produces some ointment.

Lemme hold him too, pleads the short female cop, standing on her tiptoes, arms outstretched.

We'll see, Jaruš. In a while maybe, okay?

Dang, that's a heck of a bamberflap on him, the male cop marvels, leaning nonchalantly against his copmobile. I hope they're plannin to operate on that thing.

Are you crazy, Rudolf? What would they want to operate for?

Not every guy's like you, Macinka says, bursting out laughing. The red-faced cop turns away, gazing off toward the flower beds by the main entrance.

Nobody cares about the trampled bushes now. After chasing off the usual bunch of gawkers and loiterers, the police crew get to work setting up the barricades. Fencing off the premises of the bordello. A few more copmobiles come driving up from the road.

The officer named Rudolf turns away from the spectacle. Runs his eyes along an as yet undisturbed stretch of bushes and trees.

Suddenly he gives a yell.

The girls let out a cry too.

They had heard the rumble coming from the asphalt road for a while now, but assumed it was one of the wedding guests, chugging up a side road in their old, noisy clunker. Now, though, they can see through the trees and the shrubbery the dark, powerful silhouette of a tank. And the barrel sticking out, breaking through the treetops.

37

IN THE GUARDHOUSE, DREAD AND BLEAKNESS.
WE HAVE LIBERATED YOU . . . BRAHT! BEATING,
POUNDING. A LITTLE MASONRY.

We must have word! Ivan's voice echoes in the dusky hallway.

He shoves his bulging belly up against Papa almost obscenely as he forces him onward into the house, interrupting the onslaught of blather only once they reach the door to Monča's guardhouse. The door is open.

Miran lies on the large conjugal bed.

One of the gals, or perhaps Monča herself, has pulled the covers off his face. The tattoos lend him a demonic appearance. Body rigid, bare feet poking out from under the blanket. Beneath the bed a plastic tub is filled with dirty water. There is a gruesome feeling about it all, a sense of emptiness. The most ordinary things—the decorative alarm clock, Monča's fancy mirror, a sponge—have become soaked in horror, accessories of a world whose meaning has shifted.

Occupied, Ivan grins.

Come downstairs.

Okay, braht!

Papa clomps down the stairs to the cellar, Ivan panting at his back. Now that he has no audience to perform for, he lags behind. Grasping onto the wall, he punches the stairs with his cane, groaning.

Once they pass through the cellar door, the reek from the cesspit is unrelenting. Unlike the basement in the monastery, the only light here comes from a bare bulb covered in flyspecks, suspended from a long wire.

A trough of mortar sits along the wall that Lomoz started but didn't manage to complete. Bricks. Scattered tools. Papa stares at the gap in the wall, large enough for a man to stretch through, even with a pump hose. You can see, and especially smell, the cesspool's dark, bloated surface.

Ivan slows behind him, rasping, tapping his cane. With a mighty sigh he collapses onto a heap of bricks.

You my brother. Vaska made big mistake to throw your wife out window. We did not know you not married!

The reek from the cesspit is drilling a hole in Papa's brain. It's enormous now—as it tends to be before a rain, he notes.

You inherit nothing. Now you are broke ass. But no worry, braht. You will be rich, very rich. When we will be living here together.

Papa looks around, taking it all in. Bricks. A stack of boards. Pickax. Hammer. Trowel, level. Lomoz's instruments strewn about willy-nilly.

We have required treatment in hospital, you are surprised? Monastery fell down. You are smart man to run. But me? Beams falling on my head, ai-yi! Ivan scratches at his skull, fiddling with the bandage as some stirred-up dust has worked its way into the gauze.

Yes, and Vaska? Full with bullets! From Ajvars! After journey, treatment was for us necessary. We were happy in nice Czech hospital. But who is there? There hysterical woman screaming we are bandits, robbers, murderers. Ivan shakes his head. You know who screams this? Your Soňa! She has provoked everyone!

Uh-huh.

From first moment she has seen us! You know, braht?

Hm.

She did not like me! Also not Vaska.

Oh no?

Terrible wench. Screaming, calling. Calling you! But no one was on corridor anymore. Only us.

Papa sighs. And disregarding the toxic stench, he takes in a deep breath of air. Picks through Lomoz's tools. That hammer of his is especially cool.

Be grateful! We have liberated you, braht! Your Soňa, you know what?

What? says Papa, laying the hammer aside. He picks up the pickax.

She is drug addict, drinking, what kind of mother? Eye kaput! She has leg swollen like she is carrying baby in there. What can she give? Another child freak?

Papa tosses aside the pickax, and after brief consideration settles on the trowel. Solid, big. Sharp around the edges. When it comes to tools, everyone knows that Lomoz is a true connoisseur.

And your boys? Older one can go for reeducation. They either talk him out or not! And little one—like sock! He is for nothing! These sons, shit on them! You will have many more. New Czechs, I promise.

Ivan unzips his track jacket. Papa hears a ticking, barely discernible, like a watch.

He raises his head just as the boy flashes past in the hallway above, at the top of the stairs. Seeing that his dad has spotted him, the boy crouches down and waits.

Give me your hand, Ivan. Let me help you up.

Ivan grips an oval icon bearing a portrait of the Madonna between his thumb and forefinger. Papa can hear it now loud and clear. Amid the darkness of the cellar, the regular cadence sounds like an amplified heartbeat.

I have icon from commandant of Snina. He has confiscated war Madonna from thief Serafion. His older braht is real man, commander of mountain pass. He guards borders of motherland. He has sent Serafion to camp for homosexuals. They will reeducate him. Or no. Ivan shrugs. The two men both turn their gaze to the Madonna. The beating sound quiets as Ivan slips the oval back into his track top and zips it shut.

War Madonna. With her comes war. She will move borders of homeland. Are you glad, braht?

Only now, seemingly gratefully, does Ivan accept Papa's offered arm and get to his feet. He gropes around for his cane, stumbling over the bricks. Leaning on his cane, he is no longer the hollering giant, shoving Papa ahead of him. He drags himself across the floor like a wounded dung beetle, obediently shuffling his feet, allowing himself to be led.

Son of bitch! It stinks like shit. Do you smell?

It'll be fine. Just a little bit further!

Slowly! I am old now. Not like you.

Oh no? says Papa, curiosity piqued. He pauses, one leg over the wall.

Of course no. You have still fifteen, twenty years before you will be old fireball.

That's not bad, Papa chuckles. You don't have that much time.

I don't?

Definitely not.

Then listen, braht. I will tell you best part, says Ivan, swaying unsteadily by the unfinished cesspit wall.

You already told me everything.

Our father is no dead. He has survived attack on monastery. Will live with us here. In Bohemia. Czech lands. Here is like garden. Father will recover. You are happy?

As Ivan leans toward him, a smile sliding across his mouth, Papa yanks away his cane and kicks him, knocking him over the wall. And as the old geezer, sunken up to his waist in the nasty sludge, tries to claw his way out, grabbing at the jutting bricks, Papa slams the cane down on his hands until Ivan lets go, sinking down deeper.

Then Papa kneels by the wall and reaches for a brick. He dips the trowel into the trough, spreads the mortar, sets the brick, and reaches for another.

The boy bends down beside him. His hands shake as he hears the screams and shouts from the cesspit. He grabs a brick and hands it to his father. Papa spreads and sets. The boy fishes out another brick. Hands it to Papa. Papa spreads. And again and again and again.

With all the gasping and sloshing, you would think there was a giant catfish thrashing about in the sludge. And there is something else they hear. Ivan must have peeled off his jacket. The beating of the War Madonna, pounding machinelike and precise, permeates the foul-smelling air. The wall appears to be solid, though. Lomoz always was proud of his mortar.

Keep em comin, murmurs Papa, getting to his feet. The boy, now standing on tiptoe, continues to pass him bricks.

Once the size of the hole in the wall is down to two or three bricks, Papa tilts his head back, stares a moment.

When the boy tries to hand him another brick, he holds up a finger and pushes it away.

Mercy, son, he says. He spits in the muck at their feet. They stand in a pool of foul-smelling scum that has leaked out onto the floor from the cesspit. Peering up at the opening, they half expect a hand to appear, strong and hairy, with daggerlike nails, and start to tear down their wall.

But nothing happens.

Papa pitches the trowel into a corner, tells the boy, C'mon, let's go, and they go.

38

TRACKS AND VIEWING SLIT. A SIREN FALLS
SILENT. LAST WARRIOR. THROUGH THE GULLY
AND THE WOODS. BY THE WATER WITH MONČA.
AND ONTO SHORE.

The tank crawls slowly out of the bushes, Solder's viewing slit obscured by torn-down branches . . . Faster, for God's sake, Napalm roars . . . This wasn't how he had pictured their entrance. What he sees fills him with anger and bewilderment. Solder, on the other hand, can't see squat.

It was a great trip, everything went smoothly. Speeding through the morning dawn, Napalm booming directions from the turret, Tater Tot giggling as he watched over the ammo carriage . . . emerging from the woods onto the asphalt road, metal ringing, tracks singing . . . The mere fact the scrapped junker was up and running swelled Solder's chest with pride . . . After his dad's and Miran's deaths, he had had the feeling he would never be happy again, but sonuvabitch, he was wrong . . . he did it!

He pays no mind to Napie's warning cries from the turret as he takes in the whole to-do, the wail of the police sirens, the yellow barricades being moved into place . . . the police car parked in front of the bordello, the female officer crouched behind it wielding a gun . . . and the armed hulk standing amid the cluster of girls.

The exhilarated Solder is still expecting to find a band of kindred spirits waiting for them on the lawn . . . maybe Black Lukáš could even bless the tank, he thinks, grinning to himself for what may be the hundredth time now in the course of this sensational ride.

He gives the young Tater Tot a merry slap on the back . . . yes, they came prepared to salute the guests with live fire and get the funeral party underway.

Neither Solder nor Tater Tot realize, however, that the lady cop with the bandaged head is blocking the tank's path . . . Napalm blinks in bewilderment, this lady cop is saluting them . . . And what's that she's shouting? Welcome, comrades! Then she hurls her cap in the air and yells, Hurrah! . . . She thinks we're Russkies, the dirty rat, flashes through Napalm's mind as the officer opens her mouth . . . She recognizes the long-haired, bearded old geezer bowing to them from the turret, tattoos running up and down his neck and cheeks, fishbone in his hair . . . and he's a repeat offender! Dropping behind the police car, the officer levels her gun.

They creep up the stairs, the boy trying to rip his T-shirt away from his stomach. It's completely stuck fast from the mortar. Papa's clothes are all spattered as well.

Hey, you were pretty brave back there, Papa says. Was it really bad? The boy gives no reply, not even so much as a sigh, but anyone with a gift for seeing in the dark would have caught a hint of a smile flash across his face. They come out of the cellar and nearly run right into Monča.

Sitting on a suitcase, she leans against the wall working with a mirror and comb. Making faces at herself as she adjusts her curls. She wets a finger and picks at something on her face.

Where you guys headed?

We want outta here.

I was gonna take a few things, but I don't care now. This'll do, she says, smacking a plastic bag.

So where you goin?

I'm outta here too.

Why don't you go to your mom's?

You been to see her?

Yeah.

Then you know.

Papa nods.

Let's have a look outside, says Monča, standing up from the suitcase. I hope it's calmed down by now.

They are pinned to the floor by the roar that greets them when they open the door. Quickly closing it, they reopen it a crack just in time to see the female officer jump out of the way at the last second as the tank crushes the police car under its tracks, the siren's wails suddenly falling silent . . . The other cars' sirens continue to sound their piercing alarm.

Solder and Tater Tot, inside the tank, jump under the impact as one of the tracks seems to slip loose . . . The tank continues to roll on but then gets stuck, gun barrel swiveling back and forth, twisted hunks of metal, wires, tangled wads of fabric, poke from under the belly of the monstrous machine like degenerated organs . . . and Napalm roars into the wail of the sirens, the girls' shrieking, and the bark of weapons from the barricades: We won't give up the bordello, you motherfucking pigs!

The audience inside the house gazes on as Rudolf the cop turns away from the cluster of girls, one of whom holds the tiny king in her arms, and he too aims his weapon at the thundering vehicle freshly emerged from the abyss of history.

Papa taps Monča on the shoulder and sprints out of the house, son by his side. The ropes hang over the sides of the trailer, cut through. The cords lie limp on the cart's wooden floor. The tube is gone.

As Monča settles into the sidecar, Papa unhitches the cart from the dirt bike and hops onto the seat. The boy climbs on behind him, throws his arms around his waist, Papa stomps on the gas, and off they go, wheels spitting dirt.

They blow past the stuck tank while the girls go running in every direction, their leader keeping a firm grip on her precious human bundle . . . Papa zips along the line of barricades as the agitated officers flee their posts, until, spying a gap in the fence, he breaks through the rosebushes onto the road, avoiding the parked police cars, and zooms off, taking the same route by which they came.

He turns off the road onto a trail, steering between the lindens, then turns off again, into an overgrown gully. As they jolt over stumps through the woods, Monča in particular takes a bit of a beating. There are rocks, old tires, junkers strewn on every side, washed up by the floods. They go as far as they can, and finally, when they can't go any further, Papa brings the bike to a stop by the river.

Suddenly the track snaps back into place and the tank jerks into motion, knocking the branch off the viewing slit. Solder can finally see.

They careen forward, prepared to give a thundering one-gun salute, right outside the front door, as he had originally planned . . . but something is off.

The howl of sirens now reaches his ears, and the sound right by his side is the chattering of Tater Tot's teeth . . . Their eyes, searching the scene for their brothers and friends, spy the jumble of barricades, the swarming gunmen . . . They have no idea that the policewoman is pursuing the tank with her safety off and that the other lawmen already have them in their sights.

Just then the brothel door bursts open and a monstrous figure covered in muck emerges onto the front steps . . . Gimpily dragging itself forward in full-on zombie style, it opens its gurgling mouth to discharge a rush of sludge . . . Solder is staggered by a burst of staccato gunfire drumming against the turret . . . A bullet from the policewoman's sidearm hits Napalm in the neck, and the forest man, the last warrior, tumbles into the bowels of the machine, landing right on top of Tater Tot and Solder, his dying body crushing both of the intrepid tankists. Tater Tot in turn crashes onto the detonating device. And the tank fires.

The shell wallops the muddy creature into the building's interior, and the roaring fireball sails through the bordello, demolishing everything in its path in the course of its brief flight . . . The girls, who fled the battlefield for the trees, turning their heads . . . see, floating amid the falling beams and buckled walls, panties and brassieres tangled together with floral bouquets, bric-a-brac with sprays of wedding cake jutting from the the wrecked hallways, and despite the missile having punched a hole in the taproom, a few miraculously intact drinking glasses remain standing amid the shattered brick and slivers of broken windows and beer steins . . . The stiff-faced policemen, joined by civilians from the pious flock, proceed to bombard the scorched ruins of the brothel's interior.

And suddenly the colossal figure of Black Lukáš appears among his followers, arms outstretched, blessing, or more likely cursing, the scene of desolation . . . a little kitten, coated in dust, slips between his legs . . . it's Baltie, pattering out of the rubble with a brightly colored bird clenched in his teeth.

*　　*　　*

They take a breather along the bank. Resting on the rocks. The boy, shaken by the wild ride, dashes straight into the river.

They build a fire, just a little one, more out of habit than anything else. Its time will come, though. Keep the mosquitoes away, if nothing else.

It's crazy how long it's been since the last time I saw you, Papa sighs over the burbling flow, which rises to an angry foam as it rages over the stones, and he is about to add something to the effect that he is sorry Monča lost the bordello when he realizes she has lost much more than that, and shuts up instead.

Monča gives a dismissive wave.

Her nipples are oozing milk beneath her tight T-shirt. She scoops a handful of water from the current, splashes it on herself. Settles back on the colorful blanket, lounging in a nymphlike pose.

Forget the house. I'm worried about my dad.

Oh yeah?

Lomoz always has been a wanderer, though. He probly just didn't wanna be in the way.

I've been wonderin how he was.

You should.

Did he ever wonder how I was? says Papa. He fishes through Monča's plastic bag and comes up with a tomato. She brought a bite to eat. Even made a salami sandwich for the boy. Apart from that, the only thing she has in the bag is a layette. She spreads the baby clothes out on the rocks. Then folds them back up again. Papa walks off to the dirt bike and fiddles with the sidecar. Wrestles with something using a knife, then a screwdriver, probably swiped from the cellar. Bangs it with a rock. The boy is waist-deep in the river, trying to get the mortar off. Picking at it with a stick, exposing it to the current. He repeats the process several times, letting himself dry off, then plunging in again.

Evening has fallen by the time Papa loosens the last rusted nuts. He tosses them in the bushes and proudly displays the liberated bike, as he calls it.

Course you don't remember her, he says to Monča.

No, can't say I do. Amsterdam was great for me. I'd hustled in Benešov, then Prague, and, you know, wherever, but I was still always anxious. There was this one guy dragged me over there, he was part of a whole crew. We lived all over the place. That, I was fine with. It's just, he was totally useless. Nothin but leaflets, protests, actions. But I loved him. So I got into hustling there, and at first it was great.

And after that? Papa asks, trying to carve a stick into a fishing rod—a spear or whatever.

After that, not so much.

So you came back.

Yeah, you know what? In my next life, I wanna be born a man.

How come? Papa asks, flinging the stick in the water. He hops off the rock and wanders along the bank.

So I won't be a woman.

Are you serious?

Listen, I made up my mind. I'm goin back.

Where to?

I donno. You leavin your squirt back there?

The girls'll take good care of him, I figure. How bout yours?

I donno yet. And how bout you guys? Where're you headed?

The boy is having a hard time sloshing back to shore. Papa, motor-bike at his side, reaches out his hand. Then all three of them hear it. A thundering louder than the roar of the current. Not from the skies, but engines making their way toward them. Down the trail through the gully, muffled by the woods. They're still on the forest path, for now.

Jump, boy. Go ahead, Papa says gently, offering his hand.

All right.

JÁCHYM TOPOL, novelist, poet, dramatist, journalist, is the leading Czech author of his generation. He is a winner of the Vilenica International Literary Prize, as well as his country's highest literary honor, the State Prize for Literature, and the only living writer with a work in the series Česká knižnice, a classics imprint of critical editions published by Host, in Brno. Born in Prague in 1962, in the 1980s Topol wrote lyrics for and sang with the rock groups Národní třída and Psí vojáci; cofounded the cultural review *Jednou nohou*, later renamed *Revolver Revue*; signed the human rights declaration Charter 77; and organized with the activist group České děti. In the 1990s he worked as a reporter for the investigative weekly *Respekt*, then joined the cultural section of the daily *Lidové noviny*. Since 2011, Topol has worked as the program director at the Václav Havel Library, in Prague. He is the author of two books of poetry and six novels, and his work has been translated into twenty-five languages.

ALEX ZUCKER has translated novels by the Czech authors Bianca Bellová, Jáchym Topol, Petra Hůlová, J. R. Pick, Magdaléna Platzová, Tomáš Zmeškal, Josef Jedlička, Heda Margolius Kovály, Patrik Ouředník, and Miloslava Holubová. He has also Englished stories, plays, subtitles, young adult and children's books, song lyrics, reportages, essays, poems, philosophy, art history, and an opera. *City Sister Silver*, his translation of Jáchym Topol's first novel, was featured in *1001 Books You Must Read Before You Die*. Zucker is a past cochair of the Translation Committee at PEN America, and in recent years has worked with the Authors Guild to produce the first survey of working conditions for literary translators in the U.S. and the Guild's first model contract for literary translation. More at alexjzucker.com.